ABOUT TRICIA STRINGER

Tricia Stringer is the bestselling author of the rural romances *Queen of the Road*, *Right as Rain* and *Riverboat Point*, and the historical saga *Heart of the Country*.

Queen of the Road won the Romance Writers of Australia Romantic Book of the Year award in 2013 and *Riverboat Point* was shortlisted for the same award in 2015.

Tricia grew up on a farm in country South Australia and has spent most of her life in rural communities, as owner of a post office and bookshop, as a teacher and librarian, and now as a full-time writer. She now lives in the beautiful Copper Coast region with her husband Daryl. From here she travels and explores Australia's diverse communities and landscapes, and shares this passion for the country and its people through her stories.

For further information go to triciastringer.com or connect with Tricia on Facebook or Twitter @tricia_stringer

Between the Vines

Also by Tricia Stringer

Queen of the Road
Right as Rain
Riverboat Point
Between the Vines
A Chance of Stormy Weather

THE FLINDERS RANGES SERIES

Heart of the Country
Dust on the Horizon

Between the Vines

TRICIA STRINGER

mira

First Published 2015
First Australian Paperback Edition 2015
Second Australian Paperback Edition 2017
ISBN 978 1 489 24249 5

BETWEEN THE VINES
© 2015 by Tricia Stringer
Australian Copyright 2015
New Zealand Copyright 2015

This is a work of fiction. Names, characters, places, and incidents are either the product of the author's imagination or are used fictitiously, and any resemblance to actual persons, living or dead, business establishments, events, or locales is entirely coincidental.

Published by
Harlequin Mira
An imprint of Harlequin Enterprises (Australia) Pty Ltd.
Level 13, 201 Elizabeth St
SYDNEY NSW 2000
AUSTRALIA

® and TM are trademarks of Harlequin Enterprises Limited or its corporate affiliates. Trademarks indicated with ® are registered in Australia, New Zealand and in other countries.

Creator: Stringer, Tricia, 1956- author.
Title: Between the vines / Tricia Stringer.
ISBN: 9781743693964 (paperback)
Target Audience: For general readers.
Subjects: Love stories. Vineyards—Fiction. Man-woman relationships—Fiction.
Dewey Number: A823.4

Printed and bound in Australia by McPherson's Printing Group

MIX
Paper from
responsible sources
FSC® C001695
www.fsc.org

To Dawn, Kathy and Sue

CHAPTER

1

Rosie gasped. Taylor cast her a sideways glance. Movement on the windscreen caught her eye. A brown body and eight hairy legs scurried towards her. She yelped and pulled the wheel. The van swayed bringing screams from the four women in the seats behind her. She careered off the highway and slammed on the brakes. The van slewed to a stop in the gravel.

Taylor and Rosie threw open their doors and jumped from the van simultaneously while behind them a barrage of confused questions filled the air.

"What are you doing?" Cass's voice boomed above the rest.

"Spider." Taylor clutched at her pounding chest.

An air horn blasted and wind whipped at her hair as a road train thundered past. She scrambled on wobbly legs to Rosie's side of the van. Her friend, and the bride-to-be, stared wide-eyed at the windscreen. The side door slid open.

"Oh Taylor! You and spiders!" Cass's angry expletives were lost in the rumble of another passing truck. "You could have killed us all. Where is it?"

Taylor shuddered and edged further away. Rosie was the one to point to where the ugly creature now waited, smack bang in the middle of the front windscreen.

Cass was Rosie's chief bridesmaid, the organiser of this road trip and not afraid of anything. She reached for one of the magazines that had been at Rosie's feet. The other three women climbed out of the van, shaking their heads and clutching various parts of their bodies.

"I swear I'll be bruised all over, Taylor." Mandy rubbed at her arm while Anna and Sal joined the chorus of complaints.

Cass climbed into the front passenger seat and lifted the magazine she'd twisted into a roll.

"No," Rosie and Taylor yelled in unison.

"Don't kill it," Rosie pleaded. "Poor thing gave us a fright that's all."

"You can kill it." Taylor shuddered. "Just not there. It'll splatter." The only thing worse than a live spider would be a dead one smeared across her windscreen.

Cass gave them a murderous look. "You two are the–"

"It's moving!" Rosie cut her off.

Taylor's scream pierced the air.

Cass turned, reached across and with one swift movement used the magazine to flick the spider out of the van.

Taylor's heart continued to thud. "Where is it now?"

Cass pursed her lips, strode around to the other side of the van and made a big show of stomping on the ground. She looked through the open doors to Taylor on the other side of the van. "Dead."

Taylor let out the breath she'd been holding. "Sorry everyone."

More complaints filled the air.

Cass came back around to the passenger side and stood hands on hips. "Is anyone in need of medical assistance?"

A bit of arm swinging and a few more mutters followed.

"We'll live," Anna spoke for the others.

Mandy handed around bottles of water. They had an esky full of drinks but so far the alcohol hadn't been touched.

Cass stood next to Taylor. "Would you like me to drive?"

"I'll be fine." Taylor's hammering heartbeat was steadying to a normal pace but nausea churned in her stomach. She sipped some water. The early February day was hot, reminding them it was still summer.

"The spider was just so close." Rosie shuddered. "Do you think there are any more?"

"No." Taylor spoke with a conviction she didn't feel. She pulled back her shoulders. This was her problem and she had to deal with it. "I cleaned the van from top to bottom yesterday. We parked under the trees last stop and left the doors open. It probably crawled in then." A shiver ran through her in spite of the heat. She could put up with most creepy crawlies but spiders…she put a hand to her stomach and tried to ignore the tightness in her chest. Just breathe, she told herself. It will pass.

"If your aircon worked properly we wouldn't need to have everything open," Cass said.

"It was working fine yesterday." The failing aircon added to Taylor's worries. Everyone was getting hot and bothered. Inside the van was almost hotter than out. Taylor had careered to a stop near a large gum tree which offered a small amount of shade but tempers were getting frayed. More traffic zoomed past in both directions on the busy highway between Naracoorte and Penola.

"Okay everyone, back in the van. First real drinks await." Cass waved the others back on board. She gave Taylor a sideways look, one eyebrow raised. "Are you sure you're okay?"

"I will be."

Cass gave her shoulder a gentle squeeze and climbed in. She was Taylor's best friend and understood her spider phobia.

"Do you mind if I sit with them?" Rosie had an apologetic look on her face.

"No, you go for it. I'll be fine." Taylor smiled bravely. "Not far to the first winery from here."

She slid the door shut on the hen's group and made her way around to the driver's door. She inspected the gravel all around her side of the van then leapt into the seat and slammed the door beside her. She took a deep breath and set the van in motion.

"Penola, here we come," Cass yelled. "Boy, have we got some fun lined up for you, Rosie." There was a chorus of cheers.

Taylor grimaced. She wished she was sitting in the back with them instead of being the designated driver for this hen's trip but she'd volunteered. They'd planned it just as she'd made the monumental decision to change her life. She wasn't saving money and she was sick of big Saturday nights followed by hangover Sundays. It was getting her nowhere. Taylor had made a pact with herself to cut back on drinking and partying. She hadn't even told Cass about it. She glanced in the rear-view mirror at the merry crew behind her. And anyway, she was the only one with a van. She usually used it for work, couriering goods or taxiing people, but it did make a good hen bus.

She stretched her arms straight out and pressed her back against the seat, concentrating on the road ahead. Huge gum trees lined the sides and farmland gave way to rows of sweeping vines. This weekend was going to be different. She gripped the wheel tighter and gave her full attention to driving.

"Another seven to eight weeks and you'll have to pick them." The old man rose from his stooped position beside the vines heavy with grapes and tugged his old grey felt hat down. "Maybe a bit less, if the weather stays warm."

Pete smiled. He'd thought the same but he valued Howard's opinion. The old man might not have a university degree but he'd been growing grapes in Coonawarra nearly all his life. Pete cast a look across the rows of vines, all of them loaded with his precious cabernet sauvignon grapes. He felt a mounting excitement for this new project. A tingle of anticipation he hadn't felt in years. This new clone of cabernet grapes with the code name NS18 would become Wriggly Creek's icon wine.

"What are you going to do with them?"

Pete turned back to meet Howard's steady gaze. The old man's huge bushy eyebrows hovered over grey eyes partly covered by his saggy eyelids but he missed nothing.

"Word is you haven't sold them yet."

Pete shook his head. The grape industry was a huge place and yet a small one. Everyone thought they knew everyone's business.

"What are you up to, young fella?"

"Bit soon to say yet, Howard. You know how it is."

Pete knew his reply was evasive but it was early days yet. He wasn't one to count his chickens, even with Howard. Edward knew, of course, but that was all. Word would get out soon enough, especially as Pete hadn't sought a buyer for the grapes.

"You were always one for keeping things close to your chest." Howard bent in a little closer. "I don't suppose you've heard who it is that's looking to sell their winery?"

"No." Pete shook his head and grinned. "Gossip has it there's always someone on the market, Howard. You know that."

"There's a bit more substance to this. Heard it from a few good sources. You and Edward aren't selling?" Howard pinned him with a sharp look.

"Not us. Wriggly Creek is still a fully family-owned winery. One of the few small ones left around here. We're not planning on parting with it."

"I'm glad, young fella. You've got a good head on your shoulders when it comes to wine and Eddie seems to have a decent eye for the business side of things. Your parents would be proud of what you've achieved on your own."

"Wish they were here to see it." Once more Pete looked out across the vines, their deep green colour heightened by the late afternoon sun. The NS18 was only two hectares, bounded by the winery sheds and office to his left and the cellar door further away to his right. In front of him stretched the rest of the winery with his small cottage closest to the sheds and in the distance beyond it he could see the roof of his parents' house where Edward now lived. He had helped his father plant these cabernet vines and a year later his father was dead. That had been six years ago. The pain of the loss of his parents had lessened over time but he still missed them every day.

"You've done a fine job." Howard reached up, wrapped an arm around his shoulders and gave him a firm pat. "You'll make a damn worthy red out of these grapes too, young fella. They'll be lining up to get their hands on it."

Pete twisted his head in time to see Howard wink and tap the side of his nose with his other hand.

"Time to get home to Margaret. It's roast tonight."

Howard hobbled away along the row. A knee reconstruction many years earlier had left him with a joint that was almost bone on bone but he rarely complained.

Pete shook his head. He should have known better than to think he could keep something secret from their family friend. The old bloke had become a bit of a mentor since Pete's parents had died.

He knew how badly Pete wanted to make a wine worthy of his father's original investment. But Howard was married to Margaret, a staunch community worker who attended every event in the district. She heard everything and repeated most of it, adding her own embellishments to the story.

Pete's stomach rumbled. Talk of Margaret's roast made him think of his own dinner. As usual he hadn't organised anything. There was still some of the casserole left. He would have to have that and plan some more meals tomorrow. Somehow he never thought about food until it came time to eat.

A bright blue sporty car zoomed down the road from the direction of the winery leaving a trail of dust in its wake. Felicity, their office manager, was heading home. They paid her the award rate but he wondered at her having such an expensive car. Her family were battlers but Felicity liked nice things. He hoped she hadn't overextended herself. Still, it was none of his business.

The sun went behind a thick bank of cloud. A shiver wriggled down his back. Pete looked up. A figure stood on the verandah outside the cellar door. It was quite a distance but he could tell from the stance it was Ed. Pete lifted his hand to wave but his brother had already turned away and disappeared inside. There was one vehicle out the front, a van. Perhaps they were still busy at the cellar door. Pete had meant to get back to help with the last of the customers and let Noelene go home early but he'd spent a long time with Howard walking amongst the vines and somehow the day had got away from him.

He should ask Ed to go to the pub with him for a meal tonight. They'd hardly seen each other the last few weeks. That would prevent him having to eat his casserole for a third night and give him a chance to catch up with his older brother. Ed had become elusive of late or was it Pete who'd not bothered to make enough of an effort? He could easily lose himself in the vines or the winery sheds all day. They'd never been close but they'd been strong for each other in the early days after the light plane crash that had claimed their parents.

Gradually as life had gone on they'd each taken up their roles at Wriggly Creek Wines, Pete managing the vines and wine production, Ed the finances, sales and marketing. They complemented each other and rubbed along together.

Pete shrugged his shoulders. The lowering sun combined with a breeze brought a drop in temperature. He couldn't remember the last time he'd had a conversation with his brother that didn't involve the business. The coming vintage would make a proper catch-up almost impossible. The pub was a good idea. There were several things he needed to talk over with Ed. Pete strode back between the vines, glad he'd made a decision.

CHAPTER

2

Shrieks of laughter greeted Taylor as she pushed open the cellar door. A bundle of white fluff flapped on the floor. She watched as Anna and Sal took an arm each and hauled Rosie to her feet. They all giggled and talked excitedly as they readjusted the tulle veil that had slipped sideways and fluffed out the tulle skirt they'd attached to a satin bodice for her to wear for this hen's day out. This was their fifth cellar door and the outfit was looking a little worse for wear.

Over their heads Taylor saw the older woman behind the bar roll her eyes at the guy beside her. Taylor couldn't blame her. They must see all sorts working in a cellar door, especially this one that was close to town and stayed open later than some of the other wineries. Her mini-van group would be in their motel rooms by now if it wasn't for the 'Open' sign out the front causing Cass to scream, "Stop at this one!"

More shrieks and giggles followed as her friends lined up at the bar.

"Starting with the whites, ladies?" the guy asked as the woman began to place glasses on the bar.

"Yes please, gorgeous." Cass rested one arm on the bar and leaned forward, sending up a chorus of whoops and whistles from the others.

Cass could always pick them and this guy was certainly a bit of a hunk. Taylor took a deep breath and made her way to the display of photos. They were on the wall sandwiched between two narrow floor-to-ceiling windows which looked across a rose garden to the highway. The whole cellar door was cosy, barely bigger than the average lounge room. Stone-cold sober; she distanced herself from her unruly friends. This was definitely the last stop. When Taylor had agreed to be the designated driver for this Coonawarra trip she hadn't realised how tedious it would become and it was only day one. The heat had added to her discomfort and the aircon in the van was still struggling. Thankfully the weekend weather was forecast to be mid-twenties. They were staying in nearby Penola and she hoped they wouldn't need the van much until it was time to go home.

Taylor studied the three photos hanging amongst framed newspaper clippings about openings and award wins decorating the wall in front of her. The first shot was of a man and a woman, 'Neil and Pearl Starr' the plaque read, husband and wife she assumed. Below them were head and shoulder pictures of two younger men, Peter and Edward Starr. From their appearance they had to be the older Starrs' sons. Peter had tight sandy-coloured curls with blue eyes like Pearl and although Edward had blue eyes too, he was darker like his father. He looked out from the photo with a charming smile.

"Would you like coffee?"

She spun and looked straight into that same set of intense blue eyes studying her from under a thatch of thick dark hair swept back from his high forehead. Her heart skipped a beat as his lips turned up in a grin. It was the hunk from behind the bar. Edward with the dreamy eyes from the photo. He was the only guy in the room but he had a presence that would have outshone any others.

"I'm guessing you're the desi," he said. "We've got a coffee machine out the back makes a pretty good brew or you might prefer water."

His gaze locked with hers and his smile deepened. Taylor blinked to break the spell he'd cast over her.

"Water would be fine," she stammered. "Thank you."

He moved to the jug and glasses set out on the bar, even though she could have got them herself.

Cass proposed a ribald toast which brought forth more shrieking from the group as he placed the glass of water in front of her.

"Edward Starr," he said. "Had a busy day?"

"Fairly." She took a sip from the glass. "Thanks." She realised he was watching her expectantly. "I'm Taylor Rourke." She offered her hand across the bar. He took it carefully in his and gave it a squeeze. Her heart hammered in her chest at his touch. What was going on here? She dropped her hand to her side.

He leaned closer as the voices behind them rose again. "Where are you from?"

"Adelaide." Taylor waved a hand to include her friends. "We're all from Adelaide."

"Staying the night?"

"Two. We drove down today, go home Sunday."

"How come you drew the short straw?"

She stared at him, mesmerised by the depth of blue in his eyes. It was like looking into a deep pond.

"How did you get to be the designated driver?"

There was a grin on his face. Had he noticed she was ogling him?

"I'm the one with the van and I prefer beer." Taylor grimaced. "Sorry."

"Don't be." He winked, tapped a finger to his lips and leaned further over the bar. "It takes a lot of beer to make good wine."

Taylor puzzled over his words, but didn't want to appear silly by asking what he meant. Instead, she reached for the water. A waft of his luscious male scent made her hand tremble. She knocked the glass over. "Damn!" She wasn't usually clumsy. It only ever happened when she first fancied a guy. She gritted her teeth. She wasn't going there, not on this weekend.

"Don't worry." He had a cloth in his hand immediately. "It's only water and not my best wine you're tipping out."

"Sorry." She moved a wine list out of the way as he mopped. Wriggly Creek Wines was written across the top.

"Do you have a creek?" She was trying desperately to have a sensible conversation.

"More like an indentation. You may have noticed Coonawarra is flat as far as the eye can see but the ditch across the bottom of our land is called Wriggly Creek. I'd have preferred Starr Wines." Edward gave a wry smile. "That's what the old man wanted to call the winery. Mum wouldn't let him. She thought Wriggly Creek was a better description of the property."

His gaze drifted to the noisy group at his bar then flicked back to Taylor. His intense blue eyes focused on her.

She turned away and took in the cellar door: the creamy sand-bagged walls, the polished-wood bar top and the pressed tin that covered the lower walls and sides of the bar. A keg filled one corner, topped with leaflets advertising the wine region. "Nice place you've got here."

"Mum had a flair for it." He gave the wooden top one more polish with his cloth. "We haven't changed much."

Taylor wondered at his use of past tense.

"Why don't you try some?" He put a wine glass where the water glass had stood. "We have a very good chardonnay. Unless you'd rather a red?"

"I'm driving." Once more Taylor looked away from his mesmerising eyes.

"I'm only giving you a taste. Our chardonnay has done well for us." He poured a splash into the glass. "You can't visit Wriggly Creek Wines and not at least have a sip. It's won two gold medals."

Taylor glanced at her friends. They were getting noisier except for Mandy who was looking a little pale.

"One sip," she said. "Then I'd better get this crew moving. We left Adelaide this morning and it's been a long time since we stopped for lunch at Keith. We haven't checked in yet."

She reached for the glass and bumped the stem. She snatched at it just as he did. His hand was warm and steady over hers, sending a tingle up her arm.

"Just sip it." He removed his hand.

She lifted it to her lips. The tang of liquid was crisp on her tongue then flowed smoothly down her throat.

He watched her closely.

"Very nice." She put the glass carefully back on the counter.

"Only very nice." He raised an eyebrow. "You'd better take another sip."

"Time to go I think, Tales." Cass tapped her on the shoulder. "Mandy might need a bit of a lie down."

Taylor glanced over at the friend she was supposed to share a room with. Mandy leaned back against the wall, eyes closed, a sheen of perspiration coating her white forehead.

"Back in the van everyone," Cass called.

Taylor glanced at Edward. "Sorry to rush off."

He placed a hand on her arm and fixed those deep-blue eyes on her again. "Come to the pub for a drink tonight." Her heart gave an extra thump. Damn, this couldn't be happening. Not here. Why couldn't she find a guy like Edward Starr closer to home?

Before she could answer he dropped his arm, bounded around the counter and wove through the group of cackling women to hold open the door. "Ladies." He gave a short bow and waved his arm towards the car park.

"Bye." Cass put an arm around Mandy as she passed. "Thanks for having us, handsome."

The rest of the women traipsed out after her, giggling and batting their eyelashes at Edward. Taylor couldn't meet his eyes as she brought up the rear.

"Don't forget." He leaned in as she passed through the door. "Pub at eight o'clock. You can walk there. It's just down the road from where you're staying."

"How do you know which—"

"Only one motel in town. I'll be there by eight. I reckon half of this lot will be asleep by then or wishing they were. I'll shout you a beer." Once more his face lit with a charming smile.

"I'll see how I go, can't really leave the girls."

"You can bring anyone still standing," he called.

Taylor dug the keys out of her hip pocket and unlocked the sliding door of the van. She didn't acknowledge him. She was not going to the pub to drink with a guy she'd only met for five minutes. She hadn't driven all this way to look for a man. It was a girls-only weekend.

A harsh heaving sound came from behind her van. Cass stuck her head around and grimaced at her.

"Mandy's not too good."

Taylor walked to the end of the van just as Mandy heaved again. Something wet landed on Taylor's bare toes. She looked down. Some of the vomit had splattered her feet and leather sandals.

"Great," she groaned.

Rosie peeped around the other side of the van, one hand clasped over her mouth and nose. "Do you need help?"

"We'll manage," Taylor said.

"Thanks." Cass gave Taylor an apologetic look. "I'll just clean her up and we can get going."

Taylor slipped her feet from her sandals. They were her favourites. She used the remains of her water bottle to rinse them and her toes. Thankfully they were close to Penola now. She'd drive the rest of the way barefoot. Being the desi was proving to be a tough job when it was her friends she had to be sensible for. Quite boring in fact. She was looking forward to reaching the motel.

CHAPTER

3

Taylor opened the motel room door. Cass was there, peering past her into the dim room.

"How's she doing?"

"She'll live." Taylor opened the door wider to let her friend in. They both studied Mandy curled up in the foetal position, her face pale against the white pillowcase. "She's stopped throwing up at least."

"Blimey, she's a quiet little achiever isn't she? I didn't realise she'd drunk so much."

"She hardly ate any lunch. She's dieting again."

Cass snorted and threw herself into the only chair in the room. Taylor sat on the edge of her bed.

"Trying to lose a couple more kilos before the wedding," Taylor added.

"She'll have achieved that in one go today. I didn't see her drink much."

"You probably didn't notice." Taylor thought back over their day. Cass had consumed quite a bit too but she was a seasoned drinker with more meat on her bones. She'd quickly sobered up once Mandy started vomiting. Besides Rosie, Taylor was the only one in the group who knew her roommate well. "She sampled every wine at every winery."

"Didn't we all?" Cass flopped her arms either side of the chair and stretched out her legs. "What a start to the weekend. The others are talking about going to bed."

Taylor looked at her watch. It was only eight-thirty.

"There's still some pizza in our room if you want more," Cass said.

"No thanks. I had my share and Mandy's."

"How about a drink? I reckon Rosie would be in it. She's not a piker like the rest. I've got all sorts in the esky – wine, beer, Cruisers. Or we could check out the pub."

Taylor had an image of a pair of blue eyes and Edward's face, his charming smile. What time had he said he'd be at the pub?

"Let's go out."

Cass leapt up. "Great idea."

Taylor glanced over at Mandy. "Oh, but I don't know if I should leave her."

"Hello?" Rosie stuck her head around the door.

"We're heading to the pub." Cass let her long hair out of the band holding it, ran her fingers through it and pulled it back into a ponytail. Taylor envied her thick brown locks that always looked tidy no matter what she did.

"How's Mandy?" Rosie crossed the room to look at her.

"She should just sleep it off," Taylor said. "But I don't like to leave her."

"She hasn't been sick again, has she?" Rosie asked.

"Not since we first checked in." Taylor watched the figure on the bed from the other side of the room. "She's on her second bottle of water."

"I'll stay with her if you're worried." Rosie's smile was sweet. She was such a kind-hearted person.

"It's your weekend," Taylor said. "You should go with Cass."

"I'm happy to stay here. Drinking in pubs has lost its appeal."

Cass groaned. "Listen to her. Not even married yet and she's reaching for the dressing-gown and slippers."

"Got to get my rest. Shopping and lunch tomorrow then sight-seeing and our fancy dinner in the evening. I want to enjoy it all."

Cass groaned again and rolled her eyes. Originally she'd planned a big day and night out clubbing in Adelaide, but Rosie hadn't wanted that kind of a hen's party. The suggestion of a weekend with her five closest friends had evolved into this Coonawarra trip.

Taylor glanced at her watch again.

"You keep looking at that watch." Cass studied Taylor closely. "Do you have somewhere else to be?"

"No…well, not really."

"You do." Cass pounced on her. "You little minx. Where and when did you hook up?"

"I didn't hook up with anyone. I'm not looking for a fella – remember?"

"Yeah, right!" Cass pulled on her arm. "Who is he? Come on, Tales, spit it out."

Taylor pursed her lips. Why had she even contemplated the idea of meeting Edward at the pub? She should have just climbed into her PJs and had an early night like the others.

"Is it the guy from that last place we stopped at?" Rosie's eyes widened. "Wriggler Creek or whatever it was called. I saw you chatting to the guy behind the bar for a while."

"The gorgeous hunk!" Cass screamed.

"Shhh!" Taylor and Rosie hissed in unison.

They all glanced at Mandy who turned over to her other side, let out a low groan and continued sleeping.

"I like your style," Cass said in a softer voice.

"I vowed not to rush into anything."

"Meeting a guy for a drink isn't rushing into anything." Cass's hands were on her hips. "Unless you're planning to jump into bed with him, and then it's just good fortune. Anyway, since when did you make that decision?"

"Since Larry."

"Larry the Loser!" Cass snorted and Rosie gave a giggle.

Taylor glared at one then the other of her so-called friends.

"What?" Cass opened her eyes wide trying to give an impression of innocence. "He was not your type. We all knew it wouldn't last."

"Foster was rather nice," Rosie said.

"The one before Larry? Are you kidding me?" Cass gave up the pretence. "He still lived with his mother and took her to the movies every Sunday night after she'd cooked his roast dinner."

"He always gave me the idea he was working and I believed him." Taylor had really liked Foster but his mother had been the third person in the relationship. Taylor had found it stifling.

"Gullible." Cass shook her head.

"We've all had our share of mistakes," Rosie said. "Thankfully those days are over for me but you should get back out there, Taylor."

"She's right," Cass said. "No need to be man-shy just 'cause you've dated a few duds."

"I vowed to have a break from men after Larry." Taylor was feeling a bit miffed at her friends for ganging up on her but it was true she'd had her share of 'duds' as Cass called them. Her last relationship, with Larry, had ended in a mess when she'd discovered he hadn't actually left his supposed ex-wife.

"That was at least six months ago," Cass said.

"Go and meet someone new," Rosie said. "You're only here for a weekend. Country boys might be a whole lot different."

"Come on, girlfriend. Let's make the most of the babysitter." Cass tugged at her arm. "Put some colour on those luscious lips and let's check out the pub. Who knows, the hunk might have a brother."

Taylor was about to say he did and thought better of it. What did she know about the other bloke in the picture on the wall beside Edward? He could live in the city, or another country for that matter. She hurried into the little bathroom and dragged a brush through her shoulder-length hair. No matter how often she did it, the fine blonde strands flew every which way. She tugged at the wisps that fell across her face from her part. Still, Edward had already seen her after a day of driving, anything she did now could only be an improvement. She chose a hot pink lipstick, painted her lips, did a final turn in front of the mirror and hurried out after Cass.

Edward smiled as he saw the blonde head appear round the door then had to suppress a surge of irritation as her solidly built friend followed her into the bar. He had hoped none of the cackling women with Taylor would come with her, even though he'd made the offer.

He lifted his hand to get their attention. Taylor gave a shy smile when she saw him and made her way over with her friend in tow. He only had eyes for the blonde. He was pretty sure it was her natural colour. He favoured blondes, especially good-lookers like her with decent boobs and hips that filled out her snug shirt and jeans. A simple gold chain hung around her neck. Not lots of jangly jewellery. He raised his gaze to her face as she came to a stop in front of him. And no heavy eye make-up.

"Sorry we're late," Taylor said.

"Doesn't matter. How's your friend who was a bit green?"

"Sleeping like a baby now," the other woman cut in. "I'm Cass."

He gave her offered hand a quick shake. "Edward," he said.

Cass made a show of looking around him and up and down the bar. "No brother?"

Edward frowned. How did she know Peter?

"Ignore Cass." Taylor gave her friend a playful slap on the wrist. "She's being silly."

"Can I buy you ladies a drink?"

"Thanks, Eddie, I'll have a Bundy and coke."

He turned his lips up in a tight smile. Few people called him Eddie. He'd always hated it. "What about you Taylor? Still hankering for a beer?"

"Yes, thanks," she said.

He paid for the drinks and they'd all taken their first sip when there was a crash of balls dropping on the pool table.

"My favourite game," Cass said. "Back in a while."

He watched her walk over to where two guys were lining up the balls for a game.

"Not very subtle, is Cass."

Edward turned back to see Taylor watching him with a smile on her lips.

"Hope you don't mind. She insisted on coming with me," she added

"In case I was Jack the Ripper?"

"No, she likes to have a good time. Eight-thirty was a bit early for her to turn in."

She drained the rest of her glass. The look she gave him held a hint of dare. He'd been right in thinking she was feisty behind the pretty face. He liked a woman who could take care of herself.

"My shout," she said. "You up for a shot?"

Was he? Edward's grin stretched across his face. "Yes ma'am." The night was fast improving.

An hour later they were still at the bar going shot for shot.

"You like living here?" she asked.

"There are worse places."

"It's such a different lifestyle." She turned her back to the bar and leaned on it with both her elbows. He turned to look at what she was taking in. Cass, who hadn't lost a game since she started playing pool, still had a few guys hanging around keen to take her on. Several other people were propped at tall tables and a small group were playing darts at the other end of the bar.

"Different to what?"

"I don't know. The city I guess. I've had the odd weekend in the country. Life seems quiet, not as frantic."

"Depends who's around and what's on. Some weekends you can't get to the bar for patrons." He drained his beer. "If it's a party you want I'm sure I can think of something."

She laughed. It was a deep throaty sound. "Steady up, Ed. Just drinks, remember."

Taylor's cheeks glowed pink and he drank in the sparkle in her blue eyes. She was one very attractive woman. He didn't much like being called Ed either but he would put up with it for her.

CHAPTER

4

Taylor slipped from the motel and closed the door gently behind her. She was glad of her sunglasses. After the gloom of the curtained room the morning sun was bright. Mandy was still sleeping. Taylor hoped the others were too as she walked quietly down the drive. She'd left a note to say she'd gone out for a walk. She was, that was true, but she'd omitted to say she was meeting Ed for breakfast.

A shiver swept over her in spite of the warmth of the air. Edward Starr was one good-looking guy. He was the reason she was escaping from her friends. She was meeting him at a cafe for breakfast. She turned out into the street and set off towards the shops, following the directions he'd given her last night. A truck rumbled past along the main road and then another, their engines loud in the quiet street. The motel was around a slight bend in the otherwise straight main drag, lined either side with stone houses. She passed gardens full of beautiful roses, their sweet smell wafting in the air.

It was a pretty town with plenty of space, a world away from the noisy streets of Adelaide and her small flat.

A dog barked as she approached the corner. Second street, turn left, look for an old weatherboard cottage. She could see it ahead along the wide flat street, nestled amongst similar buildings still in use as homes. It had market umbrellas in the garden and an old sign hanging from a wooden frame over the gate. She paused as she relived the feel of Ed's hands on her body, the delicious male scent of him.

He'd walked them back to the motel from the pub. Each bump against his arm had sent a tingle through her. Cass had made herself scarce. Alone outside Taylor's room he bent to kiss her. It was a brief brush of her lips. She'd wanted more and so had he apparently. Before she knew it she was pressed against the wall, their lips together, tongues probing, hands searching.

Taylor bit her lip. She took a deep breath to slow her thudding heart. Somehow she'd extricated herself from his arms. It had been a long time since she'd been with a man and she wasn't going to give in to a one-night stand. Not that it had helped with Larry. They'd been on several dates before they tumbled into bed. Waiting hadn't made any difference to her bad choice. He'd managed to keep his visits home to his wife a secret.

She took one more deep, calming breath and continued on to the cottage. Ed wasn't in the garden. She bent to get in through the low doorway and glanced around. Two couples seated at tables but no Edward.

She ordered coffee and checked out the seating. Outside was best. Keep it casual. This was the new Taylor. No jumping in headfirst anymore, besides she was only here for a weekend. There was no harm in a casual get-together with a good-looking bloke but that was as far as it would go. She took a seat at the rustic wood table and flipped through one of the magazines scattered there. Several more people came in, all couples and groups. The coffee arrived, and she drank it. Perhaps he'd changed his mind. They hadn't exchanged phone numbers. She glanced at her watch. The girls would be up by now surely. It was time to go back.

"Sorry I'm late."

She looked up into the rugged face smiling down at her. Once more she couldn't control the surge of excitement that coursed through her.

"It's fine," she squeaked. She cleared her throat. "I had a coffee while I was waiting. It's a nice spot." She glanced around at the now-full tables in the garden.

"Let me get you another. Do you want breakfast? My shout." He flashed his charming smile and disappeared inside before she could respond.

Taylor pushed her sunglasses firmly against her face, sent Cass a quick text to say she'd catch them later and leaned back in the sunshine. She was trying to avoid spending money and drifting from shop to shop with the girls would be too tempting. She was happy to let Ed get breakfast. She wanted to know more about him but his physical presence sent her common sense out the window. If they were sitting across the table from each other eating breakfast, maybe they could just talk.

The chair beside her moved. She sat up and his arm brushed hers. Once more the tingle of electricity sparked between them. There went that idea. He'd sat himself in the chair beside her instead of across the table.

"How are the others this morning?" he asked.

"Still sleeping when I left."

A phone buzzed. Ed pulled it from his pocket. He peered at the screen, frowned, then held up his hand to her and spoke.

"Peter."

Taylor glanced around. She never liked being close to someone talking on a phone but Ed didn't move away. He listened, grunted a few times then hung up.

"My brother," he said as he stuffed the phone back in his pocket. "He's a bit of an old woman when it comes to his wine. That's why I was late. We had a tanker in early this morning to pick up some wine for bottling. Peter wouldn't let it go before he'd checked everything twice. Now he's checking on some paperwork."

Taylor's phone vibrated along the table.

"My turn, sorry."

It was Cass. Taylor stood up, put the phone to her ear and moved out to the footpath.

"Where are you?" Cass asked.

"Not far. Didn't you get my text?"

"Yes, and Mandy's just come in with your note but you didn't give much information. What are you doing?"

"Having breakfast."

"With Eddie?" Cass hissed into the phone.

Taylor could hear muffled voices in the background.

"You head off shopping," she said. "I won't be long. I'll call you."

"Tell me more." Cass's voice raised a notch. "Did you come home last night?"

"I'll meet up with you soon."

Taylor ended the call. There was no way she would be grilled by Cass when she didn't know the answers herself. Besides she couldn't talk about Ed when he was only a few metres away.

The waitress was placing plates on the table when Taylor returned. She took in the poached eggs with salmon and hollandaise sauce in front of her. She wasn't a fan of salmon and she particularly detested hollandaise sauce. Ed was peppering a plate of bacon, eggs and tomato. The coffees came. Cappuccino wasn't her thing either but she would drink it.

"Enjoy," he said, not noticing her hesitation. "They do the best breakfast in town here."

Taylor's phone vibrated in her back pocket. She ignored it, more intent on how she was going to eat what he'd chosen for her. She decided on distraction.

"I think of a tanker as something that carries fuel," she said. "Why does one come to take your wine?"

"It's going to be bottled."

"Oh, is that something new?"

He stopped eating and raised an eyebrow.

"You said your brother was fussing over it. I thought it might be something new."

"No, we always outsource the bottling. It's our chardonnay. The one you tasted yesterday. We've won two gold medals for it. He's like an old mother hen when the tanker comes." Ed put down his knife and fork and picked up his coffee. "He's…passionate about the wine he makes."

"And you?"

"Of course."

Taylor noticed the slight hesitation before he spoke. He went back to his food.

Taylor fiddled with hers. Thankfully Ed was busy eating and talking and he didn't notice her slide the salmon under the Turkish bread and scrape the sauce from the egg.

"So what do you do when you're not being the designated driver?"

Taylor looked up from her plate. Ed's was completely empty. He was studying her closely.

"Tell me about you, Taylor."

Her heart did that extra thud thing again. His gaze penetrated her, as if he could see deep inside her.

"Nothing as exciting as making wine." She paused, where should she begin? "Business course at uni."

"Ditto," he said.

"Worked in a pub and also did casual office work to get enough money to go overseas. Came back and worked in marketing for a charity. Went overseas again."

"I've never been outside Australia."

His phone rang. He peered at the screen, held up his hand to Taylor again as if he was stopping traffic and answered.

"Noelene," he said.

Taylor studied him as he listened. A dark look flitted across his face.

"Okay, won't be long."

He hung up. "Sorry," he said. "Some issues at the cellar door and we open in half an hour. I have to go. Would you like to come with me? I could drop you back into town later."

"Oh, no, thanks anyway. I've got to meet the girls."

He took her hand and leaned closer. His touch sent a wave of anticipation through her.

"Can we catch up later?" he asked.

"The girls…"

"After the girls, tonight, just you and me, no girls, no phones." He bent his lips to hers. He tasted of coffee. His touch sent a tingle from her lips to her toes. She closed her eyes. Then his lips traced across her cheek to her ear. "I want to get to know you better," he said.

She opened her eyes to see the woman at the next table staring.

"We're going out for dinner, we could be late."

"I'm a night owl," he whispered. "I'll wait up."

"Okay." It was all she could manage. He was nibbling gently on her ear.

He sat back abruptly and she nearly fell off her chair.

He plucked a card from his wallet. "That's my number. Ring me and I'll pick you up." He stood up. "Sorry I have to go."

"Thanks for breakfast."

"You've hardly touched yours. I should have known someone with such a good figure would be watching their weight."

He bent down and kissed her firmly. "See you tonight." He turned away and stopped beside the woman who had been staring at them. "Enid, George," he said. "Nice morning for breakfast in the sunshine." He turned back, winked at Taylor and left.

Once more she sat back in her chair. She closed her eyes but she knew the woman was still watching her. What did Taylor care? She was savouring the feel of his lips on hers, the needling of his teeth on her ear. She opened her eyes. Enid looked away.

Taylor stood up. What was she doing? Where was this going? Was she being a fool again? She should put a stop to it now before anything happened. She wasn't a one-night stand kind of girl and tomorrow night she'd be back in Adelaide. She'd probably never see Edward Starr again.

Several people were lined up at the cellar door bar by the time Edward had finished cleaning up the mess that the broken fridge had caused. Noelene was dealing with them. Thank goodness she was unflappable and dependable. Unlike his brother. Damn Peter. No doubt he was off with the fairies somewhere. He had no idea how important the cellar door was to their business. He only saw it as a distraction from talking to his grapes.

Edward carried the bucket and mop through to the small kitchen. His breakfast with the luscious Taylor had been cut short. She was different to the last few women he'd been with. She had an inner strength that matched his, he'd seen it straight away in spite of her agitation. He thought that had been more about embarrassment for her friends' behaviour. Last night he'd thought she was going to invite him in. She was certainly hot and this morning after break-fast– He ran his tongue over his lips. He could still taste her. He'd hoped to get a bit cosier but Noelene's call had put paid to that. All he could do was hope Taylor would ring him tonight.

There was a noise in the back room. Immediately he pushed the thought of Taylor aside. He stuck his head into the bar area to make sure Noelene had everything under control.

"Back in a moment," he said.

She nodded and turned her attention to the group who were keen to buy a couple of cases of cabernet. They were in safe hands. If any-one could sell wine it was Noelene. He stepped into the back room and closed the door. Peter was in the process of swapping his shirt for one of the green-and-blue checked shirts they wore in the cellar door.

"Sorry, I'm a bit late?"

"A bit."

"I didn't sleep last night worrying about the tanker. After I spoke to you I thought I'd lie down, just shut my eyes for a few more minutes."

Edward sucked in a breath as he watched his younger brother fumble with the buttons. He could be such a klutz sometimes.

"One of the fridges died. Noelene turned up to a mess and noth-ing ready for this morning's customers. Last night you said you'd be here."

"I know, Edward. I'm sorry."

Edward sighed. Peter must have been sorry to use Edward's full name. He usually called him Ed.

"Have you given any more thought to selling the NS18?" Edward watched as Peter's fingers stopped on the last button.

"No. I don't need to," he said evenly. "I'm making our own wine with it. You know that."

"We've already got a good range of wine for a winery this size. We talked about it last night. I thought you understood. Selling those grapes is money in the bank."

"We did talk about it and I thought you understood my point. This wine will be something new. Not only for us but for the region. It will be fantastic."

"Or it might be a disaster."

Peter turned a soulful look on Edward. "Thanks for the vote of confidence, bro."

Edward stopped himself from letting out a sigh. He didn't want to put Peter offside but they could do with some cashflow. Peter never understood the money side of things. All he'd ever wanted to do was make wine. "I'm not knocking your winemaking skills. Put it off for one more year. That's all I'm asking. We'll still have a crop of new cabernet next year for you to play with."

"I'm not putting it off for another year. I'm all set to begin as soon as the grapes are picked." Peter stepped around Edward. "It sounds like Noelene's got a few customers. I've got it covered. See you after lunch."

This time Edward didn't hold back the hiss that slid from his lips. He had been so sure he'd be able to talk Peter round. There was already a buyer lined up, willing to pay top dollar for the new cabernet. He'd worked hard to broker a good deal. Somehow he had to convince Peter to put off making their own wine with it for at least a year. He thumped his fist into the palm of his hand. Or not, it didn't really matter. His parents had left the controlling interest in the winery to him. He could make the decision without Peter's approval. It would just be less hassle if he'd agree.

Edward's phone rang. The name illuminated on the screen brought a smile to his lips. He stepped outside as he put the phone to his ear.

"Mr Cheng, how are you?"

CHAPTER

5

"What are you doing?"

Taylor turned at Mandy's question, tugging at the sleeves of the jacket she'd just put back on. Her friend was standing in the door of the bathroom, eyes wide, looking angelic in soft pink pyjamas.

"Going out."

"We've only just come in. It's midnight."

"I know." Taylor took in Mandy's worried look. "I'm meeting a friend."

"The guy you met at the winery."

"Edward."

"But it's so late. Where will you go? Nothing's open in the town."

Taylor hadn't thought about that but she'd already rung. Ed was on his way. Once again she hadn't thought it through. She shrugged her shoulders.

"We'll find somewhere. Don't wait up for me."

"Taylor." Mandy took a step towards her.

Taylor gave her a wave and slipped out of the door just as head-lights lit up the car park. A dark four-wheel drive pulled in beside her. The window slid down and she was greeted by a smile and a wink from Ed. She hurried around to the other side of the vehicle and climbed in beside him.

He leaned across. The sharp scent of aftershave engulfed her as his lips brushed hers.

"Where would you like to go?"

His eyes twinkled in the glow of lights from the dash.

"I'm in your hands."

"Only place I know that's open at this hour is my place. I've made supper."

"Sounds good." Taylor smiled in spite of feeling full enough to burst. Rosie's special night out had been a plentiful dinner at a local restaurant.

"I'll take you on a town tour then the back way to my place."

They set off and drove up and back along the main street. The only sign of activity was at the pub. He turned down a side street and slowed in front of a large building. The streetlight illuminated cream walls, elegant arched windows and a dark roof.

"Mary Mackillop Centre." Ed nodded at the building.

"Australia's first saint." Taylor turned in her seat to take another look.

"We're not only famous for our wine."

They passed more houses and drove up and down a few more streets with leafy trees and tidy gardens. Few houses had lights on.

"That's it," he declared with a grin. "Now Wriggly Creek."

Away from the streetlights the passing scene was lit by a full moon. The landscape was mainly flat with row after row of vines. Ed named places as they passed. A wave of apprehension swept through her. What did she know about this guy? Here she was driving with him to who-knew-where in the middle of the night. Where was the common sense she'd vowed to listen to?

After ten minutes, he slowed and turned onto a dirt track. Up ahead she picked out the dark shape of a house. He pulled up beside it and came around to her as she opened the door. He gave her a bright smile and took her hand.

"This is our family home. Mum and Dad built it on the only piece of slightly higher ground on the property. The dip we call Wriggly Creek is down behind the house."

The night air was cool after the warmth of the cabin. Taylor wondered where Ed's parents were. She stayed close to Ed as he led her up some side steps to a verandah. She stopped. Candles in pots flickered along window ledges, from tables and beside chair legs. The air was warmer under the protection of the roof and sides that were partly enclosed and covered in climbing roses.

"It's so pretty," she said.

"Mum's doing. I try to maintain it. Have to admit to having a cleaner. I'm not good with the fancy stuff."

"Like housework." She grinned and followed him to the chairs.

"Have a seat."

Taylor snuggled into the soft cushions of the wicker couch. He put an arm on the headrest behind her and leaned in. She took in the rich brown hair swept back from his forehead, his clear blue eyes, his lips–

"Beer or wine?"

One of his eyebrows arched up as he spoke. Taylor was mesmerised.

"Beer...thanks."

He pulled away and disappeared inside. She shivered and burrowed deeper into the cushions. Edward was one gorgeous guy and she deserved a drink. Once more she'd driven everyone to the restaurant and had only had one pre-dinner drink.

He carried out two beers and a platter of cheeses, olives and crackers, put them on the low table then sat beside her. She felt his weight against her hip as he reached for the beers. He handed her one and tilted his towards her.

"Welcome to Coonawarra."

She tapped her bottle against the neck of his. They both took a swig. She looked out across the vines illuminated in the moonlight. The glistening dark rows spread as far as she could see.

"Your parents aren't here?"

His lack of response drew her attention back to him.

After a pause he said, "They died."

"I'm sorry."

The blue of his eyes darkened. This time it was Ed who looked away. "It was several years ago. Light plane crash, no survivors."

"That must have been tough."

"We get by."

"You and your brother?"

"Peter. He makes the wine and I sell it." He took another deep draught of his beer then turned his gaze on her. "What about you? Family?"

"My parents are doctors. They spend most of the year working overseas. They're in Cambodia at the moment. I have a sister. We both travelled a lot. She met an Irishman and has gone to live with him. We're a bit fractured really." Taylor tried to imagine her parents dead like Ed's. She used to miss them so much when they first started working overseas. Now they'd been absent from her life so often, they were more like good friends than parents. She berated herself inwardly for her lack of emotion. If she was honest she still missed them. She'd simply grown used to their absence from her life.

"Another beer, or would you like something else?"

Ed's question snapped her back to the present. Here she was alone with the most gorgeous guy she'd met in a while and she was being melancholy.

"I'd like some of that Wriggly Creek wine if you have any."

"Coming right up." He almost leapt from the couch.

Taylor cut herself some cheese. She could get used to this attention.

He poured two glasses.

She took a sip. She'd never thought much about the wine she drank before but she really did enjoy the crisp fruity taste.

"So this won a medal?" She took another mouthful.

"Two. Peter's pedantic about his wine. It pays off."

"And you're not so fussed?"

"It's not that. It's good wine. I'm just not as in love with the process as he is. You plant vines, you grow grapes, you turn them into wine, you sell the wine, you make money. If you don't make money there's no point in making the wine."

"There speaks a businessman." Taylor chuckled. "My sister could never understand why my parents wouldn't stay home long enough to make some decent money from their profession."

"Some people are dreamers."

Taylor took in the rigid set of his jaw. "A few dreams are good."

"Can't live on dreams. Cold hard cash is what makes the world go round."

"Yes. I'm often suffering from the lack of it. In fact I'm not sure how much longer my courier job will last."

"Maybe you need to get a job that suits your qualifications."

"Managing a business?"

"Didn't you say you worked for a charity?"

"Yes, but it was just a job to me."

"What about starting your own?"

"Charity?" She grinned at him.

He returned the smile. "I was thinking more a business."

Taylor turned the idea over. It wasn't as if she'd never thought about it before but nothing grabbed her. "There's absolutely nothing I can imagine I'd like to do."

"Plenty of businesses need managers."

"Locked in an office all day." She tipped her head to one side. "Would I enjoy it?"

"It would pay better, if money's what you want."

Taylor looked at her glass then drained the last of it. Was he judging her?

"I'm planning an overseas trip soon," he said.

"That's exciting." Taylor held out her glass as he refilled it. "Where are you going?"

"China."

"I'd love to go there. It's a big country. There's so much to see. Do you have an itinerary?"

"The Great Wall."

"A must."

"Forbidden City. Haven't decided beyond that."

They sipped their wine and talked about China. Before long they were having another glass and then another. She told him about her trip around Vietnam and her travels in Europe and her latest courier job. He talked about the local towns, marketing and tourism. They sat side-by-side. It was cosy on the couch, too comfortable, and suddenly she was struggling to keep her eyes open.

It wasn't quite the way she'd planned to spend the evening with Ed although she wasn't sure what she hoped for. He was a nice guy, a bit focused on money but she could overlook that. She stifled a yawn then jumped at the sound of a message from her phone. It was from Mandy. Taylor didn't know whether to be irritated or reassured. She wasn't used to people worrying about her. She sent a quick reply to say she was fine.

"Sorry Ed. I think I should head back to the motel."

"Uh-oh." He smirked. "Not the old 'my friend needs me' trick."

Taylor pulled away from the arm he had draped loosely across her shoulders.

"What do you mean?"

"Isn't that what you girls do? Send a message so you can escape if the guy's a jerk."

"Not this girl." Taylor stood up. She didn't like his mocking tone. "I didn't think you were a jerk but if the cap fits—"

The cold night air bit through her t-shirt. Her knees were like jelly and her head spun. Damn, she'd had too much to drink.

"I'm sorry." Ed stood. "Now I am being a jerk." He pulled her into his arms. It was warm there and he smelt so good. Taylor put her head on his shoulder, the fight gone out of her as easily as it had flared.

"We've been so busy talking I haven't kept track of the drinks," he said. "I shouldn't drive for a while but I've plenty of spare beds if you want to sleep."

It was not what she wanted. Ed's body wrapped around hers was what she desired but she knew sleep was all she was capable of. She'd had very little in the last twenty-four hours and the wine had finished her off.

"I've got to be up early," he said. "I'll wake you and drive you back."

She didn't resist as he led her inside and showed her into a room with a brass double bed. He flicked on a lamp which cast a cosy glow. She sat. The bed was delightfully soft beneath her. He pulled off her shoes and carefully helped her out of her jacket. Her body was sending all kinds of signals that her blurry brain was trying to stifle. Her eyes opened wide as he brushed her lips with his then he gently pushed her back. Her wayward body burnt with desire. He took the blanket from the rail, spread it over her then stepped back. She could see a look in his eyes, a desire that matched her own.

He moved to the door, keeping his gaze on her.

Taylor waited, wanting him to come back and yet anxious he might.

"I'll wake you in a few hours." He went through the door and closed it softly behind him.

Taylor stared at the ceiling. Was she relieved or disappointed? She certainly had feelings for Ed but was she prepared to go as far as share his bed? She rolled over and flicked off the light. The bed was so comfortable beneath her. She closed her eyes and imagined herself in Ed's embrace.

"Hey, sleepyhead."

Taylor's eyelids flew open. Hadn't she just shut them? She turned her head. Ed was standing beside the bed. His wet hair was swept back from his forehead and his jaw was freshly shaven. She dragged her gaze to his hand holding out a glass of water. She could smell coffee.

"There's coffee on the table." He nodded to the cup steaming under the glow of the lamp beside her. "Bathroom's down the passage to your right. I'm ready when you are."

She took the glass. He was gone before she could say thanks. She peered at her phone. It was six o'clock. True to his word he'd woken her and he'd provided coffee. What a guy. Thoughtful, good-looking, not attached. She wondered about that. How had he remained single this long? She'd discovered last night he was just thirty. That made him three years older than her. There had to be a trail of exes.

She sat up, drank the glass of water then took a sip of the coffee. It was freshly brewed, a little too milky but good all the same. She drank it down and made her way to the bathroom. Her face looked washed out in the light from the small fluoro above the mirror. Not that it surprised her. She hadn't even brought a lipstick. She ran her fingers through her hair and fluffed it up, rinsed her mouth and retraced her steps.

Outside she could hear voices. She paused at the front door and pulled her jacket close against the chilly morning air. Someone stood beside Ed. They stopped talking as soon as she pushed open the screen door.

"This is Taylor," Ed said. "This is my brother Peter."

"The winemaker." Taylor held out her hand. Peter looked at it a moment before giving it a shake. Where Ed's hair was straight, long and brown, Peter's was curly, closely cropped and fair but they both shared the same blue eye colour.

"Nice to meet you," he said.

"I really enjoyed your chardonnay."

"Thanks." Peter shifted from foot to foot. "Look, I'll leave you to it. Ed said he was running you back into town."

"Yes."

He looked at Ed. "We'll catch up when you get back." Peter turned hastily and set off along a track in the direction of the winery. Taylor watched as he merged into the pre-dawn gloom. The two brothers were so different.

"Ready to go, Ms Rourke?"

She turned back to Ed.

"Not really but I guess I have to." The sun cast a pink glow across the horizon. "It's beautiful here."

Ed took her hand. "Why don't you come back? You said there was nothing keeping you in Adelaide."

"There isn't but–"

He pulled her to him and kissed her. It was a quick peck at first then he repeated it long and slow. Every nerve tingled as Taylor kissed him back. Damn, he tasted good. Edward Starr was a very good reason to come back.

CHAPTER

6

Taylor thought of nothing else but Ed all the way home. She was vague with her answers to the questions fired at her by her friends.

Cass couldn't believe Taylor had stayed out all night and not shared his bed.

"You missed a great opportunity."

Rosie and Mandy hadn't said much but the other girls had echoed Cass's words. Taylor had ignored them. Let them think what they like. Ed wasn't a one-night stand. He obviously wasn't that kind of guy. Who knows, if she hadn't been so tired more might have happened between them. He could have taken her to his bed and she would have gone willingly but he didn't. There was certainly some chemistry between them. She'd like to know where it led. Thinking about Ed and the possibilities kept her awake while the girls all dozed on the final stretch back to Adelaide.

She zigzagged through the suburbs dropping everyone off until finally it was just Cass, who lived closest to her, left.

"So are you going to tell me anything about this Ed guy?" Her friend made one last attempt.

Taylor stretched her arms against the steering wheel. She was very tired and yet on full alert.

"I like him," she said.

"I guessed that. You've had a cheesy grin on your face all weekend. Give me details."

"None to give."

"You spent the night at his place!"

"Morning," Taylor corrected. "We drank good wine, talked and then I slept a few hours in his spare room."

Cass raised one eyebrow.

"Think what you like," Taylor said. "That's all there was to it."

"Are you going to see him again?"

"I may well do."

"When?"

"After the wedding."

Anticipation swept away her fatigue. She'd said it out loud. She would definitely go back.

"He's worth seeing again then?"

Taylor smiled at her friend. "Worth a second look," she said casually but she knew if she went back it would be for more than a look.

Once inside her own door, Taylor leaned against it and closed her eyes. Visions of Ed played in her head. She could feel his hands, warm and rough under her shirt. Heat coursed through her. Come back, soon. They'd been his parting words as they'd dragged their lips apart in the motel car park this morning.

She opened her eyes and looked around her little home. It was a one-bedroom granny flat in her parents' backyard. And it literally was a granny flat. She'd moved in after her gran moved out. Her parents decided to employ house-sitters for the months they were away. She didn't want to live in her own home with strangers so she'd moved out the back. The current guy was a recluse. She rarely saw him.

She carried her bag into her bathroom-cum-laundry, emptied the contents onto the floor and went in search of food. In the fridge she found some cheese and a tomato. Enough to make a toastie with the stale bread. There were three beers left from a sixpack. She opened one and drank it while the food cooked.

While she ate, she drank the second beer. Her phone rang. It was Gino with a job for early the next morning. She had to collect a group of tourists from the airport. Taylor jotted down the details and tossed her phone on the table beside the notepad. It beeped at her, signalling the battery was low. She sighed. Couriering was often interesting and the pay was reasonable but she wasn't sure how much longer it would last.

Gino was always complaining about the costs. He wanted her to drive one of his vans but she liked the extra mileage money she got. Her least favourite job was picking visitors up from the airport. She hated finding a park, hanging around inside, holding up a sign while people buzzed around. She'd much prefer to be the one going somewhere herself.

It had been two years since her last overseas trip. Somehow she hadn't saved much since her return home. She'd been invited to a few weddings that had involved trips interstate and she'd lost the knack of saving as well as she used to. She felt restless. Maybe it was time to have a good clean-out. She'd take as much work as she could get leading up to Rosie's wedding then she'd take a break. Gino would have to manage without her for a while. She'd head south again. See where that led.

She jumped up from her chair with new purpose. In her bedroom she slid open the wardrobe door and began to pull things out. By the time she'd finished she'd emptied another beer and had filled three garbage bags with clothes and shoes and odds and sods to take to the charity bin.

Taylor slumped to the floor between the bags and the mess she'd created and leaned back against her bed. She felt overwhelmingly tired. She barely had the strength to drag off her clothes. Without even bothering to clean her teeth she fell into bed.

Bright light flooded her bedroom. Taylor squinted her eyes searching for her phone. She sat up. Damn, it was probably flat. She'd forgotten to charge it last night. She lifted her arm and peered at the face of her watch. It was nearly eight and she had a nine am pick-up. Her feet hit the floor amongst the mess she'd created last night. She rummaged for some semi-tidy clothes. Gino liked to create a good impression for the customers, especially as they often stood next to chauffeurs in smart uniforms also waiting to collect people at the airport.

Her bright yellow jeans were on top of her pants pile. Luckily the soft white shirt she wore with them didn't need ironing. She threw her yellow, black and white striped scarf around her neck, brushed her hair and grabbed her lipstick. She'd put that on in the van.

Road works delayed her and the traffic was hideous so it was after nine o'clock when she rushed through the doors of the airport. There were no other drivers lined up at the foot of the escalators with cards and few people coming down. She lifted her small whiteboard with the visitor's surname, Campoli, scrawled on it and glanced across at the luggage carousel. The crowd was thicker there. She moved a little closer, holding up her board and keeping watch between the escalators and the people collecting bags.

The phone she'd managed to partially charge on her way to the airport vibrated in her pocket. Her boss's name appeared on the screen. She took a deep breath and answered. Gino's voice blared at her. He was yelling so wildly she couldn't understand him.

"Hang on, Gino," she said as she heard him say something about the lift. She turned to see a group of six people complete with luggage standing together on the other side of the lifts. She caught the eyes of one and lifted her whiteboard. Relief flooded his face and he turned to his companions as he pointed to Taylor.

"It's okay, Gino. I've found them." Taylor disconnected her phone before he could say any more.

A text binged and she peered at it, her lips turning up in a smile. *Missing you*, it read. It was from Ed.

Stuff Gino and his job, she was over it. She glanced at the screen one more time. A babble of Italian voices carried as the group moved towards her. Taylor recognised a few words. She pushed her phone into the back pocket of her jeans. She'd answer Ed's message later. For now she stretched her smile wider and greeted her customers.

They were staying in the Adelaide Hills. She took them to Mount Lofty for the view and a coffee shop in Hahndorf, keen to make amends for her lateness, before dropping them at their accommodation. Only one of the group spoke English very well but he made it clear they were all happy and had forgiven her lateness.

It was nearly two o'clock by the time she was back in the city. She pulled over to ring Gino. It irked her to apologise to him but at least she could report the customers were happy. Taylor reached into her pocket but there was no phone. She felt the seat behind her, nothing. She climbed out of the van, searched in and around and under every seat. Nothing.

"Damn!" She thumped the roof of the van. It was a battered old phone but it had everything stored in it. Losing her phone was the last thing she needed. She'd have to retrace her travels. See if she could find it. Gino would go bananas if he couldn't contact her but that was the least of her concerns. Ed's number was saved in the phone.

CHAPTER

7

Ed was already in the office when Pete got there. The bright morning sun was angling under the roof of the verandah and through the glass. Ed was standing in front of the whiteboard where they had a rough map of their tanks, hands on hips, staring.

"Good morning," Pete said.

Ed's reply was little more than a grunt. They were both tired. It had been a busy week and was only going to get worse now until vintage ended.

"What are you looking at?" Pete stood beside his brother.

"We're not going to have enough storage for this vintage."

Pete studied the rough map. "Yes we will." He pointed to some names scribbled on the board. "The rest of the whites will be transported out by the end of the week."

"It's the reds I'm worried about. This vintage is looking like a big one. There won't be enough open-tops for the NS18."

Pete felt his chest tighten. He hated conflict. He knew their tanks would be full this vintage so he'd already planned what to do with their new cabernet grapes and it didn't involve selling them off to the highest bidder like Ed wanted to do.

"Yes there is," he said. "In here." He tapped on two squares on the bottom corner of the board, where nothing had been written for years.

"Dad's original open cement tanks?"

"Yep."

"They haven't been used for years."

"I've started cleaning them up and lining them with wax."

"They won't be big enough. After Dad bought the new stainless steel open-top tanks he rarely used them."

"I know." Pete kept his voice steady. He needed to convince Ed, not stir his easy anger. "The NS18 is only two hectares. Once we've bunch thinned, we'll be lucky to have eight tonnes. The concrete open-tops will comfortably fit five tonne each."

Ed turned to look at him. "I thought we agreed not to thin too much."

"We talked about it."

"It's only mid-February. Surely you wouldn't do it yet?"

"No, but soon." Pete turned back to his brother. "These vines are still young. We don't want to cripple them with too much fruit."

"I'd hoped to have as much as possible to sell but I agree we don't want to compromise the vines. Just don't take too much."

Pete stood his ground. "I want only the best fruit for the icon wine I plan to make from this year's NS18."

Ed's jaw clenched, frown lines creased his forehead and his eyes darkened. Pete prepared himself. Ed was going to explode any moment. They held each other's gaze then Ed let out a sigh. He shook his head, walked away and slumped into the chair behind Pete's desk.

"I've told you we need to expand." Ed pushed back in the chair and put his hands behind his head. "I don't know how else to get the money other than to sell the NS18."

Pete opened his mouth to speak but Ed held up his hand.

"Just for this year," he said. "After that you can make your precious cabernet that's going to be the next best thing since John Riddoch established Coonawarra."

The spite in his tone only made Pete's chest tighten more. Ed always thought his decisions were more important.

"Why do we need to expand?"

"We've been over this before, Peter." Ed sat forward and thumped the desktop. "We've got all our eggs in one basket here. There's a vineyard for sale further north and I think we should buy it."

Pete opened his mouth to protest but Ed's mobile rang and he put it to his ear.

"Yes, Felickity."

Pete listened as Ed spoke to their office manager. He was all jokes and charm when it came to Felicity.

Ed put his phone back in his pocket and stood up.

"The tanker's here for the shiraz."

There was no more time for conversation. They both headed out the door. Ed turned left to let the tanker in. Pete turned right to reach the tanks filled with his red wine. He knew everything was ready but he couldn't relax until the shiraz he'd been working on since it was harvested two years earlier was in the bottle. He hated this part of the process. Once it went into the tanker for transportation to the bottling line it was out of his control. He looked everything over one more time and came to a stop as the tanker pulled up next to him.

Pete didn't get a chance to talk with Ed any further. Their day took them in different directions. Pete was back in his cottage with his head stuck in the fridge trying to work out what he'd eat for his evening meal when there was a tap on his back door. He looked up and his heart sank in his weary body. Ed came inside. Pete didn't have the strength left in him to discuss the cabernet.

"Everything all right?" Ed's question took Pete by surprise.

"All right?"

"The shiraz. The tanker was loaded and got away okay? I didn't get a chance to come back and see you afterwards."

Pete shut the fridge. "Oh. Yes." He put a container with assorted cold meats on the bench. "All went as well as could be expected."

"Great."

Ed shifted his feet. Pete could see there was something he wanted to say but he was in no mood to argue. He tried to deflect.

"I was just going to throw together an antipasto, do you want some?"

"No, thanks. I've still got some jobs to do." Ed ran his fingers through his thick dark hair. "I just came to tell you I'm going away for a few days."

"When?"

"Tomorrow."

Pete looked at his brother in surprise. The lead-up to vintage was a funny time to go away.

"There are only a couple more tanks to be emptied and cleaned," Ed said. "You and Ben should be able to manage that. Then we're waiting on the fruit."

"The riesling comes off as soon as we can get a machine."

"I thought you had that lined up."

"I did but Terry's giving priority to his own grapes. That's the trouble with contract harvesters."

"Don't start on that again. We haven't got the money for a machine harvester of our own."

"Just telling you why we're waiting on our grapes."

"You've got Ben, and Noelene will lend a hand. You won't miss me."

Pete was grateful for his friend Ben who worked for them as a cellar hand when they were busy. And Noelene's support could always be relied on. Pete studied Ed. He'd have thought by now his brother would fully understand the importance of timing for good wine production but he was right about one thing: their relationship was more tense than usual at the moment and Pete could do without the grief.

"Are you seeing that girl?"

Ed frowned. "Girl?"

"The one from Adelaide, what was her name?"

"Taylor."

"Yes."

"No."

Pete hovered uneasily. How had his relationship with his brother become so bad they couldn't hold a proper conversation?

"I'm spending some time in Melbourne. I've snagged an opportunity to attend a marketing meeting."

"Who will be there?" Pete's hopes rose. If Ed found new markets for their wine he might go off this buying more land idea.

"Not sure yet but I have a ticket to a sommeliers' dinner in Sydney."

"Sydney? How long did you say you'll be gone?"

"A few days. I'll keep you posted."

Pete studied Ed but he turned away.

"Ben will be here. You'll be right till vintage and I'll be back before then."

"Enjoy," was all Pete had a chance to say before Ed disappeared out the door.

Pete shook his head. There was plenty to get done before vintage. Ed didn't consider all the little clean-up jobs and preparations but he was right, Pete and his mate Ben could manage, they always had. Without Ed around for a few days, life would be less tense.

Pete opened the fridge again, took out a bottle of riesling and poured himself a glass. He swirled the wine. The citrus smell greeted him, with a hint of kerosene. The wine was aging well. He took a sip then put down the glass and looked for more things to add to his antipasto. There was still a jar of Noelene's pickled cauliflower in the back of the fridge along with some olives and sun-dried tomatoes. He began to whistle as he set the food out on the plate. It was as if a weight had lifted from his shoulders. He hadn't realised what a relief not having Ed around for a few days would be.

CHAPTER

8

The computer chimed on the desk in the corner of Taylor's living room. She glanced at her watch. Even though she'd slept in she still had a few minutes before she needed to be on the road heading to her first job. She walked slowly across the room and moved the mouse to wake up the screen. Her parents had bought the computer before they left so they could talk to each other via Skype. She rubbed a hand across her forehead while she waited, then blinked to clear her vision as the screen came to life. It was Monday morning, a whole twenty-four hours after Rosie's wedding but she still felt hung over.

She scanned the long list of emails. At least with her new phone she wouldn't need to rely on the computer. Most of the emails were junk but there was one from her parents. She sat down at the computer to read it. They were heading to a more remote location in Cambodia and couldn't Skype for a week or so. Her mother gave a brief rundown of the work they'd done that week and asked her to call on Gran and let her know they were okay. They'd tried to ring her and Gran but with no luck.

Taylor closed her eyes and massaged her throbbing temples. She had noticed a missed call from her parents late last week but between her job and the wedding she hadn't called back. Now she wished she had. She could ring her gran but she felt obliged to at least try to visit. She hadn't been there for weeks. Gran wasn't easy to be with. She didn't approve of her parents' life choices, nor Taylor's for that matter.

When Pa was alive they'd lived at Burnside. Gran had sold the big house and built this flat at the back of her parents' more humble home at West Beach but hadn't enjoyed living there. Especially because there was rarely anyone home. She'd said the granny flat was too lonely but Taylor knew it was also about location. Gran had purchased a place in a retirement village closer to where she used to live.

Taylor's mobile rang. She'd been able to keep her number but not all her contacts. Gino's, of course, was one that hadn't been lost. She glanced at his name on the screen, took a deep breath and answered. She winced as his voice boomed in her ear.

"Settle down, Gino." Taylor pulled her notepad and pen from her pocket. "Tell me the address again."

It was mid-afternoon when Taylor pulled into the car park near her gran's apartment. She looked at herself in the rear-view mirror. Her headache had retreated to a dull throb and her face looked pale. Gran was fussy about appearances. Taylor fluffed her flyaway hair and put on some lipstick. That would have to do.

"Coming," Gran's singsong voice crooned as soon as Taylor pushed the doorbell of her second-floor apartment.

Taylor pulled her face into a bright smile as the door opened.

"How fortuitous. I was going to call you." Her grandmother gave her a loose hug then held her at arms-length and studied her closely. "You look a bit pasty dear. Are you drinking plenty of water and getting lots of sleep? They're the best maintenance for your body you know."

Taylor stepped gingerly onto the white carpet as her trim, smartly dressed gran closed the door behind her.

"You're lucky you caught me. I'm going out." Gran looked at the delicate diamond watch on her arm. "I've got thirty minutes. Would you like a cup of green tea?"

"Just plain tea would be fine, thanks." Taylor followed her across the small but stylish living room to the kitchen. "Mum's been trying to ring you. They're going somewhere remote again. They'll be out of touch for a while."

Taylor heard the click of her grandmother's tongue as she turned on the kettle. It grated to think she wasn't proud of her daughter and her generosity. Gran had played the part of the doctor's wife for years, keeping her home immaculate, raising one child, entertaining and travelling overseas. Pa had always been on some committee or other but rarely Gran. She was a firm believer in charity beginning at home. Taylor's mother had followed in Pa's footsteps. Taylor sometimes wished her parents spent a little more time at home but she was used to their absence now and they certainly didn't warrant Gran's disapproval.

"Sit down, dear." Gran set two pink floral placemats on the table then gave Taylor a gentle pat on the cheek. "Tell me what you've been doing? I hope you've given up that dreadful courier job. You're capable of so much more."

Taylor sat. Once more she gritted her teeth. "I'm looking for something else," she said vaguely. It wasn't a lie. Now that the wedding was over she was giving more thought to doing something different.

"Gemma rang me last week." Gran waved a hand in the air. "She's loving paediatrics."

"Yes, we Skyped." Taylor had heard all about her older sister's latest promotion. She was glad for Gemma but she wouldn't want her lifestyle.

"Pity you didn't go into medicine. You were bright enough." Gran put a cup of tea in front of her. "Still, you must be able to get a decent income from a business degree if you'd only find something suitable. Now, I haven't much time, dear, and I have a favour to ask."

Taylor studied her gran's immaculately made-up face. She wasn't one to waste time on small talk. "What is it?"

"I have friends coming from the UK. They were going to stay with me but now I find they're staying for a month. My little apartment is too small for us to be together that long. I was hoping you could move back into your parents' house and they could have my flat."

"There's someone in Mum and Dad's place."

"I know but it's only one man. The two of you would hardly trip over each other. I'd rather they had the house but I can't expect them to move in with a stranger. My flat would be perfect for them."

Taylor opened her mouth and closed it. She had a job she no longer liked, no ties and now Gran was suggesting she move out of her home. What was she doing with her life?

"You could have your old room. It wouldn't make much difference to you."

Taylor looked at the cup of green tea and her feeling of dislocation was replaced by anger. It was as if she was invisible. If she were Gemma, Gran wouldn't be shunting her around. Ed's big smile and his suggestion to come back played in her mind. Damn it, what did she have to lose?

"As it turns out I'll be out of touch for a while too," she blurted. "I won't need the flat."

"Oh are you travelling again? Where to this time?"

"Not overseas. I'm going bush." Coonawarra was hardly the bush but Gran thought bush was any space bigger than the parklands.

"Oh." Gran's tone wasn't quite disapproving. "Have you found a new job?"

"Possibly. I'm going to check it out." She knew the vagueness of her reply would annoy her tightly scheduled and organised grandmother.

"Where exactly in the bush?"

"Haven't decided yet."

"Is that wise?" A tiny frown creased Gran's brow.

"You suggested I should try something new."

"Not necessarily 'new', just a job that better suits your qualifications."

Taylor stood up. "We'll see."

"Will you do that blab thing again?"

"Blog?"

"Whatever it's called I won't be able to access it. I used to read it on your parents' computer when I lived in the flat. It was quite interesting."

"Maybe."

That was high praise coming from Gran. Taylor had set up the blog as a way to keep her family filled in on her travels the first time she'd gone overseas. She'd kept adding to it, although not often when she wasn't travelling, just the odd quirky thing that happened. She had a reasonable number of followers besides her family.

"The computer's still in the flat. You can use that." She brushed her lips over her gran's cheek. "I'll clear my stuff out of the flat.

Nice to see you, Gran. I'll let myself out." She walked away from the untouched tea and out the front door.

Before she could think about her decision her phone rang. Once more Gino's voice rattled off instructions. *New customer* and *urgent* were repeated several times.

"Okay, okay," she said. "It's a bit of a drive but I should make it."

Taylor put the address into her phone and followed the instructions. Traffic was heavy but the car park at the back of the office was almost empty when she got there. Something about that didn't feel right. She made her way down the lane to the front door. A sign was stuck inside the glass saying the company had moved. The new address was back the way she'd come, not that far from her gran's.

"Damn!"

She glanced at her watch. They wanted a parcel delivered to the airport and she was running out of time. She rang the number on the sign, confirmed the address and ran back to her van. Once more she negotiated the heavy traffic and just as she got close to her goal she was stopped by roadworks. Taylor tapped one hand on her knee and gripped the wheel tighter. She was in gridlock with only one lane to take the huge volume of traffic.

"Come on, come on," she growled under her breath.

Finally she was through and moving along the road glancing at buildings for numbers. As she approached another intersection the voice from her phone told her she'd reached her destination. Taylor cursed. She'd missed the turn off into the driveway. She pulled into the left-hand turn lane. A horn tooted at her from behind. She ignored it and pulled slowly around the corner peering at the building. There were several different company names but not the one she was looking for. Once more there was a toot from behind. She'd have to go around the block, pull in and try to find the office on foot.

The block was huge. Several dead ends prevented her cutting through. When she finally made it back to the set of offices the tiny car park was full. Once more she cursed, venting her frustration. A woman with a small child walked across in front of the van and opened a car door. Taylor backed up. She watched with increasing frustration as the woman spent an age buckling the child in the back of the car. Finally she was done and her car edged out of the parking space.

Taylor manoeuvred into the tiny park and squeezed out of her van. She scanned the signs on the building. None of the names was what she was looking for. She walked round the corner. Once more the names were not the one she sought. A paper flapped on a glass door in a recessed entrance. Taylor ran up to it and with relief burst through the door. This was it. She followed the passage to a brightly lit reception area.

"I've come to collect a package for the airport."

The woman behind the counter looked down her nose at Taylor then at the large clock on the wall. "You're too late. The boss has taken it himself. He certainly won't be dealing with your company again."

"I was given your old address."

The woman gave her a condescending glare. "Not my problem."

"Your office has no signage."

"We only moved last week."

"And there's no parking."

"We have a back-lane access."

The woman's patronising tone was getting under Taylor's skin and the throbbing pain in her head had deepened.

"Once again, no signage," she snapped.

The woman drew herself up, pursed her lips and glared at Taylor.

"Please do not make excuses for your lack of efficiency. Not only will your company not get any further work from us but I will be informing your boss about your rudeness." With a sharp nod of her head the woman turned her back and paraded into a back area, closing the door firmly behind her.

Taylor sucked in a breath. Anger surged through her as she spun on her heel and retraced her steps to her van. Once inside she rested her head on her hands gripping the steering wheel. Hot tears rolled down her cheeks.

CHAPTER
9

"Damn it Gino, it wasn't my fault."

Taylor stood in her driveway. After her melt down in the car park she'd pulled herself together and driven home. She held her new phone away from her ear as Gino's diatribe reverberated from it.

"Will you let me finish?" She tried to get a word in. "The shop-front wasn't clearly marked and…"

His sharp words cut her off.

"What?"

She couldn't believe her ears. Had he actually, finally, fired her? He repeated it with a few foul adjectives thrown in. Yes, he had.

"Well, the same to you," she blazed into the phone. She pushed end and stared at the screen until it went blank, then she tossed it on the front seat of her van and folded her arms. She'd busted her gut for Gino and where had it got her?

She kicked at her tyre with the toe of her shoe. "Damn, damn, damn!"

"What's up?"

Taylor turned. Cass was walking towards her with a sixpack under her arm.

"What are you doing here?"

"Hair of the dog?" Cass tapped the top of the pack.

"I reckon." Taylor retrieved her phone and keys from her van and led the way inside her flat.

"Felt a bit worn out after the big wedding," Cass said. "Assumed you'd be the same but looks like you've got more than that on your mind."

"Bloody Gino's just sacked me."

"Doesn't surprise me."

"Why not?"

"He's a slave driver and a loose cannon." Cass had gone with Taylor to the staff Christmas party. She'd seen Gino in action. After a few drinks he was even more volatile. "What did he sack you for?"

Taylor thought back over the last two weeks.

"I was late collecting a group from the airport one day. But I made it up and the people were fine about it. Then I lost my phone and he couldn't call me till I got my new one. I did mess up another delivery late last week but today's wasn't my fault."

Cass expertly flipped the tops off two beers and handed one to Taylor.

"It was a shit job anyway. He's always treated you badly. You should come and work for me."

"I don't think so. Don't want to ruin a beautiful friendship."

"What do you mean?" Cass opened her mouth in mock surprise.

"You're a slave driver."

"You're a good worker."

"Let's leave it at that." They tapped the necks of their beers together.

"To the bride and groom," Taylor said.

"Rosie and Matt," Cass said then groaned. "How many toasts did we drink on Saturday night?"

"Too many."

"They certainly are happy."

"Yep." Taylor recalled the love in Rosie's look that was reciprocated in Matt's, the gentle touches, the secret smiles, the glances across the room when they were separated. They were true soulmates.

Taylor and Cass both took a long draught from their bottles. Cass wiped her mouth with the back of her hand. "I needed that."

They flopped onto Taylor's couch.

"It was a beautiful wedding." Taylor sighed.

"Thank goodness there's someone left to have drinks with." Cass gave her a nudge.

Taylor paused, her beer halfway to her mouth. She'd told her gran she was going bush but she'd only half meant it. She'd kept the idea of visiting Ed at bay until after the wedding. Well, the wedding was over. And now she no longer had a job to stay for. There was nothing to tie her down, in fact her life was going nowhere.

She sat up straight. "Not for long."

"Why's that?"

"I'm going to head off for a while."

"Where?"

"To the South East."

Cass stared at her. "You're not going to see Ed?"

"Why not?"

"You don't know him." Cass shook her head.

"There's chemistry between us."

"Lust!" Cass wiggled her shoulders and her ample breasts wobbled. "Hell, even I wouldn't mind shagging him."

"Bloody hell, Cass."

"He's fair game looking like that."

"It's more than good looks." Taylor lifted her chin and looked Cass straight in the eye. "I just know it."

"Like you did with Larry and Foster?"

Taylor felt herself stiffen. She couldn't believe her best friend was being so cruel.

"I'm sorry, Tales." Cass gave her a remorseful look. "I shouldn't have said that but–"

"It's my decision." Taylor put down her half-finished beer.

She'd thought Cass would support her. All their friends had partners. It didn't seem to bother Cass but Taylor wanted a relationship. Ed had hardly been out of her thoughts no matter how hard she'd tried to put him aside, his gaze, his touch, his kisses had been playing over in her mind for two weeks. She'd messed up another delivery last week and taken a group via some wrong turns to their venue. She had to admit she'd been distracted. Gino didn't know about those, not that it mattered now.

"You're frowning again."

Taylor looked at Cass. "Bloody Gino."

"Perhaps a trip would be good for you. I'd come too but we've got a big job on at work."

Taylor stood up. "I could be gone a while."

"How long?"

"If it works out with Ed I might stay."

"What's Ed say about that?"

Taylor looked away.

"He does know you're coming?"

"I didn't have a backup and lost most of my contacts and old messages when I lost my phone so I couldn't reply to his text."

"Why not call him at the winery? It would be easy enough to get the business number." Cass pulled out her phone. "I'll google it."

"No Cass." Taylor put a hand on her friend's arm. "I tried once. A woman answered and I got cold feet. I've decided to wing it."

"Damn Taylor, you can't just turn up."

"Why not?"

Cass opened and closed her mouth then took another swig of her beer. "I don't think this is a good idea," she muttered.

"Rosie and Matt are so happy and so in love. I want what they've got. I want a partner. A man in my life. What's wrong with that?"

"Nothing." Cass peered at her over the bottle. "As long as he's the right one."

Taylor grabbed her hand and pulled her friend to her feet. "I'm not having negativity," she said. "I've got lots to do."

Cass's look was contrite. "Don't be like that. I'm sorry. I'll help."

"No." Taylor's response was firm. "I'd rather be on my own. I'll text you when I get there." She edged Cass out the door and closed it firmly in her friend's worried face.

Taylor needed to make a change. If she couldn't go overseas she could spend time in another part of Australia. There was certainly no reason now not to go and visit Ed.

CHAPTER

10

Taylor pulled into the car park outside the Wriggly Creek cellar door. There was no 'Open' sign out the front and no other vehicles in the park. She sat back against the seat and lowered her window. The outside air was still hot.

She'd woken early and straight away been hit by nerves. Perhaps she was being hasty. She'd taken a deep breath, banished negative thoughts and set off full of eager anticipation but the further she travelled south the slower she went. Her aircon struggled in the heat again. It was late February and summer was still exerting a hold. Today was supposed to be thirty degrees. She'd stopped for iced coffee at Coonalpyn, toilet break at Tintinara and lunch in Keith. She'd idled through Naracoorte, stopped for more coffee and now finally she'd made it to Wriggly Creek Wines only to find no-one here. She closed her eyes and let out a deep breath. Now what?

Cass's words replayed in her head. "You can't just turn up."

Well she had. Taylor got out of her van, stretched and felt her t-shirt pull away from her damp skin. She walked to the door of the wine tasting room. Then she noticed the sandwich board declaring 'Wriggly Creek Cellar Door Open' through the glass just inside. She lifted her gaze to the sign stuck on the door. 'Opening hours 11am till 6pm Thursday to Monday.' Today was Wednesday.

Taylor's shoulders began to droop. Immediately she shrugged them. One small setback. She stepped off the verandah and walked to the end of the brown brick building. The land was flat in every direction and about one hundred metres away across the rows of vines she could see a stone cottage and further in the distance on the only slight rise, she could make out the grey tiled roof and cream brick of a house. It was a big house with picture windows. Edward's house. She recalled the night she'd spent there. She suspected the furnishings were much the same as when his parents had first built the house. It didn't have the look of a bachelor pad; more a family home without the family. The thought of knocking on his door sent a surge of panic through her already tight chest. Suddenly her casual, 'Hi, I've come back' sounded silly, needy. She took a deep calming breath. Further along the road from the cellar door was a group of large sheds. Maybe that was the place to look.

She went back to her van, climbed in and pulled her new phone from the console. If only she had Ed's number. She sighed and looked around. What should she do? Drive around looking for him or head into town, book herself a room and suss out the situation? The last of her waning anticipation left her.

She had her small nest egg of money. Enough to get her by for a while but she'd need to find work soon. All her worldly possessions were stashed in the body of the van behind her. After her wardrobe clean-out she had managed to squeeze her remaining clothes into a bag and a case. She had a garbage bag full of sheets and towels, a quilt, a box and esky with her kitchen supplies, and her little pod coffee machine. She had some paintings and assorted souvenirs she'd brought back from her travels, a few family photographs, a few books including her favourite cookbooks, and that was it. A couple of boxes was all she'd needed. Not much to show for her twenty-seven years. Gran owned most of the furniture and household goods in the flat. Her UK visitors were welcome to them.

In hindsight it would have made more sense for Taylor to leave her personal items in her bedroom at home. She glanced back at the stuff she'd piled into the van. Once again she'd acted before thinking it through. Gran and Cass would be laughing if they could see her now. Well, Gran wouldn't be laughing but she would say 'I told you so'. Cass wouldn't say it but Taylor would be able to see it in her look.

"Damn!" Taylor thumped the steering wheel with her hand. She didn't want them to be right. It only strengthened her resolve to make the best of it. Ed was around somewhere. She'd just have to find him. Once more she leaned back in the seat and closed her eyes.

Pete peered through the cellar door window. He'd noticed someone walking around in the car park, assumed they were checking to see if the place was open and would leave. Ten minutes later the van was still out the front and the driver appeared to be sleeping. He hesitated. Should he go and check? Maybe they were just resting.

He went to the table used as a desk in the back room and shuffled through the pile of papers once more. He still couldn't find the delivery note he was looking for. It had been a last resort to try the cellar door.

He sank to the chair ran his fingers through his hair and looked up. A large photograph hung there. His parents were planting the vines, Ed a toddler and Pete still the bulge under his mother's shirt. He loved the photo, his parents both laughing at the camera, Ed covered in the beautiful red terra rossa soil. Next to it was a more recent picture, this time he was in it with Ed and his father and they were planting the new cabernet clone that they'd named NS18. None of them looked at the camera. Their mother had taken the photo. She had captured them intent on their work. He stood up feeling a swell of pride that this vintage would see the first viable crop from those vines.

He stuck his head into the front room. The van was still there. It was getting late. He decided to investigate. He didn't want someone camping in their car park.

Pete tapped on the window of the van. The woman inside jumped and lowered the window.

"Is there a problem?" he said then paused. She looked familiar.

"Peter, isn't it?" she asked. Her lips turned up in a shy smile.

"Yes." He stepped back as she opened her door.

"I'm Taylor," she said. "We met at…I was at Ed's. You came by as he was driving me back to town."

"Oh, yes." Now he remembered. She was the attractive blonde who'd been at Ed's a couple of weeks back.

"I don't suppose…" Once more her voice faltered. "Do you know where Ed is at the moment?"

"Melbourne."

"Oh."

Pete resisted the urge to pat her arm. She looked crestfallen. "He should be back in a week. I'm hoping less. It's the worst time for him to be away."

"Oh," she said again.

She looked exhausted. What was a girl like her doing chasing Ed? She appeared far too sensible to be one of his flings but then Pete had almost given up on being a good judge of female character.

"I can give you his number."

"That would be good, thanks. I had it but I lost my phone."

Pete hesitated. Maybe Ed hadn't actually given her his number in the first place. She glanced up from her phone. The gleam of her pale-blue eyes and soft curve of her lips gave away no deception. She punched in the number as he dictated.

"Have you driven far?" he asked.

"Only from Adelaide."

She turned back to her van. "I'll get going."

"Where will you go?"

"Into town."

Once more Pete wavered. She closed the van door and he rested his hand on it.

"Was Ed expecting you? He didn't say anything." Pete recalled Ed's indignant snort when he'd suggested his brother was going to spend time with this woman.

"Yes and no." She gave him an apologetic smile. "He suggested I come back but we didn't make a definite arrangement. Then I lost my phone…"

"Did he offer work? Grape picking or something?" Pete could see there were more than clothes in the back of her van. Either she lived in it or she was on the move.

"Not exactly."

He pulled his cap off and dragged his fingers through his hair. "Ed's trip was short notice. He wouldn't normally be away at this time of year." He shoved the cap firmly back on his head. "Look, why don't you stay the night again at his place? You'll have trouble getting accommodation in town. There're a few big events on at the moment. Most places are booked out from what I've heard. You've stayed at Ed's before, I'm sure he won't mind."

"Oh no, I couldn't do that." She shook her head and her blonde hair fluffed around her face. "We're not…at least I…no." The pink of her cheeks deepened. "But thank you for the offer."

"Or there's the quarters behind my place." Something about Taylor made him want to help her. "It's basic accommodation for extras during the busy times. Rarely used."

A look of hesitation passed over her face. "I don't want to—"

"It's nothing fancy," he cut in. "It'll give you a chance to rest and think about what you want to do."

She gave him a grateful smile. "Okay, thanks."

"I'll ride with you," he said. "Show you where to go." He walked around to the passenger side and climbed into the van beside her. "Go up the road, past the sheds."

"Sorry about the lack of aircon," she said. "You're better off with the window down."

"Don't worry about it. Is this your van?"

"Yes." Her reply sounded defensive.

"I was only thinking it's not a common choice of vehicle."

"For a girl." She flicked him a questioning look.

"For anyone unless they're in a business that requires a van."

"My last job was as a courier driver and people mover."

"Turn right here." Pete pointed to the dirt track that ran past the office and sheds. "So the company didn't provide the vehicle."

"I did a lot of freelance. I didn't have any kind of vehicle when I got back from my last overseas trip. I was offered this van at a good price. It gave me a personal vehicle and one to work with."

"Turn to the left just before the stone cottage."

"Oh, what a quaint place. Is it yours?" Taylor stopped the van where the track bent off to the left.

"Yes."

She leaned out the window a little staring at his home. "I love the wood frame windows and you've made the new roof in keeping with the era."

"We put new tin on when we did up the rooms across the back. Wriggly Creek was a dairy before my parents bought it. They built a new house but kept this cottage for pickers. When I came home we did up the cottage for me and turned the old besser brick dairy into quarters for seasonal workers." He pointed to the left.

Taylor followed the track around to the quarters, about twenty metres from the cottage.

"Pull in here." He pointed to the white wooden door between two large windows set in the front of the grey brick building.

She stopped the van near the door.

"It's basic accommodation but comfortable enough," Peter said. "Luckily it got cleaned the other day. We have an extra cellar hand coming for vintage. He won't be here for another week so you've got the place to yourself."

"Thanks, Peter." She turned to him and a beautiful smile lit up her face.

Pete paused with his hand on the door handle. No wonder Ed had fallen for her. Taylor was one very attractive woman. He pulled on the handle, but his hand slipped and he had to try again to let himself out of the van and away from that smile. He pulled open the screen door and turned the knob on the old wooden door.

"This is always a bit stiff," he said. He looked back and Taylor was right behind him. "You have to put your shoulder into it." He used such force that the door flew open and catapulted him into the room.

He heard a stifled giggle behind him.

"This is great," Taylor said as she walked past him to stand in the middle of the room. "A cheerful space."

Pete glanced around at the floral curtains and bright orange vinyl chairs. His mother had made use of scrounged items to decorate the place but retro was trendy these days.

"There are four bedrooms." He led the way down the corridor that ran off from the living space. "The beds are new." He pushed open the first door and moved on to the next. "You can take your pick. There are two separate bathrooms through the end door and a back entrance with washing machine and laundry tub if you need it."

"Thanks." Taylor turned to him. The blue of her eyes sparkled despite her obvious fatigue. "This will be great."

"I'll bring you some bread and milk."

"Oh no, that's okay. I've got some things in my esky. If I need anything else I can drive in to the supermarket."

"I'll leave you to it then."

"Thanks again."

She gave him a small wave and shut the door.

Pete stared at it a moment then turned away and paced the short distance to his own door. He knew he probably shouldn't have offered the accommodation. He glanced back at the quarters then let himself in through the door of his cottage. He was only looking out for her until Ed came back. That was as far as it went.

CHAPTER

11

The morning air was crisp, but without a cloud in the sky the day promised to be a warm one. Freshly showered, Pete stood at his kitchen bench eating cereal and thinking through his plans for the day. He put down the bowl as his mobile rang.

"Morning Felicity," he said then frowned as she croaked back at him. "You don't sound good."

"Sorry, Pete, I'm still not well," she rasped.

"Don't worry. I'll manage. You take it easy."

He brushed over her apologies, told her to get better soon and ended the call. Felicity had been away a few days already. Normally she didn't work every day but this time of the year she always put in extra hours. It was tricky without her help, especially with Ed away.

Pete had just put his phone in his pocket when it rang again. This time the name on the screen was his mate Ben. Pete's finger hesitated over the answer tab. Ben was meant to be coming in today. Pete hoped this call was just to confirm arrangements and not to cancel.

"Hello, Ben."

"Hey mate. Bit of trouble with some stock. I can't come in."

Pete scrunched up his face. The son of a local farmer, Ben needed extra work to supplement his income. Pete was grateful for his help but the farm came first. He kept his tone jovial. "No worries mate, we'll be right. You do what you have to do."

Once he'd ended the call Pete stared at his phone a moment. It was a bugger Ed was away. He wondered how much longer till his brother came back. The riesling was in but their Limestone Coast supplier would be picking the sauv blanc grapes any day and then the chardonnay would be ready. He had more wine to truck out and tanks to clean. There wasn't time to man phones or help Noelene in the cellar door. There were a lot of extra tourists around this week. He hoped Noelene would manage on her own.

He glanced at his watch. It had been his father's. How he wished his dad and mum were still here. He swallowed the last of his coffee, stacked his dishes in the sink and lifted his head. No amount of wishing would bring his parents back. The tanker for his riesling would be here in an hour. He had to make sure all was ready, divert the office phone to his mobile and check the cellar door was ready for Noelene. Sometimes he thought it would be easier if they opened it every day but then he or Ed would have to be there and that wasn't always possible.

He picked up his phone and selected Ed's number. Perhaps he was on his way home.

It took a while before his brother's croaky voice answered.

"Pete? Bloody hell, what time is it?"

"Seven o'clock here. Where are you?"

"Sydney and still in bed. I've had a big couple of days. What's up?"

Pete hesitated. He didn't want Ed to think he couldn't manage the place on his own but they were two staff members down.

"Just wondering when you'll be back," he said.

"Everything all right there?"

"Yes. It's getting busy, that's all."

"I'm not sitting on my bum here, you know." Ed's tone was defensive.

"Any luck with new markets?"

"I'll tell you all about it when I get home."

"When will that be?"

"I don't know yet, Peter."

Pete hated the way his brother spoke sometimes. He was Pete's senior by two years but sometimes he spoke as if he was an adult chastising a child.

"Soon…a few more days. I have to make a stop off in Melbourne overnight again. Someone I missed on the way over." Suddenly his voice lightened. "Now that I'm awake I'm going to make the most of the morning without appointments. I'll be in touch."

The call ended. Pete stared at the screen. This trip had come up out of the blue. Not that that was unusual in the wine industry. If there was an opportunity to make a deal you had to take it when you could but Pete felt totally in the dark about Ed's current trip.

A text beeped from his inbox.

"What now?" he murmured as Noelene's name appeared. He read her message.

Cracked a tooth. Going to the Mount. Ben should be fine till I get back.

Pete groaned. What was with the world today? Three staff members not available. He hoped that was the end of his problems. He took his hat from the back of the chair and headed out the front door. First things first. Check everything was ready for the tanker in case it came early. Then he might get some office time in.

Taylor sat in the sunshine that poured through the big living room window and sipped her coffee. She'd only unpacked the bare necessities from her van last night. Her coffee machine was definitely a necessity. The morning sun was warm on her shoulders but she imagined it wouldn't be too long and she'd have to pull the blind down if the day was going to turn out anything like yesterday.

She looked around the room. Peter had been right about the place being comfortable. The chair she sat in was an old one, the fabric on the arms was worn and grubby, but she nestled easily into it. And she'd had a fabulous sleep. The bedrooms were cell-like with high ceilings. There was only room for a single bed and the window above it was also small. There was a clothes rack, a bedside cupboard and thankfully a ceiling fan which had helped stir the air till the temperature had dropped in the early hours and she'd pulled up the sheet. Little light came in through the window and the thick brick walls cocooned her from outside sounds. She hadn't woken until eight o'clock. It had been a deep, refreshing sleep.

Taylor stretched her legs then tucked them up beneath her. Her energy had returned along with a tingle of anticipation. She didn't know what the day would bring but she didn't want to lose that feeling.

She gazed out at the vines stretching away beyond her window. She couldn't see any grapes amongst the deep green leaves basking in the morning sun. The roof of a house was just visible in the distance. She didn't have her bearings yet but she assumed it was Ed's house.

She glanced at her mobile perched on one of the wide arms and willed it to ring. Once she'd settled in last night she'd tried to ring Ed. His phone had gone straight to voicemail. She hadn't left a message. What would she say? 'You said come back so here I am' or 'Hi, just passing through Penola, thought I'd call in'.

Peter already knew that wasn't true. He could have even rung Ed, warned him that she was here and that she was going to ring. Perhaps that was why Ed hadn't answered. She shook her head and berated herself. Already she was doing a good job of smothering the hopeful feeling. She looked back at the view. No negativity. Instead she pictured Ed's brother, so different in looks and personality than Ed and yet she liked him. He was kind, that was obvious from his offer of a place to stay, and he had the most beautiful eyes. They were the same colour as Ed's, blue, but they had a different hue. Ed's were darker. Pete's were clear light blue with a look that made you want to fall into his arms. She shook herself. Not that she was going to. Ed was the reason she was here.

Once more she looked at her phone.

She gritted her teeth and pushed out of the chair. It was all very well to sit drinking coffee in the sunshine but what was she going to do next? Did she stay another day? If she didn't where would she go? Not back to Adelaide. She'd have to admit to Cass that she'd stuffed up. She'd already sent her friend a text last night saying she'd arrived safely and all was well.

"No going back, Taylor," she muttered.

She rinsed her cup and straightened the kitchen chair she'd sat on to eat her meal last night. In the bedroom she pulled up the sheet on the bed then sat on it. Now what? She'd showered last night and her towel still hung over the door. She plucked it down and set off along the passage. Maybe another shower would help her to think.

Pete dashed back to his cottage. It was nearly time to open the cellar door. He wanted to grab a bite to eat and change his shirt. He jammed some cheese and tomato between two pieces of bread and went in search of his cellar door shirt.

His day had gone relatively well so far considering the start he'd had. The tanker had been a bit late but the process had gone smoothly. He wasn't quite sure how he was going to man the cellar door and juggle the rest of his jobs but he was hoping Noelene wouldn't be too long.

There was no work shirt in his wardrobe, so he rummaged in the laundry basket. He had three of them, usually he kept one over at the cellar door but it hadn't been there. He'd just have to wear a different shirt. What did it matter? Ed was the one who'd decided they needed the shirts. Pete tugged his t-shirt over his head and dropped it on the floor. Then he remembered he'd done the washing a couple of days ago. His shirts would be on the line. He stepped out his back door and stopped. He'd completely forgotten about Taylor. Her van was still parked at the front of the quarters.

He plucked a shirt from the line. It was a bit creased but it would do.

"Hello."

He turned at the sound of her voice. She'd come from the track that led out to the road.

"Morning," he said and slipped his arms into his shirt.

She came to a stop just beyond the crumbling fence that marked the edge of his yard. He couldn't see her eyes but she was smiling at him from under a broad straw hat. It was one of the assorted leftovers from the quarters.

"I've been for a walk but it's getting quite hot."

"Sorry, I haven't had time to call in." Pete couldn't believe he'd forgotten all about her. "Are you getting on all right?"

"Fine."

He fumbled with his buttons. "Any plans for the day?"

A small frown wiped away her smile. "Not really."

"Would you like to help out at the cellar door for a while?"

She looked at him. Her frown deepened. Why had he asked? She was just here for Ed.

"I don't know anything about wine," she said. The smile came back. "But I could wash glasses, wipe benches."

"That'd be good. I'm short-staffed today." He glanced at his watch. "I have to go. Come down when you're ready."

Pete dashed back through the cottage. He picked up the remains of his sandwich, grabbed his hat and strode out the front door. It was opening time.

CHAPTER

12

"So tell me what you do again."

Edward looked at the woman opposite. They were at a wine bar occupying two chairs at an outside table. The table was in the shade but the sky over Sydney was slightly overcast and they both wore sunglasses against the late afternoon glare. Heidi peered at him over the top of hers. She was blonde, attractive, but somehow she'd seemed more fun at the bar last night.

"I own a winery," he said.

"That's right. Somewhere south. Victoria, wasn't it?"

"South Australia."

"Oh, does South Australia have a wine region?"

Edward smiled at her. "Several." He spoke through gritted teeth. "That wine you're drinking is from South Australia. It's an Adelaide Hills sauvignon blanc."

"Really? Well you learn something new every day." She lifted the glass and peered at the wine as if it was suddenly going to announce its name. "I have to admit I don't take much notice of the label, as long as it's good wine I don't care where it comes from." She took another large mouthful and sat the glass back on the table. "Tell me more."

She tilted her head up. He couldn't see her eyes and thankfully she couldn't see his. It was difficult enough to keep the smile on his lips. Perhaps he should have caught an earlier flight to Melbourne after his last meeting was cancelled. He was wasting his time here. Still, now that he had one more night to kill in Sydney, no point in sitting alone in a hotel room. Heidi's company wasn't that bad.

"About the winery?" he asked.

"Yes. I'll pay more attention this time. What's it called?"

"Wriggly Creek."

"Oh. How cute."

Edward took a sip of wine. That was one of their problems right there. People thought the name cute or quaint or anything but a name for a serious wine.

"I've never been to South Australia. Where is Wriggly Creek?"

"Have you heard of Mount Gambier?"

Heidi leaned closer. The soft drape of fabric over her breasts fell forward revealing plump flesh. "Maybe."

Edward liked breasts that were more than a handful. He dragged his gaze to her face. "Coonawarra is in the south east corner of South Australia, not far from the Victorian border."

"Coona-what?"

"Coonawarra. It's a small town and the name of our wine region."

She raised her glass. "Do you make sauvignon blanc?"

"We do, but our chardonnay is our winery's best white. It's won two medals."

"Oh, that sounds good. I like chardy. Pity I can't try some of yours."

"I have some back in my hotel."

"Do you now? Was that the same place you were suggesting I went with you late last night?"

"No, that was the hotel bar." Edward's smile widened. "The chardonnay is in the fridge in my room."

Even though he couldn't see her eyes, her lips twitched. She took another sip from her glass then traced her long elegant fingers around the rim.

"I think I'm going to need some food soon," she said. "I didn't get time for lunch."

"Where's the best place to eat?" Things were looking up. Maybe the night wouldn't be a fizzer after all. "Let me take you out for dinner."

She leaned in closer and looked over the top of her glasses. This time he could see a glint in her eye. "The chef here has some interesting dishes. I'll pick the food, you pick the wine. Let's see where that takes us, shall we?"

Edward chuckled, a deep throaty laugh.

Several hours later he regretted his decision. They'd moved on to a club where Heidi had been all over him as they danced. That went on for a while. Now he was alone. She was out on the dance floor gyrating with several other women. Heidi was a player but he'd tired of the game. She was planning on going back to the hotel with him but he found himself no longer wanting what she was so clearly offering. It had been a long day. He slid from the booth and left.

The alarm sounded on Edward's phone. He groaned and pulled the pillow over his head. He was still tired. Added to that was his annoyance that this trip to Sydney hadn't brought the meetings with connections he'd hoped to make. He'd been to a dinner where he presented his wines to a group of top Sydney sommeliers. These men were the gatekeepers for the wine that made it to the tables of their fancy restaurants. He had been hopeful of at least getting

Wriggly Creek chardonnay accepted or their reserve cabernet sauvignon, but no such luck. They'd been more interested in a group of natural winemakers and their orange wine which was a new trend. One guy had said he played music to his wine while it fermented. The sommeliers went wild over that. Personally Edward didn't get it. He'd also had a meeting with Barry, their distributor, but there was nothing new there.

He rolled onto his back and tossed the pillow away. A night with Heidi may have made it all worthwhile but he'd never know now. Perhaps he was losing it. He'd rarely knocked back the chance to bed a woman before, especially away from home with no strings attached. After meeting Heidi that had been all he'd thought of but by the end of the second evening with her he was no longer interested.

He'd been like that with Taylor as well, but she was different. She was hot but she hadn't thrown herself at him like Heidi had. It was a pity Taylor hadn't replied to his texts but once she got back to Adelaide she'd obviously decided not to keep in touch. He'd been surprised to find a missed call from her after his meeting two nights ago. It was unexpected and he'd been busy. Maybe he'd follow up on it when he returned to Wriggly Creek.

He licked his lips. His mouth was as dry as a cockie's cage. Edward prised himself from the bed and staggered into the bathroom. In the mirror his hair looked lank, his skin sallow and there were bags under his eyes. He needed water and a shower. He had his most important meeting coming up in Melbourne this afternoon, the reason for all the secrecy, and he didn't want to be behind the eight ball before he started. With any luck his trip away wouldn't be a total waste of time.

By the time he got to his hotel in Melbourne, Edward was starting to lag again. It was a hot day, oppressive, not like the weather he'd left behind in Sydney. His phone rang. The name on the screen brought a scowl to his face. Heidi. He must have been drunk to exchange phone numbers. He let it go to voicemail. The bag he'd brought with him lay open on the end of his bed. He pulled out a clean shirt, shook it out and cursed. He'd have to iron it.

He had a strange sensation in his stomach. Nerves? He rarely felt nervous but he was certainly on edge. So much rode on this meeting. If Wriggly Creek was to survive they needed to expand. He had his eye on some vineyards north of Coonawarra but without a backer he didn't have the capital to go ahead. His few attempts to discuss this with Peter had failed. His brother wanted to keep doing things the same old way. He didn't worry about the money. He was happy to leave that stress to Edward. They had all their eggs in one basket and that wasn't good business.

The iron snagged on a button. Edward reached to smooth the shirt and brushed the tip of the iron with his finger. The sudden pain only increased his irritation. He stuck his finger in his mouth and felt sweat trickle down his back. He looked at his watch. Damn. There was no time for another shower, just a quick freshen-up before he met with Mr Cheng and his employer, Mr Zhu.

CHAPTER
13

Taylor wiped the top of the bar again and made sure all the folders listing Wriggly Creek wines were straight. She glanced behind her, willing Peter to appear through the back entrance before the group of men she'd just seen pull up out the front made it inside the cellar door. There was no sign of him. He'd said he wouldn't be long, but something had happened in the sheds that required his attention.

Yesterday he hadn't left her side all afternoon. His cellar door manager, Noelene, hadn't turned up. She'd sent a late text to say she had an abscess and would need another day at home. There was a friend, Ben, who helped out but he couldn't come either and their office manager was away sick. With nothing else to do Taylor had offered to stay and help in the cellar door again.

She didn't understand half of what Peter said but he was obviously passionate about his wine. Observing him, working alongside him, listening to him talk to customers – it had all piqued her interest. She was actually enjoying the experience.

They'd been busy for a couple of hours but it was late afternoon and the cellar door had been empty for a while. This group would probably be the last for the day.

Taylor glanced at the typed sheet she had on her side of the bar. Just use the tasting notes Peter had said. That's how the others who worked in the cellar door learned. She hoped she could sell some wine without his help. She looked up and smiled as the men came in.

"Welcome, gentlemen," she said. "Are you all tasting today?"

"We have a meeting." The first man through the door spoke for them all. He was tall with gingery hair and freckles on his pale face, a sharp contrast to the other two who were shorter and of Chinese origin. They were neatly dressed in suits, like businessmen.

Taylor looked back at the tall man. Did he mean they were having a meeting here or in a hurry to go to a meeting?

"Where is Mr Starr?" he asked.

"He's been called away," she said.

The tall man looked at the first Chinese man who turned to the other and spoke in what Taylor assumed was Chinese.

There was a quick exchange and then the first Chinese man spoke to her. "I am Mr Cheng. This is Mr Zhu." The man beside him gave a deep nod. "Mr Zhu has a meeting with Mr Starr at four o'clock."

Taylor glanced at the clock on the wall. They got that part right. Peter hadn't mentioned it but then he hadn't expected to leave her on her own. She flicked a look behind her. There was no help there. She didn't want to jeopardise any meeting Peter may have arranged. She took a calming breath.

"Mr Starr had to step out for a moment. Something happened in the winery he had to sort out. He should be back soon." She hoped she was right. "Perhaps we could start the tasting while you wait?"

The two Chinese men nodded and smiled. Taylor set up three glasses on the bar.

"Would you like to start with the whites?" she asked.

"We prefer the reds," the tall man said. He hadn't introduced himself.

Mr Cheng spoke to Mr Zhu who nodded.

"We will begin with the whites," Mr Cheng said firmly, ignoring the man on his other side.

Taylor took a bottle of riesling from the fridge. She noticed a slight tremor of her hand. How ridiculous. She could nail this. She glanced at the tasting notes, took a deep breath and began to speak as she poured.

"This riesling has aromas of citrus blossom and lemon zest." She glanced back at the notes. "With a touch of minerality." Whatever that meant. "And flavours of lemon sherbet and granny smith apple, a hint of chalkiness…"

The men looked at her expectantly.

"Frames the end." Taylor hoped her smile would cover up any jumbled words.

They picked up their glasses. While the tall man was all about sniffing and sipping and spitting into the barrel designed as a spittoon, the two Chinese men simply swallowed the wine and sat their glasses back on the bar. They both smiled and nodded at her.

She reached for the next white, skimmed a look over the notes and poured.

"Our sauvignon blanc grapes come from the cooler, maritime climate at Mount Benson. This wine was produced after a cold winter and a mild spring which produces the best sauvignon blanc." She paused. Once more the tall man was sticking his nose in the glass while the other two simply smiled and swallowed. "Er, you might notice, er–" she glanced down, "–melon, passionfruit and gooseberry…it's clean and crisp with a bright zippy finish." The last words came out in a rush as the two Chinese men placed their glasses on the bar and smiled.

Where was Peter? She felt so out of her depth. The chardonnay was next and then the sparkling shiraz. She worked her way through the wine list, providing a more and more garbled rendition of the tasting notes. By the end she was making it up. At least Mr Zhu couldn't understand her and Mr Cheng's English was a little stilted, but she had noticed the other man raise his eyebrows once or twice when she'd stumbled over her words.

By the time they had tried the shiraz and the cabernet sauvignon, Mr Zhu and Mr Cheng were very merry and tall guy very serious.

"Can't you call Mr Starr?" he asked her. "I have to drive Mr Zhu back to Melbourne tonight."

"Tonight?" That would explain the spitting.

"It's a five-hour trip."

Taylor looked around. Did she leave them here and walk up to the sheds looking for Peter? There was one more bottle of red sitting beside those already tasted. It had a different label and was a cabernet reserve, whatever that meant. Perhaps something special. She hoped so as she picked it up.

"One more to taste," she said. She flipped over the tasting notes. Nothing mentioned a reserve wine. This one had a cork instead of a screw cap. After some difficulty she tugged the cork from the bottle and poured. This time she noticed tall guy swallow instead of spit, although he didn't down his glass as quickly as the other two.

"I'll take a dozen of these," he said when he finished savouring the wine. "How much will that be?"

Taylor's mind went into a spin. "Excuse me a minute," she said. "I'm only new here." She sifted through all the tasting notes and lists she could find but nothing mentioned a reserve cabernet sauvignon. She found a box of them under the bar. There was one missing, no doubt the bottle she'd just opened. "I've only got eleven," she said, lifting the box to the bar.

Tall guy had his card out of his wallet. "That's fine. How much?"

Taylor did a quick calculation. The other cabernet sauvignon on the list was thirty dollars a bottle. Perhaps reserve meant special. If that was the case should she double it? She looked up at the man who was looking down his nose at her. He hadn't been that polite. What did she care if he bought the wine or not?

"It's usually ninety dollars a bottle," she said, "but as I only have eleven I can take ten dollars off the total."

He didn't even blink. "Done."

Damn, Taylor thought, I should have asked for more. She hoped she was doing the right thing as she processed his credit card. Without Peter to help her she just had to make it up.

"I'll put these in the car," the guy said to Mr Cheng.

There was a clatter behind her and Peter burst into the room. His face was sweaty and he was puffing slightly as if he'd been running. His shirt was streaked with red.

"Welcome back," Taylor said with a smile. "Your guests have been waiting a while."

"Guests?"

Peter looked at the two Chinese men on the other side of the bar and then to their companion as he came back through the door.

"This is Mr Starr," Taylor said.

"About time," murmured the tall guy.

"Very pleased to meet you," Mr Cheng said. "May I introduce the head of Zhu Trading, Mr Zhu."

Taylor noticed Peter wipe his red-stained hand down his jeans before he extended it over the counter. "Peter Starr," he said. "How can I help you?"

"No, no." Mr Cheng shook his head vigorously. "We have a meeting with Mr Edward Starr."

Taylor stared at Peter who opened and closed his mouth.

"Edward's not here," he said.

Mr Cheng began speaking to Mr Zhu in Chinese.

"What time do you expect him back?" tall guy asked.

"And you are?" Peter said.

"Frank Lister." He stood up straight, making him a head taller than Peter. "I don't know what kind of show your brother runs but Mr Zhu had a meeting with him at four pm today. We've driven from Melbourne especially and we have to drive back tonight so that Mr Zhu can catch his flight tomorrow morning."

"Look, are you sure the meeting was to take place here?" Peter asked.

"Where is Mr Edward Starr?" Mr Cheng cut in. His voice was low but firm.

"Well that's just it. I'm fairly sure he's in Melbourne for a meeting. I don't know who with but–"

Lister cut Peter off with a muttered burst of expletives.

A pained expression crossed Mr Cheng's face. He took a deep breath then pulled a thin smile to his lips and looked from Peter to Taylor. "There seems to be a mistake," he said slowly and clearly. "I myself rang last week and spoke to the young woman." He nodded at Taylor then turned back to Peter. "I told her Mr Zhu had found time to visit the winery in person. Instead of meeting Mr Starr in Melbourne we were to meet here." He looked pointedly at Taylor.

She shook her head. "It wasn't me."

"Taylor has only been here two days." Peter defended her. "You must have spoken to someone else and the message wasn't passed on. What were you meeting Edward about? He is the business manager but I am his brother and the winemaker here. Perhaps I can help?"

Mr Cheng spoke to Mr Zhu and there were a lot of short words exchanged back and forth and head shaking before he turned back to Peter.

"I am sorry but Mr Zhu's business is only with Mr Edward Starr."

Pete pulled his mobile from his pocket. "I could try ringing him."

Once more Mr Cheng spoke to Mr Zhu. Mr Zhu shook his head emphatically.

"That won't be necessary," Mr Cheng said. "It was meant to be a meeting in person. We thank you for your hospitality, Miss Taylor." Both Chinese men inclined their heads to her. Taylor fought the urge to laugh.

Mr Cheng turned back to Peter. "We enjoyed your wine very much. You are a very good winemaker. Now we must go." Both men inclined their heads again and turned on their heels.

Lister leaned over the bar and spoke in a low voice to Peter. "Bad luck about your brother but good job with the last red."

"Last red?" Peter said to Lister's back as he let himself out. He turned to Taylor. "Was that the shiraz or the cab sauv?"

She chewed her bottom lip as she took in his puzzled expression. "Neither," she said.

He frowned.

"I hope I haven't done the wrong thing." She held up the reserve bottle she'd opened. "I sold him this one."

Peter's eyes widened. "That's not on the tasting list."

"I know, but I was trying to stall for time. It was sitting on the bench, so I opened it." She grinned. "That Lister guy really went for it."

"How many bottles did he buy?"

"I could only find the box this one had come out of. He took the lot."

Peter ran his fingers through his short curls. "Eleven bottles?"

"I'm sorry." Taylor was worried by his reaction. "Was it the wrong thing to do?"

"It's all we had left of our best cabernet. I was keeping it for any of our weekend tasters who showed a special interest."

"I'm sorry," Taylor said again.

"Look, you weren't to know. We'll have a replacement bottled soon. Lister reckoned it was okay did he? I wasn't going to try it tonight but now that you've opened it let's give it a go."

He poured some of the wine into two glasses. Taylor stared at the glass he offered as if it would bite her.

"It won't keep."

She took the glass from him and watched while he swirled his and sniffed it like Lister had, then took a sip.

Peter's face lit up. "That is good, even if I do say so myself. Come on, try it."

Taylor took a small sip. The wine rolled around her tongue and left a smoky taste as she swallowed.

Peter took another sip. "What do you think?"

"It tastes fine to me but I've no idea about wine. I feel bad I sold your last box."

"Don't worry about it. I couldn't have managed without your help so we're even."

Taylor took another sip. The wine was smooth and the taste lingered after she swallowed. She could get used to it.

Peter's brow furrowed. "There was no price. How much did you sell it for?"

Taylor set the half-drunk glass firmly on the bar. She'd quite enjoyed herself even though the whole experience with the three men had been stressful. Now she was a bit worried. She'd sold his best wine.

"Ninety dollars."

"For the box?" Peter took another sip of wine.

"No, per bottle."

Taylor's eyes widened as he almost choked and spat his precious wine into the sink.

"Well, a bit less." She'd obviously not charged enough. She'd thought Lister crazy to spend that much. Who paid all that money for wine? "I took ten dollars off because he bought what was left of the box," she added.

Peter's lips twitched in a smile. "How did you come at that price?"

"I was put on the spot. Your other cabernet was thirty dollars. I thought I'd double it and then that Lister guy annoyed me, so I trebled it." Taylor lifted her chin. "He was happy to pay."

Peter started to laugh then he grabbed her and gave her a hug. "Well done, Taylor."

Her cheeks suddenly felt warm. She'd thought him kind of pudgy when she first met him but now that she'd seen him without a shirt she knew his chest was tanned and chiselled. That same chest was now pressed against hers.

She put a hand to her cheek as he let her go. "I thought you meant I'd got it totally wrong."

"We were selling it for fifty last year."

"Oh, so I did charge too much."

"It's aged well. Did he complain?"

"No."

"Because he knew how good it was." Peter chuckled even louder, rounded the counter and let himself out the door. Taylor watched him go, enjoying the deep sound of his laugh along with a warm feeling inside that she was the cause of it. She picked up the glasses from the bar and put them in the sink. He brought in the 'Open' sign and locked the front doors.

"Leave the glasses," he said. "I'll wash them and do the stocktake tomorrow. It's Friday night and I do believe I owe you dinner."

"You don't have to, Peter."

"Call me Pete, please, all my friends do. Peter sounds so formal."

"Well your offer is very kind, Pete, but I don't need you to buy me dinner."

"It's the least I can do." He offered the crook of his arm. "Taylor Rourke, you are one hell of a businesswoman."

She took his arm, unable to resist the deep tenor of his voice and the look of delight in his clear blue eyes.

"Why thank you, kind sir. I'd be delighted."

CHAPTER
14

The front bar of the pub was noisy but the dining room less so. Pete guided Taylor that way with their drinks.

"What do you feel like eating?" He handed her a menu. "Their meals are all good but I can recommend their pies. My favourite is the beef and Guinness but the chicken's good too."

"You've sold me on the beef and Guinness and I'm happy to pay for my meal." Taylor held her glass up. "You've already bought me a beer."

"I insist. A meal is cheap wages for what you've helped me with over the last two days."

Taylor's smile stretched wider and her eyes sparkled. "Okay. I won't argue. Thank you."

"Have a seat." Pete pulled out a chair at the nearest table. "I'll place the order."

He almost tripped on a chair leg in his hurry to get away from that mesmerising look. No wonder Ed was taken with her. Something

Pete had to remind himself of. There was no point in losing his heart to Taylor. She was Ed's girl.

He chose a bottle of wine to go with the pies. By the time he got back to the table he had his wayward emotions under control.

"I'm sorry I didn't ask what kind of wine you like." He put the bottle and two glasses on the table. "Or even if you like wine at all."

"I feel it's wasted on me. I'm a beer drinker."

"It takes a lot of beer to make a good wine."

Taylor put her head to one side and studied him across the table. "Ed said something like that. I don't get it."

"Winemakers work long hours without a break during vintage." Pete lifted his beer glass and took another mouthful.

A frown creased Taylor's brow.

"There's no better way to unwind after a fourteen-hour day in the cellar than with an icy-cold beer." Pete grinned. "We usually go through quite a few along the way. So it takes—"

"A lot of beer to make a good wine." Taylor finished the sentence and laughed. "Now I get it."

Pete finished his beer and poured two glasses of the red he'd bought.

"This is a cab sauv, grown by another local. A mate of mine. You'll find it a bit different to the one we drank this afternoon." Pete tilted his glass towards his nose. He could smell the clove and blackcurrant. He took a sip, rolled it round his tongue and swallowed. "It's younger so the tannins are tight, but you get that earthy, blackcurrant flavour coming through on the palate."

Taylor picked up her glass and took a sip. She smiled but he could see her lips pursed at the taste.

"Sometimes it takes a while to grow on you."

"I'm gathering Coonawarra has something special going for it when it comes to red wine."

"You might say that. It's the most renowned strip of terroir in Australia if not the world."

"What's…how did you say it? Tear wah?"

"Terroir. It's a French word. It's how you describe all the climatic factors that influence a wine growing region. Like the soil, the wind, the rain and the sun. They all play a crucial part in growing grapes."

"So what's so special about Coonawarra terroir?"

"We have the terra rossa; a dark red, iron-rich soil that sits on top of a deep ridge of limestone, coupled with a good water supply, cool nights and a long mild growing season. Put all those together with talented winemakers."

"Which is where you come in."

"Of course." He grinned and she gave a deep warm chuckle. "So all together, this region makes some of the best cabernet sauvignon and shiraz in the country, recognised around the world."

"Hmmm." Taylor took another sip of her wine. Her nose wrinkled ever so slightly.

"Would you prefer another beer?" He started to rise.

She reached across and put a hand on his arm. "No, really this is fine. I'm not much of a red wine drinker."

Pete rose to his feet this time. "I'll get you a beer." He set off before she could protest. He could easily forget not everyone appreciated wine like he did.

By the time he came back with her beer the pies had arrived.

"Thanks, Pete."

Once more her warm smile sent a jolt of energy through him, stirring emotions he didn't want to acknowledge.

"My pleasure." He sat down and tucked into the pie, trying his best to avoid her captivating gaze for a few minutes. Pete had enjoyed working with her. Once she'd overcome her initial reticence, she'd learned the job quickly and shown a quirky sense of humour. She was good fun but out of bounds.

"Have you always been a winemaker?"

Taylor's question forced him to look up. She glanced at him and took another bite of her food.

"It's all I've ever wanted to do. I guess it came from being immersed in it from birth. As soon as I was old enough I always had some brew or other fermenting in the laundry."

"Your mum didn't mind?"

"I think she was used to it. Dad lived and breathed winemaking." Pete felt a deep pang of loss. The suddenness of it surprised him. He clutched the wine glass and took a steadying mouthful.

"I'm sorry." Taylor looked crestfallen. "I've just remembered Ed said your parents were killed in an accident."

"No need to be sorry. It was years ago." Pete took another sip of red. "Life goes on."

"You still miss them though."

"Very much." It was out before Pete even thought about it.

"I didn't mean to stir up the past." Her look was full of compassion.

"You didn't. I'm thankful." Pete smiled and meant it. "I'm lucky to have so many good memories. Lots of people don't." He didn't talk about his parents' loss to anyone anymore. Not even Ed. For everyone else life had gone on. It had taken Pete a while longer to come to terms with that. And he had for the most part. He was happy enough and doing what he loved. Just every so often he missed the conversations with his dad about wine and his mother's ready laugh. His parents had done everything together and for their family. Howard filled the breach a little when it came to winemaking and Noelene made him laugh from time to time like his mother had. He was also grateful for that.

"Do you think Ed will be back soon?"

Taylor's question brought him back to the present.

"Any time now. I was half expecting him today. I'm sorry he hasn't let you know."

For the first time since the day she arrived Taylor looked a little anxious.

"It's not his fault," she said. "He doesn't even know I'm here."

"You didn't get him on the phone?"

She shook her head.

Pete found himself wanting to reassure her. "Ed can be a bit focused on the job at hand. I'm sure he'll be pleased to see you."

Taylor's face lit up. She drank her beer and Pete finished his glass of wine.

"If you're ready I should get you home."

"Sure. Thanks for this." She stood. "And for your suggestion of the pie. It was delicious."

"No problem." Pete followed her to the door.

She was right to remind him. This was just a thank-you dinner to repay her for her effort on their behalf. She'd only stayed on and helped out because of Ed anyway. Once more Pete had to remind himself she was his brother's girl.

CHAPTER

15

Edward pulled into his garage and let his arms drop from the steering wheel. He rested his head against the seat and closed his eyes. Most of the trip away had been a complete waste of time. To top it off Mr Zhu, who he'd pinned his hopes of a partnership on, had been a no-show. Edward had only had dealings with Mr Cheng, his Australian contact. He'd desperately tried Cheng's number but he didn't answer. The message bank was generic. Edward had left two messages but no-one replied. Something had gone wrong but he was at a loss to do anything more but come home.

The seat was comfortable. Edward could easily fall asleep. He dragged himself out of his car and through the internal door. He'd just have time to catch a few hours' rest in his own bed and then he'd have to do some more thinking. Not that he could imagine coming up with anything new. He'd gone over every possibility on the drive back from Melbourne. There was no way to raise the extra capital to buy the land unless he took on a partner. He could scrape by if he sold the NS18 straight from the vine but Peter wasn't having a bar of that.

He fell into bed, rolled from one side to the other and then onto his back. His mind refused to rest. The strong coffee he'd bought in Casterton for the last leg of his journey still coursed through his veins. Finally he took himself to the kitchen. He made more coffee and drank it black. The milk was off and the bread was mouldy. The sun slanted through his kitchen window. Time to catch up on what had happened in his absence. Peter would be up by now and maybe he'd have something to eat at his place.

Edward picked up the jeans he'd worn yesterday from the floor where he'd only discarded them a few hours before. He threw on a work polo shirt, collected his boots and went outside. The air was fresh but not cold around him as he tugged on his boots. There was not a cloud in the sky, which was still the deep azure blue of early morning. He took in a long slow breath. In the distance he could just make out the roof of Peter's cottage and between them row after row of damned grapes. Right now he felt the business of making a living from them overwhelmed him. Edward stepped off the verandah and past the full pink blooms of his mother's Pierre de Ronsard roses. He'd walk. Perhaps it would help to clear his head.

The gentle sound of a woman's laugh pulled him up as he approached the cottage from the side. That was something new: Peter bringing a woman home. He'd lived a celibate life for years as far as Edward knew.

Peter spoke. Edward couldn't make out the words but the tone was matter-of-fact. He stepped around the corner then stopped short. Peter was sitting on the front verandah of his little cottage and opposite him sat a woman leaning in, smiling, listening to whatever he was saying. A woman Edward recognised.

"Taylor," he said.

She looked up, startled.

Peter jumped up from his chair bumping the small table. "You're back."

Taylor grabbed her coffee cup to save the contents from spilling.

"Surprise." Edward spoke in a monotone looking from his brother to Taylor. What had he interrupted here?

Taylor smiled back at him. The glint of her eyes and that shy smile of hers melting the anger that he'd felt at seeing his brother with his...girlfriend. Could he call her that?

"Hi, Ed." She clutched the mug in her hand tightly.

"Taylor's been here for a few days helping out." Peter started picking up plates. "She's staying in the quarters."

Edward ignored his brother and kept his gaze on Taylor.

"Well." Peter put the plates back on the table. "We've got a bit to talk about but I'll leave you two to catch up first. I've got some cleaning up to do at the cellar door."

"Oh." Taylor stood up. "I should help."

"No. You stay here. It won't take me long." He looked back at Edward. "I'll meet you in the office in a while?"

Edward nodded.

Peter turned back to Taylor. "Thanks for the company."

"Thanks for breakfast," she replied.

They watched him stride away.

Edward broke the silence. "You came back."

"You asked me to."

"Yes, but I didn't think you would."

Her chin dropped a little. "So you didn't want me to?"

"You didn't answer my texts, I thought–"

Taylor moved to the end of the verandah. Edward was still on the ground. It meant their faces were level. "I lost my phone for a while. It's a long story."

Her fresh, sweet scent wafted around him. He stepped up. He wanted to take her in his arms but he still felt weird about finding her in conversation with his brother. They'd been relaxed, their heads close. His stomach rumbled.

"You'll have to tell me over breakfast." He looked past her to the table. "I was hoping Peter would have something I could eat."

"I don't know. I came over to get some milk and stayed here for toast and coffee." She smiled. "I have eggs at the quarters. I could cook you some."

"Sure."

She picked up the carton of long-life milk that had been beside her chair and stepped around him heading past Peter's cottage.

He followed. Her blonde hair fluffed out and over her shoulders. She wore a light cotton shirt, almost see-through, that was tucked in at her trim waist. He liked the way her jeans hugged her bum as she walked. She was a good-looking woman and she'd come back for him. He had to hope that meant something more than kissing.

Taylor was on edge. Ed sat in the chair watching her as she set about making scrambled eggs. All the doubts she'd had about coming returned. He'd been surprised to see her but there was more to it than that. She'd seen the annoyed look on his face that he'd quickly changed to a smooth smile. Then she'd thought he was going to kiss her on the verandah but instead he wanted food.

"How was Melbourne?"

"How was the wedding?"

They both spoke at once.

He grinned. Her heart gave an extra thump. She'd seen that look before.

"You first," he said.

"The wedding went very well. They had a Valentine's theme so lots of hearts and flowers everywhere. Rosie looked divine and Matt very handsome in his suit. The food was scrumptious, the drinks flowed and we danced the night away. It was wonderful." Taylor tipped the egg mixture in the pan and watched the tiny bubbles form around the edges. It had been a special day. She'd really enjoyed it. Ed was silent behind her. Had she been too gushy with her description? She looked back. He was staring at her with his dark-blue eyes, his expression unreadable.

"I sent you a text for Valentine's Day," he said.

"I didn't get it."

"It was a few days before."

"That was sweet." Damn losing her phone. She put a coffee in front of him.

"So you came back for a visit and brought your coffee machine?"

"Never travel without it."

"Peter should have put you up in my place. I've got a good one."

What had Pete said about his name? His friends call him Pete. Funny his brother didn't. "He offered but…well, I didn't like to without you being there. These quarters are very comfortable." He opened his mouth but she cut him off. "I'm happy here. That's if it's okay for me to stay a bit longer?" She didn't want him to think he had to offer his place but once she got to know him better – well she'd see.

"No probs. I'm not sure when Antoine gets here."

"Is he the extra cellar hand?"

"Yes. He's done the last three vintages with us. He'd have been here by now but he had a wedding so he went home for a while."

"Where does he live?"

"France. At least he did. He's been working in Australia on and off for a few years. Not sure what his long-term plans are."

Taylor put a plate of toast and scrambled eggs in front of him. She'd reserved a spoonful of egg for herself. She wasn't really hungry after the breakfast she'd had with Pete but she didn't want to sit and watch Ed eat.

"Thanks," Ed said after his first mouthful. "I drove most of the night. I was starving."

"So how did it go in Melbourne?"

Ed paused, another forkful of egg part-way to his mouth. "Not so good."

"Did Mr Cheng contact you?"

"Mr Cheng?"

"I gather there was some mix-up. You thought you were meeting him in Melbourne but he came here."

"Here!" Edward pushed back his chair and stood up.

"Well, not *here*." Taylor patted the table, surprised by his extreme reaction. "He came to the cellar door with a couple of other men. He was expecting to meet you there."

"What were you doing at the cellar door?"

"Helping out like Pete said."

"Pete?" He gave her a funny look.

"Evidently two of your regular staff couldn't come and your office manager is sick so I helped him at the cellar door the last few days. Not that I think I was–"

"And Peter was there when Mr Cheng came?"

"Well, not at first. He had some emergency in the winery he had to deal with. It was left to me to go through the wine tasting with Mr Cheng. Pete came right at the end when I was so desperate to keep them occupied I ended up selling–"

He cut her off again. "Was there a Mr Zhu?"

"Yes."

"So Peter talked with him?"

"Only via Mr Cheng and not much at all. It was then we worked out you were the Mr Starr he wanted to meet, not Pete."

Taylor was going to go on but Ed's curse stopped her.

"I've got to go." He strode to the door and pushed the screen open.

She stood up, open mouthed.

He stopped abruptly and turned back. "Thanks for breakfast. I'll be back later." He gave a brief nod and was gone.

Breakfast! He'd hardly eaten any of it. Taylor flopped onto the old floral couch and slapped it in frustration. Ed's return hadn't played out like she'd been expecting. She'd pictured them falling into each other's arms where they'd left off at the end of her last visit. She felt like the last few days she'd been living in limbo waiting for Ed to turn up and now that he had, nothing had changed. Or had it? She couldn't stop the image of his brother's smiling face over breakfast, their easy conversation over dinner last night. Taylor shook her head. The brothers were quite different, like comparing chalk and cheese. Pete was the perfect gentleman. He was being kind to her, that was all. Ed with his wicked grin and the deep-blue eyes that made the heat rise in her when he looked at her, he was the man she had come to Coonawarra for. Obviously the unexpected visit of Mr Cheng had thrown him. Once he'd sorted that out they could renew their acquaintance. Once more anticipation swirled inside her. Ed was back at last and she was looking forward to finding out where their relationship might lead.

CHAPTER

16

Pete pulled the spittoon apart and emptied it. Never his favourite part of cellar door work but it had to be done. His thoughts strayed back to Taylor and Ed. Last night he'd decided to keep her at arms-length then this morning she'd called over for some milk and he'd ended up asking her to stay for coffee at his place. Ed's face, when he turned up, had reminded Pete instantly of the dangerous position he'd put himself in. There was no way he could fall for Ed's girl.

Pete scrubbed at the spittoon. Now that he'd got to know Taylor a bit better he was sorry she was with Ed. His brother had a habit of changing girlfriends as easily as he did his shirts. They never lasted long. He didn't like to think it of his own brother but Taylor seemed too nice for him. Pete hoped she could look after herself and she didn't end up as another notch in Ed's belt. He put the lid back on the barrel. There was no point worrying about it and he certainly couldn't get involved.

He glanced at the bottles stacked ready for today's tasters. He grinned. Fancy Taylor selling their reserve cabernet for ninety dollars a bottle. What a gem. He had only been going to make it available over the weekend for any visitors who showed a genuine interest. He was happy to take the money instead. He whistled as he washed the last few glasses.

Footsteps sounded from the adjoining room. Ed stuck his head around the door.

"I looked for you in the office." He came into the bar area. "What are you grinning at?"

Pete picked up a glass to polish. "Just thinking about yesterday."

Ed took up a tea towel and helped him. "What happened exactly?"

"Ben was able to spare me a couple of hours. He noticed a leak in a barrel of red. We had to drain the wine into a small portable tank. Taylor ended up here alone for a while and your Mr Zhu turned up."

"He's not my Mr Zhu. Did he say why he came here?"

"No. He didn't speak English but his friend, Mr Cheng, said they'd rung here and left a message to say they were meeting you here instead of Melbourne."

Ed stopped polishing, his jaw clenched.

"I gather you didn't get the message."

"No."

"Taylor saved the day. The guy who drove them was a bit of a pompous ass but she sold him the last of our cabernet sauvignon reserve." He smirked at Ed. "For ninety dollars a bottle."

"You're kidding."

Pete shook his head.

"Far out."

"My sentiments exactly. It's like I've been trying to tell you. We need a top-of-the-range wine and the NS18 could be it."

"It'll be years before it's ready to drink."

"We have to start somewhere."

"We need capital now." Ed tossed his tea towel on the bench.

"Why are you so hell-bent on buying more land? Why can't we keep building our wine list? We've already added three wines to Mum and Dad's original collection. The new cabernet will be the next."

"We've got all our eggs in one basket. The vineyards at Wrattonbully could give us an option if the vintage went bad here."

"Could."

"It's planted with pinot and chardonnay vines. You've always wanted to make a sparkling."

"I do make one. We have a sparkling shiraz."

"But you could make a sparkling white."

Pete stared at his brother. They'd had this conversation again and again and yet Ed had gone off to make a business deal behind his back. "Who's this Mr Zhu?"

Ed's eyes narrowed. "We want to get into the Chinese market. I heard he was looking for wine he could export."

"So this meeting wasn't to look for a partner?"

"Getting wine into the Chinese market would help our cash flow." Ed put both hands on the counter and leaned in. "Looks like we've missed that particular opportunity."

"You should have let me in on it. I could have talked to him about it."

"I didn't know he was going to turn up here. Bloody Felicity didn't pass on the message."

Pete felt sorry for Felicity. She was normally so efficient. He'd loved her once, back when she first started working for them. She was bright and bubbly and he saw her nearly every day. Then Ed had returned from holiday and it had all gone pear-shaped. Pete had found her flirting with Ed once too often. Once he'd discovered she'd been Ed's girlfriend that had been the end of it for Pete.

"He wouldn't talk to me anyway," Pete said. "And it could have been Noelene who took the message. Felicity's been away nearly as long as you. Came down with the flu. Noelene and I have been doing everything. Then she got an infected tooth, Ben had a crisis on the farm, and if Taylor hadn't turned up when she did I don't know what I would have done."

Ed pursed his lips and sucked in a deep breath. "I'm sorry. I hadn't intended to go for so long. I'd already lined up a meeting with our distributor and there was that sommeliers' dinner in Sydney. It sounded too good an opportunity to miss."

"How'd it go?"

"Should have missed it."

Pete studied his brother's gloomy expression. Ed took some things so seriously and others he brushed off.

"You may have sown a seed for next time."

"Maybe."

"There will be other Mr Zhus."

"I guess. Anyway, no use crying over spilled wine. Who's going to do the cellar door today?"

"Noelene messaged me. She'll be back on deck. I'll keep an eye on things. Why don't you spend some time with Taylor?"

Ed's charming grin returned to his face. "Sounds like we should have her in the cellar door. Why weren't you selling that bloody wine for ninety dollars a bottle when we had more of it?"

"Wouldn't have got it back then. But we do have the next lot nearly ready to bottle. All the signs are that it will be an improvement on the last. We should think carefully about the price we market it at."

"Maybe." Ed glanced around, distracted.

"Why don't you go and see Taylor. I've got everything covered today. The cleaning's finished in the winery. Just a few pumps and hoses to be packed up. The sauv blanc will be ready to pick next week. Providing we can get the—"

"Machine harvester." Ed waved his hands in the air. "I know, I know."

Pete shook his head. "I can fill you in on everything else later. Nothing urgent."

"Thanks. I'll go talk to Taylor. Perhaps the three of us can have a meal together tonight?"

"I'll leave you to it. I took her out for dinner last night."

"Did you now?" Ed gave Pete a playful punch on the arm. "Moving in on my girl?"

"It was a thank you for all her hard work."

"Yeah, I didn't think she'd come back but she has. Thanks for looking out for her." Ed winked and let out a whistle. "Ninety bloody dollars a bottle. Who'd have thought it?" He turned on his heel and left. His laugh echoed in the back room as he let himself out.

Pete collected the tea towels and went in search of fresh ones. He whistled as he walked. He'd known the cabernet reserve would cellar well. He was also glad to see Ed's good humour return. Taylor's arrival had helped. With her around Ed might stay happy and not worry so much about the money.

CHAPTER

17

Taylor jumped as two arms slid around her from behind.

"Hi." Ed drew her back from the side of her van where she'd been cleaning out the last of her things. He smelt like soap and aftershave. She twisted her head to look at him. The dark shadow that had been around his chin was gone. He rubbed his smooth cheek against hers. "I can't believe you came back."

She turned herself in his arms. "I was a bit worried when you weren't here. I lost your phone number when I lost my phone."

"Sounds like Peter's been looking after you."

"He's been very kind."

"And I hear you've earned your keep."

She smiled. "I like to help out where I can."

"Speaking of my kind brother, he's given us the day off. What would you like to do?"

Taylor thought a moment. Apart from her walk between the cellar door and the quarters she'd seen little else of the winery. "I'd like a guided tour."

"That'll take ten minutes, what do you want to do for the rest of the day?"

"I'm serious, Ed. I really would like to find out more about your winery. Pete explained to me the importance of the soil. The tessa–"

"Terra rossa."

"That's it, and the cellar door work was interesting. Your brother's passionate about his wine."

"Our wine."

"Of course. I'd like to learn more about everything you do here. Pete's been so busy."

A small furrow creased Ed's brow. "Peter," he dragged out the name, "isn't used to dealing with more than the winemaking process. It won't have done him any harm to manage the lot for a while."

Ed made it sound as if she'd been blaming him for Pete's workload. "I'm just interested to see what the rest of the winery is like," Taylor said.

"Okay, let's go."

"I'll grab my sunnies and my hat."

Ed followed her. He stood just inside the door looking around the living space. "You could move in with me, you know."

"I'm comfy here for now."

She slid on her sunglasses and walked past him to the door. He wrapped an arm around her as she passed and pulled her in close. His breath tickled her ear.

"If you're sure," he said.

A shiver went through her. Damn, he was hot but something held her back. She wasn't ready to jump into bed with him yet and if she moved in with him it would be a given. His hand gave her a little squeeze that sent another shiver through her. If he kept this up she didn't know how long her resolve would last.

"I am." She slipped from his arm and took his hand instead. With her other hand she pushed the broad-brimmed hat she'd found in the quarters and taken a fancy to firmly onto her head. "Let's go."

They walked towards Pete's cottage. To the left the track ran between the vines to Ed's house in the distance. They turned right. Ahead of them were large sheds on either side of the track that led to the gate and the dirt road.

Ed took her into a corrugated iron shed that had various sized stainless steel tanks.

"These tanks are for storing wine and these for fermenting it." He pointed at the tanks as he walked her quickly past and out the door to the shed on the other side of the track. Inside he whizzed her past a mini tractor and a trailer with a tank and what looked like giant octopus tentacles protruding from it.

She made him stop. "What's that for?"

"It's specially designed for spraying chemicals on the vines" Ed waved his arms about, swaying as he did looking like an uncontrolled drunk.

She laughed and he moved on.

There were assorted barrels, crates and pipes and then he was leading her through another door into what he called the barrel cellar. Barrels were stacked on metal cradles four high and a forklift was parked nearby.

Taylor stopped to read some of the names and codes written on the end of each barrel but Ed was in a hurry.

He took her through a door into a brick section that housed a lab and office and finally through another door into a lunchroom, Ed's office and reception area for the business.

Ed locked the front door and slipped the keys in his pocket. "That's it really. You've seen the cellar door but we'll go and say hello to Noelene, then lunch. I don't know about you but I'm hungry."

He took Taylor by the hand and walked her back between the sheds to his four-wheel drive. She glanced from side to side as they walked. It had been a quick trip and had only piqued her interest more to find out what went on behind the scenes at Wriggly Creek Winery.

"Who's the blonde?"

Pete looked up as Noelene entered the cellar door.

"Lots of curves." She jerked her thumb back over her shoulder. "With Edward at the winery. I saw them as I drove past."

Pete smiled. Noelene always cut straight to the chase.

"Taylor," he said. "Ed's friend. She's visiting for a while."

"Hmph! You want to take bets on how long?"

"No." Pete set down the pen he'd been using to tally the wine. He really hoped Taylor wouldn't be another of Ed's statistics. "How are you feeling?"

"Much better now." She gently tapped her cheek with her finger. "Ended up having the rotten tooth pulled out."

"You sure you're okay to be here today?"

"Positive. I'm feeling much better. Hubby was driving me mad. I need to be out of the house."

"How is Frank?" Noelene's husband was a long-distance truck driver and not home on a regular basis.

"He's fine but he's got a week off and he's spent it telling me what I should be doing. I'm sure that's what set the tooth off in the first place."

Pete smiled. Noelene was not one to be bossed about in the home she'd managed alone for most of her thirty-odd years of married life.

"I'm glad to have you here. I'm going to shift some more stock in. I'll be back and forth. Give me a call if you need me."

"Sold a bit without me?"

"It was busy without you. Ed was away, Ben had a crisis on the farm."

"Sorry I left you in the lurch. You know I'd have been here if I could." She gave him a concerned look.

Noelene had worked at the winery ever since the cellar door had opened back when Pete's parents were alive. She was a good friend to his parents. Now she imagined herself as a bit of a mother figure to their sons.

"Of course I do," he said. "Anyway, lucky for me Taylor turned up."

"Worked in wineries, has she?"

"I don't think so but she picked it up quickly. Which reminds me, there won't be any of the reserve cab sauv for tasting. She sold the last of it yesterday."

"Okay." Noelene worked her way along the bar wiping and straightening. All jobs Pete had already done but she was a cleaning fanatic. "Anything else I need to know?"

"Don't think so." Pete went to leave then stopped as he recalled Mr Zhu's visit. "You remember the day you did in the office last week?"

"For Felicity? How is madam? Recovered from her sniffle?"

There was no love lost between the two women but they were both good workers and one could cover for the other when needed. Pete tried to keep out of any disagreement between them.

"Not sure," he said. "She was still unwell Friday."

Noelene's finely plucked eyebrows arched higher. "She must be sick."

"Said it was the flu. Anyway, do you remember getting a call about a meeting between a Mr Cheng or a Mr Zhu and Ed?"

"I don't remember it but I logged all calls in the book as usual. Did you check there?"

"Yes."

"Perhaps it went straight to Edward."

"No."

Noelene shrugged her shoulders and looked at her watch. "Look at the time. We should have the sign out." She bustled around the counter to the front door.

"I'll see you in a while." Pete made his way back to his cottage to pick up his ute. If it wasn't Noelene who'd taken the call the only other possible woman was Felicity. Not that he cared about the Mr Zhu meeting but Ed had been so fired up about it he could go mouthing off at Felicity and the last thing they needed was to have her offside.

Taylor followed Ed in to the front of Wriggly Creek cellar door. There was no-one there apart from the woman behind the bar.

"This is Noelene. We couldn't run the cellar door without her," Ed said with a flourish.

"Flatterer." Noelene gave him a stern look then smiled at Taylor and offered her hand over the bar. "They manage quite well without me. They just need someone to keep the place clean and tidy."

"Hello, Noelene." Taylor held out her hand to the woman she recalled from her first visit to the cellar door. She wore the same red lipstick and eye make-up that included blue eye shadow. Her wavy greying hair looked like it had been sprayed with enough lacquer so as not to be moved by a gale should one suddenly spring up.

"You were with the hen's group." Noelene squeezed her hand.

"You've got a good memory."

"Never forget a face. And I hear you've been working here in my absence."

"I wouldn't call it working exactly."

"Anyway," Ed interrupted, "now that you've seen all the sights there are to see around our winery—"

"I guess that includes me." Noelene raised her eyebrows. Up close Taylor could see they were so finely plucked they were almost not there and had been redrawn in dark pencil.

Ed's chiselled features lit up in a charming smile. "I'm taking Taylor to Hollick's restaurant for a late lunch." He put a hand firmly against her back.

"You'll enjoy that, Taylor." Noelene gave a little nod. "Perhaps I'll see you again."

Taylor swivelled a look back over her shoulder as Ed guided her to the door. Noelene had turned away to the bench behind so Taylor couldn't see her face. That was a strange thing to say.

CHAPTER

18

Taylor stepped out of the shower and wrapped herself in a towel. She peered at her face in the foggy mirror.

"Damn. What are you doing here, Taylor Rourke?"

It was Monday night and she'd hardly seen Ed since their afternoon together two days ago. She stared at herself a moment longer then strolled back to her room. She rummaged for some boxers and a tank top. The brick walls trapped the warmth of the sun each day. She only needed a sheet in bed.

She wandered out to the living area. She put away the dishes she'd left to drain and wiped down the sink. The long lunch she'd enjoyed with Ed on Saturday seemed ages ago. He'd taken her for a drive afterwards to a vineyard at Mount Benson about half an hour away where someone else grew grapes for Wriggly Creek. Later she'd made them toastie sandwiches at the quarters and they'd watched TV until he'd nodded off beside her.

Yesterday Ed had spent time with Pete going over what had been happening at the winery and then doing jobs. Today they had fruit coming in. Sauvignon blanc grapes, he'd said. It had reminded her of her time in the cellar door helping Pete. She'd set off over there hoping to help Noelene but the older woman had everything under control and had made that clear, looking down her thin pointy nose and fixing Taylor with a determined stare.

With nothing else to do she'd driven into Penola and had a meander through the shops she had missed out on during her last visit with the girls. Then she'd bought some groceries and cooked up a storm, thinking Ed and Pete would both appreciate a meal. Pete hadn't come and Ed had appeared after dark, eaten and apologised but he still had some paperwork to do.

She'd been almost relieved today when she heard Felicity was still sick. She'd offered to answer the phone for them but Noelene had squashed that idea, saying she could divert it to the cellar door which was usually fairly quiet on a Monday.

Ed had to go out tonight. They'd eaten together in the brief space between him finishing work and leaving for his meeting. She closed her eyes remembering the feel of his hungry kiss and strong arms, a brief stolen moment together before he left, leaving her unsettled.

She walked around the room and came to a stop in front of the window. All she could see was her own reflection in the black glass. She pulled the curtains, opened the door and stuck her head out. There was a light on at the back of Pete's cottage. Not that it necessarily meant he was at home but it was a comfort all the same. Since Ed's return the quarters had become a little lonely. He had asked her again this morning over their quick coffee together to move in to his place but she'd declined. If he wasn't home much anyway what was the difference? She closed the door and flopped on the couch.

It was only nine o'clock. She'd been sleeping so well and doing very little. She didn't feel the least bit tired. She got up and looked in the fridge. Both Ed and Pete had given her wine. She took out the bottle of sauv blanc she'd opened with Ed earlier and poured herself a glass. Back on the couch she reached for the TV remote.

A loud burst of gunfire blared from the television. Behind her the door juddered across the floor and flung open.

"I'm here at last."

Taylor screamed, jumped from the couch and spun around, spilling her wine as she went.

"*Pardon, pardon.*" A thin guy with a short dark beard, a moustache and dark eyes flapped his hands at her. "I thought you were Pierre. Sorry."

Taylor put one hand to her barely covered chest. "Antoine?"

"You know who I am?"

"A guess. You're the vintage cellar hand? Pete said you were coming some time."

"He is not at home. I called in there. When I saw the light I thought he must be here." Antoine's gaze travelled over her body and quickly back to her face.

Taylor backed away, aware that her night attire covered very little.

"It's okay," she said. "I'll just…I'll just. I'll be back in a minute." She put her glass on the bench, turned and dashed in to her bedroom, closing the door behind her. She leaned against it until her pounding heart slowed then she put her hand to her mouth to suppress the laugh that erupted from deep inside. That was one way to meet her new housemate.

She pulled on a light sweater and a pair of trackpants over her boxers, took a deep breath and returned to the living room. Antoine was hovering just inside the door, hopping from one foot to the other.

"I should have phoned…"

"I didn't know…"

They both spoke at once.

"I'll go." Antoine turned.

"No, please. It's okay. I'm only visiting. Pete said I could stay here for a while. I knew you were coming."

He looked back at her.

"This place is yours." She smiled. "But if you don't mind sharing, I'd like to stay for a few more days." Surely that would give her long enough to see if this thing with Ed was worth pursuing.

"Not at all." He looked relieved. "I will hardly be here anyway. It's just a place to sleep."

Taylor crossed the room and held out her hand. "I'm Taylor."

"Antoine." He beamed back at her, his dark eyes glittering in the light.

"Yes," she gave a little chuckle. "I know."

"Of course, of course. I will get my bag."

"Are you hungry? I could make you something to eat."

"No, *merci*."

"A drink? I'm having a sauv blanc."

Antione paused. "Yes, thank you. That would be very nice." He went back through the door.

Taylor topped up her glass and poured another. Antoine came back carrying a bag and a backpack.

"Which room?" he asked.

"I'm in the first one. You've got your pick of the other three."

"*Bon*. I usually take the end one. It's slightly bigger." He dropped his backpack on the couch and crossed to the passage. "Yes, good," he said and carried his bag through.

He was back very quickly. Taylor passed him his glass and they sat at opposite ends of the table.

"Welcome." She raised her glass.

He did the same. "*Bienvenue.*"

They both drank. Antoine let out a long sigh and set his glass down. "It's so good to have Australian wine again. I much prefer it."

"Pete said you went home for a wedding."

"Yes, my sister."

"Where was it?"

"Le Puy-en-Velay."

"Oh, I've been there."

"Really?" Antoine leaned in. "When?"

"A few years ago now. I only stayed a few days but it was a beautiful place. I bought a lace handkerchief there for my gran."

"Ah, *oui*, the lace. My sister had some on her dress."

"That must have been beautiful."

"I have photos. Would you like to see?"

"Yes, I'd love to."

Antoine dug in his backpack and pulled out a tablet. He moved to the seat beside her and scrolled through the photos while they sipped their wine.

The door flung open behind them and Taylor yelped.

Antoine leapt to his feet. "Hello, Edward."

"Antoine! When did you get here?" The two men embraced and kissed each other's cheeks.

Taylor stood up and put her hands to her hips. "You really need to do something about that damn door."

"I see you've met Taylor." Ed strode to her side and put his arm around her.

"Yes." Antoine nodded. "We surprised each other."

"My meeting finished early." Ed gave her a squeeze. "I saw your light was still on. Looks like you weren't lonely though."

Taylor slipped from beneath his arm. It felt heavy. "Antoine hasn't been here long. He was showing me his sister's wedding photos."

"How did that go?" Edward asked.

"Very well," Antoine said. "She is very happy. I am content she will remain so. My older brother threatened her new husband he would cut off his–" Antoine flicked a horrified look at Taylor. He cleared his throat. "Let us say he would make his life miserable if he didn't look after Giselle."

"Don't worry, Antoine." Taylor laughed. "There has been the odd groom or two in Australia whose nuts have been threatened by a member of the bride's family."

"Nuts?" Antoine frowned.

"Forget it." Ed slapped his friend on the back.

"Would you like a drink?" Taylor took a glass from the cupboard. "We were having some sauv blanc."

"No thanks. Just wanted to say hello. Another early start tomorrow." Ed looked over her shoulder. "You'll be ready Antoine?"

"Most certainly. I should retire now." He gave a slight nod in Taylor's direction. "Thank you for the company."

He picked up his tablet and his backpack and disappeared in to the passage.

"You two seem to have hit it off." Ed's arms were folded across his chest.

"He's a nice guy."

"He's French." Ed rolled his eyes.

"What does that mean?"

"Women always fall for a Frenchman."

"Do they?" She tilted her face up to look into his eyes.

He held her look a moment then grinned and reached for her. "Not if they've got a true blue Aussie nearby."

He wrapped his arms around her and Taylor snuggled in to him. He'd almost seemed jealous and yet she'd only just met Antoine. His lips brushed her ear, her cheek and then reached her mouth. She forgot all about Antoine and lost herself in Ed's embrace.

CHAPTER

19

Ed walked in to the Wriggly Creek front office. "Welcome back, Felickity." He made to move behind the large L-shaped desk to give her a hug then thought better of it. "Are you completely over the wog?"

Felicity put down the pen she'd been chewing, swivelled her chair to face him and turned on her nine-carat smile. "Much better, thank you. Did you miss me?"

"Of course."

She had only been working for them for a couple of years but she'd proven her worth over and over again. She ran an efficient office.

"I see Noelene's been here." She wafted a hand over a set of books she had open in front of her.

His gaze reached higher to her low-cut blouse.

"Mostly Peter, I think. Noelene wasn't well either."

"Oh, bad luck."

Ed perched on the edge of the solid reception desk. There was no missing the sarcasm in her voice. It was probably best Noelene didn't usually work Tuesdays and Wednesdays. Give Felicity a chance to settle back in. The only two women who worked permanently at the winery tolerated each other but occasionally there was a blow-up. "Anything I should know?" he asked.

She lifted her perfectly made-up face to look at him. "I was going to ask you the same question."

"I've been away too."

"Not all work from what I hear."

"Is that so?"

"Antoine tells me you have a guest staying at the quarters."

"Taylor? She's…a friend from Adelaide."

"From Antoine's description she's good fun and gorgeous. He's totally charmed."

Of course Antoine would think that. Ed didn't like the thought of Taylor sharing the quarters with the Frenchman. He'd asked her several times to move to his place. He wanted more from her but she was holding out on him. "I'll have to bring her over to meet you."

"You must." She held his gaze a moment. Her eyes narrowed then opened wide again. "Between Noelene and Peter I've got a bit of fixing up to do. Perhaps you could help me."

"Sorry, I've got jobs to do too."

She gave a little pout. "Oh well, I'll just have to sort it out for myself."

"You're a gem, Felicity. I'm sure you'll manage."

She flashed him a smile, lowered her head and ran one long fingernail down the column of the page in front of her.

Ed stood. "A message came through from a Mr Zhu while I was away. Do you remember getting it?"

She didn't look up. "All the messages are in the book."

"It's not there."

"I don't recall a message from a Mr Zhu." She lifted her head, her gaze direct. "Was it important?"

"It was at the time."

"Why don't you call him then?"

"I tried but the number in my mobile doesn't answer. I think there was a landline number but I must have made those earlier calls from the office phone."

"Sorry, can't help."

The phone on the desk beside her rang. "Good morning, Wriggly Creek Winery, Felicity speaking." She paused to listen to the voice on the other end. "Yes, if you hold I can check that order for you." She pressed a button on the phone, put her hand to the computer mouse and leaned in closer to the screen.

From his position on the desk Ed got a good look at her exposed cleavage. He often wondered how he could forget such great eye candy. He and Felicity had been an item for a short time before she started working for them, then he'd gone interstate. Peter had employed her in his absence to cover for their previous office manager who left at short notice. When Ed returned Felicity had already established herself in the office. They thought it best to keep business and pleasure separate.

He rose and pushed Felicity out of his thoughts. No point in dwelling on past conquests. He took his phone from his pocket and scrolled to Cheng's name again. He'd done it several times this morning without actually ringing. His previous messages had gone unanswered. Ed moved away to his office and sat in his chair.

"Damn!" He thumped the desk. Noelene hadn't taken the message, Felicity was the only other female staff member who could have taken the call. She was usually efficient but he'd kept a slim hope that coming down with the flu had made her less so and that she might have had Cheng's details jotted on a paper somewhere.

He took a deep breath and let it out slowly. He had to let the Chinese option go for now. Vintage was on them and he was too busy to pursue Zhu.

Taylor stepped outside into another gorgeous morning. Only a few more days until autumn and yet the daily temperatures were still high. She crossed the track to the edge of the vines that stretched away in front of her. Underneath the canopy of green that reached above her head, she could see the bunches of deep purple grapes nestled amongst the leaves. Between the rows, strips of green grass were a vivid contrast against the red soil. She pulled out her phone and took a picture. With the vivid blue sky as a backdrop it was a beautiful scene.

She retraced her steps and followed the track as it wound behind Pete's cottage towards the shed and the winery office. She hoped she'd find someone over there. Antoine had been moving about early and was gone before she got up. It was Tuesday so she knew the cellar door was closed. Tomorrow it would be a week since she arrived.

Taylor picked up her pace. She felt restless. She wasn't used to doing nothing. Ed had stopped in for a quick coffee then gone again. The cellar door work had been fun but now that Noelene was back she needed to find something else to do. She walked past the sheds and around to the front of the winery where a low brick building abutted one of the sheds. When Ed had taken her for the tour he'd shown her their small office area. She hoped she'd find him there. She'd be happy to run messages, wash the floors even, just to have something to do.

The heavy glass door swished shut behind her as she entered. The smart young woman behind the counter lifted her head. She looked Taylor up and down then smiled.

"Are you Taylor?"

"Yes, and you're Felicity?

"Sounds like we've both been talked about." Felicity ran her fingers through her long hair and lifted her chin. Her gaze swept over Taylor. "Can I help?"

"Maybe. I'm looking for Ed."

"You missed him. He's gone in to town."

"Oh." Taylor's spirits dropped.

"He shouldn't be long. Is there something I can help you with?"

"No, thanks." Taylor turned to go.

"How are you finding it here?"

Taylor stopped and looked back at the smartly dressed young woman with the glittering eyes who was perhaps a few years her junior. "It's great. I'm just not used to being without work of some kind though. I was hoping I could be of help here."

"I don't need any help." Felicity waved one hand over her tidy desk. "And there's not a lot on offer around here except the seasonal stuff. Someone might be looking for pickers if you're game."

"Pickers?"

"Grape pickers."

"Oh, of course."

"Most vineyards are done by machines these days but hand-pickers are still required from time to time. How long are you planning to stay? You could put your name down in town."

"I'm not sure. I'll think about it. Thanks."

Taylor let herself out through the front door. She knew there was a door through the lunchroom behind Felicity's office that opened in to the work rooms behind because Ed had taken her that way before, but with Felicity the only one in the office it felt like prying. Instead Taylor walked around the front to the other side of the office.

She had the distinct impression Felicity was being cool with her even though her manner had appeared friendly, a bit like Noelene who was fiercely determined to keep her at arms-length. Taylor usually got along well with people.

She looked across the several rows of vines between her and the cellar door building. Nothing would be happening there. She followed the drive down the other side of the office. Where the brick wall joined the tin another door was set in to the shed wall, with a small verandah to protect it. She put her face to the top half, which was glass. A passage led off with more doors set in it. Once again she had a rough memory of the layout from her tour with Ed.

She pulled on the handle and let herself in. She paused. A squelching sound came from further inside the building. The first open door was an office. It was empty. She followed the sound to the next door. Pete was stomping on a plastic bag. He looked up.

"Hello."

"Hi." She loitered in the doorway.

"Looking for Ed?"

"Felicity said he's gone in to town."

"Yeah, shouldn't be long."

"What are you doing?" She could see a green mush through the plastic.

"Checking the baume level. We're picking these grapes tomorrow. I wanted to double check."

"Baume?" She stepped in to the room.

"It measures the sugar level in the juice which converts to alcohol content."

"Oh."

She leaned in close as Pete poured the mush via a sieve into a jug.

"Winemakers get very fussy about it."

Taylor spun at the sound of Ed's voice. "Where did you come from?"

"I work here." He folded his arms across his chest and leaned against the door frame. "Where did you come from?"

"I was hoping someone could find me a job."

"Cellar door's closed," Ed said. "Felicity might have something."

"I've spoken with Felicity. I don't think so." Taylor felt a little ripple of annoyance. There was something dismissive in Ed's tone.

"I can show you how to measure the baume in the lab." Pete picked up the jug and peered into it.

"Antoine does that," Ed said.

"Only when I'm busy. It would release both of us for other things."

"I'm game." Taylor had no idea how to measure baume but she was willing to learn and she didn't want to give Ed time to make any more objections.

"Go for it." Ed shrugged. He looked over her head to Pete. "I'm off to fix that faulty pipe again."

"No probs. Antoine should be there somewhere if you need help."

Ed gave Taylor a brooding look. "See you later." He spun on his heel and left.

Taylor turned to Pete. "Right, show me what I have to do."

CHAPTER

20

"I really enjoyed myself today." Taylor lifted her head from Ed's chest. They were cuddled up on the couch at his place. The day had been warm but tonight the temperature had dropped rapidly once the sun went down. There was a definite chill in the air. Ed had put on a small blow heater to warm the room. The television played softly in the background.

"Cooking my dinner?" He trailed a finger down the side of her face. "You can do that whenever you like."

"I meant working in the lab. I think I could be a mad scientist in another life."

"I can think of other options." He put a finger under her chin, turning her face to his. He leaned down. She brought her lips up to meet his, enjoying the taste of him and feeling the heat rise inside her. Ed turned her on, there was no doubting that.

His lips slipped across her cheek, nibbled and pulled on her ear then slid down her neck. She shivered.

"Why don't you stay tonight," he murmured.

Taylor put a hand over his, the one that held her left breast. She pulled away from him.

"Not tonight," she said. "You're tired and you have to be up even earlier tomorrow."

He ran his fingers down her neck. "I told you before I can manage on little sleep."

"But I can't." She slid from the couch and stood up. "I should do those dishes before I go."

He reached for her hand and pulled her back towards him. "I've got a dishwasher."

"Well I'll tidy up at least. I've left a mess in your kitchen."

"It's worth it."

His look was hungry and not for food.

"My cooking's not that fantastic."

"But you are." He stood and wrapped her in his arms so swiftly it startled her.

She pushed him away. He released her and held his hands out wide. "Hey, what's wrong?"

"I'm sorry. I just felt…" Suffocated. No, she didn't know what she felt. "I'd better go." She gave him a swift kiss on the lips. "I'll see you tomorrow."

"What's the matter?" He reached for her again. "Taylor?"

She evaded him. "Nothing. It's not you. It's me." She gave him a quick smile. She didn't know herself why she wasn't ready to leap into his bed but something wasn't right.

He gazed back, his searching eyes a dark blue. No smile played on his lips.

"Sorry." She let herself out the door, hurried down the steps and along the path until she reached the edge of the vines. The fresh scent of earth and grapes mingled in the cool air which was a relief on her cheeks but chilled her through her shirt sleeves. She untied the jumper from around her waist and pulled it on.

Taylor looked back at the house. Shadows thrown from the verandah light and foliage merged to create shapes. Her skin prickled. One of the shapes looked human. Had Ed come outside after her? If so he'd shrunk and was standing perfectly still. Something rustled behind her. She spun, peering at the space between the vines. There was no wind, probably just a bird or an animal. That thought didn't comfort her. What kind of animal would be lurking out here?

She glanced back at Ed's house. Maybe she shouldn't have been in such a hurry. Her gaze searched the shadows, light and dark, large and small, but none of them appeared human now. She let out a sigh. It was so different from the city. There was always some kind of light there. Here, once the sun went down, there was nothing but the night sky and whatever light the moon offered. Tonight with scattered cloud cover and only a partial moon that was very little.

"Get a grip, Taylor." She turned and picked her way along the rough track that ran towards the quarters, her thoughts on Ed. She was going crazy. She'd just run from the man she'd moved halfway across the state to be with. Ed ticked all the right boxes for her. He was single, employed, no obvious defects. She sucked in a breath. He had a great body and kissed her till her head spun. Damn, he was hot. He wanted to take her to his bed, and she would have gone willingly but...

She put a palm to her forehead. "What's wrong with you?" she hissed. Perhaps it was the drifting days with nothing much to do. Yet today she'd found something to keep her occupied. Pete had instructed her in baume testing. She'd got the hang of it quickly. Then she'd cooked Ed dinner knowing he'd be late and wouldn't have time to do it for himself.

Somewhere behind her a car engine purred to life. She paused, it sounded close but not big like Ed's four-wheel drive. She listened as it moved away from her and the quiet of the night settled around her again. Taylor shivered but she wasn't cold.

She picked her way along the track, the glow from Pete's cottage and the quarters behind it her guiding beacon of light. Her thoughts drifted to Pete. She'd enjoyed working in the lab today and he planned to show her a couple more jobs tomorrow. He was a good teacher, methodical and particular but with a sense of humour. He'd brushed aside her early misgivings that she'd muck something up. He was a kind guy, happy to share his passion about winemaking with her. Ed on the other hand was full of passion for her, that was obvious, but as far as the real Ed below the surface went, she felt she knew little. Taylor stopped at the clearing at the back of Pete's cottage. What was she doing comparing Ed to Pete?

She put her arm up in surprise as Pete's backyard flooded with light, the door opened and there he was, as if thinking about him had conjured him up. He stepped out, and stopped when he saw her.

She felt awkward as if she'd been caught doing something she shouldn't have.

"On my way home," she said.

"Putting out the rubbish." He waved a pizza box.

"Good night," she said.

"See you tomorrow."

She lifted her hand in a wave and hurried on to the quarters. She put her shoulder to the door. It scraped open. There was no way you could let yourself through that door quietly. The living area lights were on but thankfully there was no sign of Antoine. She needed some time to herself.

Her phone rang, echoing in the empty room. Cass's name appeared on the screen. Taylor had only sent her friend one text since she'd arrived. She'd put off calling.

She took a deep breath. "Hi, Cass."

"Hi there. What's happening?"

"Not a lot. Just heading to bed."

"Alone?"

"Yes, alone."

"Isn't it working out?"

"Taking things slowly."

"Okay." Cass dragged the word out. "So besides Ed how's it going down there?"

"I'm enjoying it. I had no idea what happened behind the scenes in a winery. The vintage cellar hand is here, Antoine. We share the quarters and–"

"What's the quarters?"

"Accommodation for casual staff."

"You're sharing a room with Antoine?"

"Not a room, it's like a house."

"I thought you were staying with Ed?"

"I told you, we're taking things one step at a time."

"What's wrong?"

"Nothing. Why do you think there is?"

"Because being cautious is so not like you."

"Really."

"Don't get all huffy on me, I'm glad you're not rushing into anything."

"Everything's fine, Cass."

"So you're not coming home any time soon?"

"Of course not. It's great down here." Taylor flopped onto the couch. Glad her friend was too far away to talk face to face.

"Well that's good 'cause I'm coming to visit you."

Taylor sat up. "What? When?"

"On the weekend. Have you got space for me? I thought I'd drive down Saturday morning."

"It's not a good time."

"Why not?"

"Everyone's busy."

"I'm coming to see you, not everyone."

"I've got work to do."

"I won't get in the way. I'll message you when I get to the cellar door."

"Cass."

"Yes."

Taylor fell back against the couch again. "It'll be good to see you."

"Great. Anything I can bring?"

"No. Plenty of spare beds. See you Saturday."

Taylor dropped the phone onto the couch beside her. A small part of her would be pleased to see Cass but she wasn't ready for her friend to inspect her life here yet, especially because she wasn't sure herself where it was going.

Taylor surveyed the room. What would Cass make of her new accommodation? At least Antoine was proving to be a tidy housemate so far. She'd have to give him the heads up that Cass was coming.

She got up and filled a glass with water. Antoine had left a couple of dishes draining. She wondered what he'd had for his evening meal. She opened the fridge. There was nothing much in there. Cheese and bread maybe?

Pete was eating takeaway pizza and she was fairly sure the only reason Ed had eaten well tonight was because she'd cooked him something. Three men, living in three different houses, feeding themselves badly. She pushed the fridge door shut. An idea was taking shape. Perhaps there was something else she could do to help out.

CHAPTER
21

Taylor didn't get a chance to suggest her idea the next morning. She'd stayed up late poring over the few recipe books she'd brought with her, writing notes and making lists. Her mind had still been buzzing when she fell into bed. She'd finally fallen asleep but then slept late.

The air was crisp on her skin as she walked to the winery. She hoped to find Ed there and run her idea past him.

Felicity looked up as she entered the office. "Ed's not here."

Taylor had barely got past the door. "Oh."

"Of course you're not staying with Edward, are you? You won't be up to speed with his movements." She leaned towards Taylor and lowered her voice. "You're wise to string him along for as long as you can. Once you've been in his bed he loses interest quickly."

Taylor's cheeks felt warm and her mouth gaped open.

Felicity waved her hand towards the doors. "They'll be busy all day. There's a lot of work to be done once the grapes start coming in you know." Without another look at Taylor she went back to her typing.

"Okay." Taylor felt her hackles rise. She'd been dismissed.

She strode out the door to find Ed in the winery somewhere, doing whatever it was Felicity seemed to think was so important. Taylor stopped at the corner of the shed and looked back the way she'd come. How did Felicity know she wasn't staying with Ed? Would he tell her that or perhaps Pete or Antoine? Taylor didn't like the idea of any of them chatting to Felicity about her...her what? Lack of relationship with Ed? And how would Felicity know what went on between Taylor and Ed anyway?

The sound of activity distracted her. Beside a row of tanks she could see Antoine bent over some pipes. She tried the door to Pete's office and lab but it was locked. She was meant to do the baume tests later. She hoped she wouldn't have to ask the frosty Felicity to let her in. Frosty Felicity. Taylor smirked. She went back to the quarters to collect her list and her keys. She had shopping to do.

When she came back from town with bags full of groceries, Pete's ute was outside his office. She stopped the van. This time the outer door was unlocked. He looked up as she stepped into the lab. He held another bag of crushed grapes.

"Oh," she said. "I was going to do the testing later."

"You still can." He poured the liquid through the sieve into a jug. "This is our chardonnay grapes. They'll be picked next."

"From the vineyards Ed took me to the other day?"

"Did you go to Mount Benson? That was our sauv blanc grapes. The chardonnay is grown here. The vines are at the back of our land, closest to the creek."

She watched as he tested the liquid. "What does that tell you?"

"I'm checking the acid level as well as the sugar. We can leave the grapes on the vine to make sure we have the flavour ripeness but then the sugar can get too high and the acid can drop too low. It's always a fine line getting the exact moment right." He peered at the hydrometer screen. "Yes." A smile spread across his face. His blue eyes sparkled. "I'm happy with that for now."

Taylor couldn't help but grin back at him. His happiness was infectious.

"I'd better get back to it," he said. "You're still okay to test the rest?"

"Sure."

"We keep that outer door locked but you can come and go through the front office. See Felicity if there's any problem."

Taylor stretched her grin into a fake smile. "Will do."

"She usually has her finger on the pulse."

"Does she live near here?"

"In town. Why?"

"Just wondered." Taylor thought of the human-shaped figure she'd seen outside Ed's last night. Surely it was a trick of the eyes and not Felicity she'd seen lurking in the shadows. "I'd better get going myself. I've got food in the van."

She turned at the door. Pete was already busy again, his head bent over the table. Thinking about Felicity had distracted her. She wanted to share her plan with someone and Ed wasn't here.

"I'm going to cook an evening meal."

Pete didn't look up.

"For all of us," she said.

He lifted his head. "Sorry?"

"I thought I'd cook a meal for the four of us."

"You don't need to do that."

"It's no more work to cook for four than for two."

"I don't know when I'll be finished today. Ed and Antoine either."

"That doesn't matter. I'll keep it warm at the quarters. Call in when you can."

He put down the jug he'd been holding and studied her carefully. "Thanks, Taylor."

She hovered in the doorway staring back. She could see the crinkles around his eyes, the smattering of freckles over his nose and cheeks. The lips turned up in a smile. Pete Starr was a genuinely nice guy.

She cleared her throat. "You haven't eaten it yet. My cooking's not flash."

"I'm willing to risk it." Once more the grin.

She looked away quickly. "See you later then."

She'd just pulled up at the quarters when Ed drove up. She got out of the van to meet him and planted a kiss on his lips.

"So glad you're pleased to see me," he said with a mischievous smile. "Sorry I didn't call in earlier. Busy morning."

"I know."

He put his arms around her waist and pulled her close.

"What have you been up to?"

"Shopping."

"Lucky you."

"For food. Have you got time to help me carry it in?"

"I was hoping for a coffee."

"Carry a bag and I'll make you one." She slid from his hold and opened the van door.

Ed leaned in and picked up some of the shopping bags. "What's all this?"

Taylor collected the rest. "I'm going to do some cooking."

"For an army?"

"For the four of us."

"The four of us?"

"You, me, Pete and Antoine. None of you have time to cook for yourselves."

He put the bags on the table and took her in his arms. "Me you can cook for whenever you like." He kissed her. "But you don't have to worry about the others."

"I'd like to." She brushed her lips across his cheek and extricated herself from his hug. "It's something I can do to help."

Ed's brow wrinkled. "We all finish at different times."

"I thought about that. I'll have the meal ready by seven and keep it warm. You can call in when you're ready, eat it here or take it home."

He took her hand. "It's a nice idea but if we want to see each other the evenings are our only chance at the moment."

"Come for dinner then. We can catch up." She squeezed his hand. "I'll make you a coffee."

Ed sat at the table, his smile replaced with a sullen look. "What will you cook?"

"Something with chicken tonight."

"You know Antoine's vegetarian?"

Taylor's finger paused over the start button on the coffee machine. She hadn't even asked if they had any food preferences. "I've got tuna."

"I hate tuna." His tone was like a petulant child.

Taylor was tempted to say hate is a very strong word, as her mother would have. Funny she was thinking more of her mother since she'd been at Wriggly Creek. "That's okay. I'll make a chicken and a tuna dish. What about Pete?"

"What about him?"

"Does he have any food dislikes I should know about?"

"You'll have to ask him."

Taylor put his coffee on the table and made one for herself. Ed's reaction to her food offer wasn't what she'd thought. She hoped

Antoine would accept or she'd have leftovers everywhere. She could freeze some for the weekend when Cass came. Something else she needed to tell Ed. She didn't like the feeling she had to tread carefully whenever she told him anything.

"You remember my friend Cass? She came with me to the pub when we were here for the hen weekend."

"The big girl? Yeah, why?"

Taylor felt suddenly protective of Cass. Ed had said 'big girl' as if she was a giant. Cass was tall and solidly built but Taylor hadn't ever thought of her as big. "She's coming for the weekend."

"You know we're all really busy with vintage." He glared at her across the table.

"Of course."

"I'm trying to spend time with you when I can."

Taylor shrugged her shoulders. "I know."

"So why invite Cass down now?"

"I…" Taylor had been going to say she didn't. "She's got a free weekend. Doesn't happen very often. I've offered her a bed here if that's okay."

Ed slurped down the rest of his coffee and stood up. "Sure. The more the merrier. Perhaps we should all move in here if it's going to be the dining house."

She studied his face for signs of humour but found none.

"Thanks for the coffee," he said.

She reached up and kissed him. A brief brush of their lips.

He looked her directly in the eye. "I'll see you later tonight."

A little shiver ran through Taylor. Was that a threat or a promise?

CHAPTER

22

Ed stared at the cordless phone he gripped tightly in his hand. He couldn't believe his luck. He was going to get a second try with Mr Zhu. Well, not with him directly but with his Australian contact Mr Cheng. At least he was still in with a chance.

He'd nearly missed this second opportunity. He'd happened to walk through the back way from the winery in to the office only to hear Felicity almost arguing on the phone declaring Edward Starr was not available. He'd caught her before she hung up on the caller. It had been Mr Cheng.

Zhu had gone back to China but he'd been impressed with the wine he'd tasted and Lister had added his praise. Before Zhu left, he'd engaged Mr Cheng to follow up with Edward regarding the possibility of a partnership.

Edward leaned back in his chair and put his hands behind his head. He didn't want Peter to know about it yet. He'd been dead set against a partnership outside the family. The only problem was

Cheng wanted to meet in Melbourne on Saturday. Edward would have to drive over first thing that morning, stay overnight and leave early the next. It would be difficult to come up with a reason for the trip, especially since he'd just been there and vintage was well underway. He had told his brother Cheng was interested in buying wine and Peter would ask too many questions if he thought that's what the meeting was about.

Perhaps Taylor could come. No sooner had Edward thought it than he canned the idea. She might be company on the long drive but he didn't want her to know about his meeting. He didn't want anyone to know until he had everything sorted. Once the partnership was locked in he'd present it to Peter. No point in discussing what may yet not happen.

Pity Taylor couldn't come with him though. An overnight stay in Melbourne might be what they needed. Frankly it wasn't working out how he'd hoped with her. He'd been surprised but pleased that she'd come back. He liked her. She was good-looking with curves in all the right places, bright and fun, or at least that's what he'd thought. He didn't know what to make of her insistence in staying with Antoine at the quarters or her developing friendship with Peter. Edward had tried his best to get her to move to his place and yet she resisted. It was as if she ran hot and cold with him. He'd never had much trouble enticing a woman to his bed in the past.

Felicity stuck her head around the door. "I'm sorry about that call earlier. Was it important?"

"I've sorted it."

She stepped into the office. "The man was difficult to understand and he wouldn't let me take a message. Insisted on talking to you in person. I tried to explain you could be anywhere on the property. He wanted me to find you."

"You should have rung my mobile."

Felicity paused. She flicked a look to the window then back at Edward. "He didn't give me the chance to try."

"Don't worry about it."

"Are you happy for me to lock up?"

He glanced at his watch. He hadn't realised how late in the afternoon it was. He still had several jobs to finish.

"Yes. I'll go back out through the winery."

"Fine." She flashed her brilliant smile at him. "See you tomorrow."

He grinned. "Night, Felickity."

He listened as she let herself out the front of the office. Her key turned in the lock. In the silence his stomach grumbled. He'd not stopped to eat lunch. At least he would get another decent meal tonight. One he wouldn't have to get for himself. He wasn't all that thrilled at the idea of having to share Taylor with the other two but he was looking forward to her cooking.

Somehow he had to think of an excuse to go to Melbourne this weekend. Maybe there was some way Edward could conjure something up that involved a weekend away with Taylor. If she came with him he'd only have to find a way to keep her busy while he met Mr Cheng. He drummed his fingers on the desk then gave it a thump. That wouldn't work. Taylor had said her friend Cass was coming. She wouldn't want to leave on the weekend anyway.

There had to be some other way. He looked out the window across the vines to the roof of the cellar door and another idea started to form. He picked up the phone.

Taylor looked at the clock and gave herself a mental pat on the back. It was nearly the time she'd said her food would be ready and it was. She took up a tea towel and began to wipe the dishes she'd used in her cooking spree. In the oven her tuna and leek mornay was keeping warm alongside her chicken lasagne. She'd made a green salad to go with the hot food if they wanted it. There was also some fresh crusty bread.

She hummed to herself as she set the table. She wasn't sure if Ed and Pete would want to eat at the quarters or take the food with them, that's if they turned up at all. Ed hadn't seemed too pleased about her idea and Pete could be forgetful.

Male voices drifted closer, then the sound of boots on the gravel surface outside. She faced the door as it scraped open. Antoine stepped inside followed by Ed, and Pete who was carrying a six-pack of beer.

"Smells good," Pete said.

Ed crossed the room and kissed her, just long enough to be more than a casual kiss.

"Beer or wine?" Pete asked.

Taylor put her hand up for a beer and so did Ed. Antoine opted for wine. Pete organised the drinks.

"Sit down everyone." Taylor waved a hand towards the table "I'll get the food." She put everything on the table and let them help themselves. Pete took some of the lasagne and the tuna.

Ed eyed his plate. "Hungry, little brother?"

"Not sure when I'll get a feed like this again." Pete grinned at Taylor. "Thought I'd make the most of it."

Taylor took a seat at the table beside Ed. "I wanted to talk to you about that."

All three men stopped eating and looked at her.

"I was thinking I could do this each night."

"Cook for us?" Pete's eyebrows lifted.

"Except for weekends," she said.

Antoine put down his fork. "No, no Taylor."

"See, they don't want you to." A satisfied smile spread across Ed's face.

"It's not that." Pete swept a kind look her way. "It'd be great but we can't ask that much of your time, Taylor."

"I don't mind and it gives me something to do."

"But the cost," Antoine said.

"I've been thinking about that too." The bit of money she'd put aside was shrinking fast. She wasn't about to feed them for nothing. "You could all put something in so we shared the cost of the groceries."

"*Oui.*" Antoine nodded. "I'd be happy to do that."

"Are you sure it's not too much?" Pete was still studying her closely. "We might need you in the cellar door from time to time."

"I'd love that."

"You're going to be busy." Ed spoke through a mouthful of lasagne.

"I prefer to be busy. How is the food?" Taylor looked at each of the men, all at various stages of devouring the meal.

Antoine and Peter were quick with their praise.

"I've enjoyed everything you've cooked for me." Ed winked at her and reached for some bread. "Still don't think you have to cook for everyone."

Antoine looked up. Taylor noticed the uncomfortable expression on his face.

"I told you it's no extra trouble. I lived on my own in Adelaide. I'm enjoying the company around the table." She smiled at each of them in turn then when she got to Ed she winked back. "I might need a stroll in the fresh air later."

His hand found her thigh under the table and gave it a squeeze.

Taylor had another mouthful of the mornay. It had leek and orange in it. This recipe was one of her favourites and it froze well. "I'm not a fancy cook but I've got a few recipes up my sleeve.

If you don't like what I make you don't have to eat it. I won't be offended." She glanced around. Their plates were all scraped clean. She laughed.

"I'm prepared to eat nearly anything," Pete said. "I hate coming in at the end of a long day and trying to find something."

Taylor was eager to make it happen. "Sometimes I can cook in advance, then if I'm needed at the cellar door, I can take something from the freezer."

"You have given this a lot of thought," Pete said.

"Sounds like you're thinking of staying long term." Ed's tone was serious.

Taylor shifted in her seat. What did that mean?

Antoine stood up and gathered the plates. "I'll do the dishes."

"I'll help." Pete stood up too. "Why don't you two go for that walk? Antoine and I will clean up."

Taylor gave him a grateful smile. He was a thoughtful bloke.

"Great idea." Ed pushed back his chair. "Oh by the way, Peter, I had a call from our distributor Barry. There's been a problem with storage in their Melbourne warehouse. He wants me to check it out."

Taylor studied Ed. His tone had been casual but his words rushed.

"What kind of problem?" Pete paused, a pile of plates in his hands.

"I don't know. There's been an accident, some pallets dropped or something. I thought I'd drive over Saturday and straight back Sunday."

"Perhaps I should go?"

"No need." Ed put up a hand. "You'll come with me, won't you Taylor." He looked at her with his blue eyes wide.

"I can't, Cass is coming to visit, remember?"

"Oh, that's right." He looked disappointed.

Taylor felt bad. They'd had little time alone since she'd arrived. Perhaps a trip to Melbourne would be a good way to spend time together without the interruptions of the winery.

"I'll give Cass a call," she said. "She can come another weekend."

"No, don't do that," Ed said quickly. "I'm only going over and back and it will be all work."

Taylor squeezed his hand. "Are you sure?"

He nodded.

"Perhaps you should speak with Barry again," Pete said. "Find out more before you drive all that way."

"I will," Ed said. "Just thought I should give you the heads up." He nodded at the two men at the sink then threw an arm around Taylor's shoulders. "Now what were you saying about fresh air?"

His lips were close to her ear, his breath warm on her cheek. Taylor smiled and let him guide her out into the night.

Back at his place, Ed poured them both a glass of sauv blanc and flicked on the television. Taylor leaned into him while he channel-surfed. Finally he left it on a political debate. She wasn't a fan of politics but he turned down the sound at least and pulled her closer.

"Are you sure you don't want me to put Cass off?" she said. "I'd be happy to come to Melbourne with you."

"Like I said it will be a quick trip and all business."

Taylor's head was against his chest. She felt the rumble of his voice against her cheek. He was solid and warm. She relaxed.

He kissed the top of her head. "Thanks for the meal."

"My pleasure."

"You know you don't have to cook for all of us."

"I enjoyed it. Which reminds me." She tipped her head back to look at him. "Would it be okay for me to use a computer in your office? I brought some cookbooks with me but I'm doing a lot of recipe searches and I'd like to post on my blog. It's a pain on the phone."

"I've got a laptop you could use. I take it when I'm travelling so I don't need it at the moment."

"Thanks."

They both sipped their wine. Taylor felt so comfortable she could easily doze off.

Ed took her glass from her hand and she righted herself as he leaned forward and put both glasses on the coffee table. He turned back to her and pressed his lips to hers as he wrapped his arms around her and pulled her tight against him.

Once more she responded to his lips, his hands, the feel of his body against hers.

His phone rang. Taylor jolted away from him as he swore and tugged the phone from his back pocket. He stared at the screen with dark brooding eyes then tossed it on the table beside the wine glasses.

"Sorry."

He turned back to her but his sudden anger had stifled her desire as effectively as a bucket of cold water. There was a side to Ed she really didn't like, she decided. Taylor stood up.

"Time for me to go. It's been a busy day."

"You don't have to go."

"Yes, Ed. I do."

She saw the flash of anger in his eyes and she couldn't blame him. Part of her wanted to fling herself back into his arms but part of her held back. Something wasn't quite right and until she knew what she wasn't going to take the next step with him.

"If you're sure," he said.

"Yes," she said with more resolve than she felt.

"Okay, I'll walk you back."

Taylor paused. "Can I take the laptop with me?"

"It's in my office over at the winery. I'll drop it off tomorrow."

"Thanks."

He threw an arm around her shoulders and walked her out the door. The night was chilly again and she was grateful for his warmth against her. They walked the track in silence. Taylor felt more and more awkward at their lack of conversation but she had nothing to say. At her front door he dropped his arm and turned to face her.

"One day you'll stop running away from me," he said. He bent and kissed her firmly on the lips then turned and strode away into the night. Taylor shivered, part from the cold and part from the recollection of his lips on hers.

CHAPTER
23

Next morning Taylor was up at first light. Antoine was still eating his breakfast when she wandered into the living area.

"Good morning." She grinned at him.

"You look cheerful."

"It's going to be another lovely day." Taylor went to the window where the first light was glowing around the edge of the curtains. She pulled them back.

"It's going to be another busy one." Antoine rinsed his plate.

"What are you doing today?"

"Plunging keeps me busy and there are barrels to be cleaned."

"Well, at least you won't have to worry about dinner."

"I don't want to put you to extra trouble for me."

"It's no trouble. I've got a couple of ideas for some tarts but I need to check the recipes on the internet first."

"Do you have access? You can use my tablet."

"Thanks but Ed's going to let me borrow a laptop from the office."

"I'll leave you to it." Antoine lifted his hand in a wave and let himself out.

Taylor hummed as she made herself coffee and toast. Last night had been a success all round. The fellas had accepted her offer to cook and even though her evening with Ed after dinner had been a mix of feelings, she felt like she'd made some kind of progress. She just wished she knew what.

She shook her head. "Taylor, Taylor, Taylor," she murmured.

Maybe it was the memory of her friends teasing her about her past boyfriends. This time she wanted to take it slower. Make sure Ed was definitely right for her before she fell into his bed. Each time she got to the point where she thought she'd give in something held her back. Last night it was the phone call that had broken the spell he cast over her with his kisses. He hadn't pressed her further. In fact he'd been quite the gentleman but she knew that she was testing his patience. Damn it, she was testing her own.

She sat down with her toast and tried to think about other things. The laptop for instance. It would make her life a lot easier. She hoped he'd do it soon. She was eager to finish her shopping list, go into town for the supplies and get started on the cooking.

She'd just got out of the shower when her mobile rang. Ed's name appeared on the screen.

"Good morning," she said.

"Hi," he replied. "Listen, I'm not going to get away from the sheds for a while. Do you want to go and pick up the laptop?"

"Okay."

"It should be on the floor beside my desk. Felicity will know where to look."

"Thanks." Taylor screwed up her nose. She wasn't keen to ask Felicity anything.

"I might see you around lunchtime but we're flat strap here."

"That's okay, I've got plenty to do."

He was gone before she could say any more. She picked up her van keys then thought better of it. It didn't take that long to walk to the winery.

Out the front of the office Taylor paused. A sleek blue car was parked to one side. Perhaps there was a visitor. Once more Felicity studied Taylor closely when she walked in and told her Ed wasn't there.

"I know. He said I could use his laptop. I've come to pick it up."

Felicity stood. "I'll get it for you."

"No need." Taylor gave her a bright smile. "I'll find it."

Felicity sank to her chair as Taylor sailed on by.

Once in Ed's office, Taylor pushed the door to behind her and looked around the room. Ed's desk was huge by any standard and took up much of his office. Beside it on the floor were stacks of papers, wine boxes and assorted items. At first glance she couldn't see the laptop.

She walked behind the desk which was cluttered with more paper piles and document holders. A computer sat slightly to one side. In the middle of the desk was a large pad with a cordless keyboard on it surrounded by scribbles and notes. Ed had made good use of it. She smiled at the little cartoon drawings, the squiggles and doodles. Her smile widened as she noticed her name written several times in curly letters. He was obviously thinking of her.

Another name caught her attention at the bottom of the page. Cheng was written in large block letters. The letters had been traced around again and again and next to them was scribbled a date – Saturday's date.

There was movement outside the door. Taylor bent down and moved some magazines to reveal the laptop she was meant to be collecting.

"Find it?" Felicity was studying her from the door.

"Yes, took a bit of looking." Taylor stuffed the laptop and its power cable into a bag lying nearby.

"Edward doesn't allow me to touch anything much in here. He likes to keep everything in his own way."

"Mm. No doubt he knows where everything is."

Felicity stepped aside as Taylor passed her. The door closed firmly behind her but Taylor didn't look back. She clutched the handle of the bag and made her way back to the quarters pondering the connection between Mr Cheng and Saturday's date.

Internet access on a bigger screen was much better. She was able to check her emails, although there was nothing personal amongst the long list, and then move on to some recipe sites. Her plan was to make a couple of tarts that were both vegetarian and hearty. With her list complete she headed to her van, shopping bags in hand.

On the way to the main road Taylor stopped at the cellar door. It wasn't quite opening time yet. She thought she'd say hello to Noelene and offer her assistance again. Taylor walked around to the rear door. A mop and bucket drained in the sunshine just outside. She stuck her head in to the back room. A strong smell of pine disinfectant swamped her.

"Hello," she called.

Before she could take a step Noelene hollered, "Stop!"

Taylor stayed where she was and Noelene appeared in the opposite doorway.

"I've just washed the floor in there." Noelene leaned in to the room. "What do you need?"

"Nothing. I just called by to say hello." Taylor pulled her face into what she hoped was a sweet smile. "Wondered if I could be of any help today."

"I don't think so." Noelene's body relaxed. "Thanks anyway. I shouldn't be that busy."

"I'm heading into town. Anything I can get you?"

"No…thanks."

"Well let me know if I can help. I'll be at the quarters cooking when I get back."

"Cooking?"

"Yes, I'm making an evening meal for the three men each night."

"That's good of you."

"They're so busy and I thought it was something I could do to help."

"Well." Noelene's shoulders did a little jiggle up and down. "Well, that's good of you," she said again.

"I like to be useful."

"What are you making?"

"Some vegetable tarts tonight and a curry tomorrow night. I have to think up alternatives for Antoine."

"A word to the wise." Noelene tapped a finger against the side of her pointy nose. "Make sure you've got something with meat in it for Edward. Peter doesn't mind so much but Edward takes after his father. Neil was always a meat-and-three-veg man. Used to drive Pearl nuts. Edward's more adventurous than his father, as long as it involves meat."

"Thanks for the tip Noelene. I'll keep that in mind."

"No problem."

"I'll be off then."

"Taylor."

She turned back at Noelene's call.

"If you're at a loose end later this arvo pop in. I shouldn't be busy. Perhaps we could have a cuppa."

"That'd be great." Taylor lifted her hand in a wave and retreated to her van with a smug smile plastered firmly on her face.

She'd win Noelene over. Just give her a bit more time. Taylor climbed into her van and turned up the radio. As her dear old Pa would have said, there's more than one way to skin a rabbit.

CHAPTER
24

Edward looked up from his paperwork at the sound of tyres on the gravel outside his office window. A silver Porsche Boxster pulled in alongside the building. He felt his jaw drop as Taylor climbed out of the passenger seat. He stood up in time to see the driver alight. She looked like Taylor's friend Cass but she was smartly dressed and had her hair up. The two women walked off in the direction of the winery lab. Edward gazed at the car. It wasn't a new model but it had been well looked after. Sleek and sophisticated, it looked like the real deal.

"Well, well, well," he murmured. If it was Cass, she had good taste in cars.

He glanced back at the notebook he'd been writing figures in. No matter which way he counted they were short several boxes of riesling. He'd have to investigate further but for now he slipped the little book into his pocket and made his way through the back door to the winery behind. He could hear Taylor talking excitedly about the grapes and sugar levels. It irritated him what a clone of Peter she'd become.

He reached the lab door and stopped. Both women had their backs to him. Taylor was showing Cass how to use the equipment. It was Cass who held his attention. He'd only ever seen her in ill-fitting jeans. Today she looked almost corporate. She wore heels and a pencil skirt that reached her knees but a side split revealed her leg as she leaned in to look closer at what Taylor was showing her. The matching top was some kind of long-line sleeveless jacket.

"Hello."

Both women turned at the sound of his voice. Taylor smiled and was across the lab at his side in a flash. Cass followed slowly, a bemused look on her face.

"You remember Cass?" Taylor said. "I sent you a text. She was able to get away earlier."

He recalled the text but he hadn't given it another thought. "Of course. Short for Cassandra right?" He held out his hand. He noticed her top button straining over her large breasts as she shook it.

"I prefer Cass." She gave him a brief smile.

"Glad you could come. I'll be away for part of the weekend. Taylor will have some company." He put his arm around Taylor's shoulders and gave them a squeeze.

"I'm giving Cass a tour." Taylor looked up at him. "Is that okay?"

"Of course."

"Pete let us in," Taylor said. "He was here with someone when we arrived."

"Someone?"

"An old guy. Grey hat and huge bushy eyebrows with saggy eyelids."

"Howard was his name," Cass said.

Taylor's brow wrinkled. "That's right. An old family friend?"

"He's been around forever. He worked with Dad to get the winery started." Edward glanced along the passage in the direction of Peter's office. He hadn't seen Howard for ages. Had practically forgotten about the old guy. "They'll be fussing over the chardonnay. It's nearly ready to be picked."

"Anyway, Cass needs a coffee. Just thought I'd show her around on our way to the quarters."

"I can't wait to get out of these clothes." Cass tugged at the bottom of her jacket. "I came straight from a work meeting first thing this morning. Dad insists we dress for the occasion." She gave an eye roll.

Edward liked what he was seeing. "Where's work?" he asked.

"Golding Hire, you might have heard of us."

"Yes." He felt his eyebrows rise. Only one of the biggest hire companies in South Australia. "Nice car."

"You like?" Cass grinned at him.

"Dad was a bit of a fan of the Porsche but never owned one. He drove an old Triumph."

"What colour?"

"Red."

"Of course."

Cass's full lips turned up in a huge smile.

"I'll take you to the quarters." Taylor broke the silence that settled around them. She led her friend towards the outer door then turned back. "Dinner will be ready at seven as usual. See you then?"

"I'll try to be on time but it will be another big day with the chardonnay."

"No worries. Come when you can."

"See you, Ed." Cass lifted a hand in a wave.

He grimaced. Was she mocking him?

Once the door had closed behind them he went in to the lab. He wondered why Howard would have been in here with Peter.

The old guy had often helped in the past. Peter had relied on his experience to assist with making the wine but Edward hadn't realised that Howard was still hanging around.

A couple of jugs drained in the sink. Beakers and tubes littered the bench along with plastic bags and tags. The lab could do with a clean-up but it wasn't a place Edward spent a lot of time. A splatter of red wine pooled on one end with a tag discarded beside it. He picked the tag up and turned it over. Scribbled in Peter's hand writing was NS18.

Edward dropped the tag back to the bench with a sigh. That's what the two of them were up to. Howard had been there back when the new cabernet vines were planted. No doubt he was still keeping his eye on it. Peter was desperate to keep this harvest. It would be the first year the NS18 would be ready to create a viable amount of wine.

It was a wait-and-see game. Edward had high hopes for his meeting with Mr Cheng. If a partnership came about that might be enough. Peter could keep his precious cabernet grapes and make his wine with it. Edward flicked off the light and went back to his office.

The sun was low in the sky by the time Edward pulled his vehicle in behind the silver Porsche parked outside the quarters. He lifted a couple of bottles of wine from the seat beside him and got out. Laughter carried from the living area. He put his shoulder to the door and walked in. He was greeted by the delicious smell of roasting meat.

Taylor and Cass lifted their heads from the laptop screen they'd been looking at. Taylor glanced at her watch.

"Oh, thank goodness. You've made it here early. I thought it must have been later than that. Time's got away from me."

"Thank goodness you've brought wine, is what I say," Cass said. "It's a dry show here."

Taylor bent to peer at something in the oven. "I was going to drive into town for beer but we've been too busy talking."

"What were you looking at?" Edward walked around the table.

"Just girl stuff." Cass closed the laptop. "Let me help you with those bottles."

Edward suppressed the urge to say it was his laptop. It was childish but Cass's bossy tone irritated him. She took the two chilled whites from his hand. He put the red on the table and wrapped Taylor in a tight hug as she stepped back from the oven.

"Shall we start with the sauv blanc?" Cass wiggled one of the bottles at them.

"Start with!" Taylor laughed. She brushed a kiss across his lips and slipped out from under his arm. "You planning a big night?"

"I'm on holiday."

"Well, I'm not." Edward lifted his chin and met Cass's gaze. "And I have an extra early start tomorrow."

She gave him an indifferent look.

"Ed's heading to Melbourne for the day." Taylor cleared the laptop away and started setting the table.

"Just for the day?" Cass poured three drinks. "How far's Melbourne?"

"You can do it in a day there and back but it's a big push. I'll probably stay the night somewhere." Edward accepted a glass from her. "I'll see how I go."

"Well here's to my holiday. Another weekend in gorgeous Coonawarra." Cass raised her glass and Taylor was quick to meet it with hers. Edward lifted his and they all took a sip.

"Mmm." Cass licked her lips. "That's good plonk."

"They don't call it plonk around here, Cass." Taylor wagged a finger at her friend.

Cass laughed and tapped Edward on the arm. "Lighten up, Eddie," she said.

Edward felt himself stiffen at the nickname. They all turned as the door opened again.

"Hello, Antoine." Taylor waved an open hand at Cass. "This is my friend Cass."

"Antoine. You're the man I've been hearing all about." Cass's round face stretched in a huge smile.

"Really?" Antoine pulled off his cap.

"I've been telling Cass about your sister's wedding. Cass and I travelled through France together so she's been to Le Puy-en-Velay as well."

"Oh that's so good." Antoine began speaking animatedly. The three of them became engaged in a conversation that excluded Edward.

He sat on the couch and sipped his wine, only half listening to their prattle. He envied their overseas travels. Somehow it had never been an option for him. His parents had needed him at the winery. Every uni holiday and then as soon as he was finished he was at Wriggly Creek. Since his parents had died there had been even less opportunity. Peter had at least done a vintage overseas. Edward was determined he would make the trip to China later in the year. Especially if the connection with Mr Zhu worked out.

He drained his glass and refilled it. Finally Peter arrived and Taylor flew into a panic because she hadn't made the gravy. Antoine went to shower and Peter joined Edward on the couch while Taylor and Cass finished preparing the meal.

"You still heading off in the morning?" Peter asked.

"Yes."

"Did you talk to Barry again?"

"Yes."

"So what's the go with it? What happened?"

"He hadn't been there either. He's in Sydney." Edward studied his glass. He didn't want to look Peter in the eye. "He's only going on what the warehouse manager told him."

"Have you rung the warehouse?"

"Yes. Don't worry about it. I'll sort it and be back before you know it." Edward thought of something to change the subject. "You haven't taken any boxes of riesling, have you?"

"No, why?"

"My stocktake's out."

"Easily done with the rate we've been going at the cellar door."

Edward pursed his lips. He kept on top of stock checks and Noelene was very efficient.

"I may have mucked it up when you were all away," Peter said.

"Maybe." Edward wasn't convinced but it was a plausible explanation for the missing boxes of wine.

"The new oak barrels have arrived at last." Peter rubbed a hand over his face. "Lucky I chased that up when I did or we wouldn't have had them in time. Anyway now we need to get them ready."

"Can Cass and I help?" Taylor came and joined them.

"It's heavy work," Edward said.

Cass snorted. "What do you think happens with a hire company? I don't always wear a suit and heels to work."

Peter stood up. "Thanks. There's a lot of washing and lugging around involved. I'll let you know if I need you."

"The cellar door could be busy as well." Antoine joined them, his hair damp from the shower. "I went into town this morning. Accommodation's full. There's a couple of weddings and a few big parties on this weekend."

"Whatever needs doing." Taylor smiled at Peter. "You just let us know and Cass and I can help. Now dinner's ready."

"Smell's good," Peter said.

"It's only lamb roast." Taylor waved them all to sit down. "Except you Antoine. I've made you a leek and mushroom pie. Hope it's turned out okay. I probably left it in the oven a bit long."

"My fault." Cass chuckled. "I kept her talking."

"I'm sure it will be delicious," Antoine said.

Edward looked at the lamb on his plate and gritted his teeth. He liked his meat dead not pink like this but he was hungry. He poured gravy over the top and ate.

CHAPTER
25

"Peter's a nice guy."

Taylor turned to see Cass looking out through the living room window. She never tired of the view from that window. The late afternoon sun cast shadows over the vines turning them a deep green.

"Yes he is," she said. "Do you fancy him? Wouldn't it be great if we fell for brothers?"

"He's not my type." Cass turned back to look at her. "How are things with you and Ed? You haven't said much."

"We're fine." Taylor gave the sink an extra wipe. "I told you we're taking it slowly. What do you fancy for dinner?"

"Oh, food again. That lunch we had at the winery was divine."

"It's a great place. Ed took me there when I first arrived."

They'd only just returned to the quarters. They'd had a big day helping wash and shift barrels, going out for lunch and a visit to a couple of wineries then helping for the last couple of hours in the cellar door. Taylor felt a little smug about that. Noelene had been glad of her support.

"I'm not sure I need much." Cass clutched her stomach. "Anyway it sounds like you've been cooking all the time. What's with this, making meals for these blokes?"

"It's something I can do to help. The three of them are flat out all day and I'm not. They contribute to the costs."

"Slave labour," Cass muttered.

"Back to us." Taylor didn't want Cass casting a shadow over her work at the winery. "We can have toasties here and watch a movie. I brought a few DVDs with me. I've got the latest Russell Crowe."

"Ohhhh." Cass knelt on the couch and leaned in to the back rest, wiggling her eyebrows at Taylor. "I do like a bit of Russell."

"You like a bit of everyone."

"Are you calling me a tart?" Cass clutched a hand to her heart. "I'm offended."

"Really? Since you've been here you've made eyes at Antoine." Taylor held up a finger on one hand and tapped it with the other.

"Made eyes at him! Hardly. Can you imagine me with him? I'd crush him. But I must admit I am a sucker for that gorgeous French accent."

Taylor wasn't to be deterred. She tapped a second finger. "You've been up close and personal with Pete."

"I was helping him shift those barrels. You know how heavy they were. Anyway, I already told you he's not my type."

"And draping yourself over Ed's shoulder yesterday when I took you in to the office." Taylor held up a third finger.

Cass chuckled. "That was for Ms Felicity's benefit. Did you see the way her eyes widened and her nostrils flared? If looks could kill I'd be dead. She's got the hots for Ed. You'd better watch out."

"That's crazy. She's just protective of him, that's all."

"Noelene's protective, Felicity is jealous. If you ask me there's something there, either history between them or she wants to make history with him."

"I must admit there is something about her." Taylor sank to a chair. "Maybe that's why she doesn't like me."

"Has to be." Cass came and threw an arm around Taylor. "What's not to like about you? You're the most likeable person I know."

"Okay, okay." Taylor pushed Cass away. "What do you want?"

"I was thinking it was drinks time. We bought that nice bottle of sparkling at the winery up the road. It must be chilled by now."

"Why not?" Taylor leapt up again. "I've got plenty of cheese and crackers."

"Are we expecting Antoine?"

Taylor put her hands to her hips and tipped her head to one side.

"What?" Cass held out her hands. "I only want to know if I can undo my jeans. They're too tight."

"I think he's already gone out to meet some friends in town. He'll be back to sleep, I assume."

Cass's lips turned up in a smug smile.

Taylor threw a tea towel at her. "Down girl."

Cass let out a deep sigh as the movie credits rolled up the screen. "Good on you, Russell."

Taylor pressed the stop button. "What time do you have to leave tomorrow? Shall we finish the bottle?"

They'd emptied the bottle of bubbly and started on a sauv blanc.

"Why not? I probably won't go till mid-morning."

"That would work out fine. Noelene might need my help in the cellar door again by lunch time."

Cass stretched. "I've only got a mountain of boring jobs to do once I get there. I've hardly been home in a month and the washing is beyond me. I had to buy new knickers to bring down here."

"I'll have to see Ed about using his washing machine." Taylor handed a glass to Cass and perched on the solid arm of the old couch. "The one here doesn't work. I've been hand washing but I'm over that."

"I'm sure he'll oblige. Especially if you do his as well."

Taylor frowned at her. "Why would I do his?"

"You seem to be doing a lot around here."

"I enjoy it."

"Are you getting paid?"

"It's been a gradual thing. My accommodation's free."

"It could get even freer."

"What?"

"Well if you end up moving in with Ed..."

"We'll see."

"Why are you hesitating? Ed seems like a hot-blooded male to me."

"He is, it's just...I don't know." Taylor slumped back against the couch.

Cass sat up straight and locked a steely glare on her. "I knew it. He's not right for you."

"Why not?" Taylor felt panic rise inside her. She wouldn't admit to herself, let alone Cass, that she was having doubts about Ed.

"If he was the right guy you would know by now. Even if it was initially just lust you haven't done anything about it."

"I told you I'm not rushing." Taylor's panic turned to anger. "Foster and Larry, remember."

"This is different. Ed treats you like you're his possession."

"That's ridiculous."

"He's always draping his arm around you, hugging you close."

"Affection."

"Possession."

Taylor opened her mouth and closed it. She did often feel Ed's arm was a weight on her rather than a cuddly gesture. "That's the way he is."

"He ogles other women."

"I guess there's no law against looking."

"If he looked any further down my cleavage he would have seen what I had for breakfast."

Taylor gripped her glass tightly. "Perhaps you shouldn't wear such a low-cut top and then he wouldn't be able to *ogle*."

Cass frowned at her. "He's got you doing things around the winery for nothing."

"That was my choice."

"Are you sure?"

Taylor leapt to her feet, the contents of her glass swirling close to the lip. "Why the inquisition? This is my life and frankly I can do what I like."

They glared at each other, the hum of the fridge the only sound.

Cass shrugged. "Look I'm sorry. I worry about you down here on your own."

"I'm a big girl, Cass. I've lived without parental guidance for a long time, travelled the world and survived. I don't need you to mother me."

"I'm not trying to be your mother although God knows you could do with one."

Taylor opened her mouth but nothing came out.

Cass leaned in. Her eyes glittered. "It's me not your mother you've poured your heart out to when you've made some monumental stuff-ups with men."

Taylor couldn't believe her ears. Cass was her friend or at least she was supposed to be and she'd made her own stuff-ups, as she called them. Why would she talk this way? "You sure you're not jealous?"

"Jealous of what?" Cass's voice raised a notch.

"Me. At least I've had some long-term relationships. Yours are usually one-night stands."

"So what?"

"Perhaps you're not capable of committing long term."

"We're not talking about me."

"No, that's right. This is my relationship. I like Ed and I'm going to see where it takes me. I won't have you casting him in a bad light."

A vehicle pulled up outside. Taylor's hopes soared. Perhaps it was Ed. He'd said he might drive straight back. She'd go home with him tonight. Damn Cass. Taylor would prove to her Ed was the right guy.

They both turned as the door scraped open. Antoine pushed through and stopped at the sight of them.

"Hello, ladies." His cheerful French accent sliced through the chilly air.

Tears brimmed in Taylor's eyes. All the anger drained out of her.

"Have a good night?" Cass asked.

"Yes. It was good to see old friends."

"It always is." Cass looked at Taylor with sad eyes.

Taylor bit her lip to stop the tears from flowing. "Time for bed I think. Night all." She fled to her bedroom, closed the door and leaned against it then jumped at a gentle tap on the wood behind her.

"Taylor?" Cass's voice was softly pleading.

Taylor opened the door a crack to reveal her friend's worried expression.

"I'm sorry, none of that came out right." Cass gave her a wobbly grin.

Taylor stared back at Cass. Best friends didn't say the things she'd said.

"I'm going to leave first thing."

"That's probably a good idea." Taylor clenched her hands tightly. Her fingernails dug into her palms.

"Tales?"

Taylor lifted her chin and stared back at Cass.

"You're wrong about me," Cass said. "I am capable of having a long-term relationship I just haven't found the right guy but when I do it will be a partnership. I'm not going to be anyone's doormat. And I don't think that's what you want either." Cass gave her a shaky smile. "Night Tales."

Taylor pushed the door shut behind her. A sob hiccupped from her chest. Tears ran down her cheeks. She stripped off her clothes and crawled into bed. A deep hurt ached in her chest. It wasn't just her fight with Cass. Seeds of doubt over Ed had been niggling inside her and Cass's words were like a big dose of water and sunshine. The tendrils were worming their way to the surface and Taylor was no longer sure about her feelings or anything she'd thought about Ed.

CHAPTER
26

Pete looked up from his clipboard at the sound of footsteps. Taylor walked past the open shed door.

"Morning," he called.

She stopped, took a few steps in his direction then stopped again.

"Cass left early," he said.

Taylor stared at him, her face pale against the dark shadows under her eyes. Perhaps they'd had a big night.

"I heard her car while I was eating breakfast."

"Yes." Taylor licked her lips. "She had to get back to Adelaide."

"At least you've had company for a while." Pete smiled at her. "We're a bit of a boring lot during vintage. All work and no play."

"I don't mind." Taylor gave him a weak smile.

She looked so sad his heart ached for her. Maybe something had happened between her and Ed. If his brother hurt this girl...Pete's chest tightened.

"Are you okay?" He took a step towards her and watched in horror as her face crumpled and tears flowed down her cheeks. He wrapped her in his arms and she pushed her face into his chest. She was soft and warm against him. His chin rested gently on her head. He closed his eyes. Her hair smelt sweet, like apricots.

Her sobs stopped just as quickly as they'd begun. She eased away from him and pulled a tissue from her jeans pocket. "Sorry," she mumbled.

"Is there something I can do?"

"You already have." She gave him a weak smile. "Thanks. What a baby I am. I'm tired, that's all. It's been a big couple of days."

Pete longed to wrap his arms around her again. He fought the urge and kept them pinned to his sides. "Where were you going?"

She met his gaze. The sadness had left her eyes. "Out for a walk." Her chin tilted up. "Then I thought I'd see if Noelene could do with some help at the cellar door."

"You don't have to do that."

"I enjoy it."

Pete studied her closely. In spite of her sudden bravado she looked exhausted.

He felt partly to blame. She'd turned up here looking for Ed and she'd done little but work for them ever since. He assumed Ed was taking care of her but he'd hardly had a lot of time. "Why don't you take the day off, relax? Ed should be back soon."

Hope lit up her eyes. "Have you heard from him?"

"No. But I'm sure he's not far away."

She poked at the dirt with the toe of her shoe. "Is it okay for me to stay at the quarters?"

"Of course."

"I keep out of Antoine's way."

"I'm sure he doesn't mind sharing. We've had extras there in the past. Anyway he's not likely to complain. We all appreciate the meals you've been making."

The smile returned to her face. "I've been working on this week's menu."

"You're a great cook, Taylor."

This time she chuckled. "I appreciate your vote of confidence."

"You haven't asked for any money yet."

"Don't worry, you'll get an itemised account tomorrow night with your meal."

A breeze flapped the papers on his clipboard.

Taylor gave a little shudder. "I'd better get walking."

"Enjoy."

"Thanks, Pete."

He frowned.

"For the shoulder to cry on. I don't know what came over me. I'm fine now." She turned on her heel and walked away.

He watched her go. The breeze made the soft fabric of her shirt puff out and fluffed her hair out around her head. He wished he could be walking beside her. He sighed and turned back to his task.

A little while later the crunch of tyres made him look up. Ed's four-wheel drive pulled up near the door.

Pete went to meet him. His brother looked as if he'd been up all night.

"Have you just come from Melbourne?"

"No, left late last night but didn't get far out of Ballarat. Pulled into a parking bay, took ages to go to sleep. Then I didn't wake up till well after sun up."

"How did you get on?"

"Fine."

"What was the damage?"

"Damage?"

"At the warehouse."

"Nothing, that's all good. Barry was worrying over nothing."

Pete frowned. "Bit of a waste of time."

"Not entirely. How about we catch up tonight over dinner? My shout. There're a few things we need to discuss."

Pete didn't like the sound of that. "Why not talk now?"

"You're busy and I've got to check stock. We can relax tonight. Have a proper chat."

"Taylor might like to see you."

"I'll call in on her later."

"She just went past for a walk. She seemed a bit glum. I guess Cass has left and you weren't here. She's probably at the cellar door by now."

Ed shrugged his shoulders. "She understands we're busy. I can't be holding her hand the whole time."

"I don't think she expects you to but perhaps a little more attention—"

Ed smirked. "Are you giving me relationship advice?"

Heat rose in Pete's cheeks.

"Hey." Ed poked him in the chest playfully with his finger. "You're not making a move on my girl, are you Peter? You know that won't work."

"You can be a real jerk sometimes, Ed." Pete spun away and strode back across the shed.

"I'll pick you up." Ed called after him. "At seven."

Pete lifted a hand to acknowledge he'd heard. Bugger Ed. They were brothers but sometimes Pete felt extreme dislike for his sibling, especially when he alluded to their relationship with Felicity, as he liked to do from time to time.

It had been two years ago but it still hurt. Ed could be a pig when it came to women. Once more he hoped his brother wouldn't end up hurting Taylor. She was way too nice and way too good for Ed.

Edward turned his four-wheel drive around. Peter could be so irritating but Edward didn't want to cause an argument, not now when he was so close to making this deal. He needed Peter to be on side. He drove back to the cellar door. When he'd come past earlier there'd only been one vehicle out the front, now there were several.

He let himself in the back door. Voices echoed from the front room and amongst them he could make out Noelene's voice and Taylor's softer tone. They sounded busy.

He sniffed his armpit. Not too flash. He'd been in these clothes since he'd left home yesterday morning. He scratched at the growth that covered his jawline. Not really a good appearance for customers. Just as he'd decided he should shower first, Taylor stepped into the room.

She put a hand to her mouth. "Ed, you gave me a fright."

"Just called in to let you know I'm back."

She crossed the room and hugged him. "How was your trip?"

"Good but long." He held her at arms-length. "I'm going to shower then I've got a stock inventory to do. Are you happy here with Noelene?"

"Of course. It's quite busy at the moment."

"Cass's gone?"

A small frown creased Taylor's brow. "She had to get back early."

A raised voice could be heard from the cellar door followed by laughter.

Taylor picked up a tray of clean glasses. "I should get back. Can we catch up later?"

"I've got a bit to do."

"Maybe dinner."

"I'm out for dinner."

"Oh."

"Sorry. I might not see you till tomorrow."

Noelene stuck her head around the door. "Can't you find them... Oh hello, Edward."

He nodded. "Noelene."

"I'll take the glasses." Noelene reached her hands towards the tray Taylor held.

"No that's okay. Ed has to go."

Taylor turned and followed the older woman back to the front room.

Edward stared after her. Had she been a bit cool? He'd thought he could wait Taylor out. He fully expected she'd succumb to him eventually but he was getting a bit sick of the chase. He'd thought she was different, worth the wait, but maybe he'd been wrong and she was just a tease. He pursed his lips. Two could play hard to get and then see what happened.

CHAPTER

27

"So what's this dinner about?"

Pete stared at his brother across the small table. Ed lifted his gaze from the paper he'd been perusing. "Let's order first."

Pete drew in a deep breath and looked back at his menu. They'd only just sat down in the quiet nook at the back of the restaurant but he was eager to find out what Ed's plans were. He didn't want it dragging out over dinner or he wouldn't enjoy the delicious food the place was famous for.

The waiter arrived and explained the specials. They ordered a good bottle of wine from one of their competitors and then the food.

Pete poured them each a glass of water. "Is it something to do with Barry and the distribution?"

"No, that's all good. I told you when I got back from my Sydney trip we've managed to get some of our sauv blanc and our shiraz into another bottle-shop chain."

Pete pressed his lips together. Getting their wine into chain suppliers wasn't the direction he wanted to go but this time he let it go. It kept Ed happy. "What's up then? What's the secret?"

Ed glanced around. Pete did the same. There were several other diners at tables in the restaurant but he hadn't recognised any of them.

"It's not a secret," Ed said. "At least not between us. I'd rather we keep it to ourselves for now though, until it's all sorted."

"Until what is sorted?"

"A new partner."

"Damn it, Ed, I told you I–"

Ed put up his hand. "Hear me out before you say any more."

The waiter appeared at Ed's elbow with the wine. He tasted it and nodded. They watched in silence as the waiter poured both their glasses.

As soon as he'd finished Pete pushed against the back of the comfortable chair and folded his arms. "Tell me."

"Aren't you going to taste the wine? It's good."

"Ed." Pete was fed up with his brother's delaying tactics.

"Okay." Ed put down his glass. "I have a Chinese businessman who is very interested in a partnership."

"Mr Cheng?"

"Yes. Well Mr Zhu actually. Cheng is his Australian contact."

"You said that had fallen through."

Once more Ed put his hand up. "Hear me out."

Pete took a deep breath. "Okay."

"I had arranged to meet Mr Zhu in Melbourne but, as you know, his message didn't get through and he came to the winery. I missed meeting him and I didn't have a contact number. I thought the chance had gone but he got Cheng to call me again."

"Cheng was with him when they came to the cellar door."

"I met with him yesterday in Melbourne."

"And?"

"They were impressed with our wine. They're looking for a unique winery like ours to be a part of."

"A part of."

"They've agreed to a partnership."

Pete leaned forward and glared at Ed. "I haven't."

"You said you'd hear me out."

Pete pressed his lips firmly together and gave a small nod.

Ed took another sip of his wine. "I offered them twenty-four per cent of my share and twenty-four per cent of yours."

"Forty-eight per cent!"

"Keep your voice down." Ed glanced around. "It still gives us the majority share."

"Only if we vote together."

"Why wouldn't we?"

"What if you and I don't agree? Your share combined with theirs would shut me out."

"I have the majority share now."

"I know. And right now we don't agree."

Once more the waiter arrived, this time with their food. Pete looked at his lamb dish and his mouth watered in spite of the tension that churned within him. He swirled the deep-red wine in the glass and sniffed. Automatically he took in the lavender and the blackcurrant and the background scents of sage and brown butter. The taste confirmed what his nose had detected. It was all there with the French oak keeping the delicate balance. He was impressed.

They both tasted their food. The lamb and its accompanying jus melted in Pete's mouth. In spite of his brother's bombshell he was enjoying the food.

Once they'd eaten a few more mouthfuls, he put down his cutlery and studied Ed. "I guess you can sell what you like of your share. I can't stop you. But I'm not selling. We pride ourselves on being a family-owned winery, that's our story."

"We still will be, Peter. Zhu will be a silent partner."

"We've seen how silent partnerships don't work out."

"And there are plenty of examples of how well they do."

Pete sighed. "Why do you want this so badly?"

"I want it for us. You make the wine. It's good wine. We're not doing too badly placing our wines in the market considering we're at the smaller end of the scale but all our eggs are in the Coonawarra basket, so to speak. If we have a bad year here it affects our whole vintage."

"Our sauv blanc comes from Mount Benson."

"But we don't own those vines. They sell to us but they could just as easily sell to someone else. I think we should look for land there as well but this vineyard to the north in the Wrattonbully region is ready to go. It's a perfect situation for us."

"It's not that far away. If things go bad here they probably will there."

"Not necessarily. You know how different the weather conditions can be just a short distance away. You're the winemaker, Peter, but I'm the business manager. I know this will be good for the future of our business. It's a chance for us to expand."

Pete studied Ed for a moment. His eyes glittered. Pete hadn't seen him this excited about something in a long time.

"If it's such a good buy why hasn't someone else snapped it up?"

"They might soon." Ed tapped the table with his finger. "I've put a hold on it."

"How much has that cost us?"

"Nothing actually. Just an old-fashioned gentleman's agreement."

Pete let out a snort.

"But they won't hold it for much longer unless we commit."

Ed took another sip of wine and returned to his food. Pete looked down at his own half-eaten meal. He ate some more. He wasn't against the idea of expanding, just the taking on a partner.

"Are you sure there's no other way to get the money?"

"I've thought of everything. I even had someone lined up to buy the NS18."

Pete's cutlery clattered to his plate. "You what?"

"If we want this vineyard and you won't come at a partnership it's the only other way. It wouldn't be the amount I need but I hope I can convince the bank—"

"You'd sell the NS18 without consulting me?" The food and wine that Pete had enjoyed turned sour in his stomach.

"No. I'm just saying I've put out some feelers."

Pete couldn't believe Ed would do something as terrible as selling their special cabernet. The new variety their parents had planted with so much anticipation.

"Do we need Mr Zhu to take up nearly half of our ownership?"

"It's the best option but we could manage on less. Forty per cent. We could sell him twenty each."

"Our individual shares are still too low. If you're so keen on selling him forty per cent you put up thirty and I'll do ten."

"So you agree to a partnership?"

"No."

"But—"

"I'll think about it."

"We don't have long."

"You've obviously been working on this deal for a while. I've only just found out about it. I need some time to think it over."

"How much time?"

"A week."

"Too long, Pete. I need to give Mr Zhu and the vineyard offer an answer sooner than that."

"Till Wednesday then. You've got to give me some time to think it over properly. I want to see the vineyard and look at your figures."

"Okay. You can come with me to the office now. I've got all the paperwork there."

"It's late Ed, and I'm tired. I'll think on what you said. How about we take a drive to look at the vineyard tomorrow afternoon and then you can show me the paperwork. I'll still have a day to think on it before I give you my answer."

"Okay." Ed picked up the bottle. "We might as well finish the rest of this. It's not bad."

Pete felt physically and emotionally drained but Ed was right. The wine was good. It would be a shame to leave it.

CHAPTER
28

Edward parked near the quarters and got out of his four-wheel drive. The mid-morning sun was warm on his arms as he stopped to look at the vines stretched out beside him. He'd been going to send Taylor a text saying he wouldn't be there for this evening's meal then thought better of it. Perhaps the personal approach was still the best for now.

The screen was closed but the old wooden door was open. Music played and he could smell something savoury cooking as he approached. It was a shame to miss Taylor's cooking tonight but he had planned to touch base with the bloke over the Wrattonbully deal.

"That's the spot."

He hesitated at the sound of Taylor's voice.

A male voice murmured a response. Edward couldn't hear what he said but he recognised Antoine's voice.

They both chuckled. It was gentle, almost intimate. He yanked the screen open and stepped into the room.

Taylor and Antoine were sitting at the table, the laptop between them. They looked up, surprise on their faces.

"Hello, Ed." Taylor's face changed to a smile. "Have you come for morning tea? I was just showing Antoine some pictures I took of his home town when I was there a few years ago. They're on my blog."

"Blog?"

"It's an online–"

"I know what a blog is. Why would you bother to have one?"

"I…" Taylor looked back at the screen. Her cheeks turned pink.

"It's quite interesting," Antoine said. "Other travellers or even those who can't travel enjoy reading this kind of thing."

Taylor stood up. "I'd better check these pasties."

"And I'd better get back to work." Antoine got to his feet.

"Morning tea's usually in the winery with the others."

Taylor straightened and gave him a sharp look. Perhaps he had been a little short with Antoine.

"It's Monday." He forced a grin. "Felicity will have brought cake."

"I know." Antoine spread his arms wide. "I came back to change my shirt. The dregs from a hose ended up all over me this morning."

"Does she always bring cake on Mondays?" Taylor asked.

She was studying Edward with a strange look. What was up with her?

"Usually."

"An office manager with many talents." Taylor's voice carried a trace of sarcasm.

Antoine patted his stomach. "With your delicious meals and Felicity's cakes I'm going to put on weight again. You ladies look after us far too well." He chuckled as he let himself out the door.

Edward and Taylor were left alone, the only sound the hum of the oven.

"I just called in to let you know I won't be here for dinner tonight."

"Okay. Do you want me to put some aside for you?"

"What are we having?"

"Pastie slice."

"Is that what smells so good?"

"I've never made it before. I hope it turns out."

"Maybe I can have some for lunch tomorrow."

"Sure."

"Sorry about tonight." He felt he should give her a hug but she was staying put, the kitchen table between them.

"That's okay. I know it's a busy time."

"See you tomorrow."

"Sure."

He let himself out the door, feeling as if he'd been dismissed. So much for the personal approach, he may as well have sent the text. He got back into his four-wheel drive. The tyres spun in the gravel as he backed away.

Taylor finished the baume testing and recorded the last of the figures in the book. She felt more comfortable in the lab now. At first she'd hardly dared to move in case she mucked something up, but after observing Pete she realised most of the clutter wasn't important. She picked up some jugs and tubes and rinsed them in the sink then took a cloth and wiped down the benches.

She left the lab, wandered out into the passage then opened the door that led to the winery offices. She'd come in that way but Felicity hadn't been at her post, though now she could hear her voice. Taylor stood in the big space that acted as a lunchroom. Set in the middle of the table were two containers. She'd noticed them on her way in. Both had the remains of cake in them. No doubt from Felicity.

There was a pause in the receptionist's speech. A male voice spoke, Ed's voice. Taylor had assumed Felicity had been on the phone. Ed's tone was jovial, almost flirty. Taylor crossed the room. Through the gap in the walkway between the lunchroom passage and the front office she could see Ed's back. He was standing, looking down at Felicity who was perched on the edge of her desk, her hands propped behind her. She was side-on to Taylor. Her low-cut shirt revealed the tops her ample breasts, aided by the way she leaned forward from the desk. Her eyelids fluttered. In fact they batted up and down so much it was a wonder Ed's hair didn't ruffle in the breeze she was creating.

"You've got something on your sleeve." Felicity slid from her desk, reached up and plucked at his shirt. "Looks like a cobweb." Now there was barely a gap between them. Taylor tensed. Felicity was openly flirting with her boss and what was he doing? Encouraging her by the sound of it.

"Hello." Taylor plastered a broad smile on her face and stepped around the partition wall.

Ed almost jumped away from Felicity, who didn't have the good grace to act the slightest bit repentant.

"Where did you come from?" Ed asked.

"I've been testing in the lab. I came through earlier but you weren't here, Felicity."

"Oh, that must have been when Edward had me in the shed sorting through the inventory." Felicity gave him a sweet smile.

"Maybe." Ed shifted from one foot to the other.

Taylor put her hand on his arm. He looked from Felicity to Taylor. Amusement twinkled in his eyes. He gave her hand a pat.

"I'd better get going," he said. "Sorry about tonight, Taylor."

He bent to brush her cheek with his lips but she turned and pushed back, kissing him firmly.

He looked at her with mild surprise.

Taylor winked back at him. Felicity's flirting had stirred something inside her. She wasn't going to sit back and let the little madam have the upper hand.

"I'd better be off," he said.

"I'll walk with you." Taylor gave a little wave to Felicity who had sat back at her desk, her lips pursed. Now there was another name for her, Flirty Felicity.

Once they were outside Ed rounded on her.

"What are you playing at?"

"What are you talking about?"

"One minute you're almost too hot to touch and the next you're cool as a cucumber. I never know where I stand with you."

"You never will if you flirt with other women while we're supposed to be getting to know each other."

"Other women?" He looked back at the office door. "Felicity?"

"She's besotted with you."

"She's not."

"Ed." Taylor put her hands to her hips. "If she had batted her eyelids any faster you'd have been blown over."

"Are you jealous of the hired help?"

Taylor glared at him. She wasn't keen on Felicity but neither did she like the way Ed belittled his secretary. "You should make the line clear between you."

"Like you have with me?" He crunched one hand inside the other. There was a sharp *clack* as his knuckles cracked.

Taylor had felt a pang of jealousy at Felicity's flirting but now that jealousy had turned to anger. She hated to think Cass had been right but ever since her friend had left Taylor had been unsettled. She'd been mulling over her feelings for Ed and was coming to the conclusion they'd lost the spark that had ignited between them. She had been annoyed by the flirtatious behaviour she'd witnessed but now she realised she had no right to be.

"Felicity's been with us for a while." Ed held his hands wide. "It's just the way we work together. It doesn't mean anything."

Taylor's stomach churned. She was no longer concerned about Felicity. Taylor knew her relationship with Ed was over before it had even begun. "Ed, I'm sorry, but I don't think this is working. Do you?"

He dropped his hands and stared at her. The blue of his eyes deepened and his brow creased in a frown.

"By 'this' you mean us?"

"Yes."

"I've tried."

"So have I."

"Have you?"

Taylor met his gaze. The anger in his eyes was frightening.

He snorted. "You were the one to jump in your car and come here without any idea what might happen."

"There was an instant spark between us. I thought you and I would be good together, but I've had a couple of bad experiences. I didn't want to rush into anything in case…"

"I knew Antoine would beguile you."

"Antoine? What's he got to do with anything?"

"He's very smooth with his French accent and his charming smile."

Taylor shook her head. "Ed, this isn't about Antoine or anyone else. It's about you and me but I'm not ready to commit to anything and you obviously want more from the relationship."

"You were hot for it."

Taylor's anger rose to the surface again. She was not going to be made a fool of because she hadn't gone to bed with him.

He pushed his face closer, his lips turned up in an ugly sneer. "You were the one who came looking for me."

She held her ground. "I seem to remember you asking me to come back. We both tried but it's just not working out."

He glared at her a moment longer then he stepped back, shrugged his shoulders. "You came here of your own free will, Taylor. You can leave whenever you want."

The churning in her stomach rose higher in her chest. She didn't want angry words between them.

"I'm sorry, Ed."

"My name's Edward." The name came out in a growl. He turned on his heel and strode away.

Taylor watched him go. Even though her insides were mush she felt a weight lift from her shoulders. She'd done the right thing but now what? Without Ed there was no reason to stay.

CHAPTER
29

Pete gave one last look around before he closed the shed door on the wine tanks. The early evening air was cool on his bare arms after the warmth inside the shed. The last of their red was being despatched tomorrow. The new season's whites were in except for the chardonnay which would be harvested soon, and with the warm weather they'd been having the reds would need to be picked earlier than expected.

The last rays of the setting sun left just enough light for him to make his way along the track that led to his cottage. He was looking forward to putting his feet up. He trudged along between the sheds casting a look over doors and machinery. Everything was shut up for the night. Ahead the walls of the cottage glowed white against the backdrop of the green vines beyond. Tiredness seeped into his core and yet he wouldn't give this life up for anything.

He'd driven out to the property on the edge of the Wrattonbully region with Ed. He could see why his brother was so keen to buy but Pete was still not happy to take on a partner. He was reluctant to change their family-owned business when they were so close to producing a special new wine with the NS18 grapes.

Pete scratched his head. He should have taken on another hand. Everything was happening at once and between the three of them there was too much to do. Ed was always worrying about the money but had his head in another place at the moment. He was so set on this partnership idea and buying more land that he wasn't concentrating fully on the current vintage.

Ed's plans threatened to change so much about the way they did things and Pete didn't know how to deal with that. More pressing was how would they manage the next few weeks? Ben's dad had injured his leg and Ben couldn't give them as much of his time as he would normally. As Pete searched for ideas he had an image of Taylor working in the lab. She could be the answer to his problem. Maybe they could take her on for the rest of vintage. He'd feel better if they could at least pay her a proper wage for her work.

Ahead of him in the failing light he could see Antoine making for his back door.

"Looking for me?"

Antoine turned and Pete could see he was carrying a plate.

"Taylor saved some pastie slice for you. I said I'd put it in your kitchen. I thought you'd be home soon."

"Just did a final check of the red that's going out tomorrow."

"What did you think of the Wrattonbully vineyard?"

"Just like Ed said. It's a good opportunity."

"But you don't want to commit?"

"We're a family business, Antoine. I'm reluctant to share with a partner we don't know."

"It could be a good thing."

Pete peered at Antoine. It was hard to see his expression in the gloomy light but he was surprised. Pete and Ed had differing opinions on various aspects of the winery from time to time and Antoine had always made himself scarce and kept right out of it.

"I'm having difficulty giving it more thought at the moment. So much to do and not enough of us." Pete took the plate from Antoine. "This smells good. Taylor's spoiling us."

"Not for much longer, my friend."

"Why?"

"I didn't like to ask too many questions but I think she and Ed have broken up."

Pete sighed. Just what he was afraid of. Ed's relationships never lasted. He looked in the direction of the quarters. "I hope Ed hasn't upset her too much."

"She doesn't seem too upset. More relieved and perhaps a little sad. I gather she broke it off but she likes living at the winery and working with us."

Pete's shoulders slumped. He'd miss Taylor. She'd been a breath of fresh air around the place.

Antoine nodded at the plate of food Pete held. "It's been good to have someone cook for us."

Pete had to agree. Food was the last thing he had time to think of at this time of year.

"I have enjoyed sharing the quarters with her." Antoine looked expectantly at him.

Pete had to admit Taylor was more like another worker than she'd ever been Ed's girlfriend. She wasn't bossy either, like Noelene, or flashy like Felicity, she just got on with the job. Half the time he wouldn't even know that she'd been to the lab unless he'd read her neatly recorded notes in the book, although he had noticed the room was looking a lot tidier lately.

"I'll be sorry to see her go," he said with genuine regret.

"Perhaps she doesn't have to."

Pete frowned at Antoine. Once more it was unusual for him to get involved.

"You said yourself you need another pair of hands and Taylor has proved capable in many ways. You could put her on the payroll."

Pete leaned closer. "Are you sweet on her yourself?"

"She is sweet but not my type." Antoine winked. "Good night."

Pete watched him start back towards the quarters. What had that wink meant? Pete went inside, poured himself a drink and sat down with the pastie and a bottle of sauce. His mother used to make pastie slice. The pastry was different but the flavours were just as good. Taylor had added swede to the mix of vegetables and plenty of salt and pepper. He savoured every mouthful then sat back in his chair.

He was tired, a deep-seated tiredness that came from stress as well as lack of sleep. And he was tired of being the one to compromise, of going along with Ed's schemes just to keep the peace. He plonked the plate into the sink.

"Damn you, Ed."

To hell with it. Ed couldn't sell without Pete's permission and he wasn't going to give it. Not this time anyway. There'd be other opportunities to expand and maybe they'd be able to come up with the money themselves. And he was going to talk to Taylor. Bad luck if it upset Ed, they could do with her help.

He picked up the plate again, pushed open his back door and strode to the quarters. Light shone from behind the closed curtains in the big window. He knocked gently at the door. Taylor tugged it open. She smiled.

"Hello," she said.

He stared at her. The light from the room behind shone through her hair giving it a golden glow and her cheeks were flushed pink.

"Would you like some more?"

He looked down as she reached for the plate in his hand.

"Oh…no…thanks. That was delicious though. Just like Mum used to make."

Taylor chuckled. It wasn't a light tinkle but a strong happy sound. Just as Antoine had said, she didn't appear upset. "I have to thank my grandmother for the cooking lessons. Possibly the only thing we've ever had in common. Would you like to come in? I was going to call in and see you."

Pete followed her into the room. There was a chill in the air outside but the living area was warm. "Is it about you leaving?"

The smile left her face. "Oh, Ed's told you."

"No, Ed hasn't mentioned it. Antoine said something when he dropped in my meal."

"He's a nice guy."

"Yes."

"I don't really want to go but–"

"Then don't," Pete blurted.

She studied him closely. "I can't stay here now."

"Why not?"

Pete found himself staring into her light-blue eyes. He'd tried to keep his thoughts neutral. She was his brother's girl, but now…

"Ed and I," she said.

"This has got nothing to do with Ed. You've been a great help to us and I've a few more jobs I'd like your help with. I was coming to see you tonight anyway, to ask if you'd keep working for us. I'll pay you of course." He meant it when he said this had nothing to do with Ed. He wanted her to stay for him but he couldn't tell her that.

"In the lab?"

"In the lab, at the cellar door, in the winery. We'd have you doing all sorts."

"Cooking?"

"Only if you want to and can still fit it in. Vintage will get busier."

"I'm not sure how Ed will take it."

"Did you part on bad terms?"

"Yes and no. We didn't throw things at each other if that's what you mean."

"Then what does it matter? You won't have to see Ed too much if you don't want to." He paused a moment, hoping he wouldn't upset her. "Look, Ed is a…well, let's say he keeps his feelings close to his chest. Even when our parents died he simply took a deep breath and got on with it. I don't think it's because he doesn't care, it's more that he doesn't waste emotion on things that are out of his control."

She raised her eyebrows.

"I'm making him sound insensitive."

"Don't worry." Taylor nibbled her bottom lip. "I was the one to call it quits. He acted surprised but I don't think he was really. It didn't work out but I don't know if it's a good idea for me to stay. He didn't seem happy about it."

"Where would you go?"

"I don't know. I'm not keen to go back to Adelaide yet."

"Then don't worry about Ed. He'll get over it. Stay. I need an extra pair of hands and I'm usually the one who employs vintage workers. Why would I look elsewhere when I've got someone capable right here?"

There was silence between them. Taylor studied him, a perplexed look on her face. She took a deep breath.

"Okay," she said.

"That's great." He grabbed her hand and shook it, unable to contain his enthusiasm. "Really good."

"Can you stay a moment?" She moved behind him to close the door. "I'd better find out what I'm signing up…"

Pete spun to look at her as her words turned to a gasp.

"What's the matter?"

Taylor was leaning forward staring through the screen into the night.

"Nothing." She pushed the wooden door shut. "I thought I saw someone outside but it's just shadows."

"We're a long way from anyone else out here. It can seem a bit lonely sometimes."

Taylor looked back at him. "It's quiet but I don't feel lonely. Especially with Antoine here and you not far away." She moved to the kitchen bench. "Would you like a cuppa?"

"Thanks." Pete sat at the table. Half an hour ago he'd been so tired all he'd wanted was to fall into bed. Now, here with Taylor, he had a new burst of energy. He watched her move methodically, filling the kettle, setting out the cups. He liked the way she absently brushed a stray strand of hair from her eyes.

"Pete?"

He sat up. She'd said something and he hadn't heard.

"Sorry, I was a million miles away."

"You said you'd pay me to work?"

"Sure will."

"I'll have to pay accommodation."

"No. That's part of the package."

"I have to admit it will be good to have some income while I work out what to do next."

"I'll get Felicity to organise the paperwork."

Taylor hesitated then turned back to pick up her own cup.

"She's good at all that—" Pete looked up as Taylor let out a squeal. The squeal turned into a scream and her cup crashed to the floor. He leapt to his feet and came round the table behind her. "Are you hurt?"

The cup was in one piece still but its contents had splashed out all over the floor and Taylor's bare feet. She pushed back against him knocking the air from his chest.

"Spider," she squeaked.

He followed the direction of her shaking finger. A black spider crawled slowly along the bottom of the kitchen cupboard. He side-stepped the puddle of tea, squashed the spider with his boot then wiped up the mess with paper towel.

"Sorry." Taylor's voice was barely a whisper.

She bobbed down to pick up the cup, all the while staring wide-eyed in the direction where the spider had been. The skin on her feet was splotched with streaks of glowing red.

"Leave it," he said. "Get down to the bathroom and run your feet under cold water."

"What?" She looked up at him, a mixture of fear and puzzlement on her face.

He reached out and took her by the shoulders. "The hot tea has burnt your feet." He turned her round.

"Sorry," she said again. "I've got a stupid fear of spiders." She looked down. "That does sting."

Her hair fluffed close to his face. Once more he breathed in the sweet smell of apricots. Her jumper was soft but he could feel the firmness of her shoulders under his fingers.

"Run the cold water over them."

She slid from his hands and hobbled away.

By the time she came back he had cleaned up the mess and made her another cup of tea.

"Okay?" he asked as she eased into her chair.

"Yes. My feet are fine. You must think I'm a sook. Jumping at shadows and going to jelly over a spider."

"Some people don't like spiders."

"It's more than that." She drew in a breath.

He could see she was struggling to keep control.

"When I was a kid we were in a park. I picked up some bark. A huge spider ran over my hand and up my arm. It got caught in my hair." She shuddered. "I can still see its great hairy legs. Ugh." She clasped her mug in two shaky hands and took a sip. "Every time I see a spider I'm right back there in that park. It must seem silly."

"Not at all." He gave her a reassuring smile.

"Anyway, that's enough drama from me for one night. Tell me more about what you think I can do to help." She gave him a wobbly grin. The vulnerable Taylor all but disappeared except for the alarm still bright in her eyes.

Pete settled back in his chair. No matter how hard he tried to suppress his feelings it was impossible to ignore how much he enjoyed her company.

CHAPTER

30

Taylor dressed in her yellow jeans and white shirt and took extra care over her hair and make-up. Ever since she'd arrived at the winery she'd spent her days in blue denim jeans and old shirts. She was about to meet with Felicity and she needed a confidence boost.

She stood on tiptoe in front of the blotchy bathroom mirror. It was the only mirror in the quarters and barely big enough to see her face and shoulders in but she was confident the clothes were a good look. She wore a gold chain at her neck. The day was already too warm for a scarf.

Thankfully Felicity wouldn't see the daggy old bra she wore underneath. Taylor hadn't done any washing for a while. She hadn't got around to mentioning the broken machine. Antoine didn't seem fussed. He was either washing his clothes somewhere else or he had a mountain of dirty clothes like she did. Perhaps she could ask Pete about it today.

Taylor stepped out into the brilliant sunlight. Even though she was going to meet with Felicity she felt a return of the confidence she'd lacked since she'd arrived at Wriggly Creek. She couldn't believe she'd been so besotted by Ed that she'd allowed herself to be manipulated by him. She could see it so clearly now. Cass had been right. A pang of regret interrupted Taylor's happy mood. She should ring Cass, tell her what had happened and apologise, explain she was going to stay and invite her friend back for another visit without it being overshadowed by Ed.

As she drew level with the winery sheds Pete came past in his ute. He pulled in beside her, engine idling.

"Good morning." His face crinkled in a smile.

"Hello." Her voice sounded so light in comparison to his deep, clear tone. Ed had a deep voice too. They both spoke well but where he sometimes was a bit lazy with word endings Pete's were always as clear as if he was reading the news on the ABC.

"Going to see Felicity?"

"Yes."

"Good. She should have the paperwork organised. I asked her to get it ready yesterday."

"Thanks."

"Come into the lab once you've finished. I'll show you what I'd like you to do."

"Okay."

He adjusted the cap on his head, flashed her another brilliant smile and drove on.

That smile. It warmed her from the inside. She flicked the hair from her eyes. This couldn't be happening. Now that she was no longer infatuated by Ed she saw Pete in a different light – but she couldn't fall for him. That would be just too difficult. She liked it here, she needed a job, so she'd keep her distance. She straightened her shoulders and strode on towards the office. Time to face Felicity.

"Good morning," she said as she pushed through the glass doors.

Felicity glanced up from her computer. "Morning," she said and went on typing.

Taylor stood in the middle of the room and waited. Felicity kept on with whatever she was busily doing, the clack of the keyboard the only sound in the office. She paused, her fingers hovering over the keys.

"Did you want something?"

"Yes, I—"

"Let me finish this and I'll be with you." Felicity went back to her typing.

Taylor stared at the top of her head. She could see a thin line of dark hair at Felicity's scalp. Regrowth, Taylor thought smugly. And here she'd been thinking Felicity was a natural blonde. She should have realised her eyebrows were too dark.

Finally Felicity paused her typing and looked up. "Now, what can I do for you?"

"Pete said you'd have some paperwork ready for me."

"Paperwork?" A tiny frown creased her forehead.

"They're putting me on the payroll."

"Oh yes, Peter did say something yesterday but I haven't had time to organise it yet."

Taylor maintained her smile. Felicity wasn't going to make this easy. "Okay," she said. "When do you think you'll be ready by?"

"I don't know." Felicity rifled through some papers on her desk. "Perhaps later today, maybe tomorrow, I'll see how I go."

Taylor dug her fingernails into her hands. Right now she'd like to slap Felicity's smug face. "I'll be busy myself so I'm not sure when I'll be back in the office."

"You'll be back if you want to be paid." Felicity had a smile on her lips and a dark glitter in her eyes.

Taylor stretched her fingers and took a breath. "Pete said you'd have everything ready this morning. That's why I'm here. I'm about to start work in the lab. I'll let him know you weren't organised." She went to step past Felicity but stopped when the younger woman spoke.

"I should have everything done by four o'clock," Felicity snapped. She looked up at Taylor. Her smile returned and widened. "See you then."

"Thank you." Round one to me, Taylor thought. But what was that smile about?

She kept going past Ed's office, the door was open but he wasn't there, and on into the lunchroom. She pulled open the heavy door that led to the passage beyond. Loud voices masked the squeak of the door. She paused. Ed and Pete were almost shouting at each other.

"You said you'd give it some proper thought." Ed's voice was angry.

"And I did. I told you last night I don't want this partnership at the moment. Maybe another time." Pete's deep tone was placating.

Taylor winced as Ed let forth with a string of swearing. "We won't get such a good chance again."

"Calm down, Ed."

"Dad left me the majority share because he knew something like this would happen. I'm the business manager, Peter. We need to expand. To do that we need capital and if you're not prepared to sell the bloody NS18 and put up a part of your share I'll have to take matters into my own hands."

"What does that mean?" Peter had dropped his voice so low Taylor had to strain to hear him.

"It means I'm the business manager and I'm going to manage this business to keep it viable." There was a thud.

Taylor shut the door behind her as Ed stepped out into the corridor.

"Hi," she said.

"You're still here."

Taylor lifted her chin. "I'm going to work here."

"Is that so?"

"We need another pair of hands." Pete appeared behind Ed. "I asked Taylor to stay."

Ed looked over his shoulder then back at Taylor.

"I'd still like to cook dinner for you all." She smiled at Ed, trying to mask her unease. If he wasn't happy for her to stay it could get awkward.

"I don't know how Peter thinks he's going to pay you," he said.

"Our finances aren't that bad," Pete said.

"We're putting a new washing machine in the quarters."

"Second-hand new."

"There's the wireless bill."

"We'd be doing that for Antoine whether Taylor was here or not."

Ed shook his head. His shoulders slumped as if the fight had gone out of him. "Stay or go, it doesn't matter to me." He passed Taylor and pushed through the door into the lunchroom.

Pete gave her a reassuring smile. She felt herself relax under his gaze.

"He'll calm down," he said.

"I'm glad about the washing machine." She grinned. "I was running out of clothes."

"You should have told us it didn't work. Antoine only mentioned it the other day."

"It's okay. Sounds like you've got it in hand. I don't want to add to your financial burdens though."

"Don't worry about that or Ed. You head into the lab. I've got to check something in my office. Won't be long."

Taylor carefully avoided brushing against him as they passed each other and turned in their respective doors. She leaned against a bench in the lab and let out a breath. That had been a bit heavy. In the time she'd seen them together Ed and Pete had always been friendly or at least civil with each other. Ed had sounded threatening. He'd mentioned needing money and having the bigger share of the business. She wondered what he'd meant by take matters into his own hands. She'd thought a few times about his recent trip to Melbourne. The date had coincided with the date on his office pad next to Cheng's name.

Taylor stood up straight again and pushed thoughts of Ed from her mind. It was none of her business what he did. She was about to learn a few more ways she could help out with work around the winery. She had a paying job again. She'd do that and keep her nose out of whatever the trouble was between the brothers.

She reached up to brush a strand of hair from her eyes and caught her wrist on something sharp. She looked down. To her horror she could see the underwire from her bra poking out above the neckline of her shirt. She grabbed it and pushed it down. How long had it been sticking out for everyone to see? Then she remembered Felicity's parting smile. Warmth flooded her cheeks.

CHAPTER
31

"This was a great idea."

Pete looked from his ice-cream to Taylor. He grinned. She had a big dob of white on her chin. "Nothing like an ice-cream at the beach to finish the day but you might need this." He plucked a serviette from the bag between them.

Taylor mopped her face and wiped her fingers. She poked the serviette back into the bag, leaned back against her elbows and turned her face to the late afternoon sun. "This is great. I had no idea you were so close to Robe. I'm glad Antoine suggested it. And that you came with us."

"Noelene can be persuasive."

Taylor chuckled. The sound was bright and bubbly like sparkling wine.

"That's one way of describing her," she said.

"She's not being too bossy, is she? She means well."

Taylor lifted her sunglasses with one hand and studied him with her blue eyes that sparkled like the ocean just a few metres away.

"We get along very well. And like she said, I'm sure she can handle the last of the Sunday afternoon cellar door crowd. She didn't need me." Taylor slid the glasses back onto her nose and leaned back again. "Anyway, Ed was around if she needed help."

"How's the burn?" Pete looked down at her feet. They were speckled with sand and tiny pieces of brown seaweed.

Taylor raised them gracefully in the air. "Fine. Not a mark or a blister."

"Lucky. I remember having sunburnt feet as a child. I couldn't wear shoes for a week."

"It wasn't that bad." She lowered her feet to the sand and tipped back her head. "This is gorgeous."

Pete couldn't see her eyes behind her dark glasses but he had the sense they were now shut. He studied the pink of her cheeks and the curve of her lips. Her chin pointed up and her neck stretched away to a thin gold chain that rested just above the round curve of her breasts. He turned away. Taylor was the perfect woman but she'd just broken up from a relationship, if that's what you could call her short time with Ed. And with his brother. Pete didn't think it wise to go there.

Ed appeared indifferent to Taylor's continued presence at the winery. He'd arrived at the cellar door as they were planning the beach trip. Ed had said he had some other things to do that would keep him close to home. Pete hadn't expected he'd want to go to the beach anyway. Swimming had never been his thing but Pete had still been surprised that he'd encouraged the three of them to head off together. It only added more weight to Pete's theory that Ed had never been that keen on Taylor in the first place. She'd been just another conquest to him.

Way down the beach a lone figure jogged along the shoreline. Antoine had gone for a run to dry off after their swim but Taylor and Pete had both opted for an ice-cream instead. Waves rolled in on the white sand below them and other groups of people were spread out along the beach. It had been a very hot day. He would have been happy to sit in the cottage under the aircon once the cellar door shut. Now that the chardonnay was in they had a small break before the reds started.

"It's fortunate you are able to do something you love."

Taylor's comment startled him. He turned. Her eyes were open now, watching him.

"Winemaking?" He chuckled. "Perhaps I didn't get a choice. My parents, Dad especially, were always talking wine, fermenting something. I was immersed in it from birth."

"You're lucky. I'm not passionate about anything. Work is just a means to an end."

"You wouldn't be alone in that."

"I know but just lately it's been making me restless. I had a courier job before I came here and I got the sack. I'm sure I could have made a case for wrongful dismissal but I didn't care enough."

"What did you courier?"

"People and parcels. That's why the van was so handy."

"Well, I'm glad you lost your job."

"Are you?"

"It's selfish I know but I'm glad you came here and you're working for us."

"Thanks, Pete, but like you said it's only seasonal. I've got to start acting like a grown-up and get a proper job."

"What kind of job?"

"That's just it." Taylor sat up. She brushed the sand from her elbows. "I don't know. I've got a degree in business marketing but I don't want to sit in an office all day long."

"That's what I love about being a winemaker. You're outside in the fresh air, cultivating the vines, growing the grapes then making the wine that people like to drink. It's the best of everything."

"I get that, from the little I've learned. It was good of you to take me on."

"We needed help."

"I don't feel as if I do that much."

"You do. And with Ben's help as well it means that Antoine, Ed and I are free to do other things. Don't underestimate the value of what you do."

She tipped her head sideways. "You're a kind-hearted bloke, Pete."

His kind heart skipped a beat at her smile, her proximity, her salty flyaway hair.

"It's not rocket science, what I'm doing," she said. "Testing sugar levels, stirring a few barrels."

"No." He took her hand and leaned closer. The glasses didn't hide the widening of her eyes. "Those barrels hold our next crop of award-winning chardonnay. Not everyone uses barrels to ferment their chardonnay. It requires more love. The wine must be stirred every day. You are helping to create the flavour and texture of a special wine. That's a very important job."

They stared at each other, with only the sound of the waves, a seagull's squawk and the distant squeals of children. Pete's gaze strayed to her lips.

"Like I said, you're a kind person." Taylor pulled away. "Here comes Antoine."

Pete turned to see the young Frenchman jogging towards them. He arrived in front of them with sweat glistening on his brown skin, puffing from his exertion.

"We should get going," Pete said.

"Not before we get fish and chips." Antoine bent and retrieved his towel. "None of us want to cook tonight."

Taylor stood. "Sounds good to me."

"How about we dine in?" Antoine said. "It's going to be hot back at the quarters. I'm not in a rush."

"I'm a mess," Taylor said and tugged her hair back from her face.

"You are most beautiful, Taylor."

Pete felt a stab of jealousy that he hadn't said the words that rolled so smoothly off Antoine's tongue.

"Anyway, this is summer on the Australian beach." Antoine smiled his big grin. "Aussies don't care about what they look like when they're holidaying at the beach, do they Pete?"

"Officially it's autumn." Pete jumped up and ruffled Antoine's hair. "Haven't you noticed the leaves starting to change colour?"

"It's too hot for autumn," Antoine groaned.

"I agree it doesn't feel like it," Taylor chipped in.

"We'll go to the cafe," Pete said. "They don't mind sandy feet and wet hair."

"At least let me tidy up a little," Taylor pleaded. She picked up her bag and made for the toilet block.

"We'll wait for you by the car," Pete called after her.

Their footsteps scrunched in the coarse sand as the two men made their way up the beach.

"She's a very beautiful woman."

Once again Pete felt a stab of jealousy as Antoine's French accent played up the word *beautiful*.

"You two make a good couple."

Pete stopped and Antoine paused beside him.

"She's Ed's girlfriend," Pete said.

"Not any more. He suggested we invite you to come with us to the beach so he can't be too broken-hearted." Antoine grinned, puffed out his bronzed chest and threw his arms out wide. "No man in love sends his woman out with these two *fantastique* specimens." He kept walking.

Pete scratched his head. It was odd that Ed had been the one to encourage them to ask Pete along. Still, it only added weight to his belief Ed no longer gave a rat's arse about Taylor. On the other hand she didn't seem too broken-hearted either. A small flutter of excitement rose inside him but he quickly dismissed it. It was too soon. Pete knew how long it had taken him to get over Felicity. No doubt Taylor was still confused about her feelings for Ed. He didn't want to do anything that might drive her away.

Edward had no sooner waved Noelene off and brought in the cellar door 'Open' sign than a sleek black car pulled into the parking area. He glanced towards the road. Noelene was definitely out of sight. He didn't want her all-seeing eyes to witness this meeting.

A man got out of the car. Edward smiled and held out his hand. "Hello, Angus."

"Edward. I was surprised to get your call. Last we spoke you weren't going to sell the cabernet."

"It's still up for discussion. I thought you might like the opportunity to have a look at the grapes on the vine. Take some back for testing if you like."

Angus Archer studied him closely. "It would be a coup for our winery to add a first-class Coonawarra cab sauv to our list."

Even though the heat was leaving the day Edward could feel perspiration trickle down his back. "With this burst of warm weather we've had it looks like it will be ready to pick soon."

"I've got machinery on standby."

Edward paused. Peter had been planning to hand-pick these grapes. He'd said they deserved the best care. Still, it didn't matter to Edward what Angus did with them as long as he put his money where his mouth was.

"Come and have a look." Edward began walking towards the vineyard beside the cellar door. Angus fell into step beside him. "At this stage I'd like us to keep this between ourselves. My brother has enough on his plate. I don't want to worry him with this at the moment."

"As long as you're sure. I'm committed to buying a Coonawarra cab sauv. Yours is the pick of what I've been offered but if you're not going to sell I need to know."

Edward felt a twinge of guilt but he ignored it. "You decide what you think it's worth to you and make me an offer."

They walked along the fence to the opening. Edward looked back towards the road. He hoped Antoine would be able to keep Peter away from home for a while longer yet.

CHAPTER
32

Taylor watched Pete walk out across the board perched over the top of a tank of red mush. He carried something that resembled a giant potato masher.

"This is the best of our shiraz." He waved one arm at the liquid below his feet. "In a few years it will be in bottles and selling well."

"Like the one I sold for all that money?"

"No. That was our reserve cab sauv. We haven't picked those grapes yet but I'm hopeful it will make our top-of-the-range wine when we do."

Taylor heard the pride in his voice. She felt a little envious that he could grow a bunch of grapes and turn them into a wine so special people would pay a lot of money for it.

"All you have to do is push the grapes from the top to the bottom."

Taylor paid attention. He leaned over and pushed the masher through the mush. Then he dragged it up, took a small step along the plank and repeated the action.

"Do you want to give it a go?" He turned the full force of his clear blue eyes on her.

Taylor glanced down. His look made her weak at the knees and this was not the time. Especially since the plank she had to balance on didn't look very wide. It was stained with the same deep red colour as the grapes underneath it. She stepped up and edged her way to where Pete still watched her. She took the handle from him and focused on the job at hand. She pushed down. The masher slid through the liquid. She gasped as she tried to pull it back up.

"That's the hard part." Pete grinned at her.

"Looks like I won't be needing to find a gym." Taylor breathed in and pulled harder. The masher released from the liquid and she wobbled backwards.

"Take it easy." Pete's strong hands steadied her.

Taylor peered down at the dark red liquid, thick with grapes. "How deep is this?"

"Over your head. I don't recommend falling in. Hold the plunger a bit lower." He put his hands over hers as she slid them down the pole. "Now push down steadily."

They leaned together. She relished the strength of his body pressed against hers and the earthy scent of him.

"And then slowly up."

The plunger came to the surface with less force than her first attempt.

She steadied herself as Pete took his hands from hers.

"You right?"

She nodded, not trusting her voice.

"Have another go."

Taylor pushed the plunger through the liquid again. This time she planted her feet and eased it back to the surface.

"That's it," Pete said. "This has to be done several times a day."

"You're kidding." Taylor thought she was fit but she could already feel the strain in her upper arms.

Pete chuckled. His eyes sparkled. All too aware she was in close proximity to his strong arms and hunky chest, she forced herself to turn away. She gripped the plunger tightly and slowly pushed down. Pete remained at her side. She could feel him watching her.

She'd hardly seen him since their afternoon at the beach last Sunday. She still made an evening meal each day but Antoine had been the only one to share her table. Ed and Pete called at different times and took their food with them. Taylor found herself watching the clock at night wondering when Pete would arrive and then feeling vaguely disappointed when he thanked her for the meal and left. She didn't feel the same about Ed. In fact she felt nothing. She couldn't believe she'd fallen for him.

Cass had been right. Taylor had got up the courage to call her last night. She'd apologised and filled her friend in. It was a relief to be on good terms again. Cass had sent a text after she'd returned home from her weekend visit but last night was the first time they'd spoken since then. Taylor missed Cass but nothing else about Adelaide.

"You seem to have the rhythm of it." Pete's voice cut through her thoughts.

Once again she raised the plunger carefully. "I think so."

"Happy for me to leave you to it?"

"Yes. As long as you're happy I'm doing it right."

"As you've said before, it's not rocket science but it has to be done. All three tanks."

Taylor looked across at the other two. Her arms were going to have to strengthen up if she was going to do this every day. "I'll be fine," she said.

"I'll see you later." The board wobbled a little beneath her as he made his way off.

"Don't fall in," he added with a grin and left her to it.

Taylor wondered if he was speaking from experience. She gripped the handle of the plunger tightly and shifted her feet. The action made her teeter forward. She steadied herself and gazed down at the chunky liquid below. Falling in was not an option.

She edged along the plank, took a deep breath and pushed the plunger down again. The dark liquid swirled below her. There was something almost therapeutic about the activity. She got into a rhythm, lift and plunge, lift and plunge. By the time she'd done all three tanks her legs and arms felt like jelly and she'd worked up a sweat. She climbed down from the last tank and went in search of her water bottle.

The air was warm inside the shed. She stepped out, closed the door behind her and stood in the shade where a slight breeze cooled her. Across the vineyard she could see the cellar door. There were a few cars there. It was Friday so Noelene probably had a steady stream of customers. Taylor already had a vegetable lasagne made for tonight's dinner. She wasn't in a rush to head back to the empty quarters.

She decided to walk down to the cellar door. She could help Noelene with the cleaning if nothing else. When she got there the older woman was saying goodbye to a group of people and only one couple remained. Taylor said hello and went into the back room to wash glasses. Noelene's day had been busy judging by the number that had to be done.

She'd just picked up the tea towel to polish the first rackful when Noelene stuck her head around the door.

"You don't have to do that. You'll put me out of a job."

Taylor smiled. "I like to keep busy. There will be more customers I'm sure."

"They've had you plunging, have they?"

"How did you know?"

Noelene pointed at her t-shirt. "I hope that's not your best shirt and jeans."

Taylor looked down. She was splattered with streaks of red. She hadn't noticed. Thank goodness she hadn't gone out to serve customers.

"I've been plunging some shiraz."

"Everyone gets a go at that at some time, except Felicity. Wouldn't want madam to break a fingernail." She winked at Taylor and ducked back into the front room at the sound of the cellar door opening.

Taylor smiled to herself at the mental picture of Frosty Felicity teetering along the board in her high heels and falling in to the thick red mixture. There was something about the young office manager. Taylor plunged her hands into the frothy hot water and rubbed at a glass, imagining it was Felicity's face.

In no time at all Noelene was back. "Freeloaders," she said. "Not really interested in buying. Just wanting free samples. Still have to be polite to them. You never know where it may lead." She began to wipe as Taylor washed. "Did you enjoy your trip to Robe last Sunday?"

"Yes. It was a beautiful day and such a nice town. I've never been there before."

"I'm glad Pete went with you. He always loved the beach as a boy. His mother used to take them quite often. Since she died he hardly goes anymore."

"I like the beach too. My parents live fairly close to the water in Adelaide so we went as kids. They're not home much to enjoy it anymore."

"What do they do?"

"They're doctors. They do a lot of overseas aid work. I don't see them much these days."

"You must miss them?"

Taylor thought about that. "I used to but now it's just the way we are."

"Bit like me and my hubby, Frank. He's a truck driver. If he's home too long we get in each other's way. Goodness knows what we'll do when he retires. I'll have to keep working for the boys until I drop off the perch."

"You obviously enjoy working here."

"I love it. Frank and I only had the one child." Noelene's face stiffened. "A daughter. She was born with multiple disabilities and only lived a few years."

"That must have been hard."

Taylor pulled the plug from the sink and Noelene took the cloth and wiped everything down.

"It almost seems a different life now." She looked at Taylor. "Edward and Peter are like surrogate sons to me. Neil and Pearl were good friends. They're not here anymore and I feel they'd like someone watching over their boys. Even though they're men I like to keep in touch. Working for them makes that easy."

Once more the cellar door squeaked.

"I'm sorry it didn't work out with you and Edward."

Taylor remained silent. She hadn't said anything to anyone about breaking up with Ed but the word had got around. Felicity was being more smug than usual.

Noelene patted Taylor's arm. "You're his type but not his type. I love him to bits but you can do better." Noelene winked then turned and disappeared into the front room.

Taylor listened as the older woman greeted the next lot of customers, not sure what she'd been trying to say exactly. She'd been almost motherly. It made Taylor think of her own parents. Cass had been right about that too. Taylor rarely had decent conversations with her mother anymore. Skype didn't lend itself to pouring out your heart. Chats and parental advice were few and far between these days. She hadn't checked her email for a while either. She had a sudden urge to have some kind of contact. Her parents should be back from whatever remote part of Cambodia they'd been to by now and she still had Ed's laptop.

She let herself out the back door and walked along the track that ran past Pete's special cabernet grapes. The leaves on the vines were no longer the bright green they'd been when she'd first arrived. Now the green was fading and being replaced with yellow and orange and even deep red. Autumn was changing the colours.

About halfway along the carefully groomed rows she stopped. At the other end of the row, on the road side of the fence, two men were leaning into the vineyard peering at the vines. One of them was tall and wide. The sun reflected off his bald head. As she watched, another car came slowly along the road and pulled up beside them. They turned and got back into their car. They looked to have a brief conversation with the old guy who leaned out of the second car's driver-side window before both vehicles moved on. The black car went back towards the highway and the other, a faded green colour, continued on up the dirt road past the winery.

Taylor wondered what that was about. Still, there were people and machines everywhere you went at the moment. Vintage was in full swing, perhaps they were something to do with picking these grapes. Funny thing was the two men in the black car both wore suits. It was probably nothing but she thought she'd mention it to Pete when she saw him next.

As she drew level with the winery she saw Felicity coming out from between the rows of wine tanks. She didn't notice Taylor or if she did she ignored her and headed back towards the office. Taylor smirked. Felicity almost hobbled along in her high heels on the rocky ground, such impractical shoes for working in this environment. Although if she spent most of her time in the office there was no need for practical footwear there, Taylor supposed. She rolled her shoulders and felt the ache down her arms. First things first. She was going to stand under the shower to ease her tired muscles then check her emails.

"What do you think, Howard?" Pete watched as the old man chewed the grapes.

Howard crunched some more, the saggy skin around his jaw jiggling up and down, then he swallowed. "I'd be picking them soon. Earlier than we thought. A few more days maybe."

"I'll have to line up my pickers."

"Count Margaret and me in."

"Thanks, Howard."

Howard rubbed his hands together. "It will be a pleasure."

"I've got a small team of seasonal pickers on standby. We've also got Antoine and Taylor. I'll give Ben a call. His wife Jane will help as well. If it's Tuesday or Wednesday Noelene might lend a hand and there's me and Ed of course. We should get it done in half a day."

"I think Noelene's best left out of it and you should make sure Eddie's busy that day."

Pete turned his head sideways. He trusted Howard's knowledge of grapes implicitly but he had noticed the old bloke say a few odd things of late that made him wonder if he was just starting to lose his grip a bit.

"Ed has to be there."

"No he doesn't. His heart's not in it, Pete."

"I don't understand."

"It's best he does something else that day. That's all I'm saying." Howard scratched his chin. The skin wrinkled beneath his fingers. "Best for everyone."

Pete studied Howard. He was talking in riddles but his gaze was as sharp as ever. There was nothing about his look to suggest he was losing his marbles.

"Do you think he'd try to stop us? That would be ridiculous. The grapes have to be picked." Pete scratched at the back of his neck.

Howard grasped Pete's shoulder in a firm grip. "Trust me on this, boy. Eddie's better off kept in the dark about this until it's all over and Noelene, well, I think it's best she doesn't know either."

"Noelene's as solid as a rock."

"I didn't say she wasn't. I just think it's best to keep this as close to your chest as possible."

Pete screwed up his face. "I wish you could explain it better."

"No need. Let me know which day you choose and what time and Margaret and I will be here." He lifted his hat and shoved it firmly back on his head.

Pete opened his mouth but Howard turned away, moving towards his old green car with his hobbling gait.

Back at his cottage Pete was restless. He replayed Howard's comments over in his head. Pete didn't like subterfuge. He could think of nothing that would distract Ed and keep him away from the winery and he knew Noelene would want to be part of it if she could.

He stuck his head out the back door. Taylor's van was still parked at the quarters but he'd heard Antoine drive off a while ago. The Frenchman was planning to have a few drinks in town. Pete could have gone with him but he was half thinking he'd see if Taylor was staying in. Maybe they could eat whatever meal she'd prepared together. This last week he'd been late every night and had taken his meal home to eat alone and then fallen into bed.

It was Friday night after all. He pulled on a clean shirt and dragged his fingers through his tight curls. He needed a haircut but there was no time to fit that in at the moment. In the mirror he looked at the stubble shadow on his chin. He should shave but splashed water on his face instead. Now that he had decided to visit Taylor he was keen to get there.

He took a bottle of chardonnay from his fridge and made his way through his backyard and along the track to the quarters. He could hear music as he approached and through the screen door he could see the wooden door was open.

"Hello," he called. When there was no answer he pulled open the screen and stuck his head inside. "Knock, knock," he called.

Taylor appeared from the passage, rubbing at her hair with a towel. Her face lit up with a smile.

"Hello, Pete."

"Are you going somewhere?"

"No. Have you come for your dinner? It's still heating up."

"Yes, but I wondered if you'd like company." He held up the bottle of wine.

"Of course. Just let me finish my hair. You know where the glasses are. I'll be right back."

Pete whistled along to the music. He opened the wine and poured two glasses. In the background he could hear Taylor's hair dryer. There was a laptop on the table. The music was coming from there. Pete couldn't help but notice the picture of the Eiffel Tower on the screen. It was a night shot, taken close to the base looking up.

"I was re-reading my blog." Taylor came up behind him. The floral scent of her freshly showered body enveloped him.

"Did you take this photo?"

"Yes."

"It's a great perspective. How long ago where you there?"

Taylor slid on to the seat next to him. "A few years now. Cass and I went together."

"I did a vintage in France straight after uni. That's where I met Antoine. I had an incredible time. I'd love to go back one day."

"Me too."

"So this blog is about your travels?"

"Yes. It was a way to keep in touch with my family and share photos."

"Great idea. I don't think to use the computer for those kinds of things."

"I've been looking at websites and Facebook for local wineries. I hope you don't mind me saying but Wriggly Creek's could do with some work."

"I have to admit I haven't looked at it for ages. Ed oversees that side of things and I think he leaves most of it to Felicity."

"Oh." The excitement slid from Taylor's face.

"Perhaps you could share your ideas with her. I'm sure she'd appreciate it. She's got so many other jobs on her plate."

"I'll give it some thought." Taylor stood up. "That lasagne should be heated through by now. Do you know if Ed wants some?"

"I've hardly seen him all day. Last I saw he was heading into town to get some hose joiners."

"I'm putting some aside for Antoine. I'll do the same for Ed."

She was quiet as she dished up. He wondered if she was thinking about Ed.

"Can I help?" he asked.

"There's a green salad in the fridge and some dressing."

He put it on the table as she set down two plates of lasagne. Taylor sat and he followed and topped up their glasses. He raised his towards her.

"Thank you," he said.

"What for?"

"For the meals, for all the jobs you do for us."

"I'm on the payroll now," she said.

"How did the plunging end up?"

"Good. I'm glad Antoine did the next couple of shifts. I'm going to be sore tomorrow." She wrapped her arms across her chest, squeezed her shoulders with her hands and groaned. "What a weakling."

"It uses muscles you don't usually work so hard."

"Well, I'll be able to lift tall buildings once I get used to it."

"I don't think we've got any tall buildings that need moving but we can have you lifting wine barrels again." He smiled at her and was rewarded by a return grin.

"Do you think you could write me a list of things I have to do each day?"

"I could."

"That would save me having to find you. If you jot down anything you can think of I'll get on and do it. If I run out of jobs or I'm not sure then I can find you."

"Sounds like a plan." Pete was a little disappointed. He'd got used to explaining Taylor's tasks each morning but she was right. She was quite capable of getting on with the jobs at hand without having to wait for him. "I can pin it on the board in the lab."

"Good idea." She went on eating.

He put another forkful of lasagne in his mouth. "This is good, thank you."

"I'd normally make a meat-based lasagne. I'm glad Antoine's vegetarian. I'm enjoying discovering new options for meals."

"I'm enjoying not having to think about meals. Mum did all the cooking and Ed and I aren't much good in that department."

Taylor put down her fork. "I hope it's not proving too awkward having me here still."

"Not for me." He studied her. The spark had left her eyes. "It's none of my business but now that you've broken it off I think it's for the best. Ed's not your type."

"How do you know what my type is?" She looked at him with amused interest.

Pete glanced down at his plate. "I guess I don't but I do know my brother." He took another mouthful and hoped she would let it go. Perhaps it was the wine or simply being with Taylor but his tongue was loose.

"You're the second person today to tell me Ed's not my type."

"Really? Let me guess. Noelene?"

"Yes." Taylor chuckled. "She said I was Ed's type but not his type. Quite mysterious of her."

Pete knew exactly what Noelene meant. Taylor was too nice a person to be one of Ed's flings. Noelene had seen it too.

"She means well," he said.

"She's very fond of you two."

"She kind of adopted us when our parents died."

"You're lucky to have someone like that in your life, someone who cares."

Taylor lifted her glass this time and he followed suit.

"To Noelene," she said.

"To our parents, wherever they are."

"Would you like some more lasagne?"

"No thanks. That was delicious but filling."

Taylor reached for his plate.

"I'll do the dishes," he said.

"It's only two plates. I'll do them in the morning. Shall we have the rest of the wine?"

He poured and they carried their glasses to the couch. She sat with one foot underneath her, her body turned to face him. Her hair shone and her face glowed. All he could do was look at her. Suddenly he had nothing to say. Here he was sharing a drink and a couch with the most beautiful and interesting woman he'd met in a while and he was speechless.

"I forgot to tell you," she said. "I saw two men looking at your cabernet grapes today. The vineyard between the cellar door and the winery."

"NS18?"

"Yes."

He wondered who that would have been. "Quite a few people know this is the first year we'll get a proper crop off it. Vignerons are like everyone else. We like to check out the opposition. They were probably just stickybeaking." He hoped that was all. After his strange discussion with Howard he was edgy.

"This is not meant to be a shot at your clothes but they were both wearing suits."

"Well-dressed stickybeaks." Pete chuckled but it didn't alleviate his concern. With Howard's comments and Ed's talk of selling the NS18 he wouldn't rest easy until he had the grapes picked and safely in the tanks.

Taylor took a sip of wine. "You know I used to think chardonnay was for the twin-set-and-pearls people. My gran drank it and I never liked it but I'm really developing a taste for this."

"A lot of vignerons steer away from the over-oaked, buttery chardonnays of the past. The style has changed. We aim for a fruit-driven wine with tight acid, texture and length."

She tipped her head to one side and raised an eyebrow. "Whatever that means I like it."

A wisp of hair fell across her eyes. He reached across and pushed it back. They held each other's gaze. He wanted to press his lips against hers, to feel their warmth, to taste them.

There was a sharp rap on the screen door and it flew open. Ed stepped inside and looked from Pete to Taylor.

"You two look cosy."

"We've just finished our dinner," Taylor sat back. "Would you like yours now?"

"Yes but I'll take it with me."

She got up and went to the fridge. Pete hadn't heard a vehicle. Ed must be on foot. Pete stayed on the couch. He felt as if he'd been caught doing something wrong.

"Did you get what you wanted?" he asked.

Ed frowned at him.

"In Penola."

"Oh yes. All good."

Pete stood up. "I really should get going too, Taylor. Thanks for dinner."

"Oh, are you leaving?" She looked surprised. "I enjoyed it. I've got used to not eating alone."

Ed gave a soft snort as she handed him a container from the fridge.

"Thanks," he grunted.

Pete was embarrassed. Ed could be so rude sometimes.

"Good night, Taylor," Pete said and followed Ed out the door.

She called good night and shut the wooden door behind them.

"Have you got a moment?" Ed asked.

"Sure." Pete didn't like the dark look on his brother's face. It usually meant trouble.

"Let's go to your place." Ed set off, taking long strides.

Pete followed behind, wondering what bombshell Ed was going to drop this time.

CHAPTER
34

Edward's anger bubbled in his chest like a fermenting wine. He barely gave Peter time to get in the door before he rounded on him.

"What are you playing at?" Edward growled.

"What?" Peter's face creased in a puzzled look.

"Taylor. You've been making a play for her behind my back."

"No I wasn't. Whatever gave you that idea?"

"I've seen you a few times making eyes at each other. That's why she called it off with me." Edward poked a finger of his spare hand at Peter. "You've been chasing her behind my back."

"No I haven't. And from what I understand you two are no longer an item anyway so Taylor can do whatever she likes now."

"You are sweet on her."

Peter sighed and held up his hands. "Say whatever you like. There's nothing between Taylor and me."

Edwards's gaze locked on Peter. There was something about the way he said the word *nothing*. It was too emphatic.

"You're taken with her."

"I'm not."

Once again the sharp response. Edward felt anger burn deep within his chest. He'd taken a liking to Taylor but once she'd spent time at the quarters her interest in him had waned. He'd blamed Antoine but maybe it had been Peter who'd been cutting his lunch.

"Remember what happened with Felicity?"

Peter's jaw dropped.

"She was mine first." Edward wanted to stop Peter going after Taylor and it was the only way he could think to do it. "It's the same with Taylor. You always go after my cast-offs and Taylor was with me first, just like Felicity. And I do mean in every way."

Peter stepped up to Edward. Anger smouldered in his eyes. "You're an arsehole sometimes, Ed."

"Just looking after you, Peter."

Edward pushed past his brother and slammed out the door. Immediately the anger left him and remorse replaced it. Why was he so riled up? He didn't even care that Taylor had called off their relationship but if he couldn't have her then neither could Peter. It would only complicate matters.

Edward had seen them together the night after Taylor had broken off with him. He'd gone to the quarters to see her but he'd heard Peter's voice and he'd waited outside in the dark. He hadn't caught everything they'd said but it had sounded like Taylor had wormed her way into Peter's affection and he'd offered her a job and asked her to stay.

Edward had ducked away when Taylor had surprised him at the door so he hadn't heard what happened after that. No doubt she would use Peter like she had Edward and then dump him. Peter would be hurt like he had been with Felicity. Better Edward throw him a swift punch in the guts now than his heart be broken like it had back then.

The brick of the quarters glowed in the setting sun. Edward sighed. He'd best go and talk to Taylor, make sure she didn't keep chasing Peter. He crossed the yard and walked along the track to the door, still clutching the meal she'd given him.

The music that had been playing when he'd called in earlier could no longer be heard. He pulled back the screen door and knocked. Taylor opened the door. The light from the room behind shone through her hair giving a halo effect.

"Can I come in?"

She opened the door wider and gestured with her arm. He stepped past her into the quarters.

Taylor stood just inside the door studying him.

"I wanted to have a quick chat," he said.

"What about?"

"You and Peter."

She folded her arms. "There is no 'me and Peter'."

She played the game just like Peter had but Edward was having none of it. "Peter is a nice guy," he said. "Too nice sometimes. He was always the one to rescue baby animals and bring them home for Mum to fix."

"What's that got to do with me?"

"He's rescuing you."

Taylor frowned at him.

Edward took a deep breath. He would have to spell it out. "He's only being nice to you."

"I don't understand."

"Letting you stay here, giving you a job that someone else could do. He's got a soft heart."

Still Taylor frowned at him.

"Don't you get it? We broke up and he feels sorry for you. The little orphan with nowhere to go. You're just another of Peter's rescue projects."

Her eyes opened wide. He'd hit his mark.

She put her hand on the door. "I think you should go, Ed."

"That's funny. Asking me to leave my own property."

She opened her mouth but he put up his hand. "It's okay. I'm going. Peter's employed you so I won't change that but as soon as vintage eases off I think it best that you leave."

He stepped through the door.

"It will be my pleasure." She pushed the wooden door shut behind him. It screeched in protest then closed with a thud.

Taylor leaned against the door. Her heart pounded and anger pulsed through her.

"Bastard."

How had she ever thought he was the one for her? She picked up a cushion from the old chair and punched it. The cloud of dust it emitted made her sneeze. She looked around the room that had become her temporary home through watery eyes. That was just it. This was only play-acting. Like she'd said to Pete she needed to find a real job, something to give her purpose.

"Taylor, you're a bloody fool."

She sagged onto the couch. The thought of Pete's smile swept away her anger. She was just beginning to realise he had all the good attributes. Ed's had only been window-dressing but Pete's were genuine. She put her hand to her head. That's what she'd thought about Ed and Larry and Foster and the guys before them. Maybe she was the one who was at fault. She fell for them then realised they weren't the men she'd thought they were. What was it she wanted in a man? She couldn't answer her own question.

She looked at her watch. It was only eight o'clock. Here it was another Friday night and she was alone. She stormed into her little cell of a room, flung clothes about and found her good black jeans and sparkly gold top. She went to the bathroom, applied some make-up and brushed her hair. She peered at herself trying to see the whole look but it was impossible in the small mirror.

"You'll do," she said and flicked off the light.

She grabbed a jacket and her keys and let herself out of the quarters. Pete's cottage was in darkness. Her steps faltered and she stopped behind her van searching for any sign of him. They'd been having such a good time until Ed had turned up. Pete was fun. He had a ready laugh and kind eyes that also reflected an inner spark. He'd gazed at her with more than kindness in his look. Or so she'd thought, but she was only another project to Pete. Someone he could rescue then move on.

Taylor turned away from the cottage and climbed into her van. She pushed the keys into the lock and paused. Once more she questioned what she was doing, where she was going. Then with a firm twist of the key she started the engine, turned the van around and headed into town.

Pete sat in the darkness, his anger at Ed long gone, replaced by a deep sadness which had seeped into every part of him. Ed had taken delight in reminding him about Felicity. It had been so long ago Pete never thought about her in that way anymore. In fact he was glad in many ways he hadn't pursued her. As an office manager Felicity was efficient and he was thankful for that, just as he was thankful he'd never chased what he'd thought was love for her.

He lifted his head at the sound of a vehicle. Headlights shone along the passage and then were gone, the engine noise fading with them.

Taylor. He wondered where she was going. Pete had watched through his back door as Ed had made his way to the quarters and gone in. The thought of the two of them together infuriated him. Taylor had arrived as Ed's girlfriend but then she'd called it off. Neither of them had appeared too upset by that but perhaps he'd read it wrong. Ed hadn't stayed long at the quarters but now Taylor had gone out. Perhaps to meet him somewhere. Pete put his head in his hands. Too many thoughts whirled in his head. He just wanted them to stop.

He lurched to his feet and took his jacket from the hook. He needed fresh air and something else to think about. He let himself out the front door and strode out between the rows of shiraz. The grapes were gone but the leaves still clung to the vines, the fresh scent of them mingling with the sweet earthy smell of the soil. He batted at the odd string of spider web. There was little moon tonight but he made his way with a sure-footed tread despite the clinging strands. Spiders were the least of his worries. When he got to the end of the row he turned and headed towards the new cabernet vines yet to be picked.

He hadn't said as much to Taylor but anyone paying close attention to his NS18 grapes made him nervous, especially after his conversation with Howard and Ed's talk of selling. He stopped as he reached the first row of vines. He picked a couple of grapes and popped them in his mouth. The sharp and sweet flavours exploded on his palette. Wednesday, he decided. They would pick these grapes Wednesday, but how was he going to do that without telling Ed?

CHAPTER
35

Taylor stepped into the noisy bar. Friday night was a busy night with a mix of people from those still in their work clothes to the well-heeled in their leather jackets and designer jeans. Several people wore hats, some of them weird and wonderful creations.

"Taylor."

She looked over to the end of the bar where Antoine was waving at her. Relieved to see someone she knew she made her way through the throng to meet him.

Antoine kissed her on both cheeks. "I thought you were staying home."

"Changed my mind." Taylor smiled at the two blokes staring at her from beside Antoine.

"Let me introduce you then I'll buy you a drink." Antoine placed a gentle hand on her shoulder. "This is our cellar hand, Taylor. And this is Tom."

The tall blond bloke reached out a hand. "Pleased to meet you."

"And Eric."

The other guy, more Antoine's height but with a shock of red hair, also shook her hand. "Hello," he said. "We've been hearing all about your cooking. No cellar hand I've ever worked with had cooking on their CV."

"Not sure I'm your usual cellar hand." Taylor chuckled. "Once I started cooking for the blokes at Wriggly Creek they found me more jobs to do. I guess I've become a bit of a jack of all trades."

"Let me get you a drink, Taylor." Antoine pulled out his wallet. "Beer?"

"Yes, thanks."

"Hello." A woman with bright red lipstick, a big smile and a wide-brimmed orange hat with flowers poking out in all directions joined the group. She took the drink Eric handed her.

"This is my wife, Tracey." He nodded. "Taylor from Wriggly Creek."

"Hi, Tracey."

"You're the cellar hand everyone's talking about." Tracey grinned. "Pleased to meet you at last."

"Oh dear. That doesn't sound good." Taylor took a big mouthful of the beer Antoine brought back. "Thanks." She gave him a grateful smile.

"This is a small town." Tracey raised her eyebrows. "You can't roll over in bed around here without someone knowing about it."

Taylor swallowed another big draught of her beer.

"One woman living with three blokes has sent the town grapevine into overdrive." Tracey chuckled.

What did she mean? Taylor emptied her glass. This was the twenty-first century. Surely she didn't have to explain her living arrangements, defend her honour.

"So you moved here to be with Ed I hear. He's quite a catch."

"Yes and no…it didn't…" Taylor scratched at her forehead. "We're not together."

"Stop it Trace." Eric gave his wife a nudge. "You're embarrassing Taylor."

"Sorry. I must have heard wrong." Tracey looked contrite. "I didn't mean to be insensitive."

"That's okay. Ed and I did date for a while." Taylor looked at her empty glass. "I'm not used to people taking notice of what I do."

"In the country they take notice and there are some that relish adding in the embellishments. Mostly they don't mean any harm. Took me a while to get used to it."

"My shout." Eric collected their glasses.

Taylor got a glimpse along the bar. The staff all had brightly coloured top hats on.

"Is there some kind of hat theme tonight?" she asked.

"They usually run a competition here once a month. Tonight it's mad hatters night. They gave out a few prizes earlier." Tracey grinned and pulled at the brim of her hat. "I won a bottle of bubbly for mine. They've had some good events here. Gets people mixing and talking."

"You're not a local?" Taylor moved closer to Tracey. The bar was getting very loud.

"Eric and I are from New South Wales. I grew up in Sydney and he comes from Newcastle."

"You're a long way from home."

"Eric's a winemaker. He wanted to learn more about red production and there was a job going here. I do relief teaching in the area." Tracey waved a hand in the air. "We've settled in. It's a small community but the people are friendly and there's always something happening." She tapped her funny hat. "Like tonight."

Eric handed Taylor a beer and joined Antoine and Tom's conversation.

"Hi, Trace." A tall angular woman squeezed past the blokes to join them. She had a long nose and large red lips, and wore a funny little green felt hat with several feathers protruding from its band that reminded Taylor of Pinocchio. "Nice hat."

"It won me a prize." Tracey beamed. "Carol, this is Taylor. She's working out at—"

"Wriggly Creek. Yes, I'd heard." Carol studied Taylor with an inquisitive look. "Nice to meet you at last."

"Hello."

"I hear you're with Edward Starr."

Taylor's mouth dropped open.

"She's not with Ed," Tracey said firmly. "Taylor's a cellar hand."

"Really?" Carol stared at her, disbelief plastered all over her face. "But I—"

"What are you doing for the weekend?" Tracey cut Carol off and began to quiz her on her plans.

Taylor took a gulp of beer. So she really was the subject of town gossip. Living out at the winery she'd not met a lot of the locals. She'd had a couple of meals out with Ed, and Pete had brought her here for a meal and now she was here with Antoine. Well, not really *with* Antoine. She clasped a hand across her mouth. She could see how that might look to someone watching from the outside. They could easily put two and two together and come up with six.

"Something wrong, Taylor?"

She looked back to Tracey and Carol who were both studying her. Taylor dropped her hand.

"No, all good." She drained her glass. "Must be my shout."

She lined up at the bar.

A young bloke with big lips and a knowing grin plastered on his face scooped up the glasses. "Same again?" He wore a tall red-and-white-striped top hat. *Terry* was embroidered on his t-shirt.

"Yes thanks, Terry."

He turned and as he did his eye twitched. He'd winked at her. Taylor shook her head. He had to be several years her junior.

"Actually no," she said. "Make mine a glass of bubbly please." She'd join the girls with their preference.

He looked at her over the top of the beer tap. "You must be Taylor."

"How do you know my name?"

"Just a lucky guess." He lined up the beers and started pouring glasses of bubbly. "Antoine said there was a better-looking cellar hand than him at Wriggly Creek. He was right."

Taylor paid and started handing out the drinks. She wasn't used to such close scrutiny and she wasn't sure she liked it. She joined the group again. Everyone was chatting and she felt on the outer with nothing to contribute to the conversation. Before she knew it her glass was empty again.

"This is my round," Tom said.

Tracey and Carol waved a hand over their glasses and kept talking.

"More of the same?" Tom nodded at her empty glass.

"Sure." She handed it over.

Eric moved to include Taylor in the group of blokes. "Antoine said you're from Adelaide."

"That's home."

"Trace and I have spent a few weekends there since we've been in Coonawarra. We were up there a few weeks ago for a couple of Fringe shows. We had a blast."

"There's lots happening at this time of year." Taylor had a pang of regret. If she was still in Adelaide she would have gone to a few shows with Cass and some of the other girls.

Tom came back with the drinks. Taylor took a swig of her sparkling.

"We saw this guy who was a contortionist." Eric described the guy's actions. Carol left and Tracey joined in. They were all laughing and joking and Taylor felt herself relaxing at last. By the time Antoine bought the next round she was enjoying herself immensely.

When Eric said they were leaving Taylor was very disappointed. "Do you have to go? The night's still young."

"Early start tomorrow," Eric said.

"Great to meet you, Taylor." Tracey squeezed her hand. "Let's catch up again soon."

"I'm not going yet." Tom put a hand on her shoulder.

"Me either," Antoine said. "I've got the morning off tomorrow."

"Must be time for shots then." Taylor pulled out her wallet. "My turn to buy."

Taylor groaned and stretched. She was cold and stiff. The back seat of her van wasn't comfortable at all but she hadn't noticed when she'd crawled in during the early hours of the morning. Now, as the first rays of the morning sun gave the sky a pink glow, every part of her ached. She pulled the old rug tighter around her shoulders and sat up. Her head pounded and her mouth was so dry her tongue stuck to it.

At her feet she saw a red-and-white-striped top hat. She groaned again and put her head in her hands. Why had she started drinking shots? She had a vague recollection of whipping the barman's hat from his head. She scrabbled forward and grabbed the water bottle from the console beside the driver's seat. She drained what was left in it and tossed the empty bottle aside.

"Damn! You said you'd never do this again, Taylor."

She peered through the windscreen. Hers wasn't the only vehicle in the hotel car park but she could see no other signs of life. She got out of the van and shuddered as the crisp morning air chilled her through the rug draped over her shoulders.

In the driver's seat, she started the engine and eased out of the car park. She frowned and peered right. She waited as one car came towards her and then another and then still more cars came. A weird and wonderful collection, mostly older vehicles that had seen better days. Was it some kind of rally?

Finally she pulled into a gap between a faded orange kombi van and a beat-up ute. She went with the strange convoy along the highway and turned off at the Wiggly Creek road. In her rear-view mirror the convoy continued on along the highway. When she glanced back the next time there wasn't a vehicle to be seen. She blinked her bleary eyes and put a hand to her throbbing forehead. Perhaps she really had fallen down the rabbit hole.

"Well, here she is: the talk of the town." Felicity's voice was sing-song but there was a hard edge to it.

Taylor stopped in the doorway between the winery and the lunchroom. She'd forgotten it was Monday morning tea. A container of Felicity's cake sat open on the table and the others sat around it. They were all there, Pete and Ed, Antoine and Felicity, even Noelene. It was only ten o'clock and the cellar door didn't open for another hour. All eyes were on her.

"I hear you had a great time at the pub on Friday night." Ed added another reminder of her terrible night. She'd felt rotten all weekend both physically and emotionally and now she was to be humiliated further.

Noelene stood up. "You young ones. You like to let your hair down sometimes don't you? Can I make you a cup of tea or coffee?"

"Tea, thanks, Noelene."

"Have a seat." Antoine patted the chair next to his.

Taylor gave him a grateful smile. They'd had a lot of fun until she'd drunk too much. Her memory of what happened towards the end of the night was a bit hazy – there was dancing and at one stage she'd snatched Terry's hat and worn it for the rest of the night – but she'd have remembered if either Felicity or Ed had been there. She also felt sure Antoine wasn't a gossip. Not in her case anyway. She sat down next to him.

"Evidently you can drink as well as any, according to Terry." Felicity fixed her with a smug smile.

Ah, so that was it. Terry the barman was obviously the one with the loose lips. Come to think of it they were rather large lips. "Terry must have led a sheltered life," Taylor said.

"He's never been out of the district." Noelene put a cup of tea in front of Taylor. "Piece of cake? It's orange and Felicity has excelled herself. She's actually managed to keep it moist."

Felicity opened her mouth. A puzzled frown creased her brow and she glared at Noelene through narrowed eyes.

Taylor sucked in her bottom lip to hold in a laugh. She had to award that round to Noelene.

"It's delicious." Pete lifted his plate towards Noelene as she cut a slice for Taylor. "I'd like some more if I may, thanks."

"Won't be any leftovers today." Noelene put a plate in front of Taylor and lifted a slice onto Pete's plate.

A phone rang in the background. No-one moved.

"That's your job to answer the phone, isn't it Felicity?" Noelene's eyebrows made their perfect arches.

Felicity leapt to her feet and crossed the room.

"Leave your dishes," Noelene called after her. "We'll do them for you."

There was silence in the lunchroom as they heard the distant voice of Felicity answering the call.

Ed stood and gave the older woman a peck on the cheek. "You can be a bit naughty sometimes, Noelene. Thanks for making the cuppa. I'm off."

He went in the direction of his office but Taylor could see from where she sat that he passed the door and went on into the reception area.

"I'd better go too," Noelene said. "I have the stocktake to finish yet. Sorry to leave the dishes but I'm sure you'll manage, Taylor."

"Of course."

Noelene set off towards the reception area as well and Antoine got to his feet.

"Just a minute, Antoine." Pete's voice was low. Antoine stopped and they both turned to Pete. Taylor thought he looked tired. Then she was hardly the one to talk. She'd seen her own haggard reflection in the mirror that morning. She was still recovering from Friday night.

Pete looked towards the reception area. They could still hear Felicity talking to someone, presumably on the phone.

"What is it?" Antoine asked.

Taylor's heart pounded in her chest. Pete was looking edgy. Was he giving her the flick? But if that was the case why would he keep Antoine around?

"We're going to pick the NS18 on Wednesday."

Antoine grinned and sat down again. "By hand?"

"Yes. I hoped you'd both be up for it."

"Picking grapes?" Taylor felt a flood of relief.

"Yes. I want this crop to be hand-picked."

"I'd love to help." Taylor smiled at him and was pleased to see him smile back.

"That's not all." Once more Pete glanced in the direction of the front office. They could no longer hear Felicity speaking. He leaned closer and lowered his voice. "I know this sounds a little strange but I'm asking you both another favour. I want you to keep this to yourselves."

"Of course," Antoine said.

Pete stared at Antoine. "By that I mean not Ed or Felicity or Noelene. I don't want you to talk to anyone about it."

Antoine looked uncomfortable. "Are we doing something we shouldn't?"

"Of course not. The grapes have to be picked. Ed and I are not in agreement on the how that's all. When it comes to business decisions Ed has the final say."

"So you're going ahead with the partnership?"

"How do you know about that?"

Antoine's cheeks coloured. "I was in the lunchroom the other day and Ed was talking on the phone to someone about it."

"It's not decided yet."

"I'm sorry." Antoine shifted in his chair. "I couldn't help but hear him."

"Don't worry about it. Ed wants to buy more land and I'm hoping we can find other ways to do it without the need for a partnership. Anyway, when it comes to the winemaking he has to defer to me. Sometimes that's not easy. I'm making it easy for him in this case."

"By keeping him in the dark until it's a fait accompli." Taylor pursed her lips.

"Exactly. It will all work out okay."

Antoine stood up. "I'm no good at this secretive stuff." He gave Pete a pat on the shoulder. "I will do my best, my friend. I'll see you later."

"Thanks, Antoine."

Pete waited while Antoine let himself back into the winery then he turned the full force of his gaze on Taylor. She tried to calm the turmoil that look generated inside her. She reminded herself that she was his Good Samaritan project.

"Fine with me." Her voice was almost a whisper. Her mouth felt dry. It certainly didn't matter to her. The only person she might have spoken to between now and Wednesday was Noelene. It was only two days. Taylor would keep her mouth shut about the grape picking. She took a sip of tea. "Does this have something to do with those men I saw looking at the vines the other day?"

"Maybe. There are some things I don't know myself."

He reached across and put a hand on hers. She relished the feel of it but knew it was there only out of kindness.

"I worry we've dragged you into something you'd rather not be a part of."

"We?"

"Ed and I."

"I'm a big girl, Pete. I can take care of myself."

"Was that what you were doing at the pub on Friday night?"

She snatched her hand away.

"I'm not criticising you," he said. "I'm worried we've driven you to—"

"Drink?" Taylor cut him off.

"No...maybe." He looked flustered. "I don't know."

She couldn't help but smile at the confusion on his face. "Don't worry, Pete. I'm fine. I let my hair down a little too far on Friday night. It won't happen again."

"I'm not judging you."

"I know." This time she put her hand on his. She looked earnestly into his eyes. What she saw there made her go weak at the knees. Somehow she had to make him see her as a potential friend rather than a rescue project. "Friday night was a mistake. I don't want to be that person anymore."

"Phone for you, Peter."

They both jumped apart at the sharp sound of Felicity's voice. She peered around the wall frame waving a cordless handset at Pete.

"Coming." He stood up. "See you tonight, Taylor."

"Tonight?"

"I'm still counting on one of your care packages."

"Oh, the meal. Of course. Hope you don't mind tuna mornay again?"

"Sounds good." He strode towards Felicity who handed over the phone, gave Taylor a glare and went back to her office.

Taylor sipped some more tea and ate the cake. Noelene was right. It was both moist and flavoursome. She made her way to the sink. Antoine had at least rinsed his own cup and plate. She ran water in the sink while Pete sat at the table behind her deep in conversation with whoever was on the phone.

CHAPTER
37

Pete paced his office, up and back. He'd come up with an idea for making sure Ed would be off the property tomorrow. He just didn't feel good about any of it. First, getting Ed away from the place was based on a lie, and second, hand-picking the cab sauv without telling him was devious behaviour. Pete had never worked like that before. They didn't always see eye to eye but they were usually honest with each other.

Pete had enlisted Antoine's help in the end. Tonight one of the pumps was going to have a breakdown and Ed would need to go to Naracoorte first thing Wednesday morning to get the part. Pete would have preferred to start picking at first light, instead they'd have to wait until Ed left and the trip wouldn't keep him away long but the job would be well and truly underway by the time he got back.

Now Pete's stomach was in knots. He was no good at deception. The door banged outside his office. He jumped. Damn, he'd be a gibbering mess by the time he had to speak to Ed. Footsteps echoed along the passage then back in his direction.

"Hello." He spun at Taylor's call. She was standing in the doorway, looking the glowing picture of health. Much better than she had yesterday. "Is something wrong?"

"No." Pete sucked in a breath. He had to pull himself together.

"Do you have a list for me today?"

He looked at the papers on his desk then reached over and plucked one from the top. "I was just working on it. I need you to do the next and the last plunging of the shiraz."

"Right."

"The rest is the same as usual." He handed over the paper and moved to the window that looked out over the NS18 vines. He'd had another look at the grapes with Howard first thing this morning. They'd sampled and tested. The time was right. Everything was in place for a six o'clock start tomorrow morning. He just had to get Ed away from the place. His stomach churned with anticipation and guilt.

"Pete?"

He turned as Taylor spoke his name. She was looking at him quizzically.

"Sorry?"

"Do you mind if I take photos of the winery?"

"No."

"I'm toying with an idea for a blog. I'll run it past you first."

"That's fine. Did you talk to Felicity about the Facebook ideas you had?"

"Not yet."

A vehicle pulled up outside. Pete turned back to the window. Tension coursed through him.

"Ed's here."

Taylor tugged at her shirt collar. "I'll get going."

"Taylor."

She stopped mid-stride and turned back.

"I hope it's not too uncomfortable for you."

She tipped her head to one side.

"Working with Ed."

"Oh, no. We're fine."

As she said it the key sounded in the outer door.

"I'll go do the plunging," she said.

She turned her back on him. "Good morning, Ed," she said brightly.

"Taylor." Ed's reply was gruff.

Taylor moved off in the direction of the winery door and Ed took her place, framed by Pete's office door.

"I see you and Howard have been checking the NS18."

Pete felt himself stiffen. How did Ed know?

"What are you looking so guilty about?" Ed grinned. "I know Howard's helping you with it. It makes sense. He helped us plant the canes. What does he think?"

"Think?"

"Is it ready yet?"

"A bit longer yet." Pete turned his back on Ed's searching eyes and pretended to look for something on his desk. How was he going to pull this off?

"Can't be far away surely. They taste right to me. I've got the machines tentatively booked for Thursday."

"You've booked machines?" Pete spun around. "I'm the wine-maker and I want to hand-pick."

Ed's eyes narrowed. "Take it easy, Peter. You've had some trouble getting machines this vintage. I know how important it is for you to pick the NS18 when it's ready. I thought I was being helpful."

Pete studied his brother a moment. It was usually up to Pete to book the machines.

"I didn't know you'd booked pickers." Ed strolled to the window and looked out, his back to Peter. "When will they be here?"

"Thursday." Pete took a deep breath. His nerves were making him overreact. "Sorry." He looked back at his desk. Damn, he was hopeless at lies.

"Are we fairly clear tomorrow?"

"I think so." Pete kept shuffling papers.

"I'm going to have to make a run to Mount Gambier."

"The Mount?" Pete straightened and risked a look back over his shoulder. "Why?"

"I've come to an arrangement with Mr Zhu."

Pete's discomfort changed to suspicion. "I thought you'd let the partnership go."

"I have." Ed turned from the window and looked him straight in the eye. "For now. But he's taken a consignment of our shiraz."

"You didn't tell me about that."

"I didn't want to until it was all sorted. I had to wait on the bottling analysis."

"Which shiraz?"

"I did the maths on the last lot we sent out. We had enough for our domestic commitments and some left over to give us a start with Mr Zhu."

"But the labels have to be different."

"All taken care of. I had Felicity help me. We've kept the Wriggly Creek design but added a sprig of eucalyptus. I'll show you later."

Pete felt pinned against his desk by Ed's gaze.

"I guess it's worth a try."

"Of course it is."

Pete relaxed and sat his bum on the desk behind. If Ed could sell wine to China without consulting him, Pete didn't feel so bad about picking the NS18 without letting Ed know. "When are you going to the Mount?"

"Tomorrow morning. I have to get the documentation there first thing. Waste of a morning but it has to be done."

"You'll be leaving early then."

"About seven, why?"

Pete shrugged his shoulders. "Just wondered."

"I might even go earlier. The pipe supply place is usually open early. I could collect those new hoses we wanted while I'm there."

"Good idea."

Ed moved over to the whiteboard where they had the plan set out of all the tanks and open-top fermenters. "It's going to be tight. Yields are well above average. I think the NS18 will be okay in that end tank."

Pete gritted his teeth. He was determined to use his dad's original open-top cement tanks for the NS18 but he didn't want to argue with Ed about it now.

Ed turned back. "I'm heading in to Coonawarra. I'm meeting Fred from Vales Wines. They've just started selling to the Chinese and I want to pick his brains some more."

"Right. I'll see you later then."

"Maybe not till tomorrow afternoon. I've got a few other things to do this afternoon. You and Antoine have the ferments under control?"

"Yes, and Taylor's been a great help."

Ed gave him a sharp look. "I'll see you tomorrow."

Pete waited until the outside door shut and Ed's four-wheel drive started up then he sank into his chair and put his head in his hands.

Relief flooded though him. He didn't have to spin his yarn to get Ed away. Ed was doing it all by himself. Pete wasn't happy he'd been left out of the Chinese deal but he was hardly in a position to take his brother to task over it. He could finish planning for the picking tomorrow. They might have to start a little later than he'd hoped but they should get a good go at it before Ed returned.

Once more footsteps echoed in the passage. This time Antoine appeared at his door.

"I don't think we're going to fit all of the cab sauv in the tank."

"Is it coming in already?" Pete stood up.

"First truck's just unloaded but they've hardly made a dent in what's to be picked."

Pete had been out at first light to watch the machines begin picking. Today's grapes would eventually be bottled as their entry-level cab sauv. He hadn't bunch thinned this block. The vines were healthy. He wanted to see how far he could push them.

Antoine had come right into the office and was studying the whiteboard just as Ed had been doing only a few minutes before. "It's going to be tight."

"You can use the tank next door."

Antoine bent closer to the board. "That's where you're putting the NS18."

"No. I haven't written it on there yet but I've decided to use Dad's old cement tanks for that."

"In the back shed?"

"I patched the roof during the winter and gave the whole place a good clean-out. I've waxed the tanks. It will be perfect."

"If you say so."

"I do. Ed's just been in. He's going to Mount Gambier first thing tomorrow."

Antoine let out a low whistle.

"We might not start picking until seven but we won't have to worry about Ed." Pete picked up his cap and squashed it on over his spongy curls. His day was looking much brighter now.

CHAPTER
38

Taylor felt a tingle of excitement as she boiled the kettle in the quarters. Outside it was barely light but she could hear an excited babble of voices from the group of people gathered ready to start picking the grapes from Pete's precious cabernet vines. Pete was moving amongst them, welcoming them, bringing them up to speed with the day's procedure. Evidently there'd been some dew overnight so not only had they waited for Ed to leave, now they had to wait for the grapes to dry.

Pete had introduced her to everyone but she remembered few of the names. Ben she knew from his work in the winery. There was his wife Jane, and Howard the old bloke she'd met in the lab and his wife Margaret, a couple who'd been family friends for years. Then there were at least six others who were in the district temporarily for vintage, backpackers mostly who looked for work to supplement their travels. Margaret was taking orders for coffee and tea and Taylor was making them. Margaret had also produced some delicious-smelling savoury scones which she handed out with the hot cuppas.

"That's everyone that wants one, dear." Margaret came back inside, the skin of her cheeks pink from the chilly outside air. "Only you and me left. Make mine tea please."

Taylor put tea bags in two cups and lifted the kettle as it switched itself off.

"You seem to be settling in very well here." Margaret pulled out a chair and sat at the table.

"I'm enjoying it."

"They can always do with an extra pair of willing hands at this time of the year." Margaret studied her with a kind gaze.

"It seems so."

"You don't miss the city?"

"Not much."

"I bet the boys are grateful for your cooking."

Taylor handed Margaret a cup of tea. "There doesn't seem to be much you don't know about me."

"Oh there's plenty I'm sure. Have you ever picked grapes before?"

"Only a few bunches from my parents' vines."

"So you have family back in the city?"

Before Taylor could answer, Howard and Antoine came inside carrying handfuls of cups.

"Enough of your gasbagging Margaret," Howard said fondly. "Time to get started."

"I'll wash these dishes first and then I'll be there."

"I'll help." Taylor felt torn. She wanted to be part of the action out at the vines right from the start.

"No." Margaret had the water running in the sink. "It won't take me long. I'll leave them to drain. You go with the others, dear. I'll be there in a jiffy."

Taylor didn't argue. She could tell there'd be no point. She picked up her camera and her jacket and stepped outside to follow the group to the vines.

Pete had gone ahead in his ute. He was waiting for them next to a couple of portable shades that hadn't been there yesterday. He started issuing buckets and snips from the tray of his ute. Once everyone was ready he plucked two bunches of grapes from a bucket at his feet.

"This is what I don't want," he said. "Anything too thin and scraggly like this." He held one hand forward. Once they'd all looked he dropped the bunch on the ground. "And no rotten or dried up bunches or ones the birds have pecked." Once more he showed around the bunch from his hand then dropped it to the ground. "Cut them but leave them on the ground." He lifted two more bunches from a different bucket. "This is what I'm looking for."

Taylor studied the perfect-looking bunch, worried she'd get it wrong. Pete was so serious.

"Antoine, Taylor and you two." Pete pointed to two from the seasonal picking group. "You take the first row. Howard, you and Margaret can have two with you in the second row, Ben, Jane, and the last two will start at the third row. I'll keep the buckets empty for you. Take a bottle of water whenever you need." Pete waved at the esky sitting under the shade. "Let's go."

There was a murmur of voices as everyone moved to their rows.

"Weather's still warm so watch out for snakes," Pete called after them.

Taylor stared at Antoine. "Snakes?"

"Amongst other things." He grinned at her as did the young man and woman who'd come with them. "You'll be okay. Stay this side with me. Alice and Leo can take the other side."

She and Antoine were on the open side of the first row. A few metres behind them was the track and the first sheds of the winery. Taylor knew Pete's office window looked over these vines.

She watched as Antoine peered under the leaves and snipped the first bunch. Taylor had a go, looked at what she'd picked and dropped it to the ground. She did the same with the second bunch. At this rate Pete wouldn't have any grapes to make wine with. But by the time they'd moved further along the row she was surprised to see her bucket was half full of healthy bunches and Antoine's held even more. Leo and Alice were about level with them on the other side, the sound of their friendly banter interspersed with the click of the snips.

Pete strode towards them holding two empty buckets. "How're you going?"

"Good," Taylor said, taking the opportunity to straighten her back.

"She's a fast learner," Antoine said.

Pete swapped their buckets. "Don't forget to drink plenty of water," he said and set off with their full buckets.

The rays of the morning sun were already warming the vines. Taylor took a few swigs from her water bottle. She'd soon be discarding her jumper and she needn't have brought her coat. With the warmth came the bees. They buzzed in and out around the grapes and the odd beetle gave her a start. Pete came and went, ferrying the loaded buckets to the bin on the back of the tractor.

They stopped for a break when they reached the end of the row. Everyone gathered under or near the shades. Margaret had a large thermos of boiling water for tea and coffee along with a batch of sweet scones, jam and cream. Taylor was glad of a coffee. She'd been drinking water but had left her early morning tea when the call had come to start picking.

She watched Pete making his way in her direction. He was a good boss, talking to people as he went, asking them how they were going. Just as he reached Taylor on the edge of the last shade his mobile rang.

"Yes, Felicity." He listened. "No, that will be fine. Ed or I will deal with it later." He listened again. "Yes, Ed's desk." He tucked his phone back in his pocket and smiled at Taylor. "How are you finding the grape-picking experience?"

"Good. It's another aspect of winemaking I'm seeing first-hand. I've managed to take a few pictures in between picking."

A car went along the road, slowed then moved on. Pete turned to watch it.

"Are you worried about Ed coming back?"

"I'm not good at subterfuge."

"What about Felicity? She would be able to see us if she came around this side of the winery."

"Felicity rarely steps outside and if she does it's not far from the office."

Pete was wrong about that. Taylor had seen her a few times now in the winery quite a distance from her office.

"Anyway, she won't know that Ed doesn't know." Pete shook his head. "Listen to me. I sound like someone from a crime novel instead of Pete Starr from little old Wriggly Creek Wines."

"Why are you putting yourself through this if it bothers you so much?"

"Howard thought it was necessary."

Taylor looked over to where the old man sat in the shade. He was slumped back in his chair, his grey felt hat pulled over his face. Margaret sat nearby talking to Jane and Ben.

"You obviously put a lot of faith in his judgement."

"I do. It was hard losing Dad. Apart from the fact that he was my dad, he was also my mentor when it came to winemaking. Howard was a good friend and support to Dad. He's transferred that support to me."

"You've got a few people in your camp." Taylor felt a little envious. She sometimes wished there'd been more senior adults she could have turned to for advice. "Noelene as well. Although you didn't invite her to help today."

"Something obviously happened that worried Howard about Ed but he won't tell me what." Pete dragged his fingers through the hair curling down the back of his neck. "Howard suggested I keep Noelene out of the loop as well. I guess I'll find out why soon enough."

Taylor recalled Noelene's pride in both Pete and Ed and her involvement in their lives. "Perhaps he knew it would put her in a difficult situation."

"How?"

"She's very fond of you both. Thinks of you as sons. It would be hard for her to take sides."

Pete looked over in Howard's direction. "I hadn't thought of that. Howard was never close to Ed but you're right, Noelene wouldn't want to have to choose between what Ed wanted and me." His eyes filled with sadness. "Howard won't care and Ben's a close friend of mine rather than Ed's but I didn't think through the position I've put you and Antoine in."

"I can't speak for Antoine but I'm okay with it. Ed and I are barely on speaking terms as it is." Taylor gave what she hoped was an encouraging smile. "I doubt he'll even give me a thought."

Pete took a step closer. Taylor's heart raced. There was something about his eyes. It was as if he could see right inside her. His hair was damp from being under his cap. His cheeks were flushed red from the warmth of the day and his lips...her fingers twitched. How she longed to twirl the hair that formed small curls at the nape of his neck, to trace the line of his jaw, to kiss those–

"Come on, young fella." Howard's call broke the tension between them. "Time's a-wasting."

Pete glanced at his watch. "Back to it everyone," he called.

Suddenly the temporary camp was a flurry of activity as people gathered their buckets and tools and headed back to the vines. Taylor put her hat back on her head and followed Antoine to the next row. Once more the air was filled with the snap and clip of the snips and the murmur of voices.

Taylor bent and reached for a bunch of grapes. Something brushed her hand. She yelped and pulled her hand back at the touch of the cobweb. Her yelp turned to a scream as a huge spider scrabbled across the bunch she'd been about to snip.

Antoine put a hand on her shoulder. She yelled again and jerked around.

"What happened?"

Ben and Jane were beside her as well, their faces full of concern.

"Are you hurt?" Ben asked.

Taylor sucked in a breath, flapped her hands in the air and stomped her feet.

Jane took her hands. "Did you cut yourself?"

Taylor shook her head. Everywhere she looked there were worried faces and they were all surrounded by leaves. Leaves that hid spiders.

"What happened?" Pete arrived and put down his buckets.

Taylor gasped in another breath. "Spider."

"Are you bitten?" Jane tried to inspect her hands but Taylor pulled them back and curled her fingers into her palms. She shook her head. Pete put a gentle arm across her shoulders.

"It's okay everyone," he said. "Taylor will be fine. I'd forgotten she's very frightened of spiders."

"This is not the job for you then," Jane said. "Is that the first one you've seen? They're everywhere."

Taylor gasped in another lungful of air.

"You guys get back to it," Pete said. "I'll take care of Taylor."

Jane still studied her with an anxious face.

Taylor gave her a weak smile. "I'm okay."

Pete guided her to the end of the row and back to their makeshift shelter. He sat her down. Taylor hunched herself up. Every stick and blade of grass looked like a spider.

"I'm sorry," he said. "I was worried about snakes with this warm weather. I didn't think about the spiders. We're so used to them. I should've warned you. Golden orbs are everywhere in the vines. They eat the bees."

Taylor shuddered again. All the time she'd been snipping, she'd been working amongst spiders.

"I'm sorry, Pete. I can't go back there." She stared at the leaves that she'd been admiring for their beautiful colours. Now she'd discovered they'd been concealing the thing she feared most.

"You don't have to."

"But I want to help."

"You can be the bucket girl."

Taylor looked at him sceptically. If there were spiders in the vines they could easily be dropped in the buckets with the grapes.

"You can run the water bottles to people as well."

Once more Taylor looked at the vines. What had once been a thing of beauty now harboured her worst nightmare.

"Sit here until you get your breath back."

"I'm okay." Taylor uncurled her fingers.

Pete unscrewed the cap of a water bottle and offered it to her. His eyes filled with kindness. Some people laughed at her fear, told her to get over it. If only it were that easy. Pete wasn't one of those people.

She took the drink from him. "You go. I'll stay here a bit longer."

He took her free hand in his. They were both sticky from the grapes. His felt rough but comforting. "I'll do another bucket run and come back."

"I'll be fine, really. Don't worry about me."

He squeezed her hand then smiled as his skin stuck to hers. He peeled it away, gave her a reassuring smile and strode back to the vines. Taylor leaned back in her chair and sucked in another long, slow breath. Her heart was still beating fast. Whether it was still because of the spider or because of Pete's touch she wasn't sure.

CHAPTER

39

Taylor turned sharply at a gentle tap on her arm.

"Sorry." Pete had come up behind her. "Didn't mean to startle you."

She put down the buckets she'd just emptied and pulled off her gloves.

"I'm still imagining spiders everywhere. Wish I wasn't so silly."

"It's not silly." His concerned eyes stared deeply into hers. "A fear like that is not something you can turn on and off."

"Unfortunately. Thanks for these." She jiggled the gloves in the air. "It helps."

"I should have given them to you at the start. Some people prefer gloves."

Pete turned back to look at the group still picking. Taylor felt like the lights dimmed when he looked away.

"I keep needing your help," he said. "I've another favour to ask."

Once more his gaze locked with hers.

"Sure," she said. There was little she wouldn't do for him at this point. "Unless you want me to pick grapes from spider-infested vines. That I won't do."

"No." He grinned. "Would you go to Coonawarra? I've ordered a picnic lunch from the store there."

"Of course."

Jane joined them. She groaned and stretched her back and legs. "Every year I forget how much hand-picking makes my back ache."

Pete gave her a peck on the cheek. "You know how much I appreciate your help."

"I do. And I'll know it even more when you pay me." She winked at Taylor.

"Would you like to go with Taylor to pick up the food?"

"Yes please."

"I think we're nearly done and everyone will be hanging out for something to eat."

"Donella's creations are always welcome." Jane looked at Taylor. "We can take my car if you like."

Taylor picked up her camera bag from the ground beside the bin. She hoped she'd captured some good shots during the morning.

"See you soon," Pete called as they set off along the track and past the winery to where Jane and Ben had parked their car near Pete's cottage.

"Do you do much hand-picking?" Taylor asked.

"No, only when Pete asks us. Ben works here as their part-time cellar hand but he hasn't been much help lately. His dad's been laid up with an injured leg and we haven't been able to get away from the property like we could before."

They climbed into Jane's four-wheel drive and headed out of the winery onto the dirt road. Along the side of the road Taylor noticed two cars, both had seen better days if their patchy paint was anything to go by.

"Picker's vehicles." Jane nodded towards them as they passed. "Ben and I just got on the road ahead of the convoy this morning."

"Convoy?"

"Quite a few of the seasonal pickers stay in town. They're all employed by the same contractor so they set off for the one vineyard at the same time and come home at the same time." Jane chuckled. "If you get stuck behind them on the highway, you never want to be in a hurry. Most of their cars only do about eighty."

Taylor twisted her head to take another look. That explained her trip home the morning after her bender at the pub. She was relieved to know she hadn't imagined the odd string of vehicles.

"Now the shit's going to hit the fan."

Taylor turned back at Jane's words. They had reached the highway and a familiar vehicle slowed in front of them. Instead of turning off the highway and onto the track to the winery, it picked up speed and kept going. "Was that Ed?"

"Yep. Looks like Pete will have a reprieve for a little bit longer." Jane looked left and right and pulled out onto the highway going in the same direction as Ed. "I don't know if you've noticed but Ed and Pete are like chalk and cheese. A blow-up was bound to happen one day. Still, what's life without a bit of drama?"

Taylor chewed her lip. It hadn't worked out with Ed but she didn't wish him any ill. She thought she might be falling for Pete big time but she was trying to keep that to herself. The idea of the two brothers at loggerheads made her very uneasy.

"Sorry to be such a stickybeak but I gather you went out with Ed for a short time."

Taylor glanced across at Jane. "Yes, but it didn't work out."

"I'm glad." Jane gave her an apologetic smile. "You're way too nice for him."

Taylor felt an urge to defend Ed. He did have a sharp side but she thought that only came out when he was provoked. "We had some fun together. It seems he wasn't my type."

"So what made you stay?"

"I was offered work."

"Oh, I thought…it's just you seem friendly with Pete."

"He's a nice guy too."

"Yes he is." Jane turned off the highway and pulled up in front of the Coonawarra store. "Uh-oh. Looks like Ed's here."

One car over Taylor could see his four-wheel drive but Ed wasn't in it.

They both got out and Jane fiddled with the keys. "He's probably called in for lunch as well. What should we say?"

Taylor's insides churned but she wasn't going to lie to Ed's face. "Hello and we're getting lunch too?"

"Hmm." Jane pushed open the door to the store.

Taylor followed her inside. Ed had his back to them, questioning the woman behind the counter about the big box of food she was trying to give him.

"Pete ordered it for Wriggly Creek Winery," she was saying. "He said someone would come to collect it at lunchtime."

"I know nothing about it." Ed said. "I've just called in for some lunch on my way north."

"We've come to collect it."

Ed turned and the woman behind the counter looked past him to Jane, relief on her face.

"Hello, Jane. I'm sorry. Pete didn't tell me who was picking the picnic hamper up."

Ed gave Taylor a nod and a questioning look.

"We'll take it, Donella." Jane stepped up to the counter and put her hands under the box.

"There's a second box."

"I can take that," Taylor offered.

"You may not have met Taylor, Donella." Ed stood like a statue amidst them all. "She's doing a bit of work for us."

"Oh, I'd heard that. Pleased to meet you, Taylor." Donella handed over a smaller box. "Hope you enjoy the picnic."

"Thanks, Donella." Jane turned on her heel and made for the door. Taylor followed her but before they reached it Ed was there, opening it for them.

"Ladies." He smiled and Taylor gave a little shiver. She had a sudden recollection of the spider on the grapes.

"I didn't know Pete had time for picnics," Ed said.

"Just a bit of a get-together." Jane stepped past him.

"Must be a few of you." Ed fixed his look on Taylor.

"Hopefully there's leftovers," she said. "Save me cooking tonight." She slid through the door and hurried after Jane.

They stowed the boxes in the back of the four-wheel drive and climbed in. Jane started the engine. She tugged her seatbelt across her shoulder. "I know you don't want to be disloyal, Taylor, but there's something about Ed Starr I just don't like."

Taylor looked at the shop door. It was closed again and there was no sign of Ed. As Jane backed out Taylor shifted her gaze to the car they'd been parked next to. She'd been so focused on getting the picnic past Ed she'd only taken in that there were two figures sitting in the front of the neighbouring vehicle. Just as Jane swung the four-wheel drive onto the road the driver turned his head. Taylor recognised him now. It was Frank Lister, the man who'd driven

Mr Zhu and Mr Cheng and who had bought the last of Pete's reserve cab sauv. She twisted in her seat to try to get a better look at his passenger. Now that she thought about it he could have been of Chinese appearance.

She wondered what Ed was up to. Perhaps Pete wasn't the only brother covering something up.

CHAPTER
40

It was well after Taylor's seven o'clock meal time as Pete walked from his back door to the quarters, a bottle of cab sauv in his hand. He was tired but far from being able to sleep. The day had gone well. They'd got all the grapes off in good time and even though he and Antoine had been putting all of today's grapes through the crusher they'd still managed to join in with the picnic.

Pete had been expecting Ed might turn up, but he hadn't. Taylor's report of running into him in Coonawarra with Lister and a Chinese man had Pete worried but whatever Ed was up to it had bought Pete time.

He came to a stop outside the quarters and took a breath. It was done. The hand-picked cabernet was now safely tucked away in the fermenter. The last of their cabernet would be harvested over the next week as machines became available and that would be vintage over for another year.

He knocked and Taylor called come in. She was sitting with Antoine on the couch. They had a bottle of beer each and the laptop open between them.

"Welcome." Taylor smiled up at him.

"Am I too late for dinner?"

"Of course not." Taylor put the laptop aside and struggled out of the saggy couch. "We've been waiting for you."

"Can I get you a beer?" Antoine also got to his feet.

"Thanks." Pete put the red on the table and unscrewed the cap. "We can have this later."

Taylor put plates of frittata on the table and they all sat.

Antoine raised his beer. "Here's to a successful day."

They touched the necks of their bottles together.

"Now the real fun begins. The dream becomes reality." Pete took a swig of beer. "Years of work have gone into these grapes. Starting with the team who came up with the original grafts, to my parents, Howard, Ed and me and you, Antoine, and even you, Taylor."

She chuckled. "That's kind of you but I can't lay claim to doing anything towards bringing this dream to reality."

"You helped today." Antoine wagged his fork at her. "Hand-picking is an important part of the journey to producing a fine wine. Now it is up to Pete to complete the process."

Once more Taylor's musical laugh echoed around them. "No pressure."

"This is the part I love. I'm sorry Dad's not here to share it but we have Howard. I respect his opinion."

Antoine clasped his hand on Pete's shoulder. "But the final decisions must always rest with you, my friend. There can only be one head winemaker."

Pete picked up his beer. "I'll drink to that."

They finished Taylor's frittata, did the dishes together and settled back at the table with a glass of red each.

"Show Pete your photos, Taylor." Antoine beamed at Pete.

"I'd like to see them." Pete's gaze met Taylor's across the table. Time paused, then she was getting to her feet, the moment gone.

Antoine said something but Pete missed it. He forced himself to concentrate.

"Pardon?"

"Taylor has captured the essence of hand-picking with her photographs."

"Antoine can be very effusive in his descriptions. At least with my good lens I didn't have to get too close to the spiders." Once more Taylor's chuckle filled the air as she squeezed in between them with the laptop.

Pete was glad she could laugh about her fear. He enjoyed the feel of her warm shoulder pressed against his.

Taylor opened the laptop and brought up the internet site for a neighbouring winery. "I've been checking out the websites of some of the other wineries in this region. Some are very simple like this one." She pointed to the screen, scrolled down then flicked to another. "And some are quite complex – with newsletters, wine clubs, news items and stories about the wineries – but most of the other websites are static." She paused.

"Static?" Pete turned to her. She was talking another language.

"Once the original site goes up nothing much changes." Once more Taylor scrolled through some sites then brought up Wriggly Creek's. "There's nothing that gives a regular update about what's happening in the region. Not a lot here to keep people coming back to visit your site."

Pete had to agree with her. The Wriggly Creek site looked rather shabby in comparison to some of the others.

"That's why I like blogs," Taylor said. "They're newsy and chatty and fun and keep people interested."

"Show him." Antoine urged from Taylor's other side.

She closed the window and opened another.

"This is just an idea."

The new window had the heading 'Picked with love' and underneath there was a close-up of a hand cradling a bunch of grapes as the snips cut the stem. Below it were more words. 'Modern vintage can be full of machines and noise and rush but this week at Wriggly Creek the winery took a breath and paused to hand-pick our newest cabernet sauvignon, destined to become a new standard amongst the unique red wines from Coonawarra.' Another photo followed of bunches of grapes piled high in buckets.

"We've only just picked it." Pete looked from Taylor to Antoine, worry worming in his stomach. "You know so much can go wrong. This is like counting your chickens before they hatch."

"Or your wine before it's bottled." Antoine chuckled at his own joke.

Taylor placed a hand on Pete's arm. "I can change the words."

He raised his gaze to her concerned look.

"This is just my ideas," she said. "You can tell me what you would like to say."

"It can be less serious." Antoine picked up his glass and grinned. "How to make a jaunty little red."

They all took a sip.

Taylor raised her glass. "A red for the picking."

Antoine raised his. "A red affair."

Pete ignored them. No matter what they called it he'd be putting his life on the internet for all to read. "I'm not sure I'm ready for this yet."

Taylor and Antoine glanced at each other and burst into laughter. He looked from one to the other. "What?"

"You're not ready." Antoine laughed louder.

Pete shook his head.

"You're not 'red-ee'." Taylor emphasised the *red* and wiggled her fingers at him making the quote-marks sign.

Pete smiled. They kept laughing. It was infectious. He laughed too.

Finally they drew breath. Pete relaxed. He held up his glass. "Thanks," he said. "Here's to good company."

"Good food," Antoine chipped in.

"And good wine," Taylor added.

Once more they tapped glasses and drank.

"What are you going to call it?"

Pete tipped his head to one side and looked at Taylor.

"Call what?"

"Your new red. It's just that other wineries seem to have names for their wines. This one will have to have a different name from your other cab sauvs."

"Wriggly Creek's sparkling shiraz is called Pearl's Starr," Antoine offered.

"Dad named it after Mum." Once again Pete wished his parents were here enjoying this moment. He was sure they would have liked Taylor and Antoine.

"There must be a story there," Taylor said. "Several of the other wineries have their family stories on their websites. We need something unique."

"Nothing much to tell," Pete said. "Dad and Mum planted the vines with the help of Howard. The winery grew. Ed and I were just starting to be useful in the family business when Mum and Dad were killed. We've been trying to hold it together ever since."

Taylor snapped her fingers. "There you are. Two orphaned brothers left with a legacy. And there's that wonderful photo hanging in the back room at the cellar door of your family planting. It's a great story, it just needs more filling."

Pete couldn't imagine how anyone would be interested.

"People who drink your wine want to know the story behind it. Was there anything else your dad was passionate about?" Taylor asked.

"They were involved in the community. They played sport. They helped raise funds for community projects. They were involved in local wine industry committees. Ed and I still do that."

"Perfect."

Pete frowned at Taylor. He felt exposed.

"She's right, Pierre. People like to meet the team behind the wine. You know yourself at the cellar door they're always more interested when you're there – the man who makes the wine."

"I guess." Pete still wasn't convinced that laying bare his family history to the world would be good for business. "Dad was very fond of old cars. He had a red Triumph he liked to drive around the district. Mum called it his midlife crisis."

"You still have it, don't you?" Antoine asked.

"Ed mentioned it when Cass was here," Taylor said.

Pete hadn't given the Triumph a thought for years. Ed was always going to do something with it. "As far as I know it's still in the garage at Ed's."

"That's it." Taylor clapped her hands. "That's the name for your new red wine. You've got Pearl's Starr and now you can have Neil's Triumph. You could put a picture of the car on the label."

Pete looked at Taylor. Her cheeks were flushed with excitement and her eyes sparkled.

"I like it," Antoine said. "Deluxe cars and good wine go well together."

Pete nodded. "I like the idea of having Dad's name on the bottle. It was his work that started it." In fact it was perfect.

He put an arm across Taylor's shoulders. "Thank you," he said softly.

Antoine topped up their glasses. "Another toast."

They raised their glasses again but Pete kept his arm around Taylor. She leaned into him. She was warm and soft and fitted against him perfectly.

"To Neil's Triumph," Taylor chirped and he and Antoine repeated her words.

The door flew open and Ed stepped into the room. "Well, isn't this a cosy party. I guess I wasn't invited."

Pete dropped his arm. Taylor pushed her chair back. "I kept some food for you."

"Donella's leftovers or your own?" Ed glared at her.

Pete stood up. "No need to be rude, Ed."

Ed shifted his dark look to Pete. "I'm not interested in food," he said. "It's you I've come to find. Where the bloody hell are our NS18 grapes?"

CHAPTER

41

Edward stood legs apart and hands on hips in the middle of the room glaring from one to the other of the three accomplices. He'd had no idea Peter would have the gumption to do something behind his back. No doubt it was Taylor who'd somehow put him up to it. Although even as he thought it he knew he wasn't being rational where she was concerned. He'd seen Peter's arm slide from her shoulders as he'd burst in on them, lined up at the table like the three musketeers. He was disappointed with Antoine. He usually did his job and kept his nose out of any differences between the brothers.

"Let's go to my place." Peter moved out of the kitchen.

"I'm guessing you've all been involved in this so why not tell me all about it here?"

"This is between you and me."

Edward stared into Peter's eyes. Usually he backed down but Edward could see a resolve there he'd not noticed before.

"Don't tell me my little brother's grown some balls."

Peter's brow creased in a small frown but his eyes didn't waver. "That's not necessary, Ed." He turned back to the other two. "Thanks again for the meal, Taylor, and for your help today. Both of you."

Edward turned his glare on Antoine and Taylor.

"Come on, Ed." Peter headed for the door. "You want to talk, we'll do it at my place."

Edward stood his ground. Peter went outside leaving him to stare at the other two, who watched him in silence. Taylor's look was not angry but a mixture of sadness and disappointment, he assumed for Peter. Antoine turned away, embarrassed and picked up their glasses from the table. Edward glared at Taylor a moment longer then spun on his heel and went out into the chilly night.

Up ahead of him he could see the silhouette of Peter as he neared his back door. Edward marched after him. All was not lost. He'd get to the bottom of this and phone Angus to organise collection. He'd barely made it inside the cottage when Peter flicked on the light. The sudden brightness made him falter. Peter blocked his way.

"You were going to sell the NS18." Peter's voice was low but not soft.

"You wouldn't come at the partnership."

"So this was some kind of payback?"

"What?" Edward screwed up his face. "No. It's to raise the capital to buy the land."

"We agreed not to go ahead with that for now."

"You did. It was too good an opportunity to miss. I've been working on a way to raise the capital."

Peter shook his head slowly. "You might have the majority share but we make big decisions like this together."

Edward ignored the phone buzzing in his pocket. If it was Angus or Cheng he didn't want to talk to them right now. "Where are the NS18 grapes, Peter?"

"I'm not selling the crop that our parents worked so hard to bring to life."

They glared at each other. Edward blew out a long, slow breath. "As you said, I have the majority share and we need to raise the capital."

Peter took a step towards him. Anger oozed from him. His face was red, his eyes blazed. Edward had never seen him like this. Frustrated and annoyed, yes, but Peter rarely got angry.

"You can't do this, Ed." Still his voice was low, controlled.

"Yes I can. I've had everything organised and as soon as my back's turned you whisk them away. Where are the grapes?"

"In the bloody tanks. All you had to do was walk into the office and look at the board." His anger burst. "Where else did you think they'd be? Do you think I'd be so stupid as to sell them to someone else? They're going to make the wine that will put us on the map as one of Coonawarra's finest cabernets. Wriggly Creek will come of age. We even thought of a name for the wine tonight. Neil's Triumph. We could put a picture of Dad's car on the label."

Edward put a hand to his chest. It was as if Peter had punched him, knocked the wind out of him, but he'd not lifted a finger. Blood pounded in his ears. Edward turned and slammed out the door.

"Where are you going?"

He ignored Peter's call and set off along the track in the direction of his house, his mum and dad's house. Neil's Triumph. The name rang in his ears. Pain radiated through his chest. All the memories he'd tried so hard to keep locked away came flooding back. *Neil's Triumph* sounded over and over in his head.

He walked through his house, switching on lights as he went. In his office he rummaged in the top drawer until his hand found the bunch of keys he was looking for. He took a torch from the laundry and made his way to the single-vehicle shed in the yard behind the house.

He fumbled with the keys, looking for the one that fitted the padlock on the side door. The metal door screeched in protest as he pushed it open. He flashed his torch over the canvas-covered shape that filled most of the shed then found the light switch. He turned it on. The fluoro flicked several times and lit the space.

He stood at the front of the shape. Layers of dust had turned the pale cover to a dirty brown. He gripped the ends and carefully peeled back the cover. Dust filled the air and he made a series of short sharp sneezes. With the canvas on the floor he turned to take in the car, Neil's Triumph. Its red duco glinted in the light from the fluoro despite its long incarceration.

Edward walked around to the driver's side. The last time he'd been in the car was the week before his parents had died. He put a hand on the door and leaned in. Everything looked just the same in spite of its years of inactivity. He opened the door and folded himself down behind the wheel. His father had let him drive that day. A rare occurrence. Edward remembered it as if it was yesterday. It had been the end of vintage. They'd driven to the coast, stopped at a pub for lunch then continued on, talking about their plans for the future of Wriggly Creek, laughing at stupid jokes and enjoying the sheer pleasure of each other's company and the fresh air. Edward had wound the old car up and she'd hummed along while he and his dad had enjoyed the feel of the old leather below them and the wind in their faces.

When they'd finally arrived home, chilled to the bone, their mother had a roast on the table. The cellar door had been busy and the takings the best they'd ever had. Peter had opened a bottle of their parents' first red. It hadn't aged all that well but they'd drunk it anyway, making up silly descriptions for it. A week later his parents were dead.

Edward gripped the steering wheel. To his horror his nose began to run and liquid leaked from his eyes. He rubbed at his face with the back of his hand but the tears wouldn't stop. He gave in and slumped forward against the steering wheel, six years of bottled-up grief overflowing in a moment.

Pete stood in the passage long after Ed had left. His all-consuming anger had frightened him. He'd wanted to lash out at Ed and strike him. Thankfully he'd kept his arms pinned to his sides. Now that the rage had dissipated he felt flat and restless. Now what? Obviously Pete had underestimated what Ed was capable of. Howard had been right to suggest they pick when they did. Pete still couldn't get his head around the idea that Ed was about to do it for someone else. No wonder he'd booked the machines.

Pete punched his fist into the palm of his hand. He walked from room to room but couldn't settle. He went outside. The light still shone from the quarters' big window. He really should go back and apologise to Taylor for spoiling the evening but the argument with Ed had only reminded him of an earlier one, when Ed had made it quite clear that Taylor had been his girlfriend first. Tonight Pete had been so happy in her company. She'd been happy too, and Antoine. Pete couldn't read anything more into her manner than friendship after a day of sharing the work.

Instead of going to the quarters he wheeled left and headed towards the winery. When he was level with the first row of tanks, a car pulled in on the other side of the locked wire gates, the beam of its headlights illuminating the yard. The vehicle was right up close to the gates. Pete put his arm up to shield his eyes and moved towards it. He wasn't expecting visitors and friends always came in the back way past Ed's house. The car engine revved then backed out and, with a scrunch of its tyres, sped back the way it had come. Probably some tourist that had lost their way but they were sure in a hurry.

Pete continued on to the shed where the freshly picked cabernet filled the old cement fermenters his father had built. He'd lied to

Ed. He'd said the NS18 was in the new stainless steel tanks. He'd never got around to changing the board. Antoine knew but he wasn't going to say anything. Ed had obviously never meant for the NS18 to reach their own tanks anyway. Tomorrow the harvesting machines Ed had booked could start on the old cabernet block that made their reserve cab sauv. By tomorrow night the new tanks would be full of cabernet grapes, just not the NS18.

Pete flicked on the light. The tanks were full of the cabernet juice with the skins floating on top. He plunged in his hand, pulling up a fistful of the deep-red mixture then letting it trickle away between his fingers. Most of the vines on Wriggly Creek had been planted when he was too young to remember. These grapes had come from vines that they'd all had a hand in planting and nurturing, even Ed. Pete felt a knife-like stab in his chest. It was hard to imagine his brother could sell these grapes when he knew how important they were to the family.

What would their parents think of them? Two brothers who had developed into opposites. Ed seemed hell-bent on changing so much. It hurt Pete to think his brother had so little belief in his ability as a winemaker but the real pain came from the idea that Ed was destroying any semblance of Wriggly Creek as a family-owned winery.

Pete put his arm against the tank and rested his head on it. How could they move forward from here?

Taylor knocked gently at Pete's back door. The lights were on inside and the door ajar but she couldn't hear anything.

"Pete?"

No-one replied to her cautious call.

She looked around. In the distance she could see the lights blazing from Ed's house. Had they gone over there? She walked back out of Pete's yard and stood on the track that went one way to the quarters and the other back to the winery. She didn't know what to do. Ed and Pete had both been so angry. Antoine had gone to bed. He knew it was best to keep out of any dispute between brothers but Taylor couldn't just flick a switch and turn off her concern for Pete and Ed. She was worried and yet it wasn't her place to interfere. When it all boiled down she was really nothing but a hired worker.

A car moved slowly along the road then turned using the winery driveway. It pulled right up to the gate and paused there, the engine idling. For a moment she glimpsed a figure caught in the headlights and then the car reversed suddenly, its engine loud in the still night as it roared away. Taylor peered into the blackness, her heart thumping. She hoped it was Pete she'd seen but what if it wasn't? She took a step closer and felt something brush her face. She batted at it with her hand. It was a spider web. She brushed madly at her hair and dashed back to the quarters where she used the small bathroom mirror to try to check herself over. No sign of a spider. She shuddered.

In her bedroom she stripped off her clothes just in case and pulled on her pyjamas and a jacket. The air outside had chilled her. She went back to the kitchen and boiled the kettle. She didn't feel like bed but neither was she going to stumble about in the dark. She'd have a cup of tea and hope that Pete might call in.

Two hours later, Taylor woke up on the couch. She looked around the empty room then remembered she'd settled on the couch to wait. She stretched her stiff limbs. Her cup of tea was cold on the little table beside her. She poured it down the sink and turned out the light. In her bed she tossed and turned for a long time before sleep finally claimed her.

CHAPTER

42

Taylor was in the lab when she heard the door from the front office open and footsteps in the corridor. She put down her jug and listened. The steps went away towards Pete's office. Her heartbeat quickened. What would she say to him? She'd hardly slept the last two nights. Now she was tired and every nerve was on edge. Yesterday morning she'd woken early to the sounds of machinery outside. Two harvesting machines had been going up and down the rows closest to the quarters. She'd only caught glimpses of Pete and not seen Ed at all. Antoine had been the only one to turn up for the evening meal. She had no idea what today would bring or where she stood in the scheme of things.

The footsteps paused then grew louder as they came back in her direction. Taylor pulled a smile onto her face. Ed appeared in the doorway. His hair was uncombed, his eyes bleary and his chin covered in dark stubble. He didn't look as if he'd slept any better than she had.

"I was looking for Peter. Do you know where he is?" His words were mumbled, tumbling over each other.

There was little sign of the man she'd fallen head over heels for several weeks ago. Who was that guy anyway? She still wasn't sure she knew.

"I haven't seen him this morning."

Ed's shoulders slumped. He half turned away.

"Can I make you a coffee?" Taylor had to do something. He looked so dejected.

His gaze met hers. "I can make my own coffee." Not a statement, more a bewildered response. Not like the outgoing, determined Ed she thought she knew.

"I know but I'm going to have one. I'm happy to make another."

He went back into the passage and she followed him through to the lunchroom. He sat. It was like looking at a shadow of the old Ed. She got out cups and placed them carefully. The hiss of the kettle was loud. From time to time the phone rang and Felicity's voice could be heard answering it. Finally Taylor put a cup of coffee in front of him.

She was about to turn away when his hand reached out and took hers.

"Thanks," he murmured.

"No problem."

"I'm sorry I…"

The door from the winery opened and Pete walked in. He looked from Taylor to Ed to their hands. She drew hers back. Pete lifted his gaze to meet hers. His face was gaunt and like Ed he hadn't shaved, but where Ed had shrunk into sadness Pete had grown in anger. What an odd trio they made.

"I've been looking for you." Ed was the first to speak.

"The machines didn't finish till late. Antoine, Ben and I have had a lot to do."

"I know, that's why I didn't come and find you yesterday. We need to talk."

"I don't think there's any more to say, do you?"

"You can just listen if you like. What's done is done."

Taylor didn't like Ed's tone or his words. What had he done?

"Would you like a coffee, Pete?" she offered.

He barely glanced at her. "No thanks."

Ed stood up. "Let's go into my office." He moved off without checking to see if Pete would follow and leaving his coffee behind.

Taylor could see the hesitation on Pete's face as he looked from her to the door Ed had just disappeared through. His eyes narrowed and he went after Ed. The office door closed. Apart from Felicity out in the front office there was no sound. Then the rumble of a low voice started beyond the closed door. She couldn't tell if it was Ed or Pete but she didn't want to be there.

Like Ed she left the coffee and went back to the lab. She finished her work with one ear listening for the door but no footsteps came. Finally she let herself into the winery and got on with the plunging, taking her frustrations out on the grapes.

Edward lifted his head at the knock on the door. For at least five minutes now he and Peter had sat in silence. The words were all out, there was nothing more to say.

The door opened and Felicity stuck her head around. "You are in here." She stepped in a little further. "Oh, both of you, good. Noelene's been on the blower wondering who's going to come over and help at the cellar door. She's got a big group booked in. Are one of you going or do you want me to send Taylor?"

"I'll go." Peter got to his feet. "Ben and Antoine have the cleaning up covered."

Edward didn't argue. It was probably best they had some space again now and the last thing he felt like doing was making cheerful banter with strangers.

"What's going on?" Felicity looked from one to the other.

"Ask Ed," Peter growled and pushed past her.

Felicity lifted her chin. "Someone got out of bed the wrong side this morning."

Edward raised his gaze to his secretary. Her make-up was particularly thick today. He hated thick make-up.

"Can I make you a coffee or a tea?" Felicity's eyelashes fluttered up and down.

He sucked in a breath over his teeth. Why did women always want to make cups of tea? As if that would fix anything.

"No, thanks, I'm fine."

"You don't look fine." Felicity came to his desk. She wore a tight-fitting charcoal shirt dress with buttons that strained over her breasts. "Are you sure I can't help?"

"There is nothing you can do, Felicity." He felt a shift inside him. Since his collapse in his dad's car two nights before, he'd felt numb. He'd been going through the paces of what he'd decided he had to do. Something about Felicity's manner, as if she had some special right to his attention, raised his anger. He felt a little better. The desperate sadness he'd succumbed to eased. "Leave me to get on with my work. There's been enough time wasted today."

Felicity's eyes narrowed then she twisted her lips into a smile. "Of course. Let me know if you need anything. Shall I close the door?"

"Yes." Edward softened his tone. None of this was Felicity's fault. "Thank you."

Her smile brightened and she wiggled out closing the door behind her.

Edward sat back in his chair. He had some calls to make but mostly all he had to do was wait. He was confident Peter would come round to his way of thinking now. He still couldn't believe Peter had picked the NS18 behind his back but he did understand why. Edward dragged his fingers through his hair and winced as he snagged a knot. He hadn't showered this morning. He'd make the calls and go home to freshen up. He picked up his phone and scrolled to Angus Archer's name. He didn't anticipate it would be a congenial call.

Pete went through the paces, pouring the wine, explaining its qualities, smiling at the customers. He felt like a man possessed. Burning just below the surface of his carefully constructed facade was an anger so strong it hurt. Edward had betrayed him, not only him but their parents' dream. Pete heard his brother's words again. 'I'm selling my share of the winery.'

Pete had first option of course but Ed knew he didn't have the kind of money needed to buy his brother out. Ed had gone ahead and found a possible buyer. Mr Zhu who had visited Wriggly Creek was interested. Pete had initially thought it was Ed's way of getting back at him over the new cabernet except he had to have been working on this deal with Zhu for a long time.

Finally the steady stream of visitors dwindled to none. As soon as the door shut on the last customer Noelene rounded on him. Her sharp gaze locked with his.

"What's the matter?"

Pete picked up a rack of glasses. "What makes you think anything's the matter?"

"Stop right there." Noelene put her hand on the glasses forcing him to put down the tray. "You've been like a bear with a sore head. It's a wonder the customers bought anything from you.

Vintage is almost finished. I know you're tired." She peered even more closely at him. "You look terrible but usually you're jubilant at this time of year."

Pete shrugged. He wasn't ready to talk about this.

"Is it Taylor?"

He pursed his lips feeling the tension in his body. He was trying so hard not to think of her. He'd let his guard down, let himself fall for her, then he'd found her with Ed, hand-in-hand. "No."

Noelene's eyes narrowed. "What then?"

Pete's shoulders sagged under her piercing look.

"Is it the new cabernet you're still fighting over?"

"It's more than that. Ed and I want different directions for the winery. He's changing everything."

"How?"

"He's selling his share of the winery to some Chinese company who knows nothing about us."

Noelene glanced towards the back door then back at Pete. "I see."

"Of course you would." He felt the anger that had abated during the afternoon surface again. "You always take Ed's side."

"Do I?"

Pete picked up the tray of glasses again. Noelene still pinned him with her piercing look but she didn't try to stop him from carrying them to the back room. He ran the water and began washing. He had a stack of glasses to get through. At least it was a job where he didn't have to think. The front door banged. He heard voices. None of them were Noelene's. Finally a voice called out hello.

Pete dried his hands and stepped out to the front room. Four people stood on the other side of the counter but there was no sign of Noelene.

CHAPTER

43

Taylor eased into the kitchen, closing the heavy door to the winery silently behind her. The two coffee cups she and Ed had left this morning still sat on the table. She could hear the sound of Felicity's nails on the keyboard. Ed's office door was open. Taylor tiptoed over and peered around the frame. The room was empty.

She fancied a cup of coffee again now. One that she'd drink this time. There was a clunk from the front office. The sound of the main door opening and then closing. Taylor froze with the kettle in her hand. She could manage Felicity if she had to but she didn't know how to deal with Pete or Ed at the moment.

"Hello, Noelene." Felicity's voice almost purred.

"I've come to see Edward."

"He went out a while ago."

"Do you know where?"

"He didn't tell me. I heard the back door and his office is empty."

"I see." Noelene's tone was dismissive. "Thanks."

"Do you know what's going on?"

"With what?"

"Edward and Peter. They've both been acting strange."

"It's nearly the end of vintage. They're tired."

"No," Felicity persisted. "It's more than that. Something's not right between them and you know who I blame?"

"No but I'm sure you're going to tell me."

"That witch, Taylor."

Taylor sucked in a breath. That's what happened when you listened in on other people's conversations, you heard things you didn't like. Another of her mother's sayings. Now Taylor worried she might make a noise and they'd discover her.

"That's unkind."

Taylor sent Noelene a little vote of thanks.

"It's true. Ever since she's come here there's been trouble between Edward and Peter."

"Rubbish." Noelene's tone was sharp, matter-of-fact. "There was always going to be trouble between those two one day. They've managed to keep it below the surface but it's been bubbling along waiting for the moment to explode. Nothing to do with Taylor."

Taylor eased the kettle back onto the bench. At least Noelene sounded as if she was a genuine friend.

"Are you sure Edward's not here?"

"Look for yourself but I heard him go through the door into the winery."

Taylor tensed.

"I'll go through that way." Noelene's voice came closer. "See if I can find him."

Taylor made a dash for the door, yanked it open and spun to face the kitchen as if she was just coming in.

Noelene stopped at the sight of her. "Hello, Taylor. Have you seen Edward?"

"No." Her face felt hot. "I was going to make a cup of coffee." She waved at the cups on the table. "Didn't get a chance to drink mine this morning."

"You don't happen to know what's going on between Edward and Peter, do you?"

Taylor started to shake her head but she had the feeling Noelene could see straight through her. "Maybe...some of it."

"How about I make us a coffee and you tell me what you know."

Taylor sat down. She felt Noelene was giving a command rather than making an offer.

Felicity stuck hershead around the corner.

"Oh," she said. "I heard voices. I thought you'd found Edward."

"No, but we're all good here, thank you, Felicity." Noelene's voice was firm. "You can go back to work."

Taylor watched the young woman's eyes narrow and her lips purse. Her look was lost on Noelene whose back was turned but Taylor felt the full force of her glare. Felicity lingered a moment then spun on her high heels and left them to it.

"There we are." Noelene placed two cups on the table and took a seat opposite Taylor.

Taylor wrapped her fingers around the cup. Today had been the first time she'd felt cold since she'd arrived. Thin grey clouds had hidden the sun most of the day and now in the late afternoon there was a chill in the air.

"Let's keep our voices low." Noelene nodded her head towards the wall behind Taylor. "We don't want madam's flapping ears hearing any more than she already has. She always adds two and two to come up with six."

"I probably don't know much more than you," Taylor began. "I think it's mainly over Pete picking the special cabernet grapes."

"I noticed they were gone when I walked up here. I thought Edward had lined up machine harvesters for that."

"He might have." Taylor paused as she recalled Pete's request she not tell Noelene about the hand-picking but it was done now. "Pete wanted to hand-pick it."

"It's a wonder he didn't call me. I could have helped."

"I guess he knew it was your day off," Taylor said quickly. "And he had plenty of pickers."

Noelene raised an eyebrow but remained silent.

"I think he was happy with how it all worked out but..." Taylor wasn't sure how much to say.

"But?"

"Ed didn't know it was going to be picked on Wednesday. He was away from the winery all day as it turned out but he was fairly angry when he got back and saw it had been picked."

"I'm sure he would have been. He did have some ideas brewing."

"More than some." Taylor felt the need to defend Pete. "Ed's been meeting with some Chinese businessmen. I'm not sure what he's meeting with them about but I am sure he's trying to keep it from Pete."

"So it's true."

"What's true?"

Noelene didn't answer. She sat back and shook her head. "Those boys. I blame Neil and Pearl. If they were still here none of this would be happening."

"I thought their plane crash was an accident."

"It was. A terrible, terrible accident. But every now and then I feel angry at them for dying. Especially when I see their two boys struggling."

Taylor sipped her coffee. She wasn't at all comfortable with this conversation.

"So." Taylor jumped as Noelene tapped the table. "What's to be done?"

"I don't know if there's anything that can be done," Taylor said. "They have diametrically opposing ideas on how to run this business."

"I don't agree. They have some common ground. They both love the place. They're proud of their parents' achievements. They both want to produce good wine. I don't know what Ed thinks he's up to but I can't imagine him walking away from Wriggly Creek."

"Why would he do that?'

"Pete seems to think he's selling his share to the Chinese. I don't believe it."

They both sipped their coffees.

Taylor thought about the other wineries she'd visited. She wondered if the same things went on behind the scenes there. The seed of an idea began to form.

"What is it?"

Noelene's question surprised her. "Nothing."

"You looked brighter all of a sudden. You've thought of something."

"I might be wrong."

"About what?"

Taylor rubbed her hands together to keep the warmth now that her cup was empty. "I think what Ed and Pete need is a business plan."

"Good idea."

Taylor's little glimmer of hope faltered. "Surely they'd already have one?"

"Maybe they do but it's not working for them. Is it something you could help them with?"

"Oh." Taylor suddenly felt silly. "I haven't done a lot of business work since I left the charity job a few years ago."

"But you must have some idea if you studied business at uni."

"Ed did too."

"But he's too close to it." Noelene jumped up. "You're right."

"I am?" Taylor eyed her doubtfully.

"They need a business plan and they need it to come from someone who's not involved in the business but someone who cares about both of them." Noelene fixed her sharp stare on Taylor. A stare that radiated hope.

Taylor shook her head. "I don't think I should—"

"You're the perfect person. You've got the knowledge, you've had the chance to see how the winery works, you've spent time with both Ed and Pete."

Taylor's cheeks warmed up.

"By that I mean you understand what motivates them, what they want from the business."

"I'm not sure I do really."

Noelene came around the table and grasped both of Taylor's hands in her own. "Yes, you do. I'm a firm believer in people coming into other people's lives for a reason. You may be the only person who can stop Edward and Peter from destroying their family business and each other in the process."

Taylor pulled her hands from Noelene's. "No." This was not what she wanted. She'd moved to Coonawarra to find new love and a change of lifestyle. She wasn't anyone's saviour. "Anyway, I doubt they'd listen to anything I said. Neither of them are speaking to me at the moment."

"Oh, that's just ridiculous. How old are they? Truly Taylor, after all you've done for those two they don't deserve you."

Taylor felt like her stomach was full of sludge. A heavy weight pressed inside her. She now knew what she'd been trying to hide from herself these last two days. There was no reason to stay. She had to move on. Look for work in another town; maybe over the border in Victoria.

"That's kind of you, Noelene. I can't help but feel I am partly responsible. I came here because Ed and I thought there was something between us. I was wrong. When I broke it off with Ed I should have gone then. Now it's so complicated. I'm better off out of it."

"What about Peter?"

Taylor lifted her gaze to Noelene who was still standing beside her, one hand on the back of her chair.

"What about him?"

"Surely you can tell he's in love with you."

Taylor felt her eyebrows shoot up.

"And it's obvious to me that you have feelings for him." Noelene folded her arms across her chest and grinned. "You two. I should lock you in a room together. I reckon there'd be enough sparks for you to sort it out."

"What are you sorting out?" Felicity bustled into the kitchen, took a cloth from the sink and began wiping down the bench.

"Nothing that you need be concerned about."

"I'm finishing up for the day." Felicity moved to the table. She leaned across in front of Taylor and started wiping. Once again her breasts were in danger of falling out over the top of her low-cut shirt. Taylor suddenly had a new name for her, instead of Frosty Felicity she should be Flaunty Felicity.

"No need to flash your boobs," Noelene snapped. "There's no-one to impress here."

Felicity straightened up and glared from Noelene to Taylor. Taylor struggled to keep a straight face. She couldn't help but think if looks could kill they'd be dead. Felicity hung the cloth over the tap and flounced back to her office where they heard the rattle of keys and the whoosh as the front door closed.

Noelene shook her head. "I still can't believe she spent a lot of money on getting a boob job."

"She did?" Taylor looked towards the office trying to imagine Felicity without all that flesh.

"Yes. She already had a perfectly good figure before she put herself through that. I'm sure she did it to impress Edward."

"Really?"

"They'd been a bit of an item before she came to work here but like all his women..." Noelene paused. "Present company excepted."

"I'm not sure I could be classed as one of his women. We hardly even dated."

"Well anyway, Felicity didn't last long. Then Edward went off on his long break, the previous office girl got pregnant and didn't want to come back and next thing I knew Felicity had the job and a bigger set of boobs since I'd seen her last. Peter was smitten with her."

Taylor was surprised by a small stab of jealousy. She knew Ed openly flirted with Felicity but she'd never witnessed Pete be anything more than his usual polite self with his office manager.

"Not for long. Edward came back and Peter found out they'd been a couple. Edward can be a bit over the top and flaunt that kind of thing. The girls are easily attracted to him. Peter has always been a bit more circumspect. Anyway, he backed right off, kept his relationship with Felicity purely professional. I'm thankful for that anyway but I've rarely heard of him showing any interest in a woman again – until you came along."

"Look, Noelene, I don't think–"

Noelene patted her arm. "I'm just saying what I see. He's a better match for you than Ed." She straightened up and glanced at her watch. "Madam Felicity must have left early. I'd better get back and help with the end-of-day stocktake. I didn't tell Peter where I was going. Can you switch off the lights and let yourself out?"

Taylor nodded. Noelene hurried away then stopped and turned back.

"How about you come visit me at the cellar door tomorrow? I could do with your help."

Before Taylor could answer she was gone. Taylor stared at the space Noelene had vacated. She heard the outer door close. The room settled into silence around her. Taylor rested her elbows on the table and put her head in her hands. She did like Pete. She liked him a lot but something always came up to make a barrier between them. She thought about what Noelene had said about the two brothers both liking Felicity.

Taylor had never fallen for the same guy as her sister. They were poles apart in taste but she'd always worn Gemma's hand-me-downs. These days Taylor wasn't one to fuss about clothes too much. She was happy to shop in chain stores and look for bargains as long as they were new. She had an aversion to hand-me-downs. Gemma still mailed her the odd fancy jacket or expensive blouse. Taylor put them straight in the charity bin.

Maybe that was how Pete felt too. Perhaps he was tired of his brother's cast-offs and that included women. She felt warm at the thought of it. If only she'd met Pete first. Things might have been a lot different. She dug her fingers into her scalp.

"What a mess," she groaned.

CHAPTER
44

Pete pushed the plunger down through the grapes. It gave him some satisfaction to imagine it was Ed he was forcing to the bottom rather than the grape skins. He eased the plunger up carefully, alarmed at his reaction. Was he capable of violence against his brother? He rolled his shoulders and plunged again. He knew the answer was no but that didn't curb his anger. Then again there was no way he wanted to taint what would one day be his icon wine with all that anger.

Damn Ed. He'd picked the worst possible time to drop his bombshell. Not that any time would be a good time to find out your brother, who owned the majority share of your business, was selling it off, but Pete couldn't spare a minute to leave and seek advice. He had no chance to make a trip to Adelaide or Mount Gambier to ask for independent professional help. He didn't even have time to call someone – providing he knew exactly what to ask them.

Pete stepped along the board and plunged again. It was hard work with only him and Antoine knowing the NS18 was in the old cement fermenters. It meant they had to do all the plunging and be secretive about it. Ed had said he'd given up the idea of selling the new cabernet now that he was selling his share of the winery but Pete didn't trust him. Besides Antoine, only Ben and Howard knew. The former was busy on the farm and the latter too old to do the work. There was no-one else he could ask, not even Taylor.

It hurt to think he couldn't trust her but he didn't know which side of the fence she was on. She'd known Ed first. He pictured her ready smile and thought about all the things she'd done since arriving at the winery. She'd thrown herself into life at Wriggly Creek with no complaint. He wouldn't have known about things like the broken washing machine if it hadn't been for Antoine. He'd hardly seen Taylor over the weekend. She had either been at the cellar door with Noelene or off the vineyard altogether. He'd noticed her van go in and out a few times. From what he could tell they'd all avoided each other. He'd not seen Ed at all for the last two days. With the start of a new week he'd have to be in the office today and Pete had asked Antoine to get Taylor to assist him. With any luck they could all keep avoiding each other.

"No-one has come in for my cake this morning."

Edward looked up from his desk to Felicity's pouting face at his door. "They must all be busy." He gave her a nod. "I'll have some in a minute."

The pout was replaced by a smile. "I'll put the kettle on."

The mobile on his desk vibrated. Edward leaned forward to peer at it. He didn't recognise the number. He pressed the green answer button.

"Hello?"

"I'm not happy about losing those cabernet grapes."

Edward tensed. Archer must be using a different phone. Edward got up and moved to his door. There was no sign of Felicity. He pushed it to. "I know but I've explained it, Angus. It's out of my hands."

He held his phone away from his ear as the big man shouted obscenities. Once he paused Edward cut in. "I told you I can let you have some of our other cabernet."

"I don't want your crap grapes. I can get cabernet from anyone in Coonawarra. You promised me the NS18. I'm giving you one last chance to come good on your promise or your name will be mud around here. By the time I'm finished no-one will want to buy Wriggly Creek wine except for some poor unsuspecting tourist."

Angus Archer was a big man, full of huff and puff. Edward put on a placating tone. "To tell the truth Angus, you wouldn't want it anyway."

"Why not?"

"It wasn't as good as Peter was playing it up to be."

"It tested fine here."

"Well, I'm not sure what went wrong on the day but he's not happy with it." Edward paused trying to think of something else he could say to put Angus off. "He says he's going to blend it."

"With what?"

"Some of our other cabernet, I assume."

"He's a fool. The flavour and tannin development in those berries was on the right track to being a darn good crop. We would have made a cracker wine with it!"

"Unfortunately as I told you Peter went behind my back. I've apologised, I don't know what else I can do."

"You'll make it up to me, Edward. I can assure you."

"Are you threatening me?"

"No, just reminding you that you owe me a favour now. A big one."

The phone went dead. Edward looked at the blank screen. He tossed the phone onto his desk. Whatever Angus said it didn't matter to him anymore.

He got up, went to his office window and looked out across the vines now stripped of their fruit and taking on their autumn colours. Once more he marvelled at Peter's daring. If someone had warned Edward his brother would go behind his back he would have laughed at them. He hoped this new Peter wouldn't call his bluff on the sale of the winery. Edward had already made a mess of one deal, he didn't want to destroy another.

"You're kidding me?" Taylor's eyes widened at the sight below her. She was standing on the metal parapet next to a red wine fermenter that had just been emptied.

Antoine chuckled beside her. "You said you'd help me today."

"You really want me to climb down there and shovel out those... those." She pointed a finger at the mush of skins and seeds that remained in the bottom of the ferment tank.

"Skins," Antoine said.

Taylor wrinkled her nose.

"So you're not keen?" he asked.

"I'll do it," Taylor said with a confidence she didn't feel.

"Great. You shovel the skins into the bins and I'll take the bins to the press."

"What for?"

"We can still extract wine from them."

Taylor looked down at the mess below her once more. She was going to trudge around in it and they were going to use it to make wine. She shook her head and wondered at the wines she'd been drinking.

"We don't waste anything," Antoine said. "We have a farmer that comes and takes the mark."

"Takes his mark?"

"The mark. It's what we call the dried skins. He feeds them to his cattle. Peter is very strong on recycling."

Taylor shook her head. "Okay. Let's get started."

"Do you want an old shirt to put over your t-shirt?"

Taylor looked down at the pale blue shirt she'd tossed on with her daggiest jeans. These clothes were already stained from plunging. "Don't worry. These are old clothes."

Antoine looked at her shoes. Most of the jobs she'd done she'd managed in her track shoes. "We'd better find you some boots and a CO_2 counter," he said.

"What's that for?"

"Ferments cause a lot of carbon dioxide. It can kill you."

Taylor gawped at him. This was sounding better and better.

"You can't get into a tank without a counter."

"So it will warn me if there's too much gas?"

"Don't worry. It'll beep like crazy. You'll be fine. Just get out as quickly as you can. I'll be within hearing distance."

Taylor gave him a brief nod. She hoped she appeared confident but there was still a lot she didn't understand.

In no time at all she was at the bottom of the fermenter shovelling the remains of the grapes into a bin. The smell was overpowering, as if she was bathing in strong wine. Taylor put her back into it. Working at the winery had developed muscles she didn't know she had, something to be thankful for – maybe.

She had hoped to put the finishing touches to the business plan she'd worked on over the weekend but Antoine kept her busy for most of the day. It was hard physical work and by the end of it she was exhausted and sticky from head to toe. She wasn't looking forward to preparing dinner. Not that she'd bother to cook for anyone but her and Antoine. If Ed or Pete had the audacity to turn up for a meal tonight she just might empty one of their bottles of wine over their heads.

"That's it." Antoine had worked hard too but he looked decidedly clean beside her. "We can finish up for the day."

"Good." Taylor put her hands on the back of her hips and stretched forward and back.

"How about we go in to the pub for dinner tonight?"

"You're joking! Look at me."

"After you've cleaned up." Antoine smiled at her. "I'd like to pay. You've cooked for me so many times."

Taylor opened her mouth to protest then changed her mind. "Sounds good."

She was exhausted but a shower would brighten her up and she'd like nothing better than to get away from Wriggly Creek for a while. With Antoine she could relax, be herself and not think, and there'd be time in the morning to have a last look at her plan. Noelene had come up with an idea for tomorrow and Taylor was nervous. It involved getting her together with Ed and Pete so she could present her plan. As she'd said to Noelene she could present her ideas well enough but it was getting the Starr brothers to listen that would be the problem.

CHAPTER
45

Edward looked up from the paper he was reading. Noelene stood in his office doorway.

"What are you doing here on your day off?"

"I've been trying to catch up with you." She came right in and shut the door behind her. "Something at the cellar door I want you to see."

"Then why have you closed the door?"

Noelene pulled up a chair opposite him. "I want to have a chat first."

"About?" Edward leaned back in his chair and tapped the tips of his fingers together.

"What's this I hear about you selling your share of the winery?"

"It's none of your business, Noelene."

She lifted her chin, her eyebrows rose and she pinned him with one of her don't-mess-with-me looks.

Edward shrugged. "I'm tired of working towards nothing. We need capital. Peter won't agree to any of my suggestions."

"If there was a way to avoid this Chinese takeover would you try it?"

"It's not a takeover." Edward slapped his hand against his thigh. "Peter and I will never agree. I'm tired of banging my head against a brick wall for little return. He can have it on his own. It's time for me to try something else."

"Like what?"

"I don't know yet but selling my share will give Peter and me both the opportunity to try our own thing."

"That's debatable, but anyway, like I said, if there was an alternative would you try it?"

Edward studied Noelene's poker face. "Maybe."

"I've asked Taylor to come up with a business plan for Wriggly Creek."

Edward snorted. "We've got a business plan."

She waved her arm at his office. "Gathering dust in a pile somewhere I'd guarantee." She stood up. "I want you to come with me now. I've asked Taylor to set up in the cellar door where no-one will disturb us."

"Us?"

"You, Peter, me."

Edward opened his mouth but she cut him off.

"I'll be there as the arbitrator and to make sure you boys give Taylor a chance and behave yourselves."

Edward shook his head. "We're not little boys anymore, Noelene. Peter and I are grown-ups now."

She glared at him, one hand on the door handle. "Behave like it then." She threw open the door and walked out.

Edward stared after her a moment then with a sigh he stood up. "This could be amusing," he murmured.

Pete slid his key into the lock at the back of the cellar door and the door swung open. He stepped inside. Noelene mustn't have locked it when she left last night, unless she was already inside. She'd said there was something urgent they needed to look at here. He glanced at his watch. He didn't have a lot of time to spare. He heard a sound from the front room, like papers shuffling. He stuck his head through the joining door. Taylor looked up from the other side of the counter, a sheaf of papers in her hands.

"I thought you were Noelene," he said.

Taylor smiled. It was a soft crinkling around her eyes, a small upturn of her lips. He looked away.

"She should be here soon," Taylor said.

Pete glanced around the cellar door. A couple of bar stools had been placed on the other side of the counter but otherwise everything looked the same. "So do you know what she wants me to look at?"

"I do." Taylor straightened the papers in her hands. "But I'd prefer we waited for Noelene…if you don't mind."

Once more Pete looked at his watch. He felt embarrassed if the truth be told. Taylor had every right not to be here, not to be talking civilly, not to be smiling warmly at him.

"Pete."

He lifted his gaze to meet hers. He should look away but he couldn't.

"Can we talk a moment before the others get here?"

"Others?"

"Noelene." She looked down at her papers. Her cheeks were pink. "This was her idea but I wanted to help."

"What was her idea?"

"I'm sorry, this is coming out all wrong. It's not at all how I imagined."

Pete shifted his weight from one foot to the other. Taylor wasn't making any sense. "What's Noelene put you up to?"

Taylor sighed. "We're both worried about you…and Ed. Noelene asked me to come up with a business plan. I know it's crazy 'cause you're bound to have one already…" Her voice trailed away.

The confident woman who'd welcomed him was replaced by one with uncertainty spreading across her face. He stepped up to the counter. She was just a metre away on the other side. Her worried gaze met his.

"Is Noelene bringing Ed here?"

She nodded but didn't look away.

"Damn, Noelene." Pete ran his hand over his hair. He paced to the end of the counter then stopped. There was a photograph lying there he hadn't noticed before. It was the picture from the wall in the back office of him with his dad and Ed planting the new cabernet canes. He looked back at Taylor. "What's this doing here?"

"My idea," she said gently. "To remind you of what's important."

Pete gave a soft snort. "It's Ed who needs reminding. He's the one who wanted to sell the grapes."

She moved down the counter to stand opposite him again. "What else do you see?"

He rested his hand on the frame and peered at the photo. He was holding a bundle of canes and Ed had a shovel, they both leaned in towards their father who was bent over a cane he'd just planted. They were all smiling.

"Dad had just made one of his silly jokes. I knew Mum had been hovering nearby with the camera but I didn't know she'd taken this photo until…one day…after they died, when we were going through their things, I found her camera and scrolled through. Ed and I decided to have this photo enlarged."

"Had you made a business plan together, as a family?" Taylor's voice was gentle.

"No. It was something Dad was going to do. We had to get legal advice after the...after they died but we still didn't end up with a proper business plan. Somehow we've bumbled along till now and it's worked. Or it did."

He was startled by the warmth of Taylor's hand covering his own. He looked up.

"Your parents are gone, Pete but not their legacy. It's not just the grapes, it's you and Ed – you're still family."

Pete took in her tender look, the soft pink of her cheeks and the fullness of her lips.

"Why are you still here, Taylor?"

The tender look was replaced by a puzzled one. "What do you mean?"

"After everything that's happened and all you've done, we've not treated you so well, why have you stayed on?"

She pulled her hand away and straightened the mat beneath the photo. "I don't...I just–"

"It's Ed, isn't it?" He cut through her bluster. "You still love Ed."

Taylor stiffened. "No," she said firmly. "I might be confused about a few things but that's not one of them. There's no future for Ed and me. For a short time we..."

"Were an item?" The words came out a little more sharply than Pete had intended.

"No." Her reply was equally as blunt. "I guess deep down I must have known he wasn't my type."

Pete felt a mixture of relief and embarrassment. "I'm sorry, it's none of my business."

He was surprised to see Taylor move swiftly around the end of the counter and come to a stop in front of him. She looked steadily into his eyes.

"Normally I would agree with you," she said. "But in this case I think it's important you know. After the initial spark died there was never much between Ed and me. We didn't have any kind of a relationship. I still like him but as a friend. I don't – I never loved him."

Pete held her gaze. If she felt nothing for Ed maybe she had room to think about him as more than her employer, more than a friend. They were less than a metre apart. Did she want him to cross that space? What would be her reaction if he reached for her?

They both turned at the sound of footsteps.

"Pete, I just need to say that my presentation today has been planned with both of you in mind. I don't want you or Ed to think I'm favouring one or the other."

Pete opened his mouth to speak but the door to the back room opened and Taylor returned to the other side of the counter.

"Come on, Edward." Noelene's voice carried into the cellar door.

Pete steeled himself for whatever was coming. He picked up a tea towel that was covering some glasses. He needed to keep his hands busy.

CHAPTER
46

Edward paused as he stepped in behind the counter at the cellar door. Noelene was just ahead of him. Taylor lifted her head from the papers she was spreading along the other side of the counter. She was hesitant as if waiting for a reaction. Peter was polishing glasses on Edward's side, his jaw rigid.

"We're all ready," Noelene said. "You boys come around here. I've brought some bar stools in so you can sit."

Edward gritted his teeth. He still objected to Noelene speaking as if they were school kids. He let Peter go ahead of him. They took their places on the stools.

"You go round the other side of the counter." Noelene put a guiding hand on Taylor's back.

Edward gave a wry smile. At least he and Peter weren't the only ones getting Noelene's mother hen treatment.

"Now you make a start, Taylor. Don't mind me. I'm going to make everyone a coffee." She got as far as the door and turned back, her pointer finger raised in the air. "Remember you blokes both agreed to listen." She left. They could hear her in the other room fiddling with the coffee machine.

Taylor cleared her throat and shuffled her papers. She looked terrified.

"You don't have to do this," Peter said.

"No." Edward gave Taylor a mocking smile. "I think she does. Noelene has spoken."

Peter's glance showed his annoyance but he didn't speak.

"Go on, Taylor, please enlighten us with your vast knowledge of the wine business," Edward said.

"I can hear that sarcastic tone in your voice, Edward Starr." Noelene called out.

Edward slapped the bar. "Oh for f–"

"Let's get started." Peter cut him off. "Taylor has done a lot for us and she's gone to a lot of trouble getting this organised." He turned to Edward. "The least we can do is listen."

Edward swallowed his simmering anger. He glanced from Peter to Taylor then he winked at her. "Please begin."

Taylor took a deep breath. She was wise to Ed's game now. He was trying to put both her and Pete offside, covering up for his own shortcomings. She also took strength from Pete's reaction to her declaration about her relationship, or lack of it, with Ed. Pete had looked like a man who'd been given a reprieve from the firing squad. She didn't have time to explore that further. She'd wanted him to be clear that she was about to present an unbiased proposal and that meant she could show no favouritism to one brother or the other.

"I want to preface this by saying this is not a business plan as such."

Ed's breath whistled over his teeth.

"As you would know, Edward." She took care to use his full name. His look met hers. "A business plan needs to have input from the key players and so far you haven't had that input."

"I already know where our money is and where it isn't."

"I don't," Pete said.

"Just like I don't know where all our grapes have gone."

"That's enough from both of you." Noelene came back carrying cups of coffee. "We're not here for you to go tit for tat. Just shut up and listen."

"I think that's the problem." Taylor got in quickly while Noelene handed around coffees. "A business plan isn't just about money or wine production. It's a tool for both of you to understand how your business is put together. A good business plan will help you monitor progress. It would make you both accountable and in control of your business's fate. And if at some stage you do look for an investor it's a useful tool."

"I've got all the facts and figures we need on paper," Edward said.

"Quiet, Edward." Noelene took a big slurp of her coffee and nodded at Taylor. "Go on," she said. "It's making perfect sense so far."

Taylor glanced between the brothers. Ed's blue eyes had deepened in colour. Pete's were clear, full of concern. She went on. "I'm sure what you have is a good start, Edward, and I know you've got a plan for your grapes, Pete, but putting together a business plan forces you both to review everything from the value of your business, operations, marketing and finance to staffing. It helps you to spot connections you might otherwise miss. For example, Edward, if you were to buy the vineyard at Wrattonbully how will you manage that? What equipment will you need and if Pete is already busy here at Wriggly Creek who will oversee the vines in the new vineyard?"

She paused.

"Good point," Noelene said and took another slurp of coffee. Ed glared at her.

"Pete, I know you focus on quality and that's very important but maybe you could up the yield of your entry-level wines. Give Edward more to sell to a bigger chain distributor. That might be a way to increase income without spending money."

Taylor stopped. Both brothers focused their gaze on her now.

"I've been checking out your competitors," she said. "You've got all the elements that the very successful wineries have. It's not necessarily about needing more vines or money, Edward. And Pete, I know you want an icon wine but you also need more bread-and-butter wine. Both of you have got what it takes. You just need to work smarter. I think developing a strong business plan will help you."

Taylor stopped again. She was getting so little reaction from them she didn't know where to go next.

Noelene broke the silence with a clap of her hands. "You see," she said. "I told you Taylor would come up with something useful."

"This is all about why we need a plan," Ed snapped. "Not an actual plan."

Taylor tried to keep her face emotion-free but Ed wasn't making it easy for her. "I didn't have access to your information to mock up a plan and I don't want to put ideas in your head without you having a go first but I am more than happy to help you go through the process."

She paused. Ed stared at her. She wasn't sure which way he was going to go.

"I'd like to try." Pete gave her a quick smile but a troubled look stayed on his face.

"I don't see the point now," Ed said.

"Perhaps it would mean you don't have to sell." Taylor held his gaze. "Expansion at any cost isn't necessarily the answer. But if you don't expand, how could you generate more revenue?" Taylor warmed to her topic. "There may be things you already do that you could do better. Efficiency improvement doesn't have to cost you anything."

Noelene stood up. "Edward, I can't believe you won't at least try."

All four of them stared at him. Finally he threw up his hands. "Okay, okay. I'll give it some thought."

"No time like the present," Noelene said. "Tell them your idea, Taylor."

"I've put some questions and suggestions on paper." Taylor indicated the papers she'd set out on the bar. "If you'd both look at them, write what you can and I'll collate them."

Ed gave a snort. "The old 'where do you see yourself in five years' time' question."

"It's the most important one on the page," Taylor retaliated. Ed's negativity was wearing thin. "No-one else can answer that one for you."

Ed squeezed his lips together.

She picked up the picture of the men planting the vines and propped it against some wine bottles. "This might help. You're a bit more than five years on from when it was taken but I thought it might help you remember."

Pete shut out Ed's grumbles and tried to focus on the page in front of him. Noelene and Taylor had left them to it but it wasn't the business plan he was thinking about, it was Taylor. Not just because everything she'd said had made sense but because of the way she'd said it. She'd been so professional, thorough and caring in her presentation. She'd obviously done her homework. He'd found himself studying her as she spoke. He loved the sound of her voice, the curve of her lips, the way she absentmindedly flicked stray hair from her eyes.

He thought back to her determined words before the others came. There was no relationship between her and Ed. She didn't love his brother. If she hadn't gone on to explain why she was in the cellar door today, if Noelene and Ed hadn't turned up when they did, he might have...

"Bloody hell." Ed's explosion broke the silence.

"What's the matter?"

"She might as well ask what colour our underwear is and what we ate for breakfast. This will take hours."

"Just do the first page so we can give it back to Taylor. The rest we'll do later." Pete studied Ed's brooding face. "I think we need this if we're to have any chance of making a future for Wriggly Creek – together."

"I've told you Zhu has made an offer."

"You don't have to accept it."

"I need to make a change."

Pete still couldn't believe Ed would sell out on him. "I thought Wriggly Creek was your dream, like it was Dad's, and like it is mine, but I'm not going to stand in your way if leaving is what you really want."

Ed held his gaze a moment, his expression unreadable, then he looked back at the paperwork. "Let's get this done. I've got other things I should be doing."

Pete studied his outline. Ed was proud, he acted tough but Pete was sure he was covering something. There was more than the Chinese offer at stake here. Hopefully this idea of Taylor's might shake out whatever was really bothering Ed.

CHAPTER

47

Taylor dropped the papers she'd been reading on the table and tugged the sleeves of her jumper over her hands. The sunshine wasn't providing the warmth in the room like it used to. Ed and Pete had called in to collect their meal the night after the planning meeting. Both had left their first page with her and made garbled promises to deliver the rest soon. That had been Tuesday night, today was Thursday. She hadn't crossed paths with them yesterday and in the evening they'd called in for their meal and left with it. There was little more than a quick smile from Pete and a half-nod and grunt of thanks from Ed.

So much about what they'd written for where they imagined Wriggly Creek and themselves in five years' time was the same. Of course Ed had prefaced his with the message that he was planning to sell but for the sake of the document he was ignoring that prospect and imagining staying on. Taylor shivered and tucked her hands between her knees. It worried her that Noelene was putting such store in her being able to get the brothers to see they both wanted the same outcome. That was the easy bit really. It was the how that differed and they were poles apart with that.

She really needed them to give her the rest of the information, the facts and figures, projections, markets, production and equipment details before she could go any further and that wasn't forthcoming yet.

She glanced across at the meat thawing on the sink. She had plans for a chicken and veg casserole tonight, a meal she could easily create a vegetarian portion from before she added the chicken. She shook her head and berated herself under her breath. Antoine appreciated her food and she was happy to eat vegetarian. She knew she should leave the ungrateful Starr brothers to their own devices. She had an image of Cass saying more than that.

She pushed back from the table and paced the room. Something kept her here. Even though she'd first come looking for Ed and that was over almost before it began, she'd stayed. Wriggly Creek had got under her skin and not only that, she had to be honest. It was Pete. His ruffled curls, his dreamy eyes, his ready smile. Taylor groaned. How could she trust herself? She'd got it so wrong with Ed.

"Hello?"

She sucked in a breath. Pete was at her door.

She put a hand to her chest. "Calm, be calm," she whispered.

He knocked. "Taylor?"

She stepped around the open wooden door and peered through the screen. "I'm here."

He pulled the screen open, his face a mask of worry.

"Is something wrong?"

"No, not exactly." He turned his lips up in a smile. "I keep asking for your help. I'm sorry to do it again but Antoine and Ben are busy and Ed's…I don't know where he is."

"I'm on the payroll now. You know I'll do whatever's needed."
She smiled at him. "Unless it involves spiders."

He frowned again. "I'm sorry."

"I'm kidding." She looked at his furrowed brow. "I know you
wouldn't intentionally put me in that position."

"No. There won't be spiders." He scratched at the curls on his
neck. "Can you help Noelene in the cellar door? She's very busy
today. It's looking like being another big Easter weekend."

"Of course. Where's the week gone? It's Good Friday tomorrow." Taylor had forgotten all about the stash of chocolate eggs and
hot cross buns she'd put away. If it was just her and Antoine they'd
have a bit of eating to do. "I was going to head to the cellar door
soon anyway. I love working over there with Noelene. I just have
to stop by the lab and I'll go straight over from there."

"Thanks, I really appreciate it."

Taylor was rewarded with a huge smile from Pete. She had to
look away a moment. Her heart thumped in her chest. When he
smiled it was as if the world lit up. He hovered a moment, then left.
She put the meat in the fridge, collected her hat and jacket and set
off. The sunshine was weak today. Scattered clouds left little room
for any warmth to shine through. The chilly breeze ruffled the
leaves of the vines, now mainly yellow with splashes of orange and
red. She passed Pete's cottage. Like the rows of vines behind her
the leaves on the NS18 vines were also changing to the colours of
autumn. She'd loved the green but the variation in colours now was
more picturesque.

She was humming as she approached the winery office. Not the
weather, or even Frosty Felicity, was going to dampen her mood
today. At the front corner of the building she paused. She could just
see the back of a sleek black car parked close to the trees by the road
rather than in the car park.

Taylor pushed open the door to the office. A big man in a suit straightened up from leaning over Felicity's desk. Felicity glanced past him to Taylor, a surprised look on her face.

"Hello, Taylor." Felicity's voice was a little too loud. "Taylor's been our extra help over vintage, Mr Archer."

The man flicked a look at Taylor. She could tell by his expression he discounted her as of no importance.

"I'll let Edward know you called." Felicity spoke loudly as if for Taylor's benefit rather than his.

He gave a sharp grunt in response and made his way outside.

Taylor watched him walk in the direction of the car. Black car, big man, bald head: was he the one who'd been looking over the fence at the NS18 grapes just before they were picked?

"Who was that man?" She looked back to Felicity.

"A business friend of Edward's." Felicity turned away, dismissing Taylor. She began to rearrange things on her desk. A sheaf of papers slipped from her fingers and fluttered across the floor.

Taylor left her to it. A small grin turned up the corners of her mouth as she let herself through the lunchroom door into the lab behind. Flustered Felicity. She was compiling a good list of 'F' words for the office madam.

Edward entered the cellar door from the front. There were three groups at the bar and another couple standing off to the side looking at the photos on the wall. He made his way behind the counter to help Noelene and baulked at the large numbers of glasses waiting to be washed.

"You've been busy," he said as she finished explaining the cab sauv to the customers.

"It's been like this since I opened the door. Did Peter send you?"

"I haven't seen him today."

"Oh well, doesn't matter. Do you want to wash dishes or serve customers?"

"I'll serve."

"Of course you will." Noelene lifted a tray of glasses and smiled at the cab sauv drinkers. "Edward is one of the Starr brothers I was telling you about. He'll help you with any wine purchases you'd like."

"Are you the winemaker?" one of the group asked.

Edward pulled his face into a smile. "No, that's my brother but we work closely together. It's a family business."

The banter rolled easily off his tongue. The room was full of happy customers, he didn't want to scare any off, besides, it was no hardship to smile here. He usually enjoyed the cellar door. This was where he felt most comfortable. He was good at talking to people. He mightn't make the wine but he knew how to talk about it, how to sell it.

When they left, the group had bought the equivalent of three dozen between them. He was happy with that. He wiped down the bar and checked the tasting stock. Noelene came in with a tray of clean glasses.

"Thanks," she said. "It's good to have another pair of hands."

"Always a pleasure working with you, Noelene." Edward turned one of his big smiles on her.

She gave his shoulder a playful slap. "Save your charm for the customers. It's wasted on me, Edward Starr." She put the clean glasses away.

He put more bottles in the remaining fridge. They still hadn't got around to replacing the one that had died months ago. The whole counter area could do with a remodel but that was another expense.

"How's that business plan writing coming along?"

He straightened up. "Getting there."

"You are taking this seriously, aren't you Edward?"

"You know how busy things are. I don't have hours to spend on it right now."

"But this plan might be the chance to salvage everything, get Wriggly Creek and you and Peter back on track."

Edward stretched his neck from one side to the other.

"You've worked yourself into a corner haven't you?" Noelene glared at him.

"What do you mean?" He tried to evade her searching eyes.

"You don't really want to sell everything? You're trying to frighten Peter into doing things your way. You've always been able to manipulate him and you thought you could bluff him into selling part of his share to get you to stay."

Edward swore in frustration. Noelene had always been able to work him out, just like his mother, only she wasn't his mother. No matter how much he tried not to think about his parents he couldn't help the reminders that he missed them. "You don't know what you're talking about. You always take Peter's side."

Noelene laughed.

"I don't find it funny," he snapped.

"Of course you wouldn't."

"It's as if I'm invisible."

Noelene's smile disappeared. "You're hardly that."

He put both hands on the counter and pressed against it. "I've busted my butt keeping us afloat but no-one cares about that. I'm the one who gets out and sells the bloody wine. Even here at the cellar door everyone wants to meet the winemaker. Peter would stay with his nose in a barrel all day if we let him."

Noelene went to speak but the front door opened and happy voices announced the next lot of customers.

She greeted them with a smile. "Welcome to Wriggly Creek. Is everyone tasting today?"

Edward took a deep breath and moved away for a moment. The vine-planting photo caught his eye. It had been hung on the wall near the head shots of his family. He turned at the sound of Taylor's voice from behind the counter. She must have come through the back door as the customers came in the front. She could help Noelene.

No doubt hanging that blasted picture was Taylor's idea. She glanced in his direction. He made for the door. When he reached it he looked back over the customers' heads. Taylor was chatting happily as if she'd been selling wine all her life. He tugged open the door and let himself out into the chilly day. Everything was going pear-shaped.

CHAPTER

48

Taylor inhaled the spicy smell of warm hot cross buns which mingled with the savoury of egg and bacon pies. Her mouth watered. She'd woken early and after tossing and turning she'd given up on sleep and snuck into the kitchen, closing the passage door behind her. She'd decided to cook but if she couldn't sleep in, at least Antoine should get the chance.

She ran water in the sink and started washing the dishes she'd used for cooking. Easter had arrived so suddenly. She didn't want to acknowledge the swift passing of time. There wouldn't be much for her to do soon and no excuse for her to stay. She hoped at least her legacy would be to help the Starr brothers develop a business plan that might keep them and Wriggly Creek together.

She'd asked Ed and Pete to come for breakfast and they'd both agreed. Even though they hadn't stayed to eat the chicken casserole she'd made last night for dinner she'd been heartened by their response to breakfast. Noelene had been invited too but her husband was home for a couple of days. Taylor had offered to cover her Saturday cellar door shift and to her surprise Noelene had accepted.

Taylor hummed under her breath. She chuckled to herself when she realised she was singing the old hot cross buns nursery rhyme. She hadn't thought of it in years. Her mum had always sung it to them when they were kids. Taylor glanced at the laptop on the end of the kitchen table. She'd sent an email to her parents once since she'd been here and had received one, or actually a few back, now that she thought about it. How long since she'd sent hers? They hadn't Skyped since before Rosie's wedding. She hadn't even sent them the photos she'd promised to take. And she'd made no contact with Gemma who'd sent pictures of a weekend trip to London.

A pang of guilt swept over her. She hadn't told her parents or Gemma anything about her time at Wriggly Creek. Now that she thought about it their last email had been full of questions. She'd been too busy to answer. She pulled out the chair and sat at the laptop trying to think up a summary of her last few weeks.

She'd just pressed send on her brief email when Antoine emerged, his normally flat hair sticking up all over his head and his eyes still bleary from sleep.

"Something smells very good out here," he said.

"Breakfast. Do you have the day off or has Pete got you working?"

"I've got a couple of things to do this morning then he's given me today and tomorrow off. I'm going to Robe overnight. Tom and some friends have rented a place there."

"Oh." Taylor wondered what she would do. She enjoyed Antoine's company, especially now that Ed and Pete hardly called in.

There was a rap at the door and Ed came in, closely followed by Pete.

"Good, everyone's here." Taylor pasted on a smile and cleared away the laptop. "The food is ready. Come and sit down." She took the pies from the oven where she'd been keeping them warm.

Ed and Pete chose opposite ends of the table. Antoine and Taylor took the seats between them.

Taylor hoped this wouldn't be too awkward. "I thought we'd start with savoury." She set out the individual egg and bacon pies with a flourish. "Yours is sans bacon, Antoine."

"Thank you," he said.

Ed and Pete murmured their appreciation. Taylor jumped up again. "I forgot the coffee." She set about making them each a cup with her coffee machine. She'd have to order more pods soon. She felt a pang of melancholy wondering where she'd get the order sent. The shine had gone from the day.

After she'd made Ed and Pete a coffee, Antoine patted her seat. "I'll make ours," he said. "You eat before it gets cold."

Taylor accepted his offer. She was hungry now and the blokes were all wolfing theirs down.

"Haven't had egg and bacon pie in ages," Pete said.

"That was delicious, thanks," Ed added. His plate was already empty.

"Hope you've got room for hot cross buns," Taylor said. "Can you get them while you're up please, Antoine?"

"Of course." He lifted out the plate she'd wrapped in alfoil to keep warm and placed it in the middle of the table.

"Everyone help themselves," she said.

"I keep forgetting to buy some." Pete selected a bun. "I think this is the first one I've had this year."

"They're good," Ed said through a mouthful. "I don't know why we don't eat them more often."

"Then they wouldn't be as special." Taylor grinned and began to sing. "'Hot cross buns'."

Pete joined in and then Ed.

Taylor stopped after 'two a penny, hot cross buns' but the brothers kept going. Their voices blended in unison. "'If you have no daughters give them to your sons. One a penny, two a penny, hot cross buns'." They ended with a chuckle.

"What's that?" Taylor asked. "Do you have your own version?"

"No," they chorused.

"I've never heard that verse before."

"Mum always sang it to us," Pete said.

"It's a long time since you two were little boys." Antoine brought Taylor a coffee. "You've probably mixed up your nursery rhymes."

"She did it every year, right up until…"

"Mum always went to church on Good Friday." Pete filled the gap as Ed's voice trailed away.

"And Easter Sunday," Ed said.

Pete leaned back in his chair, his hands clasped over his stomach. "This is like old times. Good Friday was often a relaxed day for us. A bit of a breather in the busyness of vintage."

"It was Easter when Dad bought the Triumph." Ed's deep-blue eyes sparkled.

"That's right. Mum came home from Sunday church and he had it tied up with a big bow."

"And loaded with Easter eggs."

"He drove Mum to the creek and we rode our bikes down. We'd had a downpour a few days before and there was a bit of water in the creek."

"That was the year you went to uni." Ed wiped the corners of his mouth with his fingers.

They lapsed into silence.

"Do you still have the Triumph?" Taylor asked.

"Yes." Ed stood abruptly. "I should get going."

Taylor wished she hadn't asked.

Pete sat forward. "What's the rush?"

"Things to do."

"Would you like to eat together tonight?" Taylor was keen to keep the fledgling peace going between them. "I could cook a roast?"

"Let's have pizza. I'll bring the ingredients."

She was surprised by Ed's offer.

"I've got a few olives and a bag of cheese," Pete said.

"I've got some chicken and bacon left over," Taylor added.

"There you go. Surely we can make something edible between us." Ed beamed them one of his charming smiles. "Six o'clock?"

"Sure." Taylor grinned.

"Suits me." Pete picked up his cap from the floor by his chair.

"We should open a bottle of the new reserve cab sauv that arrived yesterday."

"Good idea." Pete grinned at Taylor. "We might get you to put a price on this one."

"Yes," Ed said. "Taylor seems to be the go-to person for wine pricing."

She studied his face, not sure if he was joking or having a dig.

"I'm off," he said.

"I'd better head too." Pete moved around the couch.

Ed was already out the door and Antoine starting on the dishes.

Pete turned back. He clutched his cap in purple-stained fingers. "I should have the rest of the information for the business plan ready by tonight. I'll bring it with me."

"That'd be great."

"Has Ed given you his?"

"Not yet."

Pete pushed his cap onto his head. When he reached the door he looked back. "Ed cares more than he shows. I'm sure he'll get it to you soon."

"Whenever you can, you're all busy." The longer it took the longer she had an excuse to stay.

Pete's eyes shone. "See you later." He lifted a finger in a small wave.

The sadness Taylor had felt earlier was gone. She started humming the hot cross buns tune again as she picked up a tea towel. Things were on the improve. Ed and Pete were getting on better. Perhaps she could help them to resolve their differences after all. And not only that, now she had something to look forward to this evening rather than a night alone in the empty quarters.

CHAPTER
49

Edward flung the cover from the Triumph and walked all around it. One tyre was flat and when he'd turned the ignition the other night, he'd got no response. He assumed it was only the battery. The car hadn't been driven for six years.

He hadn't told Peter he'd been to check out the old car. It had been too painful and he didn't want to make it more so. Besides he'd been so angry with his brother over their differing opinions on the future of the winery he hadn't wanted to share the old car. He wasn't even sure Peter would have been interested. Now their reminiscing over breakfast had sparked something inside him. They rarely talked about their parents anymore and perhaps they should be. Neil's Triumph might just be the step forward he and Peter needed.

He covered the car again and went back to his house. He wandered from room to room. His parents' bedroom was the biggest with an en suite and the best view over the vines but he'd never moved in there. He did a full circuit of the rest of the house. What was he looking for? He didn't know. He'd given up the NS18 sale but there was still the Chinese offer. What if Peter didn't come round to his way of thinking? Noelene had been right when she'd said he was trying to coerce Peter into doing things his way. If Peter didn't agree to buying the Wrattonbully property was Edward really prepared to dig in his heels and give this place up? The only home he'd ever known. Give up his share of Wriggly Creek?

He ended up in the small room off the kitchen he used as a home office. He should at least answer some of the questions Taylor had listed. He had to look like he was trying. Noelene had seen through him and he didn't know if she'd tell Peter. He found the papers and picked up a pen. He read the first question then chucked the pen down again. There was something else he should try first, something that would keep Peter onside. Edward plucked his phone from his pocket and dug in the desk drawer for his father's old Teledex. He knew he'd find the number he was looking for there.

Pete had a spring in his step. In spite of creating a busy day for himself by giving Antoine some time off, he was happy. He knew the cause of that happiness was Taylor. He walked past the storage tanks, on past the new fermenting tanks and around the back of the winery to the old shed that housed the cement fermenters. He glanced around. He felt stupid with all this subterfuge but he still wasn't sure how Edward was thinking even though he'd been more relaxed over breakfast.

He latched the door behind him and waited for his eyes to adjust to the gloomy interior of the shed, then picked up the plunger and made his way to the steps he'd put at the side of the first tank. Antoine had done two plunging shifts before he left. Pete would have to do the rest.

He climbed up and stepped onto the board. The rich red of the cab sauv grapes crusting the liquid below was a joy each time he looked at it. Fixing up the old tanks and now constant hand-plunging was hard work but it would be worth it. He had a memory of the day he'd taught Taylor to plunge. He wished she could be with him now. He knew she'd be interested, like she was in all aspects of wine production.

He was sure he could trust her now but the timing hadn't been right. Maybe tomorrow he'd bring her in and show her. She'd managed the plunging in the new fermenting tanks so she shouldn't have any trouble with these. He pulled the plunger up and forced it down again through the swirling liquid. Taylor brought a smile to his lips and a tune to his head. *Hot cross buns*. He sang it in time to the up and down movement of the plunger.

The wind picked up a little more as Taylor returned from her walk. She hurried along the track which ran between the building that housed the offices and lab on one side and the shed with the rows of tanks on the other. When no-one else was around the place felt strange. Something banged to her left. She stopped. The breeze tumbled a plastic drink bottle across the track in front of her. She started forward then she heard the bang again. It sounded like a piece of iron flapping but the wind wasn't that strong. She walked to the end of the row of tanks and round the other side. There was an old shed there and the door was slightly ajar. As she watched the wind shifted it and it banged. That was the sound she'd heard. She had no idea where Pete or Ed were but perhaps she should shut the door while she was here.

A sound pulled her up short. She listened then broke into a smile. Someone was singing 'Hot cross buns'. Taylor pulled the door open. "Pete?"

The singing stopped.

Taylor peered into the gloom. There was a movement. She hesitated. "Pete, are you in here?"

"Taylor?"

"I heard the door banging." She stepped right inside. Her eyes adjusted to the light which filtered through skylights in the tin roof. She looked up. Pete was standing on something, a pole in his hand, he was red-faced and he looked worried. "Is everything all right?"

"Can you shut the door properly please? I mustn't have hooked the latch. I was going to get down and do it."

He sounded nervous. She did as he asked and turned back.

"What are you doing?"

"Plunging."

"In here?" Taylor looked around the old shed. It was mostly taken up with the large cement block shape Pete was standing over. She moved closer and looked over the cement wall which was as high as her chest. Her eyes opened wide. The cement was a crude tank and it was full of red grapes.

"Is this…?"

"The NS18."

She looked up at Pete, his face full of concern.

"Your best grapes in here?" She cast a hand in the air. The shed appeared derelict from the outside and these old grey cement slabs looked awful in comparison to the shiny stainless steel fermenters she was used to in the winery shed.

"This is the best place for them." Pete continued to plunge, his voice coming in short bursts as he moved the handle up and down. "Much better in the cement than the stainless steel."

Taylor watched as he did the last few plunges. His jeans, although not snug, defined the movement of his muscles as did the stretch of his shirt across his shoulders. Her heart beat quicker. She looked away then down at the rich red liquid and turned her mind to that. There'd been no talk of using this old fermenter that she recalled. Still, she wasn't up on all they did – but it was funny that Pete hadn't asked her to help. She looked up at his troubled expression as he made his way back along the plank towards her. Unless he didn't want her to know.

"Have you been keeping this a secret?"

He climbed down from the tank and stood right in front of her. His clear blue eyes studied her closely.

"Only Antoine and I know it's here. And now you."

"But why, I don't understand."

"It's not that big a deal really. I always intended for the NS18 to ferment here. Everyone else assumed it would go in the steel fermenters so I left it at that."

"You're worried Ed will do something?"

Pete shook his head. A pained expression crossed his face. "I don't know what Ed's capable of these days."

"Or me?" She was hurt he couldn't trust her with his precious secret.

"The less who knew the better. There was no need–"

"I'll leave you to it then." She turned away, once more reminded she was of little importance here.

"Taylor, wait." He grabbed her hand. His touch was warm on her chilled fingers. "Please don't go."

She looked back at him. He gazed at her with such longing her heart leapt. She turned. He reached for her other hand and gently pulled her towards him. Slowly they moved together. Their lips met. His were warm and soft, gentle and then more insistent. He wrapped his arms around her, his embrace tender but firm. She slid her hands around his back, her fingers felt his warmth and the solid muscles under his shirt.

He put his hands to her cheeks and gently drew away. Their faces were only centimetres apart. She took in the whiskers that darkened his chin, his lips, his reddened cheeks, his clear blue eyes. They looked back at her with such intensity a shiver ran through her.

"Are you cold?"

"No." She smiled and touched his lips with hers. "Warm as toast."

"I've wanted to do that since nearly the first day I met you."

Taylor drew back a little. Their arms dropped away. "I'm sorry I can't say the same." She frowned. Kissing Pete had felt so right but could she trust her judgement? She'd thought Ed was the one such a short time ago. She shook her head slowly. "I've stuffed so much up."

He leaned in and pressed his lips to hers again. She closed her eyes. No other part of them touched but every part of her responded to his kiss.

He stopped. Her eyes flew open. Once more he was studying her closely, a smile playing on his lips.

"This feels good to me." He kissed her again and once more the shiver went through her. His lips slid over her cheek to her ear and at the same time his arms slid around her. "Tell me when you want me to stop." His murmur was soft, his breath caressed her ear.

Taylor wrapped her arms around him again and this time she didn't let go. Pete backed her towards the wall. Something brushed her neck. She screamed and spun away catching him off-balance. Peter tumbled against the door which flew open behind him. He fell backwards with Taylor on top of him. He gave a groan. She looked at his face just a few centimetres from hers in alarm.

"Are you all right?"

"Winded," he croaked.

Taylor tried to scrabble off of him. Her knee jerked into him. He groaned and curled away from her.

"Oh!" Taylor put one hand to her mouth and the other hovered over his back. "I'm so sorry. Are you okay?"

"Gotta catch my breath." He stayed in the foetal position while Taylor flooded with embarrassment. Her knee had connected with a very delicate part of him.

"I'm so sorry." She bent over him. The gentle pat she gave him on the back seemed so inadequate. "What can I do?"

He sat himself up resting his forearms on his knees and gave her a deadpan look. "You sure know how to slow things down."

"I didn't mean to…at least it wasn't my intention to…" She flapped her hand. "You know."

"I'll live." He got carefully to his feet.

"Can I make you a cup of tea?"

"I'd rather a beer."

"I don't think I have any."

"I do." This time there was a gleam in his eye when he looked at her. "Would you like to come to my place?"

His deep voice had a husky edge to it. Taylor felt a quiver of desire ripple through her.

"Sure, but–"

His lips pressed to hers. "Let's go."

Walking quickly they didn't say a word but each time his arm brushed hers Taylor felt a buzz tingle through her. Once inside his back door he pulled her into his arms and kicked the door shut with his foot. Their hands roamed under their shirts. Taylor could feel the thud of Pete's heart under her hand and she gasped as he slid his inside her bra.

Once more he kissed her and slowly walked her backwards, their bodies pressed together. He stopped inside his bedroom door. She had time to notice a big old wardrobe and a double bed. He sat her on the edge of it, then pulled off his jacket.

Before Taylor could take hers off, he was there doing it for her. She shivered as he slid the jacket down her arms and dropped it to the floor.

"Cold?"

"Not a bit." It was warm in his cottage. She grinned. By the look on his face she would soon be getting even warmer.

He slipped one hand behind her and tugged her shirt from her jeans, all the time gazing at her with his liquid blue eyes. Just that look sent another shiver through her.

"Are you sure you're not cold?" He slid his hands over her bare skin and gently pulled her to him.

"Positive." The word was muffled by his lips, warm, soft and insistent on hers. They tumbled back onto his bed. She was very careful where she put her knees. She didn't want to spoil anything this time.

CHAPTER
50

Edward pulled his four-wheel drive up in front of the quarters. He was actually looking forward to tonight. He'd probably had a lucky escape where Taylor was concerned. At first he'd been annoyed when she'd broken off with him but now he felt a sense of relief. He'd never expected her to follow up on his invitation to come back. Jumping into bed with her might have been fun but as it turned out it could have been awkward

He hadn't wanted her to stay on once she'd called it off but she'd been useful in the end and the business plan idea wasn't a bad one. He and Peter should have made a proper one after their parents had died but somehow time had gone on and things rolled along. He'd even put together most of the information Taylor had asked for. He was sure her plan would match his ideas for Wriggly Creek anyway. Pete would see sense in Edward's expansion ideas and there'd be no need to follow through with the threat to sell out so there was no harm in Taylor having the financial and marketing information.

Edward lifted out the box of pizza ingredients and the esky with the beer. Peter would see he could be reasonable and everything would work out fine. Taylor tugged open the inner door as he opened the screen. Her skin glowed and her hair was damp as if she'd just got out of the shower.

Thankfully, he'd realised she wasn't his type in spite of her appearance. While Felicity had taken it on the chin and moved on he wasn't sure things would have been the same with Taylor. The more he got to know her, he saw more a home-and-family-type person in her than the party girl he'd first thought she was.

"Come in," she said and stepped back as he lugged his contribution to the evening's meal through the doorway. "Pete's not here yet."

Edward put his box on the table and the esky on the floor by the fridge. He lifted the papers from the top of the box and offered them to Taylor. "For the business plan."

"Thanks, Edward." She gave him a grateful smile. "Pete's bringing the rest of his paperwork tonight too. I hope I can work on it over the next few days." She placed the papers on top of the bookcase next to the laptop. "Can I get you a drink?"

"I've brought beer."

"I was hoping someone would. I'm nearly out."

They'd just popped the tops of their cans when Peter arrived. Taylor took the items he brought and put them on the table. He also had a bottle of red which he placed in the middle of the table with a flourish.

"Our new reserve cab sauv to have with our personalised pizza."

"Can't wait to try it." Taylor's eyes shone.

"In the meantime a beer looks good," he said.

"In the esky." Edward sat on the couch.

Peter and Taylor fiddled around in the kitchen behind him. As he turned, Taylor spoke.

"How hungry are you?"

"Not very," Edward said.

"Ravenous." Peter's voice was louder.

Taylor chuckled. "Let's sit for a while, drink our beers and then we can work out what we're going to make from our pooled ingredients." She sat in the old armchair.

Peter took up a position next to Edward on the couch.

"Everything under control in the winery?" Edward asked.

"Yes." Peter took a sip of his beer. "No thanks to you. Haven't seen you since this morning."

"I've been busy. Anyway, you're the one who gave Antoine some time off."

"Only two days." Peter turned away from him to Taylor and lifted his can. "Taylor's been helping."

"And you're covering for Noelene tomorrow." Edward raised an eyebrow. "When do you get time off for good behaviour, Taylor?"

"I guess I haven't been good."

Peter coughed. Taylor's lips rose higher in a broad grin.

Edward gave her a closer look but she put her can to her mouth. He watched her throat move up and down as she swallowed.

"I'll make sure the stock levels are good," he said. "You could get busy, being Easter Saturday. I'll call in but you've got our mobile numbers if you need help."

"I'll come over between jobs," Peter said.

Edward turned to his brother. "I brought the information for the business plan."

Peter studied him a moment as if he was trying to decipher what Edward had said.

Edward looked away. There was something about the way Peter had stared at him, as if he could see through him.

"That's great." Peter took another swig of his beer. "Mine's nearly done. Would have been finished but I got caught up this afternoon."

Taylor gave a hiccupped splutter.

"Without Antoine there's a lot of plunging to be done."

Taylor spat beer down the front of her. She leapt to her feet. "How clumsy I am." She brushed at her jumper and went to the kitchen for a cloth. "I'm hungry all of a sudden." She started setting out the various containers.

Peter rose quickly and joined her. "I'll help you."

Edward followed more slowly. Taylor had been right, between them they had a variety of toppings to add to the pizza bases he'd had in his freezer. Once their creations were in the oven, Peter picked up the bottle of red he'd already taken the cork from.

"Time to try our next reserve cab sauv."

Taylor got out glasses and they all took a seat around the table. Edward watched as Peter poured himself a mouthful, sniffed it and took a sip. He smiled. "I think that's a bloody good drop but I'll let you two judge for yourselves." He lifted the bottle and poured them all a glass.

Edward sniffed his. The blackberry aroma was there with a hint of mint. He tasted and smiled.

Peter reached across and clapped a hand on his shoulder. "Pretty good, wouldn't you say?"

"Well done, little brother." Edward took another sip. He had to hand it to Peter, he could make wine.

"What do you think, Taylor?"

They both looked at her, staring into the contents of her glass. Her cheeks were pink. She shook her head. "I'm sorry."

"What's wrong?" Peter's face fell.

"It tastes good to me."

"Thank goodness," Edward's eyebrows rose. "I was worried we'd have to tip out our reserve cab sauv."

"I don't get all the sniffing and swirling," she said. "Then you reckon you can taste gooseberries–"

"Not in the cab sauv." Peter chuckled.

"Whatever," she said. "I just don't get what you get."

"But you like it?" Peter studied her closely.

Edward noticed the shine in Taylor's eyes as she gazed back at his brother.

"It's delicious."

"Then that's all that matters. Don't worry about tasting black-berries." The moment was broken by another of his hearty chuckles.

Edward glanced from one to the other. What was going on here? It was almost as if there was a hidden conversation between Taylor and Peter that he wasn't part of.

"The pizzas smell good." Taylor stood up to inspect the food in the oven. She got them out and they took turns to cut their own.

"Tomorrow night we should go out for food," Edward said once they'd taken a few mouthfuls of pizza.

"Isn't Donella doing one of her special cook-ups at the hall?" Peter said.

"I believe she is."

"The woman at the Coonawarra store?" Taylor looked from one of them to the other.

"Yes," Peter said. "Every so often she has this big cook-up and the locals go along. It's a fundraiser for the upkeep of the hall. It's usually a good night."

"Sounds like fun." Taylor smiled at Peter.

"It is." He turned to Edward. "Good idea."

Edward nodded. He needed them to be off the property for what he'd organised.

They finished their pizzas in silence. Edward felt a tension in the air. Maybe it was just him but he thought there was more to it. He lifted his eyes and intercepted a look between Taylor and Peter and suddenly he knew. Something had changed between them. He'd tried to put a stop to any possible relationship but he obviously hadn't succeeded.

"Think I'll call it a night." He stood up and put his plate on the sink.

"I've got strawberries and ice-cream," Taylor said.

"No thanks. I'm going to head home." He turned to Peter who'd stood up as well. "Do you want me to do some plunging tomorrow?"

An odd look passed over Peter's face then he grinned. "Sure. Will you do the second shift?"

"No problem." Edward took the remaining beer from his esky and offered it to Taylor. "You keep this."

"Thanks."

"Night," they all chorused and Edward let himself out into the cold night. He put the esky in his four-wheel drive and turned on the engine. He sat a moment not closing the door. He looked back at the quarters, where light shone from the chinks in the curtain. He eased himself from the seat and made his way cautiously back to the big window. There were gaps where the curtain didn't overlap. In the centre of the living area, right where he'd left them, Peter and Taylor were locked in an embrace. He'd been right. He wondered how long they'd been together and he hadn't noticed. At what point had they started a relationship?

Pain knifed its way into his chest. He didn't care for Taylor but neither did he want her to be with Peter. Edward went back to his four-wheel drive and reversed away from the quarters. As he turned his vehicle towards home he slapped the steering wheel and swore loudly at the empty track ahead.

Taylor melted against Peter. Keeping away from him over dinner had been so difficult when all she'd wanted to do was feel his arms around her. Now they were, and his lips were tracing the curve of her neck. She was having trouble concentrating. Her body was reacting to his kisses with a force of its own, just like it had in the shed this afternoon before they'd overbalanced against the door and fallen to the ground.

A chuckle burbled up inside her.

His kisses stopped. "What is it?"

She opened her eyes. "Nothing. I was remembering this afternoon. All that talk about plunging and getting caught up." The chuckle bubbled out into a warm laugh.

Pete laughed too. "Obviously I'm not trying hard enough to distract you."

Taylor put a hand to her mouth. Pete had taken the brunt of their tumble to the ground. They'd both been covered in dirt and Taylor had a large bruise on her elbow.

He kept his arms around her waist. "You should have warned me you play rough. I'd have worn some protection."

Taylor grinned. "I thought you country boys liked a rough-and-tumble."

"That's in the hay." He kissed her nose, one cheek and then the other. "You might not have noticed but we don't have any hay around here."

"Plenty of wine though." She nodded towards the table where they'd left the partly drunk glasses of red. "Your new one is good."

"Are you trying to divert me with wine?"

"Not divert." She smiled. "Just taking it steady. We don't want another accident."

"The couch should be safe enough." Pete sat.

"Just a minute." Taylor collected their glasses, came back and sat beside him. "It's a shame to not drink your wine now that I'm getting a taste for it."

They gazed at each other as they drank. Taylor felt the heat rise inside her. Her attempt to put on the brakes wasn't working. Pete put down his glass. He took hers and placed it carefully beside his. Then he slid his hands beneath her and eased her onto his lap. He kissed her again.

"I'd like a follow up with a repeat of what happened after the accident."

She looked steadily into his clear blue eyes. The longing she saw there reflected her own. "So would I." She leaned in and kissed him.

Taylor laid her head on Pete's solid chest and listened to the steady beat of his heart and the regular rhythm of his breathing. They were in her little cell of a room on her single bed. She tipped her head slightly and studied his face. There was a hint of first light coming from the window above the bed but she could see no more than his outline. She liked to think he looked content. She knew she was.

Cass's voice played in her head. "It's lust, not love." Taylor smiled. If that was the case, Peter Starr had performed the best lusting she'd ever experienced. Their first love making yesterday afternoon had been rushed. Last night they'd explored each other's bodies eagerly, leaving a trail of clothes over her bedroom floor, but with a gentleness too. This time they'd taken it steady and neither of them had wanted to spoil the night with a repeat of their tangle at the shed. Afterwards they'd joked about that. Pete had a warm sense of humour. They'd talked for a long time about all kinds of things before they'd drifted off to sleep, comfortable in each other's arms.

He'd thought it best to keep their fledgling relationship to themselves and she'd agreed. She hadn't told him about Ed's saying she was just another of Pete's rescue projects and she wasn't planning to. She didn't want to do anything that might upset the tenuous truce there seemed to be between the Starr men.

Her finger traced the side of his face. She felt the prickles of his day-old beard, the softness of his lips. His mouth opened and sucked the end of her finger.

"Good morning," she whispered.

"Good morning yourself." He turned to face her. His kisses roamed down her neck, across her shoulders until she could think of nothing else.

Pete showered and pulled on some fresh clothes. He pictured Taylor's beautiful smile as she'd kissed him goodbye this morning. When they'd finally dragged themselves out of her bed they'd sat side-by-side in the kitchen eating toast and coffee together. He'd had trouble keeping his hands off her. He loved everything about her – her hair, her skin, the way her cheeks went pink when she was embarrassed, the way her eyebrows raised in surprise. He'd studied every little thing she did for so long but now they'd explored each other's bodies he felt as if he knew the real Taylor. It was as if he'd known her forever. They were good together. He hadn't wanted to leave but there was work to do.

They'd have to be careful around Ed for a while. He'd been particularly vicious when he'd thought they'd been together before. Pete hadn't been able to admit his interest in Taylor even to himself back then. Now that he'd taken the next step he wanted to protect what they had together. He didn't want his brother to have the chance to put a damper on what he had with Taylor, not yet.

Pete stepped out his back door, gave a long look towards the quarters then set off to the winery. He wanted to do the first round of plunging for the morning, including the NS18, and be well out of the way before Ed turned up to do the next plunge. The NS18 was another thing he didn't want Ed to know about for now. Pete had never changed the board in the office. The first lot of cab sauv had been pressed and stored in the tank that said NS18. They'd barrel it next week. Ed hadn't asked what stage in the process the new cab sauv was up to. Pete hoped that meant he'd given up on selling it but he still had a niggle of a doubt.

He unlocked the winery door and went into his office. He wasn't good at keeping secrets. At least over Easter there was no Felicity keeping her sharp eye on things and Noelene wouldn't be back till tomorrow. With any luck he wouldn't cross paths with Ed until dinner tonight and then they'd be with a big group of locals. The NS18 shouldn't even get a mention.

Edward tucked his phone back into his pocket with a smile. At least something was working out. All he had to do was make some excuse why he couldn't go with Peter and Taylor to Coonawarra tonight and he'd be right. They'd probably be happy without his company anyway. In fact they might want to stay home. He'd have to make sure they didn't do that.

He flexed his arms. With Taylor here he hadn't done as much plunging as he usually did. His left arm was being a bit dodgy. At least he'd made the effort to help today and Antoine would be back tomorrow.

Edward checked the time. They'd have to open the cellar door soon and he'd promised to top-up stocks. He jumped in his four-wheel drive and drove along the track past Peter's cottage to the winery. Peter was coming from the round the back of the barrel shed. Edward slowed to a stop and lowered his window.

"Everything okay?" he asked.

"Fine. Just doing the rounds."

"Whatever floats your boat. I'm going to check stock and make sure the cellar door's ready to go for Taylor."

"Great. Thanks."

"Looking forward to Donella's dinner tonight?"

"Yeah."

Edward had to make sure Peter had no excuse for him and Taylor not to go.

"Taylor's really looking forward to it," he said. "She's cooked so much for us she'll appreciate someone else's cooking."

"Yeah." Peter nodded his head. He looked distracted. "Catch you later." He went round the back of the four-wheel drive and on to the fermenting shed.

Edward drove on. When he reached the end of the track he saw Felicity's car out the front of the office. She was just coming out the front door. She locked it and gave him a wave. Once more he lowered his window, the passenger side this time.

Felicity paused then she leaned in. "Hello, Edward," she purred.

"Don't tell me you're working?"

"No, I…I dropped off a little something in the lunchroom. I was going to text you tomorrow. It was going to be a surprise."

"That's good of you. Sorry to spoil it."

"Doesn't matter." She smiled widely, her perfect white teeth a sharp contrast to the bright red lipstick she wore.

He lifted his finger in a wave and drove on. No doubt Noelene would have chocolates tomorrow as well. He should go into town and get something for them. Perhaps later, if there was time. First he had to make sure everything was in place for tonight.

Pete took Taylor's hand as they stepped out into the chilly air. It was wonderful to feel his touch. They'd been so careful all night to act like friends rather than lovers. Ed hadn't come with them so that had made it easier.

No sooner were they inside Peter's ute than he reached across and kissed her. Taylor's lips responded.

When they came up for air Pete took a strand of hair from her face and tucked it carefully behind her ear. "I hadn't thought we'd stay so late. I've been busting to do this all night."

"Take my hair out of my eyes?"

"This."

His lips met hers again. They kissed hungrily this time. Taylor felt a little shiver as he slid his hands inside her shirt; partly because his hands were cold but partly because they felt so wonderful against her skin. She tried to get closer. The console was in her way.

"Arrgh!" Pete growled. "Let's get home."

"Your place or mine?" Taylor gave him a flirty look.

"Mine. I've got more room and I've changed the sheets."

"I'm guessing that's a good thing." Taylor hadn't taken any notice of the state of his sheets last time she was there. She'd been too busy noticing Pete and how well their bodies worked together. She leaned back against her seat and groaned. "That food was fantastic but I wish I hadn't had a second serve of that delicious apple crumble."

"Donella's famous for her food."

"There were a lot of people there. I don't know how she did it."

"I see Howard and Margaret had you bailed up for a while."

"They wanted to know more about me. I think they were fishing for gossip. Here I am living with three men and what are my intentions?"

"What indeed." He chuckled. "Margaret has been known to make up what she doesn't know about people."

Taylor laughed too. "I think I've probably given her enough information to make a good story that could possibly involve Antoine."

Once more Pete's warm chuckle filled the ute. "We'll find out soon enough, no doubt."

Taylor looked out at the vines lit by the headlights on either side of the highway. Most of the grapes were gone and many of the leaves had changed colour. During the daytime the scene was full of colour from bright yellow to deep red. It was just over a month since she'd arrived here looking for Ed. She glanced at Pete. She felt guilty about Ed now. It was a part of her life she'd like to forget and yet it had led her to Peter.

He glanced back at her. "What are you smiling at?"

"You." She reached across and patted his leg. He took her hand and held it tight.

"It was good to meet a few more people tonight."

"You do like it here, don't you?" He let go of her hand to change gears.

The lights of the ute illuminated the front of the cellar door as Pete turned off the highway and onto the road leading to the winery.

Taylor wanted to say she loved it, she loved him, but she didn't want to scare him in the first five minutes. "I enjoy the cellar door work the most, although I do like helping you with the plunging." She gave him a wicked look.

"Let's get you home," he said.

Pete slowed to a stop in front of the winery gates he'd locked on the way out. Taylor watched him stride to the gate. He stopped when he got there, bent forward as if he was looking at something then swung the gates open. Instead of coming back to the vehicle he stepped into the yard and stared ahead. She was about to get out when he turned and hurried back to the ute.

"What's up?"

"I am sure I locked the gate but the padlock wasn't through the chain. The gate just pushed open."

Pete drove the ute through and pulled up again. He jumped out leaving his door open. Taylor shivered as the cold night air seeped inside the cab. Finally Pete came back.

"It's secure now." He moved the ute forward. "Maybe Ed came through after us."

"Wouldn't he go out his driveway on the other side, save locking gates?"

"Usually. Perhaps I didn't lock it properly."

"I wonder why he didn't come tonight? He was the one who suggested it."

"Got a better offer, he said." Pete stopped the ute at his front door. "Coming inside?"

Taylor jumped out and rubbed her hands together. "I hope it's warmer."

"I've got a slow-combustion fire. I left it going."

They ran up the steps. He put his key in the lock and pushed it open.

Taylor went to step forward but he put out his arm.

She turned to look at him. He had a strange expression on his face. Suddenly he bent and scooped her up.

She gave a cry. "What are you doing?"

"Welcoming you to my home." He carried her inside, kicked the door shut with his boot and kept walking.

"Isn't this for new brides?"

"I don't care," he said. "I wanted to do it."

"You do remember I've been here before?"

"How could I forget?"

Taylor wrapped her arms around his neck and enjoyed the feel of his strong arms carrying her back to his delightfully cosy bed.

CHAPTER
52

Pete slid from his bed. Taylor stirred and rolled over. He paused. Her pretty blue eyes remained shut. She was the best thing that had happened to him in a long time, and not just in bed. They worked well together, laughed at the same jokes and she'd developed a love of Wriggly Creek. He plucked a strand of her flyaway hair from her cheek and draped it with the rest fluffed around her on the pillow. Her sweet pink lips parted a little as she breathed out – he bent closer then stopped. It wasn't fair to wake her. They'd had a late night. He fought the urge to jump back into bed and wake her with a long, slow kiss. His body went into overdrive at the thought.

He took his clothes from the floor, pulled the door to behind him and made his way to the kitchen. It was built across the back of the cottage making it a dining-cum-family room as well. The cold room was nearly as good as a cold shower. He tugged on his clothes and bent to inspect the fire. It was out. The day would warm up. No point in lighting it again until tonight. He'd have to find time to collect some more wood soon. He only had a small pile left over from last year.

He boiled the kettle and made a coffee. He wanted to get the first lot of plunging done. It was only the reserve cab sauv in the stainless steel fermenter now and the new cab sauv in the cement fermenter. Once Antoine came back he'd have help again. He took some slurps of coffee while he pulled on his socks and boots. Damn, it was cold all of a sudden. He gave one more thought to Taylor snug and warm in his bed, tugged on his beanie and set off to the winery.

Not far from the shed that housed the new wine tanks he paused. He could see one of the doors was partly open. He moved closer, unease worming through his chest. There was a hose protruding from the gap and a red stain all over the ground. He covered the last few metres in quick strides. His brain couldn't comprehend what his eyes were seeing. A hose lay at his feet, red wine soaked into the dirt around it. He threw open the door and followed the hose to the second tank. Still not sure exactly what had happened here he checked the tank. It was empty, barring the last layer of wine at the very bottom.

Pete staggered back. He looked around and then down at his boots which had left a muddy wine trail across the floor. He plucked his phone from his pocket and selected Ed's name. It took a while for his brother to answer.

"What time do you call this?" Ed's voice was croaky.

"We've been robbed."

"Is this a joke?"

"No joke, Edward." Pete looked around at his tanks. There could be others that were empty. He hadn't thought of that. "Get over to the winery. Someone's stolen our cab sauv and who knows what else."

By the time he heard Ed's vehicle pull up outside, Pete had checked the other tanks. They were all full. He'd also checked the fermenters. Everything was as it should be, even the NS18.

He went out to meet Ed waving his mobile as he went. "I've called the police."

"Was that necessary?"

"A whole tank of cab sauv is gone. I'd call that necessary, wouldn't you?"

Ed looked down at the wine-stained dirt and went to step past. Pete put a hand to his brother's chest. "I've already been clambering around in there. Probably better if we let the police take a look before we do any more."

Ed shook his head. "I can't believe it. How?" He turned towards the gate. "You'd need a tanker to steal that much wine. How did they get in?"

Pete started walking towards the gate. "Did you go through here last night?"

"No."

"When we got back from the dinner, I found the gate wasn't locked but I swear I did it properly when we left."

They set off towards the gate, Ed slightly ahead.

"Did you notice anything when you came through? You would have driven right past the shed."

"I would have noticed a bloody tanker, that's for sure." Pete thought about it. He and Taylor had been so intent on getting back to his place he'd hardly taken in anything else once he'd locked the gate behind them.

They came to a stop in front of the gate. It was padlocked like he'd left it last night. He got out his key to open it just as a police car turned onto the track from the road.

He flung the gates open in time with Ed's string of expletives.

Half an hour later, Pete huddled over coffee in the lunchroom waiting for CIB officers to arrive from the Mount. The policeman was young and new to the area. He'd called in reinforcements immediately. He was still outside keeping the crime area secure or some such thing.

Ed came through from the back of the winery. "Everything's okay out there."

"I made you a coffee."

"Thanks." Ed sat down beside him.

Pete clutched the mug, trying to draw some warmth from it. "Our insurance should cover this, shouldn't it?"

"Of course but I thought you would have been more concerned. They've taken our top-of-the-range cab sauv."

"Top of the range?"

"Your bloody next-best-thing-for-the-Coonawarra icon wine. The NS18."

Pete gave him a guilty look. "It's still fermenting."

"You've got it on the board in there." Ed jerked his thumb over his shoulder. "I just checked."

Pete sat back. He'd never changed the whiteboard map. It was still labelled as NS18. Perhaps whoever had stolen it thought they were getting the NS18. He felt sick.

Ed scratched at his neck. "If it's not the NS18 that's gone, what was it?" His face was unshaven and his long hair had fallen forward over one eye. With the frown on his face it gave him a sinister appearance.

Pete studied him carefully. "The wine that was stolen was our entry-level cab sauv."

Ed stood up bumping the table. "What have you done with the NS18 now?"

"Nothing. It's still fermenting."

"Why don't you keep that bloody whiteboard up to date?" Ed waved one hand wildly towards the door.

Pete stood up too. "Maybe it's just as well I didn't."

"Why do you say that?"

"Because someone's stolen a whole tank of wine. The one that was marked on the whiteboard in my office with NS18."

"So you don't think it was pot luck?"

Pete sank to his chair and put his head in his hands. "Maybe not," he muttered. He really didn't want to think about the implications of someone looking at that whiteboard.

"But that would mean…" Ed thumped the table and swore. "That would mean it would have to be someone who had access to your office."

Pete looked up at his brother with a heavy heart. "Yes."

The front door opened and footsteps echoed across the office.

"Pete?" Taylor's voice was tinged with worry. She burst into the lunchroom and stopped as she looked from Pete to Ed and back again.

"What's going on? I saw the policeman and thought someone was hurt. He's got yellow tape everywhere."

"No-one's hurt yet." Ed smashed his fist into the palm of his hand.

Pete grimaced. "Some wine's been stolen."

"Oh no." Taylor crossed the room and wrapped her arms around his neck. She leaned forward and brushed her lips over his cheek.

He took her hands in his and gave them a firm pat. "It's only wine. No-one's hurt."

"I see you two have obviously become close friends."

Pete looked up into Ed's dark-blue eyes. A scowl twisted his brother's face making him look even more sinister.

Pete reached around and drew Taylor close beside him. He stood up so his arm was around her waist. "Yes, we are." He kissed the top of Taylor's head. "Very close."

Ed glared at him but Pete didn't look away. He'd hoped to break their news gently but there was no way round it now. Ed would have to deal with it.

Once more the sound of the front door opening distracted Pete.

"Mr Starr?" a deep voice called.

"Yes." Ed and Pete answered together.

The policeman stuck his head into the room. "CIB are here. They'd like you to come outside."

CHAPTER

53

"What a mess." Pete sat in front of the fire, his head resting on his hands.

Taylor's heart ached for him. It had been a terrible day. Not at all what she'd thought her Easter Sunday would be. Instead of a leisurely breakfast with Pete and eating chocolate eggs she'd spent her time answering questions, making cups of coffee and helping Noelene at the cellar door. Taylor thought ruefully about the chocolate eggs she had stashed at the quarters.

"What a day." She sat on the seat next to him and held her hands to the fire. Music played. She'd have liked to turn it off. It was Pete's choice and it wasn't very relaxing. She glanced at him. "Thank goodness Antoine's back."

He murmured something but he didn't look up.

Taylor reached out and squeezed his shoulder. "There's nothing more you can do now."

He lifted his head and stared at the fire. "Who did this? That's what bothers me more than anything."

"The police will sort it out."

"I'm sure they will."

Taylor put her head to one side. "Don't you want to find out?"

"That will be the terrible part." Pete turned the full force of his clear blue eyes to her. She saw the despair on his face. It frightened her.

"What's the matter, Pete?"

"It has to be someone we know, someone close, someone who has a very good idea of what happens day-to-day at our winery."

"Does it?" Taylor had imagined a faceless stranger stealing the wine.

"The place wasn't broken in to."

"Couldn't they have come from the gate on Ed's side of the property?" She remembered the first night Ed had brought her to his place at Wriggly Creek. His gate had been open then and he hadn't shut it, let alone locked it.

"They'd have to drive right through the property, past Ed's house, my place. Anyway the track isn't really wide enough for a truck. The police checked. They didn't find any tyre tracks."

"Maybe someone left the main winery gate unlocked."

"Maybe they did." His eyes narrowed.

"On purpose, you mean?"

"I am sure I locked the gate when we went to Coonawarra but it wasn't locked when we got back."

"But who...?" Taylor felt a chill run through her despite the fire. Now she knew what Pete meant. A log slipped inside the fire sending up a spray of sparks and the thudding beat of the music seemed to grow louder.

"It wasn't me and it wasn't you."

She gave him a little smile. "I'm glad you've ruled us out."

Pete turned his gaze back to the fire. "But that only leaves Antoine and Ed."

Taylor studied his profile. His jaw was clenched.

"Or Ben, or Noelene, or Felicity." She tapped her fingers.

"None of them have a motive."

"Why would Antoine do it?"

"That's the problem." Once more Pete turned his sad gaze on her. "I don't think he did."

"So you think it's…" Taylor couldn't bring herself to say it.

"Edward. My brother is the only one with a motive."

"Why would he steal his own wine?"

"Yes, tell me why I'd do that?"

They both leapt to their feet. Edward was standing in the entrance to the lobby that led to the back door. He grasped a sixpack of beer to his chest.

"I knocked," he said, "but you were obviously so caught up in your conspiracy theory you didn't hear me."

The two brothers glared at each other.

"Why don't we sit down and have a drink," Taylor said. "It's been a long day."

"That's what I thought." Ed didn't look in her direction. He kept his glare on Pete. "Now I'm more interested in finding out why my brother thinks I would steal my own wine."

Pete sighed. "Come and sit down."

"I'd rather stand thanks, better to face my accuser on my feet."

"All right, Edward." Pete took a couple of steps towards his brother. His voice rose a notch. The music continued to thud around them. "I'll tell you why I think you're the one who stole the wine. You've been trying to sell the NS18 since before it was picked."

"But it wasn't the NS18 that was stolen." Ed's voice was low, controlled. "Why would I steal a tank of entry-level cab sauv?"

"You said yourself you thought the tank held the NS18."

"I didn't know that for sure. You keep swapping things round without telling anyone."

"Perhaps that's just as well if people are going to help themselves to it."

"And when was I to get the opportunity to drive my tanker in and spend the time it would take to empty the tank?"

"I didn't say you actually did it, but you could have organised it."

"Why would I do that, Peter?"

"Insurance?"

"What about it?"

"You've been trying to raise money. Perhaps you arranged for someone else to take it. You were here alone last night. You made sure we were out of the way."

A flicker of surprise passed over Ed's face.

"You arranged for us to go for dinner," Pete said. "Then you stayed home. There was no-one else here."

Ed's eyes opened wide. "I wasn't stealing wine."

"What were you doing Ed?"

"I…" Ed lifted his spare hand in the air and let it drop. "It doesn't matter now."

The head-banging music thudded but no-one spoke.

Taylor looked from Pete's sad face to Ed's wounded expression. Her heart ached for these two men. They looked so lost.

"Have you eaten, Ed?" she asked softly. "We had soup and toast. I could get you some."

He turned his dark eyes on her. There was no sign of the self-assured arrogant Ed.

"No thanks." He looked back at Pete. "You might be interested to know the police rang just before I came over. A delivery truck driver saw a tanker turning off our road onto the highway at about four o'clock this morning. They're hopeful it's only a matter of time until they track it down. I was in my bed at that time but of course I don't have an alibi like you." He looked from Pete to Taylor and left.

The music thumped on.

Edward strode out of Peter's backyard. The lights were on at the quarters. No doubt Antoine was there. Edward had gone to Peter's because he hadn't wanted to be alone. He'd even put aside his annoyance at knowing Peter and Taylor were a couple. Antoine would be company at least. Edward hesitated then turned right on the track that led back to his house.

He was too angry now. He needed thinking time. He couldn't believe his own brother was accusing him of theft. Perhaps he'd earned Peter's distrust but Edward was astounded to think Peter could believe he'd go as far as to organise to steal their own wine. The reverse hadn't entered his head. Edward was quite sure Peter had nothing to do with it. But he had come to the same conclusion as Peter and the police. The obvious person to organise the theft of their wine had to be someone who knew their winery well.

Edward looked up at the full moon. It lit up the vineyard. You'd have to be very daring to carry out a theft with the place so full of light. Either that or desperate. The path to his house was almost as clear as daylight.

Edward let himself inside and slammed the back door behind him. He'd gone over to tell Peter the real reason he'd got him off the property but he'd been too angry and hurt to bother. He also felt a little bit guilty if the truth be known. He'd let the mechanic out through the main winery gate. Edward had been in a hurry. It must have been him who hadn't locked the gate properly. He'd told the police that. It was a help in establishing a timeline for the theft.

He'd been in the winery workshop until just before Peter and Taylor had arrived home. His rush to shut the gate had made him careless. Not that it mattered now. The theft had to have occurred in the early hours of the morning and Peter was sure he'd locked the gate. The lock wasn't tampered with so someone had used a key. Edward thought of all the people who had a key to that gate. He couldn't believe any of them were wine thieves.

Peter returned to his chair in front of the fire. He was aware of Taylor moving around but neither of them spoke. She put on another CD. Something from his jazz collection blared from the speakers. She turned the sound down and put another log in the combustion fire.

Finally she came and knelt in front of him, placing her hands on his lap.

"Can I get you a drink?"

He shook his head.

"Pete?"

He lifted his gaze to hers. Once more a strand of her hair had fallen across one eye. He carefully tucked it behind her ear.

"You don't really think Ed is capable of this, do you?"

"I don't want to but everything points to him."

"There's got to be another explanation." She put a hand to his cheek.

Pete closed his eyes at her gentle touch and covered her hand with his. "I wish I knew what it was."

"The police will find out. Ed's a lot of things but I can't believe he'd steal from Wriggly Creek. I've read the things he wrote for the business plan. His heart is here."

"He might write that on paper but it's not how he acts. He wants to sell his share!"

Taylor raised herself up on her knees. He drew her to him and they wrapped their arms around each other.

"You've got to fix this, Pete," she murmured into his shoulder. "You're brothers and Wriggly Creek needs both of you."

Pete closed his eyes again. A picture of his parents popped into his head. What would they make of this mess?

CHAPTER
54

Taylor and Pete walked into the back room of the cellar door hand-in-hand. Noelene greeted them with a smile that split her face from ear to ear.

"I'm so glad to see you two have worked it out at last." She hugged them both in such a tight crush Taylor thought she'd lose her breath. Noelene gave one final squeeze and released them.

"I did think you were close yesterday but of course with the theft and police and hoo-ha I didn't get a chance to say anything. I saw Margaret in the street this morning and she seemed to think you and Antoine were an item, Taylor. Talk about getting the wrong end of the stick."

Taylor smiled as she felt Pete squeeze her hand.

"Every person I saw wanted to know about the robbery. It's all over town. We'll probably have a few locals at the cellar door today trying to get all the gossip."

"How are you, Noelene?" Pete managed to get a word in finally.

"I'm fine. Why?" Her eyebrows arched.

"No particular reason. Anything that needs doing here?"

"All ready." Noelene turned to the coffee machine. "Still half an hour before opening. I was going to make a cuppa. Would you two like one?"

"Let me make it." Taylor reached for the cups. "You have a rest for a minute."

Noelene and Pete sat on the bar stools they'd had out the front for the business plan session. That seemed so long ago now, Taylor thought.

"Do you have any ideas about who might have taken the wine?" Noelene asked.

Taylor glanced at Pete.

He screwed up his face. "I did think it may have been Ed."

Noelene gave a hearty laugh. "You're joking."

"Not really." Pete's shoulders dropped. "He had motive and opportunity."

Noelene laughed again. "Since when have you become a policeman? Ed wouldn't steal from his own business. Nor anyone else's for that matter." She stared at Pete. "Are you serious? You'd really accuse your brother?"

"I already have."

"Oh, for goodness sake." Noelene slid to her feet. "I suppose you two have had another barney."

"Let's say I'm not his favourite brother at the moment."

"I don't blame him." She wagged her finger at Pete. "And before you tell me I always take his side that's not true either. You two are so lucky to have each other. And after everything you've been through you should be close."

Taylor handed out the coffees.

They all looked up at the sound of the screen door opening. Ed paused at the sight of them.

"I thought you'd taken up talking to yourself, Noelene."

"Come in." Noelene took him by the arm and dragged him forward. "I've just been hearing there's some sorting out to be done."

"I don't think so," Ed growled.

"I know so." Noelene crossed her arms. "Starting with Peter wanting to apologise to you."

Taylor took a breath. Would Pete do it? Last night he'd made such wonderful gentle love to her she thought her heart would burst from loving him back. This morning he'd been so sad. They'd talked it over and she knew he was feeling bad about accusing Ed.

"Well?" Noelene tapped her foot.

Taylor wondered at her approach. They were grown men not a pair of schoolboys.

Pete stood. "I was wrong to accuse you, Edward." He held out his hand. "I'm sorry."

Taylor held her breath. Ed's expression didn't look forgiving.

"There's been so much happening lately, I–"

"No." Noelene cut Pete off. "No excuses. You two need to put all your cards on the table. Be honest with each other. There's no time like the present. Taylor and I will take our coffee into the other room."

Taylor followed obediently. Now she had some understanding as to why Pete and Ed did as they were told when it came from Noelene. The older woman shut the internal door once Taylor was through then they found a patch of sunshine streaming through the window onto one end of the counter and stopped there with their coffees.

"Did you use to be a teacher?" Taylor asked.

Noelene chuckled. "Good heavens no, whatever gave you that idea?"

"Just wondered."

"This theft thing has really set the cat amongst the pigeons. I hope those two boys can sort things out. And no matter what the police say I can't believe this has been an inside job."

Taylor had her own theory on that but with all the finger-pointing that had happened already she wasn't keen to air her thoughts.

Noelene chatted on. Taylor found it hard to concentrate. She badly wanted to know how Pete and Ed were getting on. She could hear the murmur of voices from time to time but no shouting at least. Hopefully that was a good sign.

As it drew close to opening time Noelene buzzed around making sure everything was in readiness even though Taylor could see it already was. The door opened. Pete and Ed came into the cellar door. Taylor looked from one to the other. They weren't smiling but they didn't look angry either.

"Well?"

Ed held up his hand. "Don't push it, Noelene. We've made a start. Let's leave it at that until this mess is sorted out."

"And Taylor has finished the business plan." Pete reached for her hand and gave it a squeeze.

Taylor smiled at him. He leaned on the counter next to her.

"Has anyone heard anything more from the police?" Noelene asked.

"Not me," Ed said.

Pete shook his head. "We've told them everything we know. They've interviewed anyone with a connection."

Noelene blew out a breath. "It was hardly an interview. I think they only asked me three questions. It took five minutes."

"They know it isn't you who stole the wine," Pete said.

Noelene lifted her chin and pushed out her chest. "I could be the mastermind behind it."

"They've spoken to everyone and come up with nothing," Ed said.

"Except the tanker that was seen." Pete straightened up. "Hopefully they'll track it down."

"It could be anywhere by now." Ed's tone was dismissive.

"And I did notice a vehicle a few nights back stopped in our driveway."

"So did I." Taylor thought back to the night she'd seen the headlights illuminate Pete and how sad they'd both been then. At least things had improved personally for them.

"I told the police about it," Pete said. "But who knows, it could have been someone checking the place out or someone who was lost."

"Did they interview Felicity?" Noelene asked.

"I gave them her details," Ed said. "But she wasn't at work over the weekend so I don't think they were that interested."

"Neither were Ben or Antoine." They all turned to look at Taylor. "You said the police interviewed them, didn't you Pete?"

"Yes, but Ed's right. This wouldn't have anything to do with Felicity either."

Taylor took a breath. There were things that didn't add up with Felicity. "I think you may be dismissing her too soon."

"Don't be ridiculous, Taylor. If the truth be known I think you've been a bit jealous of Felicity."

Noelene looked at Ed and gave a snort. "What?"

"Ed's right in a way." Taylor bit her bottom lip. "This is a bit awkward but when I was with Ed I was a bit jealous of Felicity. I could see how she doted on you, Ed, and you played up to her."

"I'm only joking," he said. "She knows that."

"Does she?" Noelene asked. "You do realise she got her boobs enlarged and she still dyes her hair."

Both Ed and Pete howled her down.

"You know her better than anyone, Ed," Noelene said. "Didn't you notice when you came back from holidays after Pete had employed her? She had bigger…" Noelene pointed at her breasts.

Ed's mouth fell open. "I did wonder."

"And she does dye her hair," Taylor said. "You can tell."

"You can?" Pete ran his fingers through his own hair.

"I think she did it to impress you, Ed," Noelene said. "She made herself into your type."

"I've got a type?"

"Good figure, decent boobs, blonde hair…" Noelene's voice trailed away.

Taylor shifted from foot to foot. Her cheeks felt warm.

"Felicity would do anything for you." Noelene broke the silence.

"That's ridiculous." He gave Pete a sheepish look. "We were an item once but that's a long time ago."

Taylor looked up. She met Ed's gaze. "She was in love with you. But now I wonder if she's turned against you."

"I think Taylor's right," Noelene said.

"We all know you're not a fan of Felicity's."

"You are a bit blind where she's concerned, Ed."

"Rubbish."

"And you Pete, if the truth be known."

"Hang on." Pete put an arm around Taylor. "Leave me out of this."

"She flutters her eyelashes at both of you," Taylor said. "But I do think it was you she was after, Ed. No doubt there was a time when if you'd asked her to walk on hot coals she'd probably have done it."

"Rubbish," Ed said again. "She knows there's no future with me."

"She does now." Noelene's eyebrows arched. "Maybe this is payback."

"For what? Having a fling with me." Ed shook his head. "Felicity runs the office well but she doesn't know much about what happens beyond it."

"You'd be surprised," Noelene said.

"I agree. You underestimate her." Taylor looked up at Pete. "You said the other day she never leaves the office but I've seen her around the winery several times."

"Probably looking for one of us," Ed said.

Pete frowned. "She always rings me when she wants me and if she can't find me she writes the message in the book."

Ed shrugged. "Ditto I guess but–"

"I've caught her listening in on conversations." Noelene looked from Ed to Pete. "She's a nosy parker."

"That doesn't make her a thief." Ed puffed out his chest. "Nor does once having a crush on me make her one."

Taylor looked at Ed. "I know you'll think I'm being paranoid but one night outside your place, I was sure I saw someone in the shadows. And the next day Felicity seemed to know a lot about our personal relationship."

"You think she was peeping through the windows?" Ed snorted. "Listening at doors?"

Even Pete raised his eyebrows at her.

No matter what they said Taylor felt something wasn't right about Felicity. "What if she was doing her best to cause trouble?"

"What would that achieve?"

"I don't know. I was just thinking she might have been the one to take the message from Mr Cheng that you never got."

"You know we have had a few orders go astray lately," Pete said. "Things I've needed for the lab. Only minor but a nuisance. And our new barrels were late coming. She'd ordered them but when I rang they hadn't received the order."

"We didn't get much summer rain either," Ed said. "Surely we can't blame it all on Felicity."

"Do either of you know a Mr Archer?"

Pete shook his head but Ed stared at Taylor. His eyes narrowed.

"I do," he said. "How do you know him?"

"I don't. But he was in Felicity's office on Thursday. He was leaning in close and Felicity seemed flustered. She's not usually so—"

"What was he doing in the office?" Ed cut her off.

"I don't know. Looking for you? She said she'd leave you a message. Only I think he was one of the men I saw that day looking at the NS18 from the road. You remember, Pete? I told you about it. He was a big man with no hair."

Ed gripped the counter. His face was pale.

"Who is this Archer bloke?" Pete asked.

Ed looked up at his brother. "The guy who was going to buy the NS18."

Pete's arm tightened around Taylor's waist.

Noelene put a hand on Ed's shoulder. "What have you done, Edward?"

"Nothing." He shook off her hand and leaned closer to Pete. "You picked the grapes and stashed them away. I had to call it off. I told him we could sell him some other grapes another time. I didn't know he'd called in the other day. Felicity certainly didn't…" His hand went to his head. "Felicity was in the office on Saturday. She said she'd left us a surprise. I assumed she'd meant Easter eggs but come to think of it I didn't notice any. Did you?" He looked at Pete.

"No, something's not right here, is it? We should tell the police."

Taylor saw a car cruise to a stop in the car park. "You can tell them now. They're here."

"Oh, look at the time," Noelene yelped. "I haven't put the sign out yet."

CHAPTER
55

Taylor cooked them dinner that night at the quarters. Noelene stayed to eat with them and Antoine was there. Taylor could see that Pete, and Ed especially, were still shocked by the news the police had brought. Felicity had been the insider for the wine theft. The information they were able to give the police helped them tidy up the loose ends. Felicity had been taken to Mount Gambier police station and the Archer guy was being tracked down in Adelaide.

Everyone but Taylor, who was checking the roast, was sitting around the table.

Pete got up to hand out beers. "I can't believe this Archer bloke thought he could steal our wine and it wouldn't be noticed."

"Thieves are usually the kind of people who think they'll get away with it." Noelene popped the top on her can.

"He was under pressure from his employer to get a quality Coonawarra cab sauv," Ed said. "He thought he had ours."

"And when he didn't, he stole it." Pete shook his head.

"So how did he connect with Felicity?" Antoine asked.

Noelene leaned in. "Margaret heard from someone who'd been speaking to the new policeman that they'd met some time before."

"Here we go." Ed pressed his fingers up and down against his thumb like a quacking duck.

"Need any help?" Pete was at Taylor's elbow as she stirred the gravy.

"All good, thanks." She gave him a quick kiss. He kissed her back.

"Oh, can you two get a room," Ed groaned.

"Leave them be, Edward." Noelene said. "You'll find the right woman someday soon."

"Yeah, well, I haven't been too good a judge, have I?"

"I can't believe the beautiful mademoiselle Felicity is a villain." Antoine shook his head.

"She had you fooled as well." Noelene gave a smug nod.

"I still don't really understand why," Pete said. "She told the police Archer had been paying her for some time."

"That would explain the expensive car and the flash clothes," Noelene said.

"She didn't admit it," Pete continued, "but they think she and Archer were lovers."

Taylor shuddered at the thought of them together. It took all kinds. "What was he paying her for?" she asked.

"To feed him information." Ed took up the story. "Evidently he wanted more than just a tank of wine." Ed paused. "Archer got wind that we," he glanced at Pete, "I might be selling. He had his eye on taking over our winery."

"And Felicity was helping him," Pete added. "I thought she liked us."

"She did," Noelene said. "In fact she loved Edward."

"Funny way of showing it," Ed grumbled.

"Her love wasn't reciprocated. Not in the way she'd hoped. I imagine she'd planned to be Mrs Edward Starr."

"Really?" Ed shook his head. "She knew it was over between us."

"You know what they say about a woman scorned."

They all looked at each other. Taylor could easily picture the Felicity she knew scheming to get back at Ed.

"Archer must have come along at the right time and she saw a way to get back at you. To hurt you like she'd been hurt," Noelene said.

They all sipped their drinks. Taylor turned back to the gravy, gave it a final stir then set it aside. She took another sip of the red Pete had poured for her. It slipped smoothly down her throat. She was starting to prefer it over beer. Especially now the weather was cooler. Everyone was silent, no doubt contemplating the turn of events. Taylor tried to think of something to lighten the moment.

"I know it's probably not appropriate," she said, "but I had a string of 'F' words for Felicity and I've just thought of another."

"No swearing." Ed raised his eyebrows.

"Felonious Felicity."

Ed's eyebrows went higher. Pete and Antoine smirked while Noelene laughed out loud.

"What were the others?" she asked.

"Let's see." Taylor held up one thumb and tapped it with the finger of her other hand. "Frosty Felicity, Flirty Felicity." She gave Ed a quirky grin. "Flaunty, Flustered and now Felonious." Taylor held up her hand. "That's a different persona for every day of the working week."

"It seems a bit harsh," Pete said.

"You always were a softie," Noelene said. "Take the blinkers off. Felicity tried to harm your business."

"She was all those things." Taylor looked directly at Pete. "I just put a name to them that's all."

"I only ever saw Flirty and Flaunty Felicity," Ed said.

"That'd be right," Noelene said.

"What about Flashy?" They all looked at Pete. Noelene laughed.

"So does anyone know what will happen next with Felicity?" Antoine asked.

Ed opened another can of beer. "The police said they were charging her, she'll get bail and she'll have to appear in court later."

"Will we?" Taylor asked. She didn't like the thought of it.

"Maybe Pete and I. I doubt they'll need anyone else."

Taylor's phone rang. "Hi, Cass."

She moved into the passage away from the noisy conversation. Cass was full of questions about the robbery. It took Taylor a while to fill her in. By the time she came back Noelene had taken charge of serving the meal.

"That was Cass," Taylor said. "She heard about the wine theft on the news."

"We're famous," Ed said.

Pete raised his eyebrows. "Not the kind of fame we're looking for."

"Any publicity is good publicity." Ed helped Noelene hand out plates of food.

Taylor picked up her jug of gravy and offered it to Pete. "Evidently there was a picture of our cellar door and one of Felicity being bundled into a police car."

"So it's still all about Felicity." Ed shook his head.

"Let's change the subject." Noelene joined them at the table. "I've had enough of Madam Felicity, or should I say Felonious Felicity?" There was a wicked twinkle in her eye. "What about we talk about the business plan?"

"No, Noelene," Pete and Ed chorused as one.

* * *

Pete walked back to his cottage with his arm wrapped around Taylor. The night was cold. They walked quickly but in easy step with each other.

"I haven't had a chance to ask how your talk with Ed went this morning." Taylor looked up at him. "Have you sorted anything out?"

"We washed the dishes together."

"That's a good start."

"To be honest I don't know." Pete opened the door for her. "We were mates once but somehow we've drifted apart. We're chasing different dreams."

Taylor turned to him as they reached the kitchen. "You're not really, you know. I believe what Ed wrote on his business plan was how he truly felt. You both want to be here at Wriggly Creek in five years' time with a solid wine list and good markets. There has to be a way to achieve that and in a way that suits you both."

"So you'll keep working on it."

"Of course. If I don't keep finding myself a job you might fire me and then I'd have to leave."

He frowned. He didn't want her going anywhere. "We always need to eat."

"Hey!" She gave him a playful poke in the chest. "I didn't mind cooking for vintage and being paid for it but I'm not turning into anyone's full-time cook."

He laughed at her frowning face. She eyed him suspiciously.

"I can run an office you know."

"Damn, yes, I hadn't thought of that. We'll need someone to cover Felicity."

"Replace her, you mean."

"Would you be interested in the position?"

"I might. Depends if there are any perks."

Pete laughed again and wrapped his arms around her. "You're one very special woman, Taylor Rourke."

She looked up at him. Her eyes sparkled and her skin glowed. "You're not so bad yourself, Peter Starr."

"Anything I can get you?"

She shivered. "Some heat. It's freezing in here."

"I didn't get around to lighting the fire today." He leaned forward and nuzzled the soft skin on the side of her neck. His lips tracked upwards and found hers. Damn, she tasted good. "I've got another way to keep warm."

"Really?"

She locked her gaze with his as he scooped her up and carried her to the bedroom.

"I could get used to this," she said. His lips found hers again and there was no more talking.

CHAPTER
56

Taylor sat at Felicity's desk and looked around. Everything was neat and tidy. Her filing was up to date and in good order. So far Taylor couldn't fault the other woman's office management skills. Faultless Felicity. She smiled to herself. Perhaps not.

With little to do but answer the odd call, Taylor had checked out Wriggly Creek's Facebook page and their website. She hoped Pete and Ed would let her have a play with them. She was bursting with ideas for improvement. At the top of the list was to get some decent background photos and then to start a blog. She visualised a picture of Ed and Pete together – the Starr brothers of Wriggly Creek Wines.

She logged in to her email account.

The first email to drop into her box was from her parents. It wasn't the usual newsy email but a carefully worded message full of concern. Taylor's mood dampened. Her parents were so far away. They must hang out for her emails and she'd hardly sent any.

Watching the tussle between Pete and Ed had made her think more about her family. Her parents might often be away but that didn't mean they didn't care about her and want to share her life. Perhaps she'd been the one to put up the barriers, relying on her friends more than her family for support.

Taylor sat up straight and hit the reply button. She began to type the usual beginning to the nondescript emails she sent her parents. She paused, her fingers hovering over the keyboard. Then she continued.

I am having a wonderful time in Coonawarra. I've ended up finding work in a winery where I've done all kinds of things. It's been a steep learning curve.

Once more she paused.

But the best thing is I've met this wonderful man. His name's Peter Starr and he owns Wriggly Creek Winery with his brother Edward.

Her fingers hovered over the keyboard.

I know you're going to be surprised but I think he's the one! Let's organise a Skype session soon, maybe this weekend, so you can meet him.

Taylor finished the email and pressed send then she picked up her mobile phone.

"Hello, Gran. It's Taylor, how are you?"

Gran's reply was short and sharp as usual.

"That's good. And your visitors?"

Taylor listened to her gran's story on the shortcomings of her overseas friends. And evidently they were staying longer than expected.

"No, that's okay. I'm not planning to come back anytime soon but you'll be pleased to know I'm using my business skills."

There was some background noise.

"No, that's okay Gran, you answer the door. Just wanted to let you know I'm fine."

Taylor hung up. Gran would always be Gran but at least Taylor had made the effort.

She scrolled through her emails to the last one from Gemma. As usual it was all about how hard they worked and their latest holiday, a weekend in Paris. Taylor leaned forward and re-read the last two lines again. Gemma made mention of feeling unwell. It wasn't like her at all.

Taylor looked around at the sound of footsteps. Pete appeared from the passage behind her. Her face lit up. She couldn't help it. He made her feel like she was bursting with happiness.

He came behind the desk, spun her chair to face him and bent down to kiss her. "Good morning sleepyhead."

"I can't believe you let me sleep in on my first day in the office. What if the boss had sacked me?"

He nuzzled her neck. "He's had you in the sack," he murmured. "Does that count?"

She grinned back at him.

"I see you've worked out the computer." He nodded to the screen behind her.

She turned back. "It wasn't hard. You must change the password. I worked it out in a flash."

"Really?"

"No, but Felicity did have it written on a piece of paper stuck inside her top drawer. Not very secure."

"Who'd want to…?" Pete's voice trailed away.

She tapped the desk with a fingernail. "You should keep everything as safe and secure as you can. You and Ed should each have a separate log-on to the network."

"You think?"

"Yes, I think."

"It seems to me a little bit of power has gone to your head, Ms Rourke."

He pulled his mobile from his pocket and answered it. "Yes, Ed."

Taylor felt a wriggle of discomfort. She didn't know what Ed's reaction would be to her working in the office.

"Over in the front office." Pete winked at her. "Yes, we're both here."

Taylor pointed to the phone and mouthed, 'did you ask him'?

"Okay, see you in a minute." Pete ended the call. "What was that?"

"Did you ask him about me working here?"

"I told him. He's happy for you to do it for now. We'll talk about the future later."

"That's fair enough. Is he coming here?"

"Yes. Said he's got something to show us."

They both looked up at the honk of a funny-sounding car horn.

A look of surprise swept over Pete's face. "That sounds like Dad's old car."

Taylor stood up and followed him. At the door she turned back and took her keys from the desk.

Pete gave her an amused look as she locked the door but he didn't say a word. She followed him round the side of the building. Ed was grinning and waving to them from the front seat of a small red sports car.

"Is that your dad's Triumph?"

"Yes it is." Pete strode to the driver's side and ran his hand along the door. "I didn't think it worked."

"It didn't." Ed opened the door and unfolded himself from the seat. He looked from Taylor to Pete. "This is why I wanted you out on Saturday evening. I tracked down the guy who maintained it for Dad. I couldn't get it to start so we towed it to the winery workshop. He brought it back to life." Ed put his hand on Pete's shoulder. "I'm sorry. It must have been me that didn't lock the gate properly after him. I was in such a rush to get the Triumph back to the garage before you came home. I wanted it to be a surprise."

"It wouldn't have made any difference. The police said the truck came in the early hours and Felicity supplied the key."

"I know but I should have told you as soon as the wine was stolen. You were blaming yourself for not locking the gate."

Pete gripped Ed's shoulder. "It doesn't matter, Ed."

Taylor batted at the tears that filled her eyes. She thought of Gemma all the way over in Ireland and feeling unwell. It must have been more than a sniffle for her to mention it. She would ask Pete if she could use the office phone to ring her sister later.

"Let's go for a ride." Ed ran around and held open the passenger door waving for Taylor to get in.

"Thank you, Edward." She slid into the seat. She felt as if she was almost sitting on the ground.

He shut the door and leaned in. "You can call me Ed. I don't mind."

She smiled up at him. "Thanks…Ed."

"You drive, Pete."

"Are you sure? Where will you sit?"

"I'll perch in between you on the back of the seat. We can only drive inside the winery anyway. It's not registered."

After a jerky start Pete managed to turn the car around.

"Flatten it," Ed shouted as they headed off back towards the cottage.

Taylor let out a yell as Pete accelerated along the track. The wind whipped her hair around her face. She lifted a fist into the air. "Neil's Triumph, as smooth as a fine red wine."

Taylor paced the floor in Ed's kitchen as the two brothers read the business plan in the lounge. Ed had cooked but she'd offered to clean up while they read. She'd stacked the dishwasher, washed and dried the extra pots, wiped down the benches and now she was left with nothing to do. All she could hear was the occasional rustle of paper from the other room. She badly wanted them to like her ideas, for all their sakes. She picked up the glass of wine she'd carried with her to the kitchen. Pete had opened another bottle of their reserve cab sauv to accompany the steak Ed had cooked.

Taylor stopped pacing at the murmur of voices and took a few silent steps closer to the door. She jumped as Pete appeared in the doorway.

He grinned at her. "We've read it."

"What do you think?" She looked from one to the other as she followed Pete into the lounge.

"Interesting," Ed said. His face didn't give anything away.

"I like it." Pete gave Ed a poke in the shoulder. "We both do."

"There's a bit of fine-tuning to do." Ed started flipping through the pages.

"Of course," Taylor said. "These are my thoughts based on your information but it's got to be your plan."

"I like the idea of buying our own harvester instead of the Wrattonbully vineyard." Pete sat next to his brother.

Ed gave a soft snort. "You would."

"You agreed with me a minute ago."

"Don't get your undies in a twist. I do agree but if we're to do it without an investor it could be tricky." He looked steadily at Taylor.

"You've money put aside and I've some other ideas. It might not be possible to achieve by next vintage but definitely the one after that."

"This idea of getting extra tanks to process other people's fruit could work but once again it comes down to money." Ed tapped his finger on the page.

"That would go hand-in-hand with some streamlining of our processes though," Pete said.

"Still means money," Ed said. "And I would like to have a holiday in China. I don't see that factored in."

"Yes it is." Taylor took his plan and flicked to the appendix at the back. "It's a market exploration trip."

Ed's face slowly lit with a smile.

"You haven't mentioned much about starting up our icon wine." This time it was Pete who gave her the enquiring look.

"That's tied in with my loose idea to display the Triumph but I need a bit more time to think it through. By the time your wine is ready to drink I'd like to see us have some kind of display of the Triumph attached to the cellar door."

"Maybe we'll need a bigger cellar door." Ed nudged Pete.

"Maybe. Letting people rent the quarters outside vintage could work."

"There would need to be a few improvements." Taylor folded her arms. "Like fixing that front door."

"That adds character,' Pete said.

Taylor ignored him. "None of the improvements would involve a big outlay."

"I don't know if we want people traipsing through the place."

"This needs more work." Taylor picked up their copies. "Now that you've written all over these I can go back to the drawing board and refine it again."

"I'm excited by this." Pete stood up and gave her a hug. "I like the job description you've outlined for the office manager."

"Yes," Ed chipped in. "Sounds like it may have been written with a particular person in mind."

Taylor jumped at the sound of a phone ringing.

Ed frowned and rose to his feet. "No-one rings on the landline these days. .

"It could be for me," Taylor looked around for the phone. "I hope you don't mind. I've been trying to contact my sister. I gave her your number for tonight."

"Go for it." Ed said. "It's in the office off the kitchen."

Taylor dropped the plans back on the side table and made a dash, anxious to get there before the phone stopped ringing.

"Another drink?" Pete suggested.

"Good idea." Ed put another log into the combustion fire and headed to the kitchen. "I've got a shiraz from up the road we should try." He came back with the bottle and fresh glasses. "The phone must have been for Taylor. I could hear her talking to someone."

"She's hardly mentioned her sister before." Pete settled back in the chair. "I didn't think they were close."

"I remember she said her sister was a doctor and lived in Ireland. That's all I know."

Pete gripped the glass Ed offered tightly. He still felt a bit sensitive about Taylor being Ed's girlfriend first. Although he had no doubt about the strength of his feelings for her and he was fairly sure she felt the same way about him.

"She was never my girl, you know."

Pete looked up. Ed was staring at him, his look intense.

"There was nothing much between us from the start."

Pete took a sip of the wine. "Not bad."

Ed did the same. "Not as good as yours."

They both sipped again.

"I'm glad you two met," Pete said.

Ed glanced at him, a puzzled look on his face.

"If you hadn't then I may never have met Taylor. I can't imagine life without her."

"That sounds like a commitment."

"It will be, if she'll have me."

Ed reached his glass across and tapped Pete's. "Good luck. If it's any consolation I agree with you. You two are like an old married couple already."

Pete chuckled. Ed hadn't seen them sitting by the fire before they'd come out for tea; a chair drawn up, a beer in hand, and their socked feet resting on the hearth. He'd felt content despite all the drama of the last few weeks.

"This business plan, we should have done it back when Mum and Dad died, you know," Ed said.

"Past history now."

"I'm the one with the business degree. I should have been the one to get it organised."

"Don't beat yourself up." Pete stared into the flames of the fire. "We've both made mistakes."

"You're happy with the plan?"

"It will need some tweaking but the basic ideas are good. What about you?"

"It's a good start."

"So no more talk of selling to Mr Zhu."

"I wouldn't have sold everything you know. I thought you'd be prepared to give up a percentage to get me to stay."

Pete looked steadily into his brother's eyes. "I know."

"Guess what?" Taylor burst back into the room her face all aglow.

"What?" Pete and Ed said together.

"I'm going to be an aunty." Taylor clapped her hands. "Gemma's having a baby. Well, two actually. She's having twins. And they're going to move back to Australia so she can be close to family. She thinks Mum and Dad might hang around a bit more if they've got grandchildren."

Pete stood up and wrapped her in his arms.

She looked up at him with shining eyes. "Pinch me. I'm so happy I must be dreaming."

He kissed her instead.

Ed poured another glass of wine and offered it to Taylor. "We'd better drink to that."

Taylor took a sip and nearly choked.

"What's wrong?" Pete gave her back a gentle rub.

"That's not what I had before?" She stared aghast at her glass.

"I should have warned you, Pete's cab sauv is all gone." Ed held his glass up. "This is a shiraz. It's a bit rough around the edges."

"A bit," Taylor gasped.

"You don't have to drink it." Pete went to take her glass but she kept hold of it.

"That's okay," she said. "I'm going to have to learn all these different wines if I'm working in a winery."

"Yes." Pete winked at her. "Yes, you will."

CHAPTER
58

Taylor had just put down the phone when Pete stepped into the office.

"Are you busy?" he asked.

"Not very. There could be lots of things I'm not doing. Noelene's going to call in this afternoon after she's done her shopping and show me the ropes."

"That's a good idea."

"My suggestion." Ed came in from his office. "Felicity was efficient but she didn't leave any handover notes."

"Funny about that," Pete said. He looked back at Taylor. "I was hoping to steal you away for a while."

"What for?"

"I'm giving the new cab sauv its last plunge. I thought you might like to help."

Taylor jumped up. "I'd love to." The phone rang. "Oh, but–"

"You go," Ed said. "I can manage the phone for a while."

"Thanks, Ed." Taylor gave him a grateful smile and linked her arm through Pete's. "Let's go. My boss is a slave driver. I can't be away long."

"You bet I am," Ed called behind them.

Outside it was a beautiful day. The sun was shining and only a slight breeze stirred, tossing some autumn leaves across the ground.

"Do you want to change?" Pete asked.

Taylor had put on her yellow jeans and a long-sleeved white shirt to work in the office. "I've got flat shoes and I'll take off my scarf." She'd become pretty efficient at plunging, hardly splashed a drop anymore.

They made their way around to the old shed and Pete opened the door.

"So this is the last time we have to plunge the NS18?" In spite of getting better at it, Taylor had to admit she'd found it hard work and she had only done a small amount compared to Pete and Antoine. She hoped it might be one of the things she could change about the way Pete processed the wine.

"It gets pressed next and then we'll barrel it."

"How long till it's bottled?"

"Two years."

"It's a long time to wait for an end product."

"But worth it." Instead of picking up the plunger Pete turned to her and took both her hands in his. He locked his gaze with hers.

She closed her eyes and leaned in ready for his lips to reach hers. It was almost this very same spot where they'd first kissed. Taylor pursed her lips together to stifle a grin. That had ended badly for Pete.

"I don't have much," Pete said. "This wine was the most special thing I had. Until you came along."

Taylor opened her eyes. He looked so serious she wondered what on earth he was going to say next.

"I want to share it with you, Taylor. Me and everything I have. Will you stay here and be–"

Taylor pressed her fingers to his lips, cutting him off. "Wait a minute." Her heart raced, not from excitement but from fear. She was so happy but she didn't want anything to spoil it. She hadn't known Pete all that long and it had sounded like he was about to propose. "I want to stay here with you. But can we take things, slowly?"

"I'm not my brother. I've fallen in love with you, Taylor. That means forever to me."

"And for me. I...well, I've made a few blunders in the love stakes and... I want to be sure."

Pete looked crestfallen.

"I'm not going anywhere. It feels right to me. I just need a bit more time to make sure. Then you can ask me." She peered at his sad face. "Can you cope with that?"

"If it's what you want?"

"You is what I want." She hugged him tight. "I'm sorry I can't say more than that for now."

"Okay. I can wait." He kissed her and let her go. "I'm a wine-maker, I know what patience is." He sighed. "I also know we need to get this plunging done. Antoine will have the press ready to go." He took up the plunger and climbed up onto the plank.

Taylor leaned her arms on the cement edge of the tank and watched. It was hard to imagine this wine had to go into a barrel for two years before it could be drunk. How could he trust it would come out all right at the other end? She watched Pete's strong arms lift and push the plunger, his face intent on his work. Her heart went out to him. He'd put himself on the line for her and she'd knocked him back. Why couldn't she make up her mind like he had? It was what she wanted after all. Someone who she truly loved and who loved her back. Someone she could share her life with. She already felt she knew Pete well. They had so much in common. Her resolve deepened. Like a barrel of wine she had to trust it would turn out okay.

She put her foot on the step, steadied herself and climbed on to the plank. Pete was halfway across. He looked back at her, surprise on his face.

"Can we do it together?" she said. "So in two years' time when we drink it together we can look back on this moment."

"You've changed your mind?"

"No. I've made up my mind."

He lifted the plunger as she stepped up to him but instead of taking the elbow he offered she reached for the handle. It rose higher, upsetting her balance. She waved a hand in the air and let out a scream as she felt herself falling. She felt Pete's fingers slide across her hand but she slipped from his grasp.

Taylor hit the lukewarm liquid and slid below the surface. Her feet scrabbled on the slippery bottom and she rose to the top as Pete's hand gripped her arm. She stood in the liquid up to her chest gaping up at him.

"Are you all right?"

She was horrified. "I've ruined your wine."

He hiccupped. "It'll be fine."

She peered closer. He was laughing at her.

She gritted her teeth. "I'd like to get out."

He moved to the side and helped her slide up onto the plank. She lay there a moment listening to him laugh. She pushed herself up, slid her feet over the edge and rounded on him.

"We are definitely changing from this manual plunging."

"No we're not." He reached over and plucked a grape skin from her hair. "It's part of the process that will make this wine so special."

Taylor glared at him. She ran her tongue around her mouth, pushed out a grape skin and spat it to the ground. She froze. There was a flavour, almost imperceptible. She licked her lips, ran her tongue around her mouth again and grabbed Pete's arm. "I can taste it." She started to laugh. "I can taste the blackberries."

Pete pulled her close and pressed his lips to hers. "Mmmm. So can I."

A chuckle burst from both of them forcing them apart. Pete scooped her into his arms.

"I reckon you're going to need a long shower or you'll be the colour of a good red for a while."

Outside the wind chilled her through her wet clothes. Taylor rested her head on his shoulder and let him carry her. She had a fair idea her yellow jeans would never be that colour again but it didn't matter. She didn't care about anything but being here with Pete. She was sure about that. Wriggly Creek was home and she planned to stay.

ACKNOWLEDGEMENTS

The inspiration for this story developed on visits to the beautiful Coonawarra wine region of South Australia. There are such a variety of wineries and cellar door experiences and so many different wines to sample, all in the name of research of course, however there's far more to wine than just drinking it.

To get a feel for what happens when producing a good wine and find out what is special about Coonawarra wineries, I had some interesting chats with Wendy Hollick who co-established Hollick Coonawarra in 1983 and John Rymill who is following in his great-great-grandfather's footsteps producing wine at Rymill, Coonawarra. I would like to thank them both for their willing and thoughtful support with my research. I also listened to many passionate winemakers from other wineries who helped to round out the picture, however, words cannot express my gratitude to my son Jared and his partner Alexandra for their fantastic help with the background for this story.

It has been very handy to have a son who is a winemaker and Alexandra who has worked in various aspects of the industry. They've patiently answered my many questions and given suggestions when I've been stuck. Jared also read the early manuscript and replied to my desperate emails at all hours. How lucky am I? Thank you both so much. Your name's not on the front of the book, Jared Stringer, but I hope you're happy to see it here.

So with all this wealth of winemaking knowledge you would hope I've got my information correct. I am a storyteller and some-times we storytellers can't help ourselves – we can't let the facts get in the way of a good tale so any mistakes within are my own. Most of the places mentioned in the story are also fictitious. I want you to discover the real Coonawarra for yourself.

This writer's journey is assisted by all the usual suspects. In particular I'd like to thank my dear friends Dawn Greig, Kathy Snodgrass and Sue Barlow who have accompanied me on various road trips including a few to Coonawarra. We've had some great times, shared so much and I've managed to fit in some research along the way. Cheers to you, girlz.

Fellow writers are an important support. We're from all over the planet but the willingness to share and encourage is always there. Thank you all from Career Boosters, to Masterclassers, to Romance Writers of Australia and all those in between. And a special thank you to Meredith Appleyard. We've had a couple of very productive writing catch-ups and retreats this year. So good to have another writer just across the table to bounce ideas off when you need it.

The folks at Harlequin are a wonderful team. Thanks to Jo Mackay for her ongoing support and initial feedback and to Annabel Blay for her insightful editorial work – who knew commas were so versatile? And cheers to you both for your quirky quips and delightful senses of humour; timely reminders that I'm not really alone at the keyboard. I know it's hard to single people out but I also want to thank Laurie Ormond and Sarah Fletcher for their proofing expertise, Romina Panetta and the design crew who've excelled with another beautiful cover and Adam Van Rooijen for all the marketing ideas and ready support. So many other wonderful people at Harlequin have had a hand in the publishing of this book. You're a fantastic bunch. Thank you all.

I am also very lucky to have the backing of my other grown-up children and their partners. My daughter Kelly is my number one reader and together with my two young grandsons, my family is the best cheer squad a writer could have. I also have a wonderful extended family and dear friends whose encouragement I appreciate very much. Thumbs up to my husband, Daryl, who keeps me grounded, fed and watered (or should that be wined) and is a steady support in my often crazy writing life. Thank you all.

Last but by no means least, thank you to readers, librarians and booksellers who champion my books, give such valuable feedback and encourage me to write the next story. I appreciate it so much and...I'm onto it!

The first chapter of *Heart of the Country* by
Tricia Stringer follows.
Heart of the Country is an epic historical saga of three
Australian families forging their paths in a land both
beautiful and unforgiving...

Available where all good books are sold

One

1846

The biting wind tugged at Thomas Baker's hat as he turned the corner. He pressed it tightly to his head with his hand and bent into the wind. Another miserable day in Adelaide but he would not be deterred from his purpose. He kept to the wooden palings that served as a footpath in front of the assorted stone buildings that made up Hindley Street. Most were single storey, and on this part of the street there were no verandahs. The few people brave enough to be out huddled against the cold with bowed heads and moved quickly. Horses and carts churned along the muddy street. Thomas hunched his shoulders and pulled his coat tighter against the chill, thankful at least that he wasn't wielding a shovel trying to keep the road passable.

He came to a stop in front of a white picket fence and peered up at the sign suspended from a wooden post. The Black Bull Hotel was written in bold lettering and beside it someone had painted a picture of a serene-looking bull. This was the place. He pushed open the gate. Below the name of the hotel there were more words in smaller print.

The bull is tame, so fear him not, so long as you can pay your shot.
When money's gone and credit's bad, that's what makes the bull
go mad.

The warning in the words fitted the brooding appearance of
the grey stone establishment. A short sharp shower of rain pro-
pelled him forward. He shook the drops from his coat and ducked
his head through the door.

Inside the hotel, he stopped and peered through the smoky air
and was pleased to see a fire flickering in the grate. A bar ran the
length of the large rectangular room and several rough tables and
chairs were scattered along the opposite wall. Most of the occupants
stood, crowding the space in front of the bar. They were a rough-
looking lot; from their dress they were mainly sailors and bushmen.

Raucous laughter and a jaunty female voice drew his gaze to
the bar. A barmaid was flirting with the men in front of her as
she set down their drinks. She glanced in his direction, but he
looked away. He had no intention of buying a drink. With any
luck he could conduct his business and be on his way quickly. He
sought one man in particular but he could see no-one who met
the basic description he'd been given. He squeezed behind two
sailors arguing about whose turn it was to buy the next drink.
One of them swayed and someone knocked hard against him.
Men complained around him. He collided with a chair.

"Steady up."

"Beg your pardon, sir." Thomas dipped his head to the seated man
he'd almost fallen over. Even though his clothes were unlike any
Thomas had seen a gentleman wear, the tone of the man's voice and
his stature put him a cut above the rest of the patrons. The man gave
him a good look then went back to eating the food in front of him.

Thomas edged into the corner. The sight of the gentleman's
steaming bowl reminded him he'd eaten nothing since the pitiful

porridge he'd been given at his lodgings that morning. He eased off his damp outer garment and hooked it over the back of the chair. At least from here he could better inspect those at the bar and he would see anyone who came in the door.

Slowly the warmth of the room thawed him. So far the fourteen grey, damp days he'd passed in Adelaide had done little but remind him of the miserable cold of England. They had shown no signs of producing the fresh start his father had predicted. But today would be different. The fledgling hope that had been with him as he stepped ashore all those weeks back, and which had gradually ebbed away, was strong in his chest again. Today was the start of something new.

A pot of ale hit the table in front of him with a thud. He lifted his eyes to those of the barmaid. She leaned in. He pulled his head back from the smell of sour beer and sweat.

"If you're going to sit here you have to buy a drink."

The lilt of her Irish voice reminded him of the girl who'd been the cook's assistant back home, but the barmaid was nothing like Bernadette, who'd made his face heat with her flirting. There were deep lines around this woman's eyes and mouth and her cheeks were ruddy. From across the room it had looked like a youthful glow but now he could see the skin was rough and the glow probably the product of her employer's slops.

"No, thank you." He frowned at her. "I don't want it."

"This is a pub. Everyone wants it." She rolled her eyes and pushed her barely covered bosom closer. "Especially a good-looking feller like you."

Thomas started to rise but the barmaid put a hand on his chest and pushed him back.

"Sure, you've enough for one drink."

He looked over her shoulder through a gap in the crowd to the bar, where the bartender was watching them intently. The woman was right: if he was going to sit here any longer he needed a drink or he'd draw more attention to himself than he wanted.

He slipped a hand into his pocket for his money pouch. The pocket was empty. He patted his pants and reached for his jacket. No pouch there either. He must have left it in his trunk when he repacked it that morning. "I don't have my pouch."

"Cut the games." The barmaid fixed him with her small round eyes. "Pay for your ale or leave."

Thomas hesitated. He recalled the menacing words painted on the sign outside. He had notes concealed inside his shirt but he was reluctant to reveal them here.

A large hand appeared between them and slapped some coins on the rough wooden surface. Thomas looked up into the eyes of the gentleman from the next table. In spite of his clean-shaven face he had a rugged appearance, but none of that changed Thomas's earlier impression that he had the air of a gentleman.

"I'll shout the gentleman; and one more for me thank you, Mary," the man said.

Before Thomas could protest Mary had scooped up the coins. "Thank you, Mr Browne." She did a small bob and was gone, weaving skilfully through the crowd to the bar.

Thomas studied the man who'd come to his aid. "You're Mr Browne?" he said.

The man's sharp gaze locked on Thomas. "That's me. Who are you?"

"Thomas Baker. I've come about the job. I'm sorry I didn't recognise you. I was told you had long hair and a beard."

Mr Browne gave a hearty laugh. "I did until this morning. I've been out of town a long time with only sheep for company. I've just come from the barber shop." He studied Thomas. "You're early, and not what I was expecting."

"I can work as hard as any man." Thomas pulled back his shoulders and lifted his head as the older man looked him over. This was not how he'd intended to approach his prospective employer.

"Well, Thomas, since we're sharing a drink, is it all right if I move myself to your table?"

Before he could answer, Mr Browne took up his bowl and moved it across, then shifted his large frame into the chair alongside. The smell of some kind of stew reached Thomas's nostrils. His mouth watered and his eyes were drawn to the bowl.

Another pot of ale appeared at the table.

"Mary, bring us another bowl of whatever this is." Mr Browne waved his hand over his food and dropped more coins on the table.

"It's Irish stew, Mr Browne, me old mam's recipe."

"Whatever it is, we'll have another for my new friend."

Once again Thomas began to protest but Mary had taken the coins and gone.

"You look like you could do with a good feed."

"It's very kind of you, Mr Browne, but –"

"The name's Andrew James Browne. People call me AJ." He reached out and gripped Thomas's hand in a firm shake. His face crinkled into a smile then he pointed to his bowl. "You'll be hard pressed to find much mutton in the stew. Mostly potatoes and onion, but it's tasty all the same."

"Thank you. I'm not sure how I can repay your kindness."

"It's not necessary."

Thomas sat back quickly as Mary plonked a bowl of stew in front of him. His stomach rumbled in anticipation.

"Eat your fill." A deep chuckle gurgled from AJ's throat and he ate from his own bowl.

Thomas did the same, and by the time he'd swallowed the last mouthful the stew had warmed his insides and the ale had warmed his blood.

AJ sat back and folded his arms across his broad chest. "So Thomas Baker. What brings you to the new colony of South Australia?"

"It was my father's idea originally." Thomas paused, not sure how much of his story he should tell his prospective employer. "He worked back in England managing a farm. After my mother died he decided we should make a new start."

"I'm sorry for you loss. What kind of work are you and your father looking for or has he already found employment?"

Thomas hesitated. "My father died aboard ship on the way here."

The sharp gaze that studied Thomas softened. "Once more, I am sorry," AJ said.

Thomas clenched his jaw. The promise of a new start had been the only thing to brighten their days since his mother's death. They'd heard Australia was a wonderful new land with plenty of work and money to be made. His father had taken their meagre savings and accepted cheap passage to South Australia but he had not taken to ship life, succumbing to constant sea sickness which had finally killed him just before they'd reached Adelaide. For a moment, Thomas was transported to his father's burial and the memory of the weighted shroud as it slid from the board and plunged into the rough ocean below. The mournful tolling of the bell marked the moment, as Thomas braced himself against the railing, gusts of wind ripping at his coat and wailing through the rigging. The waves had swallowed his father's body, and slammed against the wooden hull.

He took a deep breath. Their employers, the Dowlings, had made a mockery of his father's decision, called them both fools as they'd left and warned them not to come crawling back looking for handouts. Perhaps the Dowlings had been right ... Now there was only Thomas, the last of their money hidden inside his shirt, and the two trunks of basic items they'd brought with them.

"Have you worked before with animals?" AJ's question cut into Thomas's thoughts.

He swallowed his grief once more and gave his full attention to the man opposite. "Yes. The farm I worked on had sheep and there were cows to be milked. We also helped with the horses."

AJ studied him closely. "You're not quite what I was expecting."

Thomas felt as if his deception was written all over his face. His job at the Dowlings had been footman. He'd only assisted his father in his rare moments of spare time.

"In what way?"

"I was hoping for someone more robust."

"I was very sea sick on the trip out," Thomas said quickly. "I've lost weight but I'm strong." He hoped the good Lord would forgive him his lies but he needed this job and after the labouring work of the last few weeks he had certainly built up some strength. The rain that had fallen on his arrival in South Australia had hardly let up and the streets of Adelaide had turned to slush. He'd been given rough lodgings in Emigration Square and in return he'd been sent to work with a few other men. No sooner had they shovelled and scraped the roads into a traversable surface than it rained again and a fresh lot of horses and drays passed by, causing the ruts and pot holes to return.

AJ pursed his lips and drew a watch from his top pocket. He opened it, peered at the face, then snapped it shut. "I'm sorry for all that's befallen you, Thomas, but I don't know if you're suited to my needs."

Thomas drew himself up. "I am quite used to hard work if that's what bothers you."

"Rest assured," AJ reached across and gave him a firm pat on the shoulder, "I didn't take you as a man not prepared to work for his living. I was hoping for someone with a little more experience. There were a couple of men interested."

Thomas held AJ's gaze. He could see the older man was weighing something up.

"Whatever the work is, I am sure I am up to it," Thomas said.

AJ studied him a moment longer then his face relaxed into a smile. "You remind me of myself ten years ago. I came to Australia in similar circumstances, although not orphaned, I had only the clothes on my back and little money. I learned as I went. Hard work has stood me well." He leaned forward and the smile dropped from his face. "I'll tell you what I need, Thomas Baker. You may well change your mind once you've heard me out."

Thomas recalled his father had used nearly the same words before he'd told of his plan to leave England. He needed to do this, not only for himself but for his father. He pulled back his shoulders and clasped his hands firmly together.

"I don't believe I will, Mr Browne."

"Very well. There's plenty to be made from this land if you are prepared to work. I have property in the north and I've stocked it with three thousand sheep. It's rugged country. Water's not so abundant and it's no place for the faint hearted. There are wild dogs up there and there's also been trouble with the natives. In spite of that the sheep don't need shepherding as you would know it in England." AJ leaned closer. "I have other land to see to and I need an overseer."

The word hung in the air between them.

Finally Thomas spoke. "So you would want me to be your overseer?"

"I need someone reliable. It's no easy job. I've left one shepherd up there, a redheaded Scot with a quick temper. McKenzie's his name but he's little more than useless when left to his own devices. He needs a master."

Thomas held Mr Browne's look across the table. He was a footman. What did he know about shepherding in the bush of South Australia?

"So now you know," AJ said. "I need a man I can trust. I am in a hurry but I can wait for the others." He paused. "Unless you believe you could be that man."

Thomas swallowed his doubts. "Will there be some guidance?" he asked.

"You seem a bright enough fellow to me. McKenzie knows sheep; you'll learn from him. He's just not what I call reliable." AJ lowered his voice. "I'll pay you sixty pounds a year."

Thomas's reply died in his throat. That was a decent sum of money. It would come with a lot of hard work but he had nothing to lose and he needed the experience a job like this would give him.

AJ was watching him closely. "I'll loan you the money to buy a horse and saddle. If you do well, I'll increase your salary each year."

Thomas's mind raced as he calculated the income. Maybe he could make enough to get his own place one day. His father would have been proud. "It's a good offer, Mr Browne."

"Call me AJ." The older man reached his hand across the space between them. "Do we have a deal?"

Thomas hesitated then thrust his own into the firm grip of his new employer. With not much to lose and a lot to gain, he felt a surge of optimism.

"Well done, Thomas. It's a good opportunity I'm offering you. It won't be a ride in your English countryside but I'm sure you're up to it. Come on." AJ rose to his feet. "No need to wait around here any longer. There's a lot to organise. We might as well make a start."

Thomas reached for his jacket. No longer would he have to wield a shovel in the endless job of keeping Adelaide's streets passable. He would still be working for someone else but for a good wage and AJ was already proving to be a most agreeable employer. Outside, the heavy clouds had lifted and broken apart. Sunlight reached his patch of the street. Thomas was happy to take that as a sign his life was improving. He pushed his battered hat firmly onto his head and strode purposefully after Mr Browne.

Coming in May 2016,
the second in the Flinders Ranges series,

Dust on the Horizon

talk about it

Let's talk about books.

Join the conversation:

 on facebook.com/harlequinaustralia

 on Twitter @harlequinaus

www.harlequinbooks.com.au

If you love reading and want to know about our
authors and titles, then let's talk about it.